RAWHEAD

JON

BEBBINGTON

RAWHEAD

JON BEBBINGTON

For Permission requests, write to:

YBR Publishing, LLC
PO Box 4904
Beaufort SC 29903-4904
contact@ybrpub.com
843-597-0912

RAWHEAD

JON BEBBINGTON

ISBN-13 978-1-7339992-1-2
ISBN-1-7339992-1-3

Front Cover art by Ayana Bibbs and Jon Bebbington
Back Cover photo source www.britishbattles.com
Editing by Bill Barnier
Cover design and Interior formatting by Jack Gannon

RAWHEAD

"Jon Bebbington has truly caught the atmosphere of the Cheshire countryside, so familiar to me. His knowledge of life on a rural tenant farm in the early 1900s brings this book to life. Vivid descriptions, combined with historical accuracy, capture the cruel turmoil of the Great War and the fears of the unknown by those on the battlefields, and the loved ones left at home. Combining the horrors of war and the tears of a loss, I found RAWHEAD an excellent read."

~Dr. Lynn Bristow Cook, Ph.D.

Born in England 1953, Lynn studied European history for over forty years, completing her studies at the University of Sterling, Scotland. In 1997 she moved to South Carolina, where she took up the position of Operations Director at the historic Frampton Plantation in the Lowcountry, in Yemassee, South Carolina.

RAWHEAD

JON BEBBINGTON

"A thoroughly enjoyable read!"

~Alan Westcob, Major, Retired
Duke of Wellington's Regiment, 33rd Afoot

RAWHEAD

Review by Author K.C. Finn for Readers' Favorite

Rawhead is a work of historical and military fiction penned by author Jon Bebbington. Based on the real experiences of the author and his family during the First World War, we find ourselves in the idyllic Cheshire countryside of England. A family of tenant farmers is about to encounter the most terrifying prospect the human population has ever seen: a world war. As the impact of the war is felt at home on the farmland, the young men of Cheshire are sent off to fight, causing yet more heartache for those left at home. But the horrors those men face on the European mainland are secrets that they will either take home deeply buried in their minds or be buried with them.

What I enjoyed most about this immersive work of historical fiction was the comprehensive view it gives of both those facing battle and those at home with very little idea of the reality of what their loved ones are facing. There was an acute sense of fear throughout the tale which was very well created, and it's clear that author Jon Bebbington used both accurate research and strong personal memories to build the tale. The narrative often feels like a memoir, contributing to that powerful, nostalgic sense of realism, and the details given of the battlefield are not so graphic that this book couldn't be read by all ages who are curious about the real experiences of people in the Great War. Overall, Rawhead is an important and engaging piece of historical fiction.

(Publisher's Note: This novel is based upon the experiences of the author's grandfather and his siblings, not of the author himself.)

RAWHEAD

AUTHOR'S NOTE

RAWHEAD is a fictional story based on a true-life family and events.

The family featured in the story indeed lived and worked as tenants on a dairy farm named RAWHEAD in Cheshire, England. Five of the nine brothers in the family served honorably in World War I as members of Her Royal Majesty's Navy and Army. Their ultimate fates described herein are true, as is the history of the war and the great personages named.

All other names, characters, businesses, events and incidents are fictional. Any resemblance to actual persons, living or dead, or actual events is purely coincidental.

RAWHEAD

ACKNOWLEDGEMENT

I could not have produced this book without the involvement of historians and researchers in the United States and across "The Pond". These include Geoffrey Crump of the Cheshire Regiment Museum, Rob MacAdie for his research at the National Archives, and Joan Hewitt for her research at the Cheshire Record Office. Acknowledgement is also made to D. H. Rowlands' *For the Duration: The Story of the Thirteenth Battalion, the Rifle Brigade*, by D.H. Rowlands (Simpkin Marshall Ltd, London); Col. Arthur Crookenden's *History of the Cheshire Regiment in the Great War* (Naval and Military Press, Sussex); Col. R. H. Beadon's *The Royal Army Service Corps* (Naval and Military Press, Sussex); Lt. Col. Sir Richard Verdin's *The Cheshire (Earl of Chester's) Yeomanry* (Willmer Brothers Ltd, Birkenhead); and Wendy Bawn, Rebecca Dakin, and Carol Shadbolt's *A Local History of Broxton, Duckington & Harthill* (Local Heritage Initiative).

I extend wholehearted thanks to Tony and Julie Cureton and their two sons, who have served as resident managers of Rawhead Farm since 1984. I am grateful to Brian Sheen of Chester for sharing his detailed records about Rawhead and the subject family's tenancy there.

Special gratitude is extended to Robyn Bebbington Hiltner for her early review of the manuscript.

Finally, a heartfelt expression of gratitude to my patient relatives in Cheshire, too numerous to list here, for their anecdotes and cordial guided tours of Cheshire.

Jon Bebbington

Beaufort, South Carolina

March 2019

RAWHEAD

"All will be well. We have, I believe, within us the life-strength and guiding light by which the tormented world around us may find the harbor of safety, after a storm-beaten voyage."

~Winston Churchill

RAWHEAD

For my father and best friend,
Philip Joseph Bebbington,
and for my grandfather,
Philip Henry Bebbington,
whose story figures prominently in this book.

RAWHEAD

HMT *Royal Michael*
2 miles off the Pelion Peninsula, Aegean Sea
October 1915 9:51 p.m.

Arriving in the Mediterranean, fact overcame rumor. The ship's complement was briefed that they would land at Salonika, Greece, intending to use the city as a base for an offensive against pro-German Bulgaria. On the tenth day, the Allied Salonikan Force sailed northeast between the Pelion Peninsula and the island of Skiathos, one day from the Port of Salonika. The sea was calm, the night black and windless. Below decks a group of foot soldiers played cards in a stuffy smoke-filled cabin strewn with hammocks.

Bertie tossed in his cards and stood.

"Where are you going?" Sam asked, indignant that Bertie would leave the game.

"On holiday," Bertie announced in defiance, and walked out.

Benson, still clinging to a hand of worthless cards, asked Sam, "Didn't your brother just check on the bloomin' animals?"

"Yes, so what? It's not like he's had much luck tonight anyway."

"He's a farmer," Wainright volunteered, a cigarette dangled from his mouth. "Loves animals." He lifted Bertie's cards slightly to see his hand. A Royal Flush. "Besides, 'e 'ad nothing. Call."

Sam, Benson and the others revealed their unlucky hands.

"Ha!" Wainright crowed, throwing down four twos. While he raked in pound notes, an announcement was passed from the bridge.

"All hands! The General Emergency alarm will sound momentarily," voices repeated throughout the ship.

"Not again," Wainright groaned.

Within seconds, the alarm sounded. The men grabbed life jackets and moved to stairwells while some went below to retrieve their gear. After descending a stairwell a few steps, Bertie turned and made his way back up the way he had come. A passing sailor tossed him a lifejacket. On deck, Bertie arrived at a lifeboat station.

Ten minutes later, the words "General Muster Drill concluded" was passed from the Bridge, and the crowds of milling soldiers and seamen on deck began to disperse. Bertie removed his lifejacket and headed back down to the cargo hold where the mules and horses waited in their stalls. Most of the men followed to re-stow their equipment.

The first officer turned from entering the exercise in the watch log and looked at his pocket watch. It was 10:04 p.m., nearing the end of his watch. He walked out of the bridge and surveyed the night with binoculars. A new moon in a cloudless sky made it the most pleasant evening he had seen in weeks. The fresh, cool air was welcome, comforting. A search off the starboard beam revealed nothing but gentle swells and an occasional white cap. He strolled past the wheel house to the port beam. After another full sweep, he again saw nothing that worried him. Lowering the binoculars, he started into the bridge then paused. *One more scan for my watch and I'm off to bed*, he promised himself.

The captain had plotted a course into shallower water that took them close to shore to minimize the possibility of submarine attack. It was a bold decision. The course took them through a narrow channel at night, between the Pelion coast and the island of Skiathos. Sinkings were occurring further to the southeast in the main shipping lanes and the course also meant the ship had no allied support in the channel, except for other transports following.

Uneasy, he stepped back to the railing and leaned against it, studying the horizon through the binoculars. He looked back and forth carefully, but it was so dark and quiet, the ocean and sky appeared as one. He could barely see the ship's wake.

Suddenly, out of the port quarter, he saw a streak of green phosphorescence churning toward the ship. The first officer managed two steps toward the alarm when the torpedo struck. A thunderous boom sounded as the torpedo ripped through the inch-thick plating of the hull and exploded. The blast rocked the *Royal Michael* six feet off center just below the engineering deck, tossing sailors and troops like toy men on a shaken table. A massive cast iron boiler deflected the blast upwards, blowing through several decks including the officer's and captain's quarters. In the cargo hold, horses and mules were slammed screaming against the sides of their stalls, terrified by the noise and the rocking of the ship. Cold seawater roared through the wound in the ships' side with a vengeance, flooding every open space in its path. Seconds later, the General Emergency alarm was sounded, adding to the noise and confusion. Instinctively, men jumped out of their hammocks and ran through bulkheads and up stairwells to the main deck.

"All hands to lifeboat stations!" voices shouted over the noise. "This is not a drill!"

"Bloody obvious, I should think!" Sam yelled, reaching for his lifejacket.

He started down a smoky stairwell but was stopped by men climbing in the opposite direction. Dozens of seamen were still deep below decks, following the order given only minutes before to re-stow their gear from the practice. An enlisted officer grabbed Sam.

"You're goin' the wrong way! We've been hit by a torpedo! Get up to the lifeboats!"

"Is this part of the drill?" called Wainright from below. "We just had one!"

"My brother's down there!" Sam yelled, pointing down the stairway.

"We've been hit hard on the port side! We don't have time! Help the injured!" The NCO hurried off, bellowing orders to men in other compartments.

Two decks below, Bertie pushed past seamen who were shouldering injured sailors up the steps. Another explosion knocked him against a bulkhead and his life jacket fell to the floor.

On deck, the first officer met the third officer of the watch. "Why aren't you lowering away?"

"She's listing hard to port, sir," the third officer shouted to be heard over the cacophony of alarms and grinding metal. "All the starboard lifeboats are swingin' over the deck!"

"Cut 'em loose and toss 'em over the side!"

The ship groaned loudly then righted itself for a moment, before rolling back to port. The single exhaust funnel had been badly damaged and was creaking ominously, threatening collapse. Men near it jumped overboard in fright.

Two sailors climbed rapidly past Bertie descending on the stairwell. One grabbed him by the shirt.

"Where are you going? Are you bloody daft? She's sinking!" he growled in Bertie's face.

"I gotta let the horses out!"

The sailor started pulling Bertie up the stairwell by his shirt while the other seized his arm. Bertie whirled around and punched him in the jaw, knocking him backward. Released, Bertie continued down the stairwell and vanished into the smoke and steam. The two men hurried on their way, the second massaging his chin.

Deep in *Royal Michael*'s core, Bertie splashed through cold waist-deep water, now filled with oil and debris, and began opening stalls. The panicked animals bawled, their wide eyes rolling in panic. A cargo door had fallen away, creating a large passageway into the sea. Bertie grabbed a horse by its mane and led it to the opening, but it balked. He shoved the animal's backside but it refused to jump into the ferociously swirling water. Bertie looked around wildly, then, grabbing a whip off its hook, he snapped it in the air and shoved a few horses toward the cargo door. The animals just bunched up at the opening, rearing and bellowing. Then, a big brown gelding leapt out the door and into the ocean.

"That's it!" Bertie commended him. Just then, a third explosion sent debris and steam shooting through the hold. The ship listed further, allowing a clear escape. The horses and mules started slipping through the opening, swimming freely, following the gelding.

On deck, the aft section of the superstructure was ablaze, providing some light in the dark night. Dozens of men leapt overboard and swam toward the few life boats that had been lowered. On the starboard side, two seamen produced knives and cut the lines holding one lifeboat in place, then lifted it over the rail and let it go to slide down the side, grinding against exposed hardware and splashed into the water. Other sailors scrambled to another lifeboat still hanging from its davit and began cutting it free. Just then, the funnel split away from its base, shrieking and juddering as it fell. Terrified, the men on the starboard deck ceased cutting the lifeboat free and leaped over the side.

In the water now, Bertie caught up with the horses, swimming aimlessly for their lives. He spotted the big gelding and hauled himself over its back, looking around desperately for a reference to swim toward. He saw a flicker of light to the north, so with fists full of mane, he guided the gelding in that direction, looking back at the others to see if they were following. Several of them veered off to the east.

Bertie looked up at the funnel on deck and kicked his horse to get out of its way. The stack broke away with an ear-splitting screech and plunged into the water, creating an upsurge of water just feet from his small group of survivors. For a moment, he was overwhelmed by a sucking wall of cold, black water. He saw one horse thrash and disappear beneath the surface. Next to him another one kicked frantically, floundered and sank. Horrified, Bertie shouted: "Come on!" to the beasts around him. "It's not that far! This way!" He waved his arm, gesturing northward.

The *Royal Michael* was fully engulfed in flames. The occupants of the lifeboats watched in awe as the burning ship upended and began its descent to the bottom of the sea. They saw the animals bobbing on the surface, heading away from the ship. Sailors and soldiers, some on fire, were still vaulting into the water and swimming to the life boats.

The first officer made it to a boat and clambered in. Chest heaving, he wiped the salt water off his face and squeezed himself in amongst the others. He caught sight of the man and animals in the water. "Will you look at that!" he exclaimed to the others. "Where's 'e takin' those daft creatures?" The other seamen in the boat looked at the flotilla. It was such an unlikely sight it might have inspired a joke if the circumstances had not been so desperate. "He's a right stout lad, our Bertie," Benson commented under his breath.

The men huddled in the lifeboat began calling out to Bertie, cheering him on. Bertie resembled a valiant crusader riding on the back of his mighty steed. "By God, I hope he gets himself and them beasts to safety," a sailor offered.

Another explosion lifted the ship's stern a few feet, blasting debris in all directions. The men in the lifeboats leaned over and covered their heads with their arms. The few boats that had been lowered were now full and could only serve as floats for men in the water to hold to. Some were injured and without life jackets. They bobbled perilously in the water, snatching for the rims of the boats or anything that floated.

"There's men in the water there, sir!" a sailor called to the first officer, pointing to an overturned lifeboat fifty yards away. Though he could not swim, Sam had his life jacket on and was anxiously clutching the bottom of the overturned boat. He caught sight of Bertie and the animals.

"Berteeee!" Sam yelled. Bertie could not hear him.

An NCO and the first officer were watching Bertie, too.

"Where's he going, sir?" the NCO asked.

"Hey!" the first officer yelled. "Hey youuuuu!"

"How far is the shore, sir?"

"About two, maybe three, miles," the first officer estimated.

"What do we do, sir?" asked another.

The first officer looked around at the six lifeboats drifting near them. In the distance, men were struggling to escape the cold water and drape themselves onto the one lifeboat that had flipped. He looked at Bertie and the animals who were now almost out of sight. Everyone looked to him for a decision.

"Shouldn't we go after him?" one of them asked. "The captain—"

"The captain's dead! Row southwest!" the first officer ordered.

The men obeyed and the boats swung around. The first officer took a last look at Bertie, now 100 yards away, then lost sight of him in the smoke. A cargo hatch blew open from a pocket of air, sending it hurdling off the stern. Moments later, the *Royal Michael* gave a mighty exhale and slipped into the depths of the Aegean Sea.

"Berteeeee!" Sam screamed repeatedly. He looked at the first officer. "You can't leave 'em, sir! You can't!" His voice cracked. "Berteeeee!"

"Damned cheesemaker," muttered Max Wainright, as he pulled on an oar. "God be with him."

Sam called over and over to Bertie. He let go of the lifeboat and kicked his legs in the direction his brother had taken. Other soldiers in the water grabbed him and pulled him back.

"Berteeeee! Berteeeee! Berteeeee!"

Out of earshot, Bertie and the animals disappeared into the night.

Rawhead farm, c. 1905 (photo courtesy of the author)

PART I

1908 – 1914

--- 1 ---

Malpas Parish, Cheshire, England
October 1908

Joseph Bebbington looked across the cornfield to see who was driving up the road. The large stand of pine trees west of the farm, known as The Clump, obscured the approach. Daily events on the Cheshire plain were fairly predictable. Rent collections from the estate landlord were predictable, for example, though the arrival of Edgar, the village postman, was not. Milking time for cows was predictable, though the image of his twelve children hard at their chores was not. A patient man, he stood and waited for whoever was coming. He could hear the clatter of a one-horse trap.

Joseph stepped forward squinting against the mid-morning sun. It was a fine Cheshire day with few clouds and a slight, chilly breeze. He made out his landlord Gilbert Bryden and the Ballantyne Estate land agent William Cutter in the carriage. He relaxed his shoulders.

The Brydens of Ballantyne were pleasant to deal with, as far as landlords went. They asked much of their tenants, but on the other hand, they invested in their farms and rarely evicted anyone. In fact, the Brydens were known for their efforts to improve the condition of the humbler classes in general. Nearly every good cause aroused their sympathy. They favored building schools and churches, for example, and supported other local Christian and philanthropic causes.

Joseph Bebbington tried to make himself presentable as best he could without using the watering trough in the courtyard. He was already within view of his landlord. Joseph knew Bryden trusted the Bebbington name because the family consistently produced top quality Farmhouse Cheshire cheese and superior dairy products. The Bebbingtons of Rawhead worked very hard and were considered expert dairymen and cheesemakers by landlord and peers alike.

"Clem!" Joseph called to his son. "Put Bo and Wendy in their pen!"

A handsome young man of twenty-two stepped from the cheese room into the courtyard. He wore a long white apron and cap. His brown rubber gloves were slimy from packing cheese into forms.

Clem peered out the open gate at Joseph and saw the approaching carriage. "Yes, Father!" He whistled for the pair of sheep dogs.

The farm was typical of those within large estates throughout England. It ranged over a broad hill a quarter mile south of the Rawhead Escarpment. A landmark in the area, the escarpment was the highest point in the Peckforton Hills and Cheshire County. Measuring 745 feet in height, the distinctive red sandstone cliff, sculpted by ages of wind and rain, was a landmark visible for miles across the Cheshire plain on a clear day. The lofty heights offered sweeping views of the Mersey River, Birkenhead and Liverpool, roughly forty miles away.

Family photo c. 1908. William and Martha Evans' Wedding
Photo courtesy of the author

The Rawhead Farm buildings consisted of a two-story sandstone brick house and a U-shaped barn made of the same material. The bricks were hand cast from the mottled red sandstone native to the area. Both house and barn abutted a rectangular, cobblestone-paved courtyard. The barn housed the livestock, milking floor, farm implements, conveyances and winter feed stores. The cheese parlor was next to the house to one side of the courtyard.

Over forty years old, Rawhead Farm represented the newest addition to the Ballantyne holdings. The Estate's other farms included Lower Rawhead, Droppingstone, Bankhead, Oak Bank, Ballantyne Hill, Old Inn, Little Ballantyne Hill and still others further away. A different family had worked Rawhead Farm for four years before old Robert Bryden hired Joseph Bebbington in 1884 "to grow it to profitability." When he assumed tenancy of Rawhead, Joseph moved his new wife, Mary

Richardson, into the sturdy farmhouse. Robert Bryden died a year later at eighty-seven, at which time his only son Gilbert took over ownership and management of the estate. Gilbert Bryden had advised Joseph when he hired him "to have a large family". He knew children were made to help with the work and "children didn't get paid".

Joseph's wiry 6'2" frame was deceiving. He was powerfully muscled, his facial features, chiseled. He had a full head of dark hair shot with grey. His eyes were brown and deep set and he had leathery skin, toughened by more than four decades of raw Cheshire weather. He was fifty years old and practically illiterate, though he had wisely married a woman who could compensate for his educational shortcomings. When he asked for her hand, she had already lost two husbands and was a few years his senior.

Joseph wiped his hands on his overalls and finger-combed his hair. He buttoned the top button of his dark blue cotton shirt and frowned at his clothes. He was too clean, he knew, despite a busy morning. He was normally covered with dirt by this time of day, but he had spent a few minutes with Mary on the accounts that morning, hence his clothes appeared cleaner. Reaching down, he grabbed a handful of mud and smeared it across one knee. "Blast!" Joseph muttered, feeling ridiculous. He strode out to meet the carriage, raising his hand in greeting. Gilbert Bryden did not return the gesture.

The economy of rural Cheshire in 1908 was healthy because the demand for its dairy products was high and growing. Dairy farming was the primary industry followed by salt and coal mining. Four out of five people were gainfully employed. Cheshire cheese had a reputation for creamy texture and tangy bite. Prevailing opinion held that the rich green pastures of the Cheshire plain lent a salty flavor to the milk produced by the cows that grazed on them.

The region's prosperity was propelled forward by the arrival of the railroad in 1850. The railroad brought jobs and forged trade relationships with other parts of England and the European countries. The service economy thrived while manufacturing burgeoned and diversified. Farms were more productive due to improved methods. Rents rose and arrears fell, all of which pointed toward prosperity.

In 1908, Cheshire County encompassed 600,000 acres of fertile land. Largely flat, the county is bordered by North Wales to the west, the Mersey River to the north, Derbyshire to the east and Shropshire and Staffordshire to the south.

Many farms in the parish were owned by wealthy estates. Rawhead Farm originated in 1750 when a gentleman named James Burrows commissioned the construction of a stately home built of locally quarried red sandstone. He called it Ballantyne Castle. Since then, the land and hall had passed through many hands. In 1836, the Castle was purchased by Robert Bryden, a Scottish entrepreneur who relocated from Ayr to Cheshire to establish a cotton textile business in Manchester. To augment his wealth, he acquired a 100-acre parcel near Ballantyne Castle in 1865 and constructed a two-story red sandstone farmhouse in the center. He named the farm Rawhead after the escarpment, amending the name from two words to one.

"There is a cleanliness of everything about the place," William Cutter said to Bryden about Rawhead as they bounced along in the carriage toward the farm. "A model of what a dairy farm should be." The kitchen and the great room in the house were stocked with dark wood furniture. Above an ornately carved chest of drawers, good china tableware stood in plate racks and shelves. There was an oak settle in the kitchen and a wood-burning fireplace in the great room.

The farms of Ballantyne and other nearby estates were not created by accident. Since the Middle Ages, the land in the area was deemed ideal for dairying because of the salty, mineral-rich soil. The author Daniel Dafoe wrote about the region in 1720:

> *The soil is extraordinarily good and the grass they say has a peculiar richness in it which disposes the creatures to give great quantity of milk and that very sweet and good.*

Robert Bryden read Dafoe's words in school and decided that perhaps he would buy a piece of that land someday. He had followed through.

In 1836, the Brydens of Ballantyne were newcomers to Cheshire society. As many as sixty noblemen owned rental properties in the area each worth £20,000 or more. Another sixty gentlemen owned portions valued in the £5,000 range. But it was the great landowners who owned over half the county's acreage. Among these were the Duke of Westminster at Eaton Hall, the Earl of Stamford at Dunham Massey, the Marquis of Cholmondeley at Cholmondeley Castle and Lord Tollemache of Peckforton Castle. As many as thirteen of these lofty personages owned residences in both Cheshire and London. The Brydens were known as squires or prosperous farmers as opposed to titled noblemen or gentry.

In 1908, Gilbert Bryden was sixty-seven. He was of medium height and portly. Mostly bald, what remained of his dark grey hair fringed the lower back of his head from ear to ear. He sported arduous sideburns that reached nearly to his chin. Well educated, he graduated from the Harrow School in London followed by Oxford University, obtaining both bachelor and master's degrees in economics and a Doctor of Law. Soon after completing his education, he took up the post of Director of the

Manchester and Liverpool Regional Bank which was founded by his father, Robert.

Both father and son were members of the Cheshire Yeomanry, Gilbert for thirty-two years. He rose from Cornet to Captain and participated in the first Boer War. In 1869, he married Ella Whyte of the McGregor Family of Steersgun Castle in Scotland. They had a son in 1876 and named him Robert after Gilbert's father. Robert arrived after seven years of "enduring" as Gilbert lamented, the births of six daughters. The arrival of his long-awaited son was such an event he threw a gala celebration on estate grounds and invited his entire acquaintance.

As Gilbert and the land agent approached Rawhead farm, Cutter remarked, "Mr. Harrison of Hill Farm wants to supply Bickerton Farm with marl and bone." He wrapped the reins of the two horses in harness. He was referring to a form of crumbly earth much prized among farmers for its calcium and lime content.

"Tell him no! Why deplete his own land of minerals?" Bryden asked as he surveyed the passing fields. He occasionally gestured to the heavens to punctuate his remarks. "Cutter, I hired you to be my land agent because I heard you were a man of experience, probity and sound judgment. I expect regular reports on rent collections and condition of the farms."

"Yessir," Cutter murmured.

"Take this fellow at the Moss Farm for study," Bryden went on, pulling a rolled ledger from his jacket pocket. "What's his name?"

"Tydd, sir," Cutter supplied as they turned onto the Rawhead Farm road. "James Tydd."

"Tydd!" Bryden spat. "That's him. Tydd the Fat Irishman! Cutter, here we have a man with a large family who takes no account of his receipts or disbursements and wastes land in his allotment. He delights more in serving hunters and falconers than in tilling my land! I know he's given to his stomach. The sorry man's grown so obese he can hardly walk. I tell you if the man ate less of the cheese he makes and sold more, he might make better of himself!" he harrumphed. "And me!" he added.

Cutter's eyes cautiously drifted to Bryden's large belly. Bryden scowled. Clearing his throat, Cutter quickly turned back to the road ahead. "Mind me, I won't stand for this type of mismanagement by the tenants, Cutter!"

"Inexcusable, sir. I'll look into it directly. Now, here we have Rawhead Farm, sir." Cutter deftly steered the conversation away from James Tydd. "Currently, it occupies one hundred acres at a rent of two pounds per acre per annum. Produced sixteen thousand pounds of Cheshire cheese in 1907!"

"Ah yes, the Bebbingtons," uttered Bryden. "Well, being mad Methodists carries no weight with me, mind you! Quite the contrary."

"Yes, sir."

Joseph greeted them as Gilbert Bryden and his agent drove into the cobblestone courtyard. He took the bridal of the nearest horse and walked it tightly around so both animals were headed toward the exit. There were no circular or drive-through outlets like at Ballantyne Castle. The large, smooth river stones which paved the courtyard always felt uncomfortable under Joseph's booted feet. He would like to have the surface replaced with macadam; the crushed rock surface developed by Scotsman John Macadam in 1820. Macadam-covered roads were easier to navigate by foot, horseback or carriage but he suspected his landlord might not approve the expense.

"Good day, Joseph," called Bryden. He and Cutter climbed down from the carriage.

"Good day, Squire Bryden, Mr. Cutter," Joseph replied, smiling.

Bryden extended his hand and they shook. Bryden surveyed Joseph's appearance, noting that his clothes looked remarkably clean for a weekday morning. "You're not just starting the day, are you?"

"No, sir!" assured Joseph. "We've been awake since 4:30 this morning! The cows are milked and out to pasture. Clem is in the cheese parlor. Sam is in Broxton delivering the milk and Bertie is…in the east field." He gestured vaguely toward a horse-drawn hay mower raising dust in the distance. "Andrew is…baking bread or out hunting with Dave. Can never be sure."

Gilbert Bryden looked around. "And your other children?"

"Philip, David, Jim and Mollie are in school, sir. Bickerton. I didn't see the need for them to stay home."

"And your other children?"

Joseph grinned. "Jack and Tom are in the house with Mary. They're just four and five. George is a miller's apprentice now. In Tilston."

"And your other children?"

Joseph looked at him quizzically. "I believe that's all, sir. You did suggest I have a large family, to work the farm?"

Bryden managed a grin. "And you?"

"Working on the trap, sir. One of the axles broke—nearly threw Mary when she drove to Chester Market last week."

"Goodness," Bryden exclaimed. "I hope she's all right. I won't take up much of your time. I've come to see your books. I trust they are current?"

"Yessir. Mary's good about that."

Joseph led his landlord and the agent through the cheese parlor and into the kitchen, normally a hive of activity. The combined aromas of meat roasting and fresh bread cooling in pans on the hob greeted them. Buckets of turnips rested on the floor waiting to be processed. A long oak table, with fourteen ladder-back chairs around it, was set neatly for the upcoming lunch.

Breakfast at 6 a.m. consisted of bread, butter, marmalade, cheese, hard-boiled eggs, porridge, ham, and fruit. On Sundays, they all enjoyed a traditional English breakfast of bangers, kippers, black pudding, and scrambled, fried or poached eggs. On weekday mornings there was never enough time to cook it or eat it because school started early and the milking had to be done. They all drank mugs of strong, hot tea or milk with their meals. They paused for a tea break at 10 a.m. then gathered for the largest meal of the day at noon. They ate a variety of foods for lunch: stew, soup, cheese, potatoes, tomatoes, homemade bread, savory and sweet pies, hard-boiled eggs, apples, pears.

If away from the farm at lunchtime, pubs offered a ploughman's lunch as a quick and economical bite. These consisted of rolls, butter, a generous portion of cheese, pickles and salad, and was usually washed down with a pint of beer. Sunday dinners as well as breakfasts were special. After returning from chapel in the late morning, the family sat down to a large meal of roast beef or pork with potatoes, parsnips, peas, Brussel sprouts, green beans, bread, Yorkshire pudding and gravy. Yorkshire pudding was a moist egg batter baked in roast beef drippings. The farm maintained a large vegetable garden and regularly harvested fresh vegetables for the table. Jars of fruit preserves, jams, butters, piccalilli, chutney, relish, and pickled onions lined the Rawhead larder.

Another break for refreshment took place at 4 p.m. This meal, known as Tea, represented the evening meal for small children. They were put to bed in the early evening while adults and older children sat down to a more formal repast at 8 p.m. Tea usually consisted of sandwiches, fruit, breads, and hot tea. The formal three-course cream tea, with its requisite selection of at least three kinds of sandwiches, biscuits, preserves, fresh berries, clotted cream and a rich selection of iced cakes, was served in commercial tea establishments and in the homes of the wealthy. Working farmers rarely interrupted their regimen to sit down with the family for a snack at 4 p.m. After the noon meal, they grabbed a jar of tea and a hunk of bread to take with them as they headed back to work. Dinner generally consisted of leftovers from lunch, sometimes cold. It was also referred to as supper.

Now, as the three men walked through the cheese parlor, Gilbert Bryden helped himself to a sample of the Cheshire.

"May I?" Bryden asked.

"Of course," Joseph answered.

He studied it and sniffed it before taking a bite. "A tad salty," he remarked to Cutter, though he thought it tasted delicious. Cutter quickly scribbled something in his ledger. Bryden reached for another slice of cheese. Mary Bebbington called from the kitchen. "Squire Bryden, how good to see you this morning! And Mr. Cutter."

"Mary," replied Bryden, smiling.

Joseph's wife Mary was a study. At fifty-three, she stood 5' 3" tall and appeared to be almost as wide as she was tall. She had a broad face, several chins and bright, intelligent brown eyes. Her dark hair was scraped off her face and pinned to the back of her head. She smiled at the men. "Will you join us for lunch?" she invited. Bryden and Cutter politely declined.

She wore a "Cheshire bed gown": a long-sleeved, short jacket open in front and tied at the waist. Underneath the jacket her dress was long and plain, generally blue or black. She wore this ensemble for every occasion except, despite its name, to bed. She had never been seen in a coat, preferring shawls and never seemed to be ill. She was a strong, hearty, country soul, accustomed to farm work and childrearing.

Joseph led the two men to a small room down the hall where an open, roll top desk sat open. The farm's accounting ledger and receipts were neatly stacked on the desktop. Such reviews were normally accomplished by Cutter. But a surprise visit from Bryden was not uncommon. He picked one or two of the estate farms to drop by on a rotating basis. Bryden produced a pair of spectacles and lifted the ledger that Mary had updated just the hour before and paged through it quickly.

"You've…150 heifers at this time?" inquired Bryden.

"Yessir."

"And how many acres of winter corn planted?"

"Eighty now, sir."

Bryden put down the ledger. "A good cow will produce 400 pounds of cheese per year and the plough is the servant of the milk pail, Joseph. I expect at least one hundred acres to be planted!"

"Working on that, sir."

"Your sons Clement and Samuel are of marrying age. I trust they will convey their trade to your younger sons before starting their own families? Particularly how to make Ballantyne Cheshire?"

"Certainly, sir." Joseph rarely considered the possibility of his sons leaving the farm. He vaguely remembered his own inclination to leave his father's shoemaking business thirty-five years previously. He had apprenticed with a dairy farmer in Broxton because he preferred not to cobble shoes. Bryden and Cutter soon concluded their visit and departed with no substantive complaints, requests or praise. Joseph and the family returned to work.

This was Rawhead. It was home to a family of fifteen, self-contained and sustaining. It was a place that required many hands to make it work and it was an important component of the Ballantyne Estate. The country had been at peace for decades and the economy was bountiful. In the words of A.G. Street, "It was not a luxurious existence of any kind, but there was a spaciousness and an aura of solid well-being."

--- **2** ---

Philip Henry Bebbington struck the cricket ball so hard that it split the bat in two. It was Sunday, and cricket was the game of choice. After the game, Philip picked up the bat pieces and tossed them aside. The family attended church that morning and rested for a few hours on the lawn at Rawhead snacking on ham and buttered bread, and samples of Bertie and Sam's homemade ginger beer. For supper, they ate roast beef, Yorkshire pudding, suet gravy, and boiled turnips.

Around the long dinner table sat Joseph, Mary, George, Martha, Elizabeth, Sam, Clem, Bertie, Andrew, Philip, Dave, Jim, Mollie, John "Jack" and Tom. George was the eldest at twenty-four and Tom the youngest at five. Those in between the two were born one to two years apart, ten in the big bed upstairs with a midwife in attendance. Joseph, Andrew and Bertie had thick hair. The rest of the boys had thin hair which predetermined baldness in their maturity. Joseph and George were tall and lanky at 6'2", while Dave and Jack were the shortest at 5'5." Sam was stocky and the rest tended to be lean. Bertie had a gentle, childlike nature and was generally amiable. The others were more serious and guarded.

Finishing a noisy Sunday dinner, Dave stared pointedly at Clem, urging him to make good on a promise he made earlier that day. Clem nodded at him but Dave began nudging him under the table.

"Father, do you think I could teach Dave to plough?" Clem said, irritated.

Their father thought the request over and shook his head. He looked at Dave. "You're what, ten now Dave? Another year, son."

Alarmed, Dave made a face at Clem wanting him to press the issue. "I won't be here next year," Clem informed his father which got everyone's attention. Not looking at anyone, he reached for another piece of bread. "I joined the Navy." They were stunned, never expecting such a revelation.

"Oh, Clem…" Mary murmured, her hand covering her mouth.

"When did you do that?" His father asked.

"Yesterday in Chester. I don't want to make cheese anymore, Pa. I don't want to plough or milk cows or any of it." He looked mutinous.

"There's not a war on," Mary reminded him.

"Something's always going on somewhere," Clem informed her. "The Navy's building lots of ships and needs men to sail 'em. I haven't seen any of the world, except here. I'm eighteen. It's time."

"Can I have your rifle?" Andrew asked hopefully.

"Yes, but you must let me show you how to use it," Clem said.

"I already know how."

Joseph knew Clem was restless. He understood the lure, and the danger, of the world outside of the farm. Hours of ploughing allowed the mind to wander to places learned about in school books.

"You're a grown man now Clem. You must do what you think is best. We shall miss you, son."

"Who's going to teach me to plough?" Dave worried.

Jim flipped a piece of wet biscuit at Dave with a spoon, striking his neck.

"Mum!" Dave said, wiping it off. "Jim spat in my face!"

As the Bebbington family ate dinner, so did the Brydens of Ballantyne Castle, but in significantly different surroundings. Seated high in the Broxton Hills on sweeping grounds made up of lush lawns, formal gardens, and wooded areas, Ballantyne offered a spectacular view of Chester, Liverpool and the Welsh mountains. Constructed of red sandstone brick, the three-story residence had wide, canted bays and a castellated roofline. The centerpiece was a four-story tower with turrets. Encircling the house and grounds were sandstone walls punctuated by graceful steps leading to upper and middle terraces. Some were large enough to accommodate sporting events. There was a gate house, stables, a bridge over a fish pond, a gazebo beside a small lake, and a boat house. A grand manor, indeed.

Ballantyne Castle could not rival the nearby Cholmondeley, Delamere or other estates for sheer size, but held its own in a handsome, charming way. The estate staff in 1909 included a tutor, butler, footmen, housekeeper, cook, maids, a dressmaker, coachmen, gamekeepers, grooms, stable hands, and a small fleet of gardeners and groundskeepers, excluding the tenantry on the farms.

Family dinners were formal affairs. Young Robert Bryden observed his father Gilbert at the head of the table, who was focused on his plate. Gilbert engaged in polite conversation only when the family entertained guests for dinner. He discussed business with his associates in the solitude of the library. Ideally, he liked to take his male guests shooting before dinner which afforded ample opportunity for serious conversation. Seated around the Bryden table were Gilbert, his wife Ella, Robert, Meredith, Melissa, Lesley, Lindsay, Bethany, and Megan.

"Tell us about your trip to London, Gilbert," Ella urged. Perversely, she liked to interrupt his silences. Bryden masked his irritation by touching his mouth with his napkin.

"Father's been elected to the presidential chair of the British Dairy Association!" Robert volunteered. The family applauded the news.

"How wonderful, father!" exclaimed Meredith. "Lord Belper has done a lot to help you reach that post!"

"Lord Belper had nothing to do with it," Bethany said. "He achieved the distinction by making the finest cheese in all of Britain."

"It might be good of you to send notes to the farmers," Ella suggested. "I mean, they are the ones who actually produce the cheese."

Gilbert Bryden acknowledged her comment with a curt nod. He had already arranged for a Harthill printer to send letters to his tenants and to place news of his appointment in the *Liverpool Journal of Commerce* and the *Chester Chronicle*. He had not told his wife this. He was too much of a gentleman to shrug off her suggestions, and wanted people to believe they had provided him with advice that had not yet occurred to him. His father passed that bit of wisdom to him years before. "Excellent idea, dear," he graced Ella with a smile.

Ella looked across the table at Robert. "That is a position I should like you to hold as well, Robert. And High Sheriff, like your father, when the time comes."

"I have an announcement to make," Robert announced abruptly. "I am going to be married."

His father choked on a piece of the aged pheasant he bagged a week earlier. He covered his mouth with his napkin. Everyone looked at him with concern as they reacted to Robert's news.

"Married?" croaked Gilbert Bryden. "To whom?"

Robert took a sip of tea. "To Miss Heidi Allerton Moore," Robert answered, staring at his tea cup.

"How wonderful!" Merideth beamed.

"Of the Manchester Moores?" asked his father, trying to summon his knowledge of the family.

"The same," Robert confirmed, reaching for a West Indies orange. "And Galloway County. Her family wants the ceremony to be at Cally House Chapel in Gatehouse of Fleet on the 28th," he answered. Gilbert Bryden choked again.

"Gilbert, stop eating!" Ella ordered.

"So romantic," Merideth whispered dreamily.

"Of October?" Bryden asked, glaring. "But that's only a month away! I had no idea you were keen on a particular woman."

"I am, father," Robert affirmed as he stood, peeling the orange. "Now if you will excuse me." He bowed politely to his mother and laid his napkin on his chair. Before his father could stop him, he turned and left the dining room.

"I wonder whom I shall marry," Lindsay said, smiling at her sisters from under her lashes.

"No one without our permission, I can assure you!" Gilbert told her vehemently. The girls frowned in unison.

Robert Bryden decided to go for a ride. He had much preferred congratulations from his father rather than the inquisition he usually got every time he mentioned a female acquaintance. In 1907, he and his best friend A.G. Wilkinson caught a steamer to the Olympic mountains in Washington state, for a shooting holiday. At a Yeomanry function before the trip, both men met marriageable young ladies. After the round of social functions, neither man grew enamored of any of the women. Over Highland scotch and cigars, they decided to leave Cheshire for a time rather than risk being talked into what was probably a sensible arrangement for them both. By the time they had met most of the eligible young women in Cheshire and surrounding counties, they had become disappointed in the prospect of ever finding love.

"Robert!" he heard his father call from the hallway. Ella Bryden appeared behind her husband. Robert halted in stride. With his back to his parents, he rolled his eyes. Gilbert said firmly: "I would like a word with you. Please come into the library."

Robert reluctantly followed his father into the windowless library a few steps away. The walls were sheathed with hundreds of books. Robert never liked the room. It was dark and airless, and smelled of cigars and dusty, old tomes. It reminded him of his seemingly endless days at the Harrow School and Oxford. He had not been the scholar his father had been, preferring active, outdoor pursuits. He had barely managed to graduate and take his place at the bar.

"What's the meaning of this?" his father inquired.

"Nothing ambiguous about it, father. I simply want to marry the woman I love."

Bryden placed his hand on his son's shoulder.

"What happened to that charming girl from Cholmondeley Castle who—"

Robert half-turned and ripped his orange apart. "If you insist on tying me to one of these boring gentry' families, I'll leave again. I'll go to New Guinea to shoot!" Bryden waited for his son to finish.

"With that fool-on-a-horse friend of yours? Wilkinson? He's a bloody miscreant!"

"He's been my friend since Harrow!" Robert said defiantly.

"Well, you've made a poor choice in friends, Robert. You made good marks at Harrow and Oxford. Wilkinson hardly attended instruction. His family's acquaintances got him through!"

"Harrow doesn't award grades for money," Robert told him through clenched teeth. "If it did, I'd have been a scholar. I barely scraped through and you know it!"

Robert strode to a five-inch thick world atlas resting on a spindly easel. He began flipping through its pages. The easel swayed and creaked, threatening collapse. He arrived at a plate illustrating Colonial Africa.

"We'll go to Kenya this time. And shoot," he hesitated, searching for an appropriate target. "Rhinoceros!" he announced triumphantly.

"Well, I hope Wilkinson gets trampled by one!" Bryden said. "He is a disgrace to the Yeomanry! It's only out of respect for his father that I--"

"You've misjudged him based on a few minor mishaps."

"I did not raise you to run away with your mates every time responsibility confronts you!" Bryden spat.

"Getting married is not a responsibility I recognize," Robert declared. "Rather it's spending the next fifty years with a dull woman I worry about."

"And what is your idea of responsibility? Running off to shoot game in far-flung Mongolia?"

"Father," Robert said calmly, closing the atlas with a clap, then facing his father. "I do not wish to avoid responsibility. I welcome it as a matter of fact. That is precisely why I am going to marry Heidi Moore on October 28th in Cally House Chapel in Gatehouse of Fleet."

Robert started for the door.

"Where are you going?" his father demanded.

"For a ride. Do I require your permission for that?" Robert asked, his eyes boring into his father's.

"Do you know how the Moore family made its money?" Gilbert Bryden threw at his son, who was fast making his escape out the door.

"I don't care!" Robert threw back, turning to face his father. "Our family's wealth is based on slave trade, is it not?"

"No, it most certainly is not!" Gilbert Bryden shouted, horrified. "I only named the business Ballantyne. I did not name it after that Liverpool slave trader from a century ago. That wretched fellow was not a Bryden. Our wealth is derived from cotton and textiles!"

Robert Bryden leaned into his father's face. "And who picked that cotton in America?" His son had the high ground now, and Gilbert knew it. Before his father could speak, Robert added, "If you attend the wedding, bring your guns for afterwards. Her father is the best shot in Galloway County!" Robert turned and left the room, briskly making his way to the stables.

A shoot! Gilbert Bryden pondered the prospect. Any man who was a good game shot could not be half bad. Brilliant!

Robert felt a good ride would be best about now. A good ride was far better than a drink. It was quite understandable why Robert Bryden chose to give up his bachelorhood for Heidi Moore. She was as beautiful as she was intelligent. For anyone who saw her, and especially to anyone who knew her, he was a fool to not marry her. To say she was beautiful was not enough. Heidi Moore had a flawless complexion, thick cherry brown hair framing large eyes of the richest shade of green. She walked, rode, and danced with wonderful grace, and sang and played both piano and harp with uncommon skill. Robert concluded that it was her parents, not his, who should be questioning the marriage, if at all.

Gilbert Bryden observed his son through a bay window as he walked to the stables. As much as he loved his seven daughters and could easily influence the selection of their husbands from Cheshire society, Robert was a different story. He was the pride of his life, following in nearly the footsteps he had. School at the prestigious Harrow School in London, Oxford, admission to the Inner Temple, Justice of the Peace, Doctor of Law, and then becoming an officer in the Cheshire Yeomanry. But above all else, he was a servant to his tenants.

Nine years earlier, when the young Lieutenant Robert Bryden was ordered to South Africa to fight in the Second Anglo-Boer War, his father confronted him at Ballantyne and begged him not to go, despite his insistence that he become a leader in the Yeomanry a decade earlier. On the morning he departed from Liverpool, Bryden accompanied his son to the SS *Lake Erie* at dockside and pleaded with him one last time to stay, on the suggestion of "a last-minute illness". Gilbert Bryden could not, and would not, lose his only son and heir after thirty years of rearing. Yet, all his pleas failed. They parted tritely with Robert's overly noble words, "Am I to lead men for the Yeomanry as I have trained or continue to entertain civic dignitaries and young ladies over tea?"

With his son aboard ship, Gilbert Bryden's driver closed his door and assumed his seat behind the wheel.

"Back to Ballantyne, sir?" he asked.

"No. My insurance broker on Essex Street."

"I have doubts they'll be open, sir."

"He'll be open," Bryden said as he opened a copy of the *Financial World*. "If not, I'll call and advise him to reopen. I have an insurance policy to purchase!"

Robert Bryden arrived at the stables and arranged for a mount. The stable boy knew Robert favored riding the spirited gelding named Carlton. Seated comfortably he rode to a high point overlooking Ballantyne and Harthill. From there, he could see the dining room in the castle still lit. He then whipped his horse into a gallop and headed in the direction of the cemetery.

Bertie Bebbington had taken a Rawhead horse for a trip to Chester via Harthill to obtain medication from a veterinarian. A hundred yards to his right he observed Bryden on a horse, bucking and recoiling. Bertie kicked his horse into a run towards them, jumping a hedge in route. Bertie galloped up to Bryden and began efforts to calm his horse. Bertie knew from experience that some horses tended to be scared easily or get 'spooked'. A horse's emotions depend on its surroundings and the emotions of its rider. Sometimes spooking occurs because a horse comes into contact with an unfamiliar object, sometimes because of an alteration of its routine, and sometimes inexplicably. Bryden dismounted and stepped away to catch his breath.

"Are you all right, sir?" Bertie asked as he grabbed Carlton's reins. He rubbed his withers and whispered soothing sounds in an effort to gently calm the horse.

Bryden nodded. "Yes. Thank you." Bryden couldn't quite recall the young man's name, though he should have. His father always made it a point to know all the employees and tenants in his charge, and those he did business with, no matter how many. It was just plain good business.

"Bert, is it? Of the Bebbingtons at Rawhead Farm?" Bryden recalled.

Bertie smiled. Being called one's name by a landlord he rarely saw was like soothing music. It confirmed he was someone and not just a name on a list.

"Yes, sir." Bertie said.

"I don't know what happened!" Bryden said. "He was fine and then he started bucking."

"Just spooked, sir." Bertie offered. "Something he saw, maybe."

"Maybe,"

"Will you be all right, sir? I can ride with you to the stable."

Bryden remounted Carlton. "No, thank you. Have a good evening, Bert."

Bertie watched his landlord slowly ride back toward the stables. He led his horse around the immediate area looking for something that might have startled Bryden's horse, but saw nothing.

In the weeks before Robert Bryden and Heidi Moore's wedding, the Ballantyne butler, Lloyd Green, knocked on an office door.

"Come."

"Miss Moore is here and wishes to see you.

Bryden sat in a leather chair looking through a bay window.

"Please send her in. Thank you, Lloyd." Bryden stood.

Heidi Moore appeared and Lloyd closed the door quietly. Her mere presence was overpowering. The two walked to each other and embraced.

"I had to see you, Robert. There are some wedding details I wanted to discuss with you."

"I am sure they will be fine," Robert said touching her hair.

Robert turned and walked to the fog shrouded window.

"What's wrong?" she asked.

"Heidi, I need to talk with you about something that weighs heavily on my mind."

"Of course."

"As you know, I will become landlord of this estate soon. Responsible for the welfare of tenants and employees. Building and serving as County Sheriff."

"I know that, my love," Heidi responded curiously.

"And I am also many other things, including being an officer in the Yeomanry. All duties my father and his father had will be passed on to me. These things will take me away from you from time to time. For weeks or months, perhaps even years. I wonder what else lies beyond that fog."

Heidi stepped closer to her fiancé, wondering what he was thinking before the tall window.

"Years? If you're gone that long, I will come to you."

Robert turned to her, taking her hands. "Not if I am in Palestine or South Africa, or some other place where conflict always seems to erupt. It would be unsafe for you, my love. I wanted you to know that."

"You're being elusive again, Robert. Please step out of the fog and speak plainly."

He looked into her beautiful eyes. "I will love you Heidi, and only you. There will never be anyone else. If I should ever be killed, please always know that."

Heidi pushed him away. "Don't do this, Robert!" she demanded. "You're not going to be killed! Why are you doing this?"

"I don't know Heidi," Robert said solemnly. "I just sense the years ahead of us. Things going on in the world."

Heidi wiped away a tear. "Well if you keep thinking that way, you will be killed. Stop!" Accept some money from your father and quit the Yeomanry and your duties. You already served in South Africa! How many wars must you serve in? We'll go away somewhere."

"Quit the Yeomanry? And what would my tenants say of me when they are asked to go in my stead?"

"Robert, you don't owe them anything!"

"I wish I owed nothing to anyone," Robert replied, his true feelings coming to the surface. "But I always will. Don't you see it? That's the life I have inherited."

"Your father again! Oh, what are you telling me, Robert? You don't want to marry me?"

"I am telling you that you have a choice. You're a beautiful woman and you can have any man you wish," his voice trailing to a whisper.

Heidi stepped to him.

"Please, Heidi," Robert said halting her. "Please think about us and what I've told you." Robert withdrew his gold pocket watch from his vest and observed the time. "I must be off. I've a meeting with Cutter."

Heidi took his hands into hers, tears streaming down her face. "Robert Bryden, I have thought about us," she cried. "I love you and want to spend my life with you. But I don't want to see you torture yourself with your father and the responsibilities he and this place have laid upon you! If things ever begin to destroy you, we can just go away. To…South Africa or India."

Robert looked into her eyes, now glassy with tears. He felt his strength eroding. "And do what, Heidi?" he asked. "There's no place on earth we could go that would be far enough."

"Then I will protect you," Heidi promised. "I will be your savior."

--- 3 ---

Two very different weddings happened in the autumn of 1909. Robert Bryden married Heidi Allerton Moore, the daughter of a wealthy Scotsman, and George Bebbington married Elizabeth Arrowsmith, daughter of a tenant dairy farmer. Robert Bryden was thirty-three and Heidi Moore twenty-one. George Bebbington was twenty-seven and Elizabeth Arrowsmith, eighteen. The Ballantyne couple were married at Cally House Chapel in Gatehouse of Fleet. The Rawhead Farm couple at the Primitive Methodist Chapel in Nantwich.

In Gatehouse of Fleet, guests came from as far away as Cape Town and Bombay. The wedding was conducted by the bride's uncle, the Reverend Hubert Moore. For many years, Cally House had been rented in the summer months by the Moore family for shooting, and Heidi Moore had fond memories of those times. She suggested the venue to Robert after his proposal during a secret weekend escape there. An 18th-century country house located in the Civil Parish of Girthon, Kirkcudbrightshire, Cally House stood within an extensive estate on the southern fringes of Scotland. It was adorned with riding trails and scenic gardens with sweeping views of the Solway Coast. Built wholly of granite in 1763, the chapel included a splendid marble vestibule filled with fine sculptures and contained a fine collection of paintings, including some by Clande Lorraine, Poussin, and Sir Joshua Reynolds. It also contained the Sèvres wedding casket of Marie Antoinette.

Guests had been arriving for an hour and gathered in the vestibule for pre-wedding drinks and samples of various cheeses from England and abroad, including of course, all varieties of Cheshire cheese. Standing before the altar, Robert Bryden made a handsome, gallant figure. He wore his Cheshire Yeomanry uniform adorned with medals and awards he had earned over fifteen years of service. Beside him was his best man, A.G. Wilkinson.

Heidi Moore wore a white satin dress that had a high collar neckline with decorative bretelles running from the slightly raised waist to cover close-fitting sleeves. She carried a bouquet of flowers selected from Cally greenhouses. She was beautiful. Robert knew he was the envy of many men in attendance.

Robert Bryden and Heidi Moore affirmed their promises to love, honor, and cherish each other for as long as both of them shall live, in accordance with the Anglican Church *Book of Common Prayer*. After the ceremony, the Moore family hosted a wedding feast and served a lavish selection of roasted meats, pastries, cakes, pies, fruits, and vegetables. Local wines and beers were offered. Then, of course, there was the traditional wedding cake nearly four feet tall with a uniformed groom and his bride at the crest. An accomplished band, consisting of a violin, cello, and piano, performed Gilbert and Sullivan, gypsy dances and Viennese waltzes, as well as pieces from the great classical composers.

At his small cottage in Tilston, George Bebbington put on his glasses, straightened his clothes and pinned a flower to his lapel. Minutes later, Bertie picked him up and delivered him to the Primitive Methodist Chapel. The little country chapel was filled to capacity with neighboring farmers and friends. Being the first of her sons to wed, Mary Bebbington was enormously proud. Elizabeth Arrowsmith wore beige chiffon and velvet with a hat of matching material, and satin shoes. She carried a bouquet of chrysanthemums. Bertie was the best man. A simple reception followed at Elizabeth's parent's home with fruit, cakes, tea, roast beef, cheese, and Yorkshire pudding. That night, fireworks exploded above Harthill to celebrate the wedding of their landlord. But the Bebbington family believed the fireworks were for both couples. The boys drank beer and the girls had tea while resting on chairs placed in front of the Rawhead farmhouse. After the reception, George and Elizabeth departed for a five-day honeymoon to Blackpool while the Brydens took a three-month wedding trip to the Far East.

The trip from Mumbai to Colombo, Ceylon took three days by steamer, too long for Heidi Bryden. She much preferred to travel by land whenever possible as sea sickness made ship travel sheer agony. But Robert Bryden begged her to extend their honeymoon south to Ceylon. If sufficiently entertained by the exotic sights, perhaps she would embrace an extension as far as Japan. Robert Bryden sensed that he would not see that part of the world again.

September 1909 saw Philip Bebbington's introduction to cheese making after years of working the farm. He received most of his instruction from his elder brothers and visiting labourers.

He had worked as an assistant to waggoneers, carters, ploughmen, and horsemen. He also took care of the horses for the skilled labourers. Farm work included ploughing and harrowing, cultivating, rolling, drilling, manure carting, mowing and reaping, cutting the chaff, feeding the animals, and carrying hay and straw. Philip had learned how to harness and groom, how to value the quality of corn and hay. He had learned to milk, to clean the mangers, stalls, gutters, and to fetch cows in the fields with Wendy and Bo. He took the milk to market or the railway station twice daily and delivered cheese to warehouses. Later, he learned to make bread, all the while attending school in Bickerton.

Philip knew how Cheshire cheese tasted, smelled, and looked. He briefly witnessed its preparation as a young boy but never actually made it. He remembered liking its taste but grew to favor it less and less because it was always available at Rawhead. But if making cheese took him from his current chores which included cleaning out the midden at 4:30 a.m., he would give it a go. He could no longer bear the stench of the gutters and stalls of the cow houses. He detested clomping around in manure only moments after waking in a warm bed and listening to the infernal crowing of roosters, moans of cows, and the confounded "ee-yawing" of peacocks. He felt farm work just didn't suit him. There had to be some other way to live.

Clem entered the Rawhead cheese parlor carrying a fifty-pound wheel of Cheshire cheese wrapped in cloth. He placed it on the bench before Philip and began to carefully remove the cloth wrapping. For the first time, Philip noticed the cleanliness of everything about the room.

"First, wash your hands," Clem instructed. Philip looked at his hands, which were not particularly dirty, but did as he was told.

"This is Cheshire cheese of the red variety, because annatto is added, giving it the red-yellowish color."

Clem explained that Cheshire cheese is thought to be Britain's oldest named cheese. It was originally the generic name for cheese produced in Cheshire and the surrounding counties of Denbighshire, Flintshire in Wales, Shropshire, and Staffordshire. One of the oldest varieties of cheese made in Britain, Clem explained that the first Cheshire cheese is believed to have been produced by the Romans as mentioned in the Domesday Book in 1086 AD. Cheshire had to have been being made from cow's milk by the late 1600s. A London tavern dating to 1660 even bears its name: The Ye Olde Cheshire Cheese. It is believed that until the late Middle Ages it was made from goat's or sheep's milk, as cows were rare and prized mainly for their ability to give birth to oxen for the fields.

Until the late 19th century, different varieties of Cheshire cheeses were aged to a sufficient hardness to withstand the severities of transport by horse and cart to London. But not all dairy farms in Cheshire made the cheese. From around 1840 the production of Cheshire cheese shifted to Shropshire, as markets for solely milk were developing in the North. Conditions evolved such that younger, fresher, more crumbly cheese was the predominant variety made in the region simply because it was less expensive to make and required less storage. Yet, there were consumers in London and abroad who had grown to prefer the harder Cheshire and as such, turned away from the younger type. Highly prized, some individuals on one occasion even tried to pass off Dutch cheese for Cheshire, labeling it "Pure Cheshire" but were quickly caught and convicted. The court summons cited the fraudulent cheese as not being of "the nature, substance, and quality demanded by the Cheshire cheese customer". The incident was so serious, some said it had the characteristics of a murder trial.

Clem took a knife and cut a one-inch wide wedge from the wheel. Philip noticed the Ballantyne label with a cat expressing a broad, fixed grin.

"What's with the smiling cat?" asked Philip.

Clem grinned. "He's the Cheshire Cat. From *Alice's Adventures in Wonderland*."

"But why is it on the cheese?"

"Branding. Next time I go to Chester to sell some cheese, maybe you'll see why. The cats sitting on the Chester warehouse dock on the River Dee wait for the rats and mice to leave the ships that carry Cheshire cheese to London. They're the happiest cats in England!" They both laughed.

In the course of the day, Clem went through the steps of making Cheshire cheese. Farmhouse Cheshire is of course unpasteurized and was still produced from a unique recipe. Although the instructions were available on a well-fingered sheet of paper tacked to the wall of the cheese parlour, Clem and his older siblings knew it now by heart. And, they never "experimented" by trying different things to improve the product. There was a large demand for Ballantyne Cheshire and that was reason enough not to waver from "true quality and goodness", as Ma put it. From exhaustive experiments conducted at Rawhead and other farms years ago, each pound of fat present in the milk was found to increase the yield of cheese by almost three pounds. On average, one gallon of milk made one pound of cheese. The distinctive tangy flavor is owed to the salty soil from which the cattle graze, as Cheshire was once an inland salt lake.

In a fifty-gallon vat, Clem combined morning and evening's milk which, per the recipe, was collected at 6:30 a.m. and 4:00 p.m. After a period of coagulation, Clem heated the curds in the whey for about forty minutes. As the vat heated, Clem turned to a second vat and drained off the whey, a byproduct used for pig feed. He then had Philip cut the curds with a long knife and tear them into small pieces. As instructed, Philip then salted, milled and placed the pieces into molds for slow pressing over twenty-four to forty-eight hours. In the subsequent days, Philip watched Clem and Sam cut curd in a large tub.

"How is it somebody would decide to add juice from a cow's innards to milk to make cheese?" Philip asked.

"That's a good question," Clem answered as he placed a large chunk of curd into a press. "It's called 'rennet'. Taken from a cow's fourth or true stomach."

"A cow has four stomachs?" Philip inquired.

"Yes. One stores the hay it eats and the others are for digestion.

"I think Sam has four stomachs, seeing the way he eats!" Philip joked.

Hearing him, Sam threw a cheesy towel at Philip.

"I recall Mum saying that a Middle Age traveler once stopped for refreshment with milk they carried in a bag made from an animal's stomach," Clem continued. "After several days of travel, the milk became a soft white paste. As tired and hungry as he was, the traveler ate the stuff and was surprised by how good it tasted. The rest is history, so Ma says."

Mary Bebbington was probably correct. In fact, many recipes over the ages were the result of "accidents". It is believed that the pioneer of the famed Blue Stilton was an innkeeper in the village of Stilton who supposedly discovered a distinctive blue cheese in 1730 while visiting a small farm in rural Leicestershire, some one hundred miles south.

"This part of the process takes only three hours," Clem went on. "It is then pressed for one to two days, as Sam is doing. The cheese is then ripened, or aged, anywhere from one to two months."

Some farms went beyond that in aging, from four to nine months. Cheeses aged that long were usually sold as "Farmhouse Cheshire" and were wrapped in cloth soaked in lard before aging.

"What makes blue cheese blue?" Philip asked. "Is it rotten?"

Clem smiled and stepped to a stone lined spiral stairwell and gestured for Philip to follow.

The stairs led to the cheese cellar, a damp, dark, cool, stoned cave with shelves of cloth wrapped cheese wheels.

Philip lifted a wheel of Cheshire Blue. Clem took the wheel from Philip and began poking holes through the skin where the blue veins were absent.

"It's done by piercing the skin, like this, to expose it to air. The air in the cellar makes the cheese grow bluish molds that give it a different flavor and appearance. Kind of like when you see moldy bread in Ma's pantry. But it's good mold." Clem cut a piece and slid it over to Philip. "Try some!"

Philip looked away. "I'm not hungry," he said, placing his hands in his pockets. "Didn't know it was made this way."

Clem laughed. "Phil, if you've the inclination, we can visit Stinton's Butchery in Broxton to buy a roast for Sunday and if we're early enough Mr. Stinton will show you how bangers are made. Maybe butchery will suit you better."

"I haven't the...inclination," Philip said. "Why are they called 'bangers' anyway?"

"Cuz' they 'bang' from all the fat when they get cooked.

Philip rolled his eyes and looked away, his stomach wincing in protest.

"Well Pa wanted me to teach you something before I leave. Wanna' clean animal stalls instead?"

"I would not."

"Or maybe go to work in the salt or copper mines?"

"No."

"So, you hate something when you don't know much about it."

"I know something about it now."

"Then go fetch some water from the well, Cheese making requires lots of water."

Thus, twelve-year-old Philip Henry Bebbington learned to make cheese at Rawhead just as his older brothers and sister Martha had. After several weeks of instruction, he asked his father if he could work with Andrew to learn how to shoot and help him with baking as his primary chore. Over the years, Joseph observed his fifth son's meandering from chore to chore before mastering each, and knew to put a stop to it. His father approved the request but under the condition that he continue making cheese for two more months under Sam and Clem's supervision, and that the quality of the cheese met with their approval. Philip reluctantly agreed. In July 1910, Philip left the Bickerton School to work full time at Rawhead, as there was just too much work and labour was in short supply. His father needed his help.

--- **4** ---

There was an air of excitement the morning Clem left to report to the Royal Navy. It was peacetime on the high seas. He knew how to swim and was as personable and intelligent as any young man from his background could be. He was proficient at farming and had become a master cheesemaker. He was looking forward to the future.

For the past century, the British Royal Navy's approach to conflict was shore bombardment. The last significant campaign was the Second Boer War ten years earlier. The priority of the Royal Navy at the time was to maintain a battle-ready fleet large enough to deal with any adversaries. For that the service required a steady supply of men.

Clem descended the stairs and paused to observe the familiar walls around him. Rawhead had been his home for 18 years, and he wanted to fix a mental image of it in his mind. Wearing a wool cap, an old suit from his father, and a white shirt buttoned to the top, he carried his father's old suitcase down the hall, through the kitchen and out into the courtyard. Everyone except George and Elizabeth waited for him in the yard. Joseph, Mary, William, Martha, Sam, Bertie, Andrew, Philip, Dave, Jack and Mollie were clustered around, waiting to tell him goodbye, while young Tom stood close to his mother. Postman Edgar Miller had delivered the mail and stayed to take a photograph of the family at Joseph's request. Secretly, he was hoping to be invited for tea and a biscuit after Clem's departure.

"When did you acquire the bicycle, Edgar?"

"Last Wednesday," he responded with glee. "With that I'm the mayor of Chester!"

"You look splendid, Clem," Mary smiled at him.

Joseph handed the camera to Edgar. The family gathered in the garden with the house behind them, the older ones standing in back and the youngsters sitting on chairs in front. Tom and Jack argued over who would hold the dogs still.

"Okay, everyone… smile! Say, cheese," Edgar called and snapped the picture.

"Bloody thing better work," Joseph said. "Spent a whole pound on that box. We'll take the next photograph when you visit next, Clem."

The farm wagon was hitched and waiting in the courtyard, Bertie sat holding the reins. "I'm off to see the world," Clem proclaimed with excitement. He kissed his mother, shook his father's hand and climbed onto the seat next to his brother. Bertie wrapped the reins and they drove off to the train station in Chester.

Mary and Joseph watched them disappear around The Clump. There was an ache in their hearts. Though proud of the fine man their son had become, they silently feared he might not return.

Later that day, Mary heard Mollie, Philip, Jack and Jim fussing at each other and went outside to quell them. "If you don't get along, Rawhead and Bloody Bones will come to get you!" She warned them.

"Rawhead and Bloody Bones?" Mollie inquired. Philip had heard of them but Jack and Jim listened warily.

"Yes. He lives in caves and sometimes goes by the name 'Tommy Rawhead', or just plain 'Rawhead,' Mary explained. "He lives near places where there's water, under sink pipes and the like. Rawhead and Bloody Bones reward good children but punish bad ones by climbing into their bedrooms at night and dragging them down the drainpipes or into wells and drowning then. He can turn them into pieces of trash or spots of jam, anything he's of a mind, only to get thrown away when they're found!"

Horrified little faces stared up at her.

"And by all means watch out for the ghost of Mad Allen!" Mary continued. "It's the ghost of a man who lived in a cave for forty-six years!"

The stories had evolved out of ancient folklore. Mary heard the same tales from her own mother. The stories gave her nightmares, but she did not forget to do her chores again. Bloody Bones was a fiend invented to keep children in line. *The Oxford English Dictionary* cites 1550 as the earliest written account of the creature. The Dictionary referred to the beast as hobgoblin, rawhed or bloody-bone.

Some stories told of Bloody Bones living in a dark cupboard under the stairs. If someone dared to peer through a crack, they might catch a glimpse of the ugly, hunchback ogre sitting on a pile of bones that had once belonged to children who told lies, spoke disrespectfully or failed to do their chores. Mad Allen was the name given to a man who, in the 18th century, embraced a hermit's life after his family refused to sanction his marriage to a young woman they did not like. He moved into a cave and lived there for decades. When adults told these legends to children, they did it to frighten the little ones into compliance.

"It's south of the farm! Here…!" Philip said pointing to a map hanging in their classroom at the Bickerton School. Jim, Jack and Mollie leaned forward to look. They had arrived a few minutes early so they could view the map Philip had told them about. Their mother mentioned a cave during supper the evening before, intriguing them. *A cave? On a farm?* They decided to investigate right away.

"We should go after school," Philip proposed.

"You'll miss your chores," Mollie reminded them. "You'll get into trouble."

"Not if you tell her the headmaster has given us an assignment," Philip suggested carefully.

"I won't lie to Mum!" Mollie insisted. "Besides, I want to go, too."

"No, you can't go. It's a boy's cave not a girl's cave," Jim stated.

"Why did you tell her, now she wants to come along," Jim complained. Mollie, who was considerably larger than Jim, pushed him.

"It's Bloody Bones' cave and he'll drag you down a water pipe," warned Mollie.

Philip thought a moment. "All right, we'll all go. We'll just make it a quick visit this time and then go home."

After school, Mollie, Jim, Jack and Philip left their books behind and ran across the fields to the Rawhead Escarpment.

"Wait!" Mollie called from behind.

Jim turned to Philip. "Let's leave her."

"No, she'll just tell," insisted Philip. They waited impatiently for her to catch up, then reached an old well and peered down into it.

"Is there water down there?" Dave asked.

"Sure!" Philip replied. He dropped a stone into it. Three seconds later, there was a splash. "It's called the Droppingstone Well."

"Why? Because people drop stones in it?"

"You can tell how deep it is by dropping a stone in it. Count when you drop it."

Dave grabbed a stone and dropped it in the well.

Philip counted out loud, "One-two-thr—" and again there was a splash.

"Three seconds," Mollie said. "Maybe two."

"Now, times that by ten," Philip instructed.

"Thirty feet?" chirped Mollie, wrinkling her nose in thought. "That's not so deep."

Jim pushed Mollie toward the edge. "Don't do that!" screamed Mollie. "I'm telling Mum."

The trail to the Rawhead Escarpment took only a few minutes to find. Once he reached the cliff, Philip paused and waited for the others. The three cautiously peered over the 100-foot cliff. The view from the Rawhead Escarpment was impressive. It was also the first time they had seen the Cheshire plain and Liverpool in the distance. "Amazing," Philip whispered.

"Is that Chester?" Jim asked.

"No, that's Liverpool." answered Philip.

"Is not! It's Chester!" Jim said.

"It's Liverpool," Mollie said flatly. "You can't see Chester from here. It's past those trees."

"See?" said Jim.

"Where's the cave?" Philip inquired, looking down the Escarpment. "It's got to be down there," he said pointing.

Mollie had been investigating. "It's around here!" Mollie said, climbing over a large rock and beckoning to them.

They stepped into the mouth of the cave. In the dim light, they could see an old frying pan, a pile of ragged clothing, animal bones and a well-used sleeping pallet. Further back, a passageway led to a separate room in the cave. They bravely walked toward it. Suddenly, a dirty face with a scar appeared out of the darkness, staring with piercing blood shot eyes at the intruders.

"What are you little blighters doing in here?" growled the face.

"It's Bloody Bones!" Mollie shrieked. She turned and bumped into Jack on her way out. The boys pushed each other in their haste to follow their sister.

"It's Mad Allen!" Jim shouted.

Philip tripped on a rock and fell to his knees. He looked up at the skinny old man in grubby clothes standing over him. The man stooped and lifted Philip to his feet by his belt. Philip could smell his foul breath.

"Go away and don't come back," the man growled.

Philip was petrified, but he managed to nod before scrambling after the others who were already far down the trail.

"I'm Bloody Bones and I don't fancy naughty young'uns like you comin' round 'less I can 'ave 'em for supper!" the old man yelled after them.

The frightened explorers reached the farmhouse pale and breathless. Throwing fear of punishment to the wind, they told Mary what they had seen. She explained it was not Bloody Bones at all but a former Cholmondeley estate worker who had gone to the cave after his wife died of influenza years earlier. He wandered the county for months, she told them. The man's name was Oliver Goldford. He took shelter in the old cave after losing all his money in taverns. The cave had a history. It supposedly dated back to the Bronze Age. In the 18th century, it was occupied by brigands who terrorized the surrounding farms, stealing food and valuables. They even resorted to grave robbing. Their reign of terror ended in 1834 when they were caught and hanged.

"That's not Mad Allen," Mary told her panicked children. "He's naught but a poor man and that's his home. Leave him be."

After school days later Philip saw the man again near the Droppingstone Well. He was picking bilberries. The man turned toward Philip. "What do you want, boy?"

Philip held out his lunch. "Would you like something to eat? Cheese, ham, bread?"

He studied Philip for signs of trickery, then snatched the bag from Philip's hands. He withdrew a lump of cheese and a tomato, then bit into the cheese eagerly. Philip did not stay to watch him finish.

--- 5 ---

Clem's train arrived at Devonport after a circuitous daylong route from Chester via Birmingham and Bristol. Before then, Clem had not seen much of England. Devonport was formally known as Her Majesty's Royal Naval Barracks Devonport but was more commonly called Devonport Dockyard. It was located west of Plymouth and was the largest naval base in Western Europe at the time. Clem thought the word "barrack" was taken from the French word "baroque" meaning booth or hut, but he had read that barrack in Spanish meant "soldiers' tent". Sailors jokingly preferred the definition for the Spanish word "barercoon", meaning "slave pen". The barracks were named "Vivid" after the Commander in Chief's iron-built steam yacht, HMS *Vivid*. Politicians considered the Edwardian Royal Navy an exclusive yacht club, despite the changes that were taking place.

Clem joined the Royal Navy at the height of one of the longest periods of peace enjoyed by Britain, interrupted only by minor digressions when it became necessary to send a gunboat to repress "mosquitoes" in a distant colony. One such venture took the Royal Navy to the Nile River. A young naval officer named Winston Churchill took part in the British Army's last cavalry charge at the Battle of Omdurman in 1898. They were chasing the Khalifa and his Dervishes in central Sudan.

These were gracious, spacious days. The British Empire was at its peak of power and prestige, and the Royal Navy was the instrument for maintaining that peace. Its size and strength were almost always in flux, and the nearby dockyard was building a new dreadnaught yearly. Unbeknownst to Clem and the rest of the nation, the frenzy of construction was timely. That gracious, spacious era was coming to an end.

Clem's tram stopped at the enduring limestone gates of the Royal Naval Barracks, Devonport. He stepped off with nine other men carrying suitcases or carry-all's. They slowly passed over the threshold, looking around.

"Halt you lot! Papers," a guard demanded. Clem handed over his folded orders. A clock tower in the distance read 5:03 p.m. He withdrew his father's pocket watch and compared the time. The watch was spot-on. The guard read Clem's orders quickly and pointed at a large stone building behind him, then moved on to the next man.

Clem looked around the dockyard. There were dozens of ships everywhere he looked. There were 19th century sailing ships, ships in dry dock and ships in various stages of completion, or being dismantled for scrapping. There were even ships that had sunk in the harbor with only the tops of their masts exposed to warn pilots of the hazard they posed. In the distance was the skeleton of the largest ship he had ever seen in the early stages of construction. Clem replaced his pocket watch and stepped into the stone building.

--- 6 ---

"The name is Plunkett, Ma'am," a tall, lean man in a khaki uniform called from the gate at Rawhead. He leaned his bicycle against the wall and removed a brown campaign hat from his head. "George Plunkett. With the Boy Scouts of England in Liverpool."

Mary walked to the gate from her doorstep. The man standing before Mary was positively brimming with enthusiasm.

"Oh yes, the program for boys!" Mary said. "Lord Baden Powell's boys."

"Yes, ma'am. He started the movement on Brownsea Island two years ago and we've formed a troop in Liverpool," he said. "I was wondering if you might permit us to camp on your farm."

"Oh," Mary said with relief. "I thought you were from the British Army coming to get my boys. I'm sure the Brydens wouldn't mind if you camped here. You'll have to be careful where you set up. The manure, you know?"

Plunkett laughed.

"We'll take care…and your name, ma'am?"

"Mary Bebbington. I've got nine boys who could learn some things."

Mary estimated the man was in his late-twenties. She invited him into the kitchen where she made him a cup of tea and introduced Dave and Jim who had come in from school a short time before. After a brief discussion, it was agreed Plunkett would return two weeks later with twenty-five boys to camp near The Clump.

Lt. General Robert Baden Powell was a soldier, painter, educator and prolific writer. A few of his books, though written as training manuals for military intelligence, had been read by many boys. Popularly known as B.P., Baden Powell had served in South Africa prior to the Second Boer War and was involved in actions against the Zulus. At the time, he had been the youngest colonel in the army, responsible for organizing local settlers. He created decoys that were credited with the success of various conflicts. Trench warfare was the battle style of the time. One of his innovations entailed planting simulated minefields and ordering his soldiers to avoid the non-existent hazards while they moved between trenches. The general had performed much of the reconnaissance himself.

Boys under fighting age were employed to perform relatively minor tasks such as standing guard and carrying messages between locations. This practice freed soldiers to perform their military duties. Baden Powell had been impressed with the success of this practice and had it in detail in his book *Scouting for Boys*, published in 1908. While he was writing, he tested his ideas with Plunkett and a group of boys on a camping trip on Brownsea Island in 1907.

Two weeks after he had spoken with Mary, Plunkett arrived at Rawhead with twenty-five boys clad in khaki uniforms and campaign hats. They explored The Clump wearing backpacks and carrying walking sticks.

"Looks like the British Army!" Bertie said as he and his brothers watched from the gate. "Jack, go tell Mum."

Jack ran off and Mary soon bustled out to join them. She and her sons led the troop to a clearing near The Clump. Plunkett introduced the 14-year-old leaders of the group, Eddie McFie, Ernest Hewett and Lewis Briscoe. The three were models of British youth, full of energy, courtesy and good health.

Mary watched the scouts set up camp in orderly fashion. They rolled logs out from The Clump for seating and made a ring of stones to serve as a fire pit with a steel tripod over it for cooking. Their canvas tents were pitched neatly in rows. Two boys started a fire and began boiling water while others hung a bucket of water for drinking from a tripod made from walking staves.

"This is my sister, Mabel Jean," Plunkett said, introducing a girl of ten standing behind him. "I call her Mabes." Mabel Jean had insisted on accompanying her older brother and the troop of boys to the farm for camping.

"You must be a girl scout," Mary suggested warmly.

"There aren't any girl scouts," she told Mary.

"Well, I think there are. It just takes one girl!"

"Girl Scouts?" Jim cried in a derisive tone. He had a campaign hat on his head that he had borrowed from one of the scouts. "There will never be any girl scouts!"

"There will, too!" Mabel Jean assured him.

"I think he likes you, Mabes," Plunkett said with a smile.

"Arrrrgh!" groaned Jim and Mabel together through their teeth.

The Girl Scout movement began in 1909 at The Crystal Palace in London where Baden Powell encountered girls in scout uniforms. He recognized there was a demand for a program for young women and girls. The program started out as Girl Guides but soon became Girl Scouts.

"Mollie is in the barn if you would like to learn how to milk, Mabes," Mary told the girl.

"I would!" She stuck her tongue out at Jim as she turned to leave.

"I'll show her where the barn is," Jim volunteered cheerfully.

"I think they like each other," laughed Plunkett. Mary chuckled agreeably.

In the milking barn, Mollie sat on a stool next to a big white cow. Jim told Mollie about Mabes when they found her. "Would you like to be a milkmaid?" Mollie asked Mabes. Both girls grinned.

"Yes, I think that would be fun!"

"Be careful. You might tire of it."

"I don't think I will!" Mabel Jean commented as Mollie resumed milking.

"See? Squeeze and pull," Mollie demonstrated. Mabes did not find it easy at first but eventually got the hang of it. "Be sure to finish well," Mollie said. "The last milk from the cow is the richest." Mabes helped Mollie milk more of the cows.

Mary, Joseph and Plunkett had tea in the Rawhead kitchen as they watched the scouts busy themselves through the window.

"How long have you been living in Liverpool?" Joseph asked.

"My family? Oh, a long time," Plunkett answered. "Since 1805. My father is a Vicar."

"And how did you become part of the scouts?" Mary asked.

"I was a lieutenant in the army, an instructor. I met Lord Baden-Powell at one of his lectures."

Boy Scouts in Rawhead Courtyard c. 1909

Girl Scouts visiting Rawhead. Date unknown
Photos courtesy of the author

"I hope you'll join us for supper."

"I accept with gratitude, ma'am," Plunkett replied.

Mollie, Mabel Jean, Sam, Bertie, Plunkett, Mary and Joseph were the only ones at the table. Bertie had just returned from Droppingstone Farm where he had gone to loan the tenant a hay thrasher.

"I must take the boys their pudding!" Mary remarked as everyone finished their pieces of cake. She began to cut a pan of the cake into pieces for the scouts.

"I think they might surprise you with a dessert of their own," Plunkett interrupted. "They're very inventive. Cooking is one of the first skills they learned. The movement is preparing a set of ranks for them to earn. To advance in rank, they acquire a series of skills organized in 'merit badges.' The army loves the movement."

"I hope more boys join scouting and not the army," Mary stated. "It might help prepare them for university."

Plunkett looked across the field to the distant groups of boys huddled around camp fires. "Well, whatever they choose to do, they will do it well. They're fine young men."

Three days later, Plunkett's scouts struck their camp and began to pack up. Mary walked out to them to say goodbye and offered them biscuits. After starting to roll the logs back to The Clump and dismantling the fire ring, Mary stopped them.

"What are you doing?" Mary asked.

"We are putting the camp back the way we found it," scout Eddie Briscoe answered.

"You don't have to do that here," Mary said. "I want you to come back."

The scouts looked at each other, unsure of how to respond. It was against their nature to leave a campsite like that. But they did as Mary asked and every few months or so, they returned to camp there, rain or shine.

--- 7 ---

Sam's face twisted as he tasted a fresh batch of Cheshire. "This is ruined!" Sam shouted at Bertie. "What did you do to it? Six bloody weeks and it's gone! It's pig food!" He spat out the sample. "I should have made it myself! Did you add the rennet? Drain the whey?"

"Of course!" Bertie said vehemently.

"Did you use clean utensils? Wash your hands?"

"Yes."

"We've only weeks until the fair! Now we're short a batch!" Sam was beside himself. "You better stick to animals, Bertie. That's the only thing you're good at." Bertie hung his head.

Sam left to inform their father, passing Jim and Dave who had been listening. They exchanged looks. "We better not," Dave told Jim as they ran out to The Clump.

"No one will know," Jim assured him. "We can switch a wheel from the Belton Farm! Mrs. Nunnerly won first place last year."

"But how do you know her cheese is good this year?" Dave said.

"Mum said Mrs. Nunnerly thinks it's her best cheese ever. Mum tasted it."

"But that'd be cheating!" Dave insisted.

"But we'd be winning," Jim countered, smiling.

The Cheshire Dairy Association cheese fair and judging took place annually in October. The show was considered one of the most prestigious cheese competitions in England. Similar events included the Nantwich and Whitchurch shows, held in different months. Held in Chester on the old Roodee racecourse, the Cheshire show brought scores of people from surrounding counties. Families made a day of it. There was something at the fair for everyone. Even though Philip did not care for cheese, he enjoyed sausages, boiled sweets, and all the excitement. Entries from many of the current master cheesemakers made the contest fiercely competitive. In addition to the cheese contest, there were sheep herding trials, foods to buy, a stock show, a flower show, farm equipment exhibits, a band, dancing and a large beer tent.

Sam lifted his wheel of Cheshire cheese from the wagon and carried it to the entry table to register for the contest. The weight seemed lighter and the wrapping a bit different, but he paid no attention. The smiling Cheshire Cat logo and Rawhead Farm label were there and that's all he noticed. Rawhead Farm was not going to win this year anyway, Sam thought sadly. No thanks to Bertie.

A contest attendant accepted his entry and wrapped it in a plain white cloth to hide the label. He wrote the number "23" on the cloth and placed Sam's cheese on a long table amid dozens of other entries from far and wide. Cheese was judged for taste, texture, color and how closely it met the accepted standards. Champion First Prize winners were presented with a ribbon, twenty-one pounds sterling and a congratulatory letter from His Royal Majesty, King Edward VII. The reigning monarch always received a few wheels of the winning entry. The remainder was sold by weight at the fair until it was gone.

Jim and Dave stood watching the activity at the cheese tables. They exchanged sly smiles, then darted off. Philip and Andrew wandered through the crowds. The sound of an engine buzzing and sputtering over their heads caught their attention. They looked up and saw an airplane for the first time; a Cody One biplane.

"That's one of those flying machines. An aeroplane, they call it," Andrew exclaimed.

It looked more like a big, rickety kite than a machine with a man making it fly, Philip thought. He shielded his eyes from the sun and watched as it headed northwest towards Liverpool. Amazing, he thought, shaking his head. He wondered how it would be to fly.

Everyone was having a good time. Judges meandered around the tables sampling the entries, pausing now and then to take notes. They were careful not to disclose their opinions to anyone within earshot. Farmers stood along the walls watching the judging. After an hour of sampling the entries, comparing notes and voting amongst themselves, the judges stepped onto a raised platform to announce the winners. The lead judge held up a bullhorn to signal for quiet.

"Third prize of the 1911 Cheshire Dairy Association cheese contest goes to the Morton Hill Farm of the Cholmondeley Estate!" The crowd applauded politely.

Sam looked at Bertie. "I thought that one was ours."

"There's next year, Sam." Bertie consoled his brother. "I'll make it up to you. Would you like to grab a pint? I'm buying." Sam nodded and the two eased themselves through the crowd toward the beer tent which had drawn a host of men already.

"Second prize of the 1911 Cheshire Dairy Association cheese contest goes to the Woodhouse Farm of the Telomere Estate!" There was louder applause, obviously a surprise.

Mrs. Nunnerly, the cheesemaker for the Belton Farm on the Cholmondeley estate, clapped. A woman in the crowd next to her uttered "Looks like it will be yours again, Mrs. Nunnerly!"

"Oh, I don't know about that," she said humbly.

"Two pints of bitter, please," Bertie requested of the attendant at the table. A row of kegs stood on the table. The young man drew the pints and sat them in front of Bertie, the thick foaming head spilled down the sides of their mugs. Bertie licked his lips in anticipation and paid the two shillings for the beer. Sam reached for his but the attendant stopped him. The ritual of pouring beer and allowing the head to settle was not merely a custom, it was the law. Too many fights had occurred in pubs over patrons accusing keepers of cheating them of a full pint. Finally, after waiting an excruciating three minutes in the noon heat for the head to settle, Bertie and Sam were permitted to drink. They clinked glasses and swallowed a third of their beers in one pull.

"And the Champion Prize of the 1911 Cheshire Dairy Association cheese contest goes to..."

The rest of the announcement was not audible to Bertie and Sam due to the roar of applause from the crowd.

"What'd he say?" Sam inquired indifferently. He took another sip.

"I guess they announced the Champion Prize winner," Bertie surmised. "Another pint it's Mrs. Nunnerly of the Belton Farm! She always wins."

"At's a wager, Bertie!" Sam accepted. Several free pints were on his mind and Bertie was not good at wagers.

Faces of the crowd turned toward Bertie and Sam at the ale table. "Bertie, Sam, you've won! Rawhead won!" Sam spit his last swig of ale onto his shirt and coughed. Bertie and Sam looked at each other.

"What?" Sam managed. They set down their classes and started walking back to the cheese tables. The crowd patted them both on the back as they passed. Mary and Joseph were equally amazed. Well, maybe not too amazed, Mary thought. Rawhead Farmhouse Cheshire was well known for its quality and was a competitor in any contest. But to Mrs. Nunnerly? Her Belton Farm Cheshire placed nearly every year. She was the one to beat.

A judge pushed his way through the excited crowd and a large blue ribbon was handed to Sam. The crowd cheered and patted them on the back. Jim and Dave looked on from the sidelines, both with Cheshire Cat grins.

"Who says I don't work?" Jim asked Dave, joining the crowd in applauding his brothers.

Gilbert and Ella Bryden made their way to Sam extending their hands, and beaming with pride.

"Well done, Sam Bebbington!" Gilbert Bryden said. "Well done. We can always count on the Rawhead Farm!" Bryden shook Sam's hand long and in an overly up and down fashion to make sure his congratulations were observed by the crowd. A photographer snapped a picture. Mary and Joseph hugged each other for another successful year. Dave and Jim laughed hysterically. They then snuck off to see what other mischief they could cook up.

Supper that evening was held later than usual because of the considerable food and drink that had been eaten at the show. Bread, stew, cheese, milk, and tea were served. Around the table were Joseph and Mary, Clem, Bertie, Sam, Philip, Dave, Jack, Tom, Mollie, Martha and William Evans.

Philip, full of news and gossip from the show, spoke up. "I heard a man named Woodrow Wilson was elected president of the United States, a college professor."

"That's why you must go back to school and spend less time on the farm," Joseph answered. "Your schoolmaster says you show some promise."

"I also heard an American Indian won the Stockholm Olympics!" Philip continued. "A man named Jim Thorpe."

Bertie and Sam helped themselves to more stew.

"Another well done," Mary said. "Thanks to Bertie and Sam for winning the cheese contest today." Everyone applauded.

Jim covered his face with a cup. Dave knew what Jim was smiling about and playfully kicked him under the table. Annoyed, Jim kicked him back but harder, making the table shake.

"Dave and Jim, stop fussing under the table!" Joseph ordered.

"It wasn't me, it was Jim!"

"It was not!" Jim defended. "Ouch!" Jim yelled, acting as if he had been kicked again by Dave.

"Dave, go outside!" Joseph scolded.

"Jim swapped cheeses!" Dave blurted out.

Silent eyes looked over at Dave. Jim dropped his jaw, hearing the betrayal from his younger brother.

"I did not, he did!" Jim returned instantly, pointing across the table.

"What are you talking about, Dave?" Mary asked.

Jim and Dave stared angrily at each other.

"Dave switched Sam and Bertie's cheese with Mrs. Nunnerly's cheese for the contest! He should be flogged!"

Suddenly it all came to Sam. The cheese he had entered in the contest that morning was not his but from another farm. Mrs. Nunnerly's cheese: she was impossible to beat.

Joseph stood and bolted towards Jim. Jim pushed away from the table and ran towards the door. As Jim started outside, his father's long arm grabbed his hair and pulled him back into the house.

Knowing what was about to happen, Mary ran to them. "Joseph, no! He didn't mean to do it!"

"Yes, he did! He misses chores, too!" Joseph said as he carried a squealing Jim into the court yard and entered one of the stalls. He threw him over a trap wheel and began to whip his behind with a crop. Jim wailed louder but exaggerated the pain in an effort to ease the punishment.

"Your behind isn't healed yet from missing your chores this week and you do something again? Well this time is the last!"

Behind Mary, Dave appeared in the kitchen doorway. He had missed some chores as well and knew he was an accomplice in Jim's caper. Seeing the punishment being administered, he instinctively looked to his right and bolted through the courtyard entrance gate.

Jim screamed from the whipping. Mary appeared in the stall and pulled at Joseph's arm.

"Stop, Joseph!" she insisted. "He'll return the prize and money to the judges and apologize to Mr. Bryden and Mrs. Nunnerly! That's his punishment!"

Furious, Joseph threw the crop against the barn wall and stormed off. Mary lifted Jim off the wagon wheel and held him.

"I did it for him! I did it for everyone!" Jim cried. "Twenty-one pounds and the ribbon! And I get a whipping for it!"

"But it was dishonest, Jim." Mary said. "What do the Scouts say? A scout is…"

Jim thought a moment and looked down. "Trustworthy."

"And what else?" Mary asked.

"Loyal, Helpful, Friendly…," Jim stopped. "I can't remember the rest."

"Yes, you can," Mary corrected.

Jim thought a moment and continued. "…Courteous, Kind, Obedient…Cheerful, Thrifty, Brave, Clean, and Reverent."

"And were you?" Mary asked.

"I was brave," Jim said, looking at the house and pointing. "I have to be brave around him."

By now, Dave was already at The Clump and disappeared into its thick grove of pines. Dave would not be heard from again until the next day after spending the night in the cave with Oliver Goldford. Dave had felt his father's crop before and knew to avoid it.

And so it was that Jim Bebbington returned the prize and apologized to the judges of the 1911 Cheshire Dairy Association annual cheese show contest, and the Brydens, Mrs. Nunnerly, Bertie, and Sam. But he would experience the crop and buggy wheel again.

The year 1912 was a sign that things were changing. George's wife Elizabeth died two weeks after the birth of their first child. Carden Hall, a 15th century medieval castle near Chester burned to the ground, allegedly after someone dropped a lit cigarette at a party. The great ocean liner RMS *Titanic* departed Liverpool, struck an ice berg and sank with the loss of over 1500 lives. Aggression overseas began to dominate headlines. Work hours were long, conditions were bad, and pay was low. As such, a labour shortage compelled Dave to quit school to work at Rawhead, as Philip had done years earlier. Something was coming, Mary sensed. But she did not know what.

Preparing the horse and trap in the Rawhead courtyard.. c. 1912
Photo courtesy of the author

Rawhead as seen from The Clump c. 1910
Photo courtesy of the author

PART II

1913 – 1918

--- 8 ---

Over the next two years, the conversation at the Rawhead dinner table turned from countryside gossip, cheese making, livestock and farming to national and global politics.

"They say there's going to be a war, Pa," George said one evening while visiting from Tilston. He was preparing to move back to Rawhead with his baby daughter, since his wife Elizabeth had passed.

"It does look that way," Joseph agreed. "So long as it isn't here, let's try not to worry."

"If there is a war, I'm joining up." Philip announced. He had declared his intent several times so no one appeared surprised. Bertie and Sam were thinking about it too, but didn't say it.

"Not me," Will Evans said. "There's no possible justification for killing. It's not Christian. But I don't object to saving lives," he clarified. Martha smiled approvingly and patted his shoulder.

"If England goes to war, we must join up! Do our duty," Bertie told his brother-in-law across the table.

William shook his head stubbornly. Andrew offered nothing as he listened. He just looked at his rifle sitting in the gun rack against the wall.

"I'll have nothing to do with it," Will said. "I'm for peace, not war."

"Pacifism, put that way, signifies nothing," Sam said. "No matter where you live."

Becoming irritated, Sam pointed to Philip. "Philip wants peace. Mum wants peace. And Father and Andrew as well. The only time you're guaranteed peace is when they put you in the ground and post a 'rest in peace' sign over your head! Is that the kind of peace you want, Will?"

"I'm as much a patriot as you, Sam." Will said quietly. "I just don't want to kill for it."

Andrew, Bertie and Sam did not like that their sister had married Will Evans. Before meeting Martha, he had bounced from job to job, never developing competence at any one. He most recently signed on as an electrician's helper, but a fire had started shortly after he rewired a Chester solicitor's office and he had been fired. Now he was working at Rawhead. Everyone expected he would not be content with farming either. He would have to work or he'd be shown the door, with or without Martha, Joseph informed them, leaving no other option.

All knew Andrew's thoughts on the subject. He was a skilled marksman and anxious to put his talents to the test. He had given thought to joining up years earlier, but with the country at peace he didn't see the point. The topic at the supper table shifted to practical matters: errands to town, animals that were poorly, chores to tackle.

When the "Great War to End All Wars" broke out on August 4, 1914, precious few Englishmen understood why.

Outside of the rumblings from Germany, the conflicts in faraway places like Hungary, Turkey, Bulgaria, Egypt, and Palestine seemed unrelated to England. Yet, Lord Horatio Kitchener called for 100,000 volunteers and the appeal was met with overwhelming enthusiasm from every corner of the United Kingdom. Men from all walks signed up by the tens of thousands and the War Office faced overwhelming numbers of recruits almost overnight. The prospect of marching to war generated a patriotism not seen for a long time. The promise of Army pay was a big enticement to the thousands of unemployed men who had families to support. They believed they could count on the Army to feed them.

At first, the new force was all-volunteer. It rose in the United Kingdom following the outbreak of hostilities in Belgium and France. The regulars and Home Guard were reporting heavy casualties in the first weeks of the war. The response to Kitchener's ardent call for volunteers signaled a turning point in British military history. For the first time, men were committed to a massive land force to fight against other European powers. Some of the new soldiers saw action almost immediately while others faced little for years.

Within days, Clem was transferred from the tender HMS *Exmouth* to the battleship HMS *Canopus* to help ready her for service in the Channel Fleet's 8th Battle Squadron. Robert Bryden and the Cheshire Yeomanry were activated the same week and began driling immediately. George, Sam, Bertie and Andrew took the wagon to Chester to join the army. Dave, Jack, Jim and Tom were too young. George was denied admission right away. He had aged out and had poor eyesight. William Evans chose not to join, drawing the formidable scorn of his brothers-in-law. *How would Mary and Joseph run the farm with so many of the men gone?* William reasoned aloud.

Philip was seventeen and therefore did not meet the age requirement of 18. If Joseph had signed permission, Philip might have been able to go but his father refused. Philip decided to try anyway. He ran across the east field to catch up with his brothers as they made their way to the recruitment office.

A lengthy queue of men extended from Chester Castle down Grosvenor Street. It was Thursday, September 3, 1914.

"Look at this line!" Sam exclaimed. "You'd think they was giving away free beer, not signin' up to fight!" Within an hour they were inside Chester Castle. Sam and Bertie were met with a suggestion from the recruiting staff.

"Try the Service Corps," a recruiting officer told them. "You're not big enough for the Yeomanry or the Cheshire Regiment."

The two stared at him. "What's the Service Corps and where do we apply?" Sam finally asked.

"They're the supply arm of the British Army. In Ripon, North Yorkshire" the officer told them. Undeterred, Sam and Bertie caught a train for Ripon.

Andrew was met with more enthusiasm after the recruiting staff sized him up. Andrew had brought his rifle with him and held it with confidence. The recruiters accepted him right away. He was told to leave his rifle at home when he reported. Philip ran into more trouble. Sam and Bertie told him of their failed effort to join an active unit, but he made up his mind he would not be turned away because he was short and underage.

He moved to the next station and watched a Medical Corps officer examining a shirtless applicant in his late thirties. The officer pointed to a tattoo on his arm reading "BC".

"What is this?" inquired the doctor. The applicant shrugged. "What do you make of that?" the doctor asked a nearby ranking officer. Battalion Commander William Harkness studied the tattoo.

"BC. Stands for 'Bad Character'. If you see a 'D' tattoo it means 'Deserter'. We've been seeing more and more of them. Where'd you get the marks, coal miner?"

The man hesitated.

"Speak up!" demanded Harkness.

"In the Second Boer War, sir. South Africa."

"Well we haven't any need for bad characters or deserters in the Cheshire Regiment!" Harkness started to leave.

"I paid my penance, sir!"

"What's your name, deserter?"

"Heathcote, sir. Herbert Heathcote."

Harkness walked a circle around Heathcote, rubbing his chin.

"What do you think, Lieutenant? Think he'll give us trouble when we order him out of a trench and Maxim machine guns are spraying six hundred bullets a minute at him over No Man's Land? Or when he sees men step on mines and get blown to bits? Or when canisters of poison gas start landing at his feet and burning out his eyes and his skin starts to blister? And seconds later he starts bleeding on the inside, choking because he doesn't have any lungs left? Think he'll desert again and leave his mates to watch his back while he runs back to the nearest tavern for a pint?"

The medical officer frowned. "Can't be any worse than the spears he ran away from in South Africa!" he said. Heathcote looked away and clenched a fist at his side. The physician noticed. "Maybe he's changed, sir." A silence followed.

"We'll see. Move on," Harkness ordered.

Heathcote shuffled to the next station, humiliated.

Harkness looked at the next recruit. He pointed his baton at the five-foot, six-inch mark which was exactly three inches above Philip's head. "You're too short," Harkness told him.

"I can fight just as well as a taller man. Better!"

"The average is Hun five feet, seven inches," the lieutenant said. "You'd be at a disadvantage!"

"Well you're taller than me and I could give you a go!"

"Why, you insolent puppy," the lieutenant snarled, advancing on Philip who stood his ground in defiance. Harkness and another officer separated them.

"You want to be a soldier, eh? Kill Huns?" Harkness demanded of Philip. "Well you're not off to a good start insulting an officer! You want a BC tattoo like that bloke? We can put it smack in the middle of your forehead!"

Philip glared at the physician, unperturbed.

"You best brand me with a 'D', because that's what I'll be if you don't let me fight!"

"Try the Service Corps."

Philip shook his head. "No Service Corps for me! I've two brothers headed for the bloody Service Corps now. I don't want to tend mules or drive lorries! I want to fight!"

Harkness studied Philip. "There's talk of a bantam battalion forming up. If you can wait,"

"Bantam, sir?" Philip asked.

"It's a regiment of short…" Harkness paused to rethink his words. "A bantam is a person of diminutive stature who possesses a combative disposition."

"Well that sounds like me, sir."

"Let's move on, shall we?" the lieutenant suggested.

As Philip moved to the next station, Harkness and the doctor exchanged looks.

"Sir, he's too short! We've the pick of the lot here!" he reminded him, gesturing to the long line of half-naked men. He read from a clip board. "Regimental requirements are eighteen to thirty-five years, height of at least five feet, six inches, chest measurement of thirty-four inches. The fellow's lying about his age too, I'm sure of it."

Philip waited to be addressed at the next station.

"A deserter and a little farmer, anxious to die," Harkness muttered to the lieutenant and walked on. "They undoubtedly will be," the medical officer said to his departing back.

In addition to "BC" and "D" tattoos, enlistment recruits were examined for moles, scars or any other identifying marks should they ever be rendered indistinguishable by obvious means. Any such marks were then described on the recruit's enlistment papers.

By the end of the day, a Medical Corps officer marked "Fit" on Philip's enlistment form. He crossed out the number 'one' and wrote in a 'three' indicating the number of years he would be in the army. Philip had lied and said he was nineteen years and one month old.

Andrew and Philip swore an oath of allegiance, accepted the traditional King's shilling and returned home to Rawhead to await their call-up. At 165 pounds and five feet, five inches tall, Andrew had a 36-inch chest and 20-20 vision. He had a formidable presence, despite barely meeting the physical standards. He had a certain air of confidence and intense brown eyes. He had boasted of his shooting ability and expressed his desire to fight. The Army agreed to oblige him.

Later in the war, the standards for physical requirements for enlistment were lowered so the army could accept more men. But at the outset, the minimum requirements in September 1914 remained eighteen to thirty-five years, five feet, six inches tall and the chest measurement of thirty-six inches. When they were in their teens, the Bebbington brothers had hoped they would grow taller. They often wondered why they and many other men of the day were so short. They speculated that it was the plight of Englishmen and they were partially correct. The average height of early 19th century Englishmen was 5'6". But it was their inadequate diet that was the real culprit. Consistent meals of cheese, meat, bread, potatoes, and few fresh vegetables or fruit were largely to blame.

--- 9 ---

"What do you mean?" Robert Bryden asked A.G. Wilkinson as they rode their horses down a trail near Harthill.

"Just what I said," Wilkinson replied as he unbuttoned the top button of his uniform. "They will never send the yeomanry to war. Not this war. We'll spend months parading in town squares before the public. Just imagine all those young women throwing us their handkerchiefs!"

"We will be sent," Bryden argued. "And must I remind you I am married, A.G.? I have no interest in such dalliances."

"So is Delverson but that doesn't stop him." Wilkinson said. "I find the prospect quite inviting."

Bryden studied his friend. "Wilkinson, you best get used to the idea that we will be deployed to Europe to fight the Germans. And we as officers are sure to be in the thick of it. We may be back by Christmas but I have doubts on that."

--- 10 ---

In Devonport, Clem boarded the HMS *Canopus* and spent most of the day in orientation. He had been thoroughly trained in shore establishments and in other ships. While walking, Clem observed a sale of items on deck following a sailor's death. The deceased sailor's effects were displayed on a blanket and sold to his mates at inflated prices. Any money raised was given to the deceased's family.

"I'll take that," Clem said, pointing to a small string instrument. He tossed two pounds on the blanket. Sailors who were also looking at the display stared at him, no doubt for offering such a princely sum. Clem took the ukulele from the petty officer overseeing the sale and walked away plucking chords. His hammock was slung between the deck beams opposite the mess deck. He sat in the roomier broadside mess to eat, write letters, play his ukulele, and read. There was a tiny library on board and a small naval band. To Clem's delight, Cheshire cheese was served in plentiful amounts.

Named for the ancient city where the Battle of the Nile occurred in 1798, *Canopus* was a handsome ship, Clem thought. She was a two funnel, pre-dreadnought battleship and the lead ship of her class. Well-fortified, she bristled with weaponry and included four, 18-inch submerged torpedo tubes. Weeks later, *Canopus* was sent to the Cape Verde, Canary Islands Station, to back up a cruiser squadron. On September 1, 1914, her sister ship HMS *Albion* relieved her and *Canopus* moved farther south. She arrived at the Abrolhos Rocks on September 22nd to support another cruiser squadron. Trained as a torpedoman, Clem was anxious to see one of his fast-moving sub surface weapons sink a German vessel, but the opportunity would have to wait. *Canopus* left the Falklands for the Mediterranean on December 18, 1914.

--- 11 ---
Ripon Camp, North Yorkshire
September 1914

While in route to Ripon, Bertie and Sam speculated about the unit they would join. They preferred to be part of a local unit from the Cheshire area. Barring that they hoped to get into a unit with a dashing name such as the Cheshire Regiment, the King's Liverpool Regiment, or perhaps the Lancashire Rifles, or perhaps even the Liverpool Pals. They knew their abilities would be considered in their assignment. Unlike Clem, Sam wanted to be on land, so the Royal Navy was out. He also knew he was not tall enough to be in a combat unit. He had experience driving lorries and horse drawn wagons, and he could take care of livestock and make cheese. But he definitely hoped he would be asked to do more exciting jobs than those. Bertie on the other hand was an experienced animal wrangler and liked the idea of stewarding horses and mules for the army. Both men wanted to wield weapons, fight their country's enemies and defend their homeland on the battlefield. But they were obligated to do what was needed and go where the army sent them. And they had promised their mother they would return home safely.

While Andrew and Philip waited at Rawhead for their call up date to arrive, Bertie and Sam arrived at Ripon Camp, hearing the insults that passed for humor from other British soldiers along the way. Soldiers referred to the Army Service Corps or ASC as the "Alley Sloper's Cavalry". A British weekly comic strip about the rent-dodging con man and drunkard had first appeared in the late 1880's. "Alley Sloper" was slang for a person who snuck down an alley to avoid the rent collector. From the ranks of the cavalry, the jibe referred to those who cared for the thousands of draught horses and mules deployed to the Western Front.

The ASC, like many other support units, was not a combat element but the supply and transport leg of the British Army. This essential service was responsible for feeding the quarter million labourers hired to assist the forces. The workers came from multiple nations and had diverse diets. The officers and enlisted of the ASC were trained to drive motor vehicles and maintain engines. They also were taught how to take care of horses, mules, camels, oxen, dogs, reindeer and even pigeons. The pigeons were used for communications and Bertie didn't like working with them. They were messy, dirty creatures, he thought.

Considerable supply improvements had been made during the Second Boer War in South Africa a decade earlier but would not be tested until now. The British Army had never embraced the age-old concept of supplying its needs by raiding the stores of the countries it passed through. The Romans and Napoleon took whatever they wanted, for example. The ASC supply chain started in the home country and extended to the sailors and front-line soldiers, wherever they were.

Ripon was a sea of uniformed khaki. Located just south of the city, it accommodated 30,000 troops. By war's end, over 350,000 soldiers would pass through the camp. Once trained, units would travel by road or rail to a channel embarkation point and await deployment to whatever theater of the war they were assigned. As part of the indoctrination, formal photographs were taken of each man and made into post cards for sending home. After standing in line for an hour, Bertie entered a photographer's tent where a civilian photographer stepped back and observed Bertie. He dug through a box of scrap and handed an empty rifle bandolier to him. He helped buckle it across Bertie's shoulder.

"For looks," the photographer said. "To impress your folks and lady friends."

Days later, Bertie and Sam received a stack of postcards with their portraits. On the back read a preprinted slogan:

If thou wants a fight just come down to Ripon and
I will give thee a whipping.

Whenever they could, Bertie and Sam mailed one home.

In January 1915, several ASC companies were ordered to Salisbury. NCOs directed Sam and Bertie and hundreds of other recruits to waiting lorries. They sat opposite each other, swatting flies with batons to pass the time.

"Do you think we'll get rifles today, Sam?" Bertie asked.

"We're animal stewards, Bertie, not soldiers."

"But...aren't we all soldiers?"

"I suppose, but...not fighting soldiers" Sam replied, pointing to a platoon marching through the depot with rifles. "Those fellows will fight."

Bertie frowned. "But why?"

Sam observed a line of mules and horses being led by a driver. "Cause we're farmers. Army figures we drive mules and lorries for a living so they saved city folk for fightin'."

The lorry roared to life and lurched forward. A lean, bespectacled recruit across from Sam lit a cigarette. He had been observing the two farmers with amusement since they climbed aboard.

Sam at Ripon Camp
Photo courtesy of the author

"Farmers, ay?" he inquired, taking a drag. "Well I'm a city bloke and never drove nothin', though you could say I drove my father insane." Bertie and Sam stared silently at him, not understanding. He shrugged and studied the burning end of his cigarette. "So he says, anyway." He took a puff and exhaled.

"What did you do in the city? London was it?" Sam asked him.

"I worked in Paxton & Whiteland's Cheese Shop on Exeter Street in Westminster. It's one of the oldest cheese shops in England."

Sam thought a moment about that and smiled. "Tell me, what do you think of Cheshire cheese?"

"Cheshire?" inquired the man as he put his boot on the opposite bench and crossed it with the other. "Which variety? White, extra mature, red, blue? They're all a bit mild for me. I've sold a lot of Cheshire to the navy and army. I prefer the stronger, smellier cheeses like Vieux Boulogne, Camembert or Limburger. But it don't really matter what I think. It's whatever the customer likes, I suppose."

"Those aren't even English cheeses!" Bertie exclaimed.

"Don't listen to him, Bertie!" Sam said. "He's all mouth and no trousers!"

"Well my tongue don't discriminate. Except against a cheese I heard they make in Sardinia where they use maggots and sheep's milk." He knew he had their attention and watched them out of the corner of his eye. "Heard tell of an American man named Kraft who is making a product called 'American Cheese.' He has a technique he's calling 'processed'," Wainright said, shaking his head. "What in the world is that?"

Sam and Bertie exchanged surprised looks. "Maggots in cheese?" Bertie could not imagine such a thing.

"We made Cheshire cheese on our farm," Sam offered. "And we didn't use maggots!"

The shopkeeper leaned back. "Cheesemakers, are you?" He rubbed his chin. "What did you sell a 50-pound wheel of Farmhouse Cheshire for, let me guess, at the Chester Market?"

"Five pounds or so," said Sam.

"Five pounds!" The shopkeeper whistled.

"Yes, but to a broker in Broxton, who sends it on to Chester and London."

"You're on the wrong side of it, cheesemaker," Wainright chuckled. "I sell it for twelve and pocket a good bit of the difference, less whatever the Board of Revenue steals, of course. Bloody bastards."

Sam was astonished. *Twelve pounds sterling for a wheel of good Cheshire which took two men eight weeks to make from 70 gallons of milk at four pence a gallon?* Seeing Sam thinking, the shopkeeper laughed again.

"Don't work it, cheesemaker," the shopkeeper said. "It's a good quality cheese and if you've a brand it's worth something! Branding's the future you know!" He finished his cigarette and dropped it on the floor, stepping on it.

"Which brand?"

"Brand?" Bertie asked.

"Brand of cheese! You know, Cropwell Bishop, Cornish Yarg, Cotherstone."

"I never heard of those names."

"Usually it's where the cheese is from."

"Rawhead Farm...Ballantyne Estate," Bertie answered.

The shopkeeper rolled his eyes and rubbed his chin. "Ballantyne. Sure, I think I've heard of it."

"Heard of it?" asked Bertie. "It's won Third Prize at the Cheshire Dairy Association Chester Show for the last five years!"

"Easy, mate! Save it for the 'uns! I'm sure it's a good cheese. Cheshire's well known for its cheese. I take it you both have names besides cheesemaker? Or shall I call you 'Red' and 'Extra Mature'?"

"Bert Bebbington." Bertie informed him, reaching out to shake the shopkeeper's hand. "This is my brother Sam." Sam and Wainright shook hands. "But you can call him Red if you want and me, Extra Mature!" They all laughed.

"Max Wainright," the shopkeeper said, offering Bertie and Sam cigarettes from his crumpled packet.

"Well, I'm pleased to make your acquaintance, Misters Bebbington. You're friendlier than the sorts I'm used to dealing with in London. When we get some leave, I'll take you to one of the Tom and Jerrys in Piccadilly for a pint. Or maybe a good London cheese shop so I can give you an education."

The lorry took a sharp turn and the soldiers gripped their seats. They had been bouncing on the hard, wood benches for hours. The riders in the cab with the driver got to sit on cushioned seats and watch out the windows. But the ones in the back could only see out the rear flap if it was pulled open. When that happened, they caught whiffs of the lorry's exhaust fumes. By the time they reached their destination, Bertie and Sam felt nauseous. It was a grey, cold day. Clouds hung in the sky.

"Why have we stopped?" Bertie inquired when their lorry came to a halt.

Wainright whipped open the rear flap, exposing a view filled with NCO's shouting orders, hundreds of recruits, a raft of white tents, trucks, jeeps, and piles of supplies and equipment.

"Salisbury. We train here 'til they ship us overseas," Wainright speculated. "Be here for months, I'd wager."

"Months!" Bertie exclaimed. "Well what were we called up for, then?"

"To train, boys." As a shopkeeper, Wainright seemed to have all the answers. "And train and train and train. And after that we'll train. And then when we're all done training we'll train some more. And maybe we'll get to put the supply chain in order. From here, to London to the front, whether the destination is across the channel or all the way to India."

The ASC workers quickly climbed out of the lorry. It felt good to get out of there and stretch. Some of the riders stumbled because their limbs were so stiff. A sea of a thousand canvas bell tents stretched before them as far as they could see.

"Hey, Mature, wait up!" Max Wainright called to Bertie.

"It's Bertie."

"Bertie, yeah. Sorry, Bertie."

A portly NCO wielding a baton summoned the newly arriving recruits to muster. "Step in line!" he yelled. The men hustled to form up before him. The NCO strutted back and forth in front of them.

"You are now part of the Fourth New Armies 'orse Transport of the Army Service Corps!" barked the NCO. "The British Expeditionary Force in France and Belgium depends 'eavily on horses and mules for the transport of men and materials. Mules, when the bloody animals cooperate, are 'ardier than the 'orse. 'Ere in Salisbury you will learn proper care of the beasts and 'ow they are used by the Army. Fully trained, you will be caring for the animals on land and ship. You will lead them in 'auling munitions and supplies from depots to battlefields o'er seas. You've been picked for this duty based on your experience with animals. Those of you who want to fight will 'ave plenty of opportunity. But, you'll prove 'ere first. You are the blood of the army at the front of battle. Without you, they'd perish. It takes a trained Service Corpsman to think, predict, do, and surmount 'cumbrances as quickly as they appear," he paused a moment, eyeing them. "These are the animals in your charge," he said, his baton sweeping back and forth. "You can start by feedin' 'em." He withdrew a book from his bag and handed it to Sam.

"Read this," he ordered. "And return it when you're done."

The frayed book cover read *Horses, Saddles, and Bridles* by General William Giles Harding Cutter. The NCO walked away toward another incoming lorry.

Bertie and Sam were not impressed by their introduction to the ASC.

"Am I to read a book about horses for this duty?" Bertie asked. "Do they think we know nothin' about 'em?" Bertie stepped closer to the two dozen horses and mules the NCO had pointed them to. They were corralled by ropes. He noticed a three-number brand on each animal's rump.

"Can't call a horse '921'," Bertie said. "I think I will call you Errol," he told the gelding. He turned to a brown mare with a black mane next to him. "And I will call you Bess." Bertie looked at a very large middle-aged gelding at the end of the corral. He was standing at an empty tub and was marked with a 426 brand. Bertie strolled toward him. The gelding turned his head to look at him and nickered quietly.

Bertie noticed Wainright talking to a group of other ASC soldiers who had wandered away from the horses. They were laughing, probably hearing of his tales about the London ladies, Bertie surmised. Max Wainright had probably never fed a horse, much less saddled one.

"And I will call you Max," he told the big gelding, stroking his neck.

Bertie liked naming his new equine friends. He found that each animal reminded him of a person he had met at one time or another over the course of his eighteen years.

--- **12** ---

Andrew received notice in October that he was assigned to the 13th (Service) Battalion, Rifle Brigade. The battalion was part of the infantry rifle regiment of the British Army formed in January 1800 as an experiment to provide sharpshooters, scouts, and skirmishers. Renamed several times, the unit was finally named the "Rifle Brigade" and the 13th Battalion was commanded by LTC Pretor-Pinney.

Philip was to report to Winchester in the Salisbury plain, post haste. After barely passing his physical exam and waiting for nearly two months, Philip was assigned to the 9th Battalion of the Cheshire Regiment. The 9th Battalion was the second in the "New Army", under the command of Lt. Colonel Harkness, with Major W. E. Dauntessey, second in command. Harkness was in his mid-sixties and not a well man. But he was an experienced soldier and dedicated to the training mission ahead of him. The men in the battalion would require a great deal of attention before embarkation for parts unknown.

The 9th Battalion initially billeted near Chester Castle on the old Roodee race course with the grand stand serving as field headquarters. The battalion was composed almost entirely of men who joined up in their oldest clothes right off the street. Rain and muddy conditions created such a hardship that within days, they moved by rail to Codford in the Salisbury plain for training.

On the train, an energetic lieutenant walked down the aisles with a roll of red ribbon and asked each man what their civilian jobs had been. Farmer, labourer, brickmaker, millworker, shopkeeper, lorry driver, blacksmith, miner, cook, and cheese maker they variously answered. As part of the "New Army", this represented an attempt at organization. The young officer asked more questions. "Do any of you have previous military experience? The Second Boer war perhaps?" he hinted. There were no responses. The lieutenant searched their faces. "Were any of you policemen?" he asked. No responses. "Were any of you cadets? From an officer training program in school?" The officer sighed when still no one raised a hand. "Were any of you Boy Scouts?"

Heads turned, looking around. A hand slowly went up in the back of the train car. Amazed, the lieutenant walked rapidly toward him. He tied a ribbon around Philip's left arm.

"Right!" he said. "You're now an acting NCO. I'll brief you on your duties later." He continued down the aisle asking questions and tying a few more ribbons to arms. Bewildered, Philip looked at the ribbon on his sleeve. Must have been purchased from a lady's dress shop, he thought. Soldiers seated around him looked Philip over and wondered why he was made an acting NCO because he was a Boy Scout. Philip wondered if he would regret raising his hand.

By the time they arrived in Salisbury, the battalion had been organized into four companies. Each company consisted of four platoons. Each platoon was commanded by a lieutenant with a platoon sergeant as his deputy. Each platoon was divided into four sections and these were headed by corporals. Philip was assigned to Second Platoon. Mail was delivered while they were on the train and Philip received a card from the King and Queen.

"Look at this," Philip showed his card to the private next to him, surprised. One side showed a photo of Queen Mary and King George V. Philip turned it over and read:

With our best wishes for Christmas 1914. May God protect you and bring you home safely.

Mary R. George R.

As the train approached Codford Station, it started to rain. Philip observed the hundreds of bell tents standing in the fields. Ordered to disembark, the 988 men of the 9th Battalion Cheshire Regiment marched through the rain to a piece of empty ground where piles of stakes, poles and tent canvas was heaped. The lieutenants directed the newly appointed NCOs to organize the men into teams. These groups were then instructed to assemble the 20-man tents.

The rain intensified to a deluge. There were briefings about the importance of camp sanitation and the construction of privies. Food consisted of tea and bread purchased from grocer's carts brought in from town. The men slept and moved in a river of mud several inches deep. Illness such as influenza and dysentery made appearance and spread rapidly.

This was Philip's introduction to the plain and what lay ahead. He thought, I should have gone with Andrew. He imagined that Andrew could not have been as wet, cold and miserable as he was. They were issued 'drill' rifles which were not much more than broom handles. They did not receive uniforms for weeks. Initial training consisted of conditioning and strengthening exercises followed by drill, inspection, bayonet practice, maneuvers, and musketry. Marching 30 miles a day for five days straight was common. The road marches would begin before dawn in the rain and would end well after dark in the rain. Finally, mercifully, it stopped raining. The mud began to dry and harden. Work parties were formed to fill in rutted roads and dig channels for draining fields that remained under water. Most had no change of clothes and there were no bathing facilities. Philip and the other NCOs ordered their platoons to the River Wylye where they disrobed, rinsed off in the freezing river and air dried themselves by jogging around in circles. Some sat naked on the river bank to dry off, which appalled passing town folk.

They had to inspect their clothes for lice, a practice called "chatting". Philip knew all about delousing from living on a farm. Lice were known to have lived for thousands of years. William Shakespeare references to them in his writings, which brought the tiny irritants some notoriety. Comprising over 5000 species, the creatures thrive on the skin and blood of their living hosts. Philip swore he had seen every one of them. Crowds of people living in close quarters are often afflicted with lice infestations. Philip dreamed of the facilities at Rawhead, especially the hot baths he had enjoyed. He could only hope that better days lay ahead but that winter conditions worsened in the tents. Illness was rampant. An entire battalion deserted and another came close to rioting. The commander ordered extra rations of beer and assigned battalion NCOs to complaint duty.

Finally, after six weeks of these appalling conditions, experienced marine sergeants were shipped in. They continued the drills and inspections but allowed the men to play football games. They introduced trench digging to condition the men. But the state of affairs at the training camp remained unacceptable. Col. Harkness wired Lord Kitchener about the situation.

Kitchener gave Harkness permission to move the men into billets at Basingstoke. The townspeople collected blankets and clothing for them. Wounded men arriving from the front gave talks on their experiences. More strenuous training commenced as a result, and Second Boer War-era rifles were issued. The young lieutenants, most of whom had been exposed to officer training programs in their schools, were distributed books on modern warfare, strategy and tactics from libraries and book shops. The young men formed discussion groups to educate themselves. Col. Harkness sickened and was forced to resign his command of recruitment and training. LTC Dauntessey assumed the post.

--- 13 ---

Like Philip, Andrew made the best of Salisbury training. The unrelenting rain, fouled mud, poor food, and sickness were the same. But he always sought out better tents and floor boards and bargained for foods over card games. In the 13th Rifle Brigade, naturally there was more attention given to target practice.

A British sergeant instructor stood before Andrew and his platoon and instructed on how to fire the SMLE Mk III Lee–Enfield rifle. The Lee–Enfield bolt action rifle was known for its smooth operation and was often associated with the "Mad Minute", a pre-World War I bolt-rifle speed shooting exercise used by British Army riflemen.

"Which is your dominate eye?" the instructor asked.

"My right, I guess." Andrew said. "But I can shoot on the left if I have to."

The instructor was dumbfounded.

"Show me."

Andrew then proceeded to shoot several rounds on the right side, the target was switched, and then he fired several rounds on his left. When the targets were retrieved, the right-side effort was more accurate but the left not far off the right.

"Can you teach that?" the instructor asked.

"No, sir. I just can do it."

"Now that you know how to shoot," the instructor said, "I'll teach you to shoot faster!"

The instructor stood before Andrew and two dozen soldiers at a firing range.

"The exercise is called 'The Mad Minute' or more formally as 'Practice number 22, Rapid Fire' and you can find it in Part One of the *Musketry Regulations.*"

The instructor grabbed Andrew's rifle, replaced the magazine and readied to fire at a target down range.

"You are required to fire fifteen rounds at a second-class target at 300 yards by using a sort of 'palming' method where you use the palm of your hand to work the bolt, and not your thumb and forefinger, while maintaining your cheek weld and line of sight. All within one minute."

The instructor then fired an astounding fifteen rounds in fifty-five seconds and included removing each five-round clip, retrieving a full one from his bandolier, and inserting it in the rifle again. A runner brought the target sheet up and all examined his accuracy. All rounds fired at the target of two concentric circles were bull's eyes.

The soldiers stood in awe of the instructor's shooting ability. His Mad Minute hand motions were nothing short of fine poetry.

"Mastering the Mad Minute may be the difference between life and death in France! The world record is 38 hits in four minutes."

Soldiers looked amongst each other.

"Private Bebbington!" barked the instructor. "Try it."

Andrew laid in prone position and practiced what he just saw without firing. He took a breath and began the exercise. The first two shots got off easily enough but then he fumbled from the speed and resumed. After firing the last clip, the instructor looked at his stop watch.

"Eighty seconds," the instructor said. "Too slow, you're dead. Next man…"

And so passed the Mad Minute. Andrew was not sure why they were being trained to fire so fast at a target hundreds of yards away and expected to hit what they aimed at. He had heard that the battles consisted largely of the exchange of artillery and long-range rifle and sniper fire over "No Man's Land". But on the other hand, the tactic of climbing out of a trench and running open field towards enemy lines across No Man's Land made little sense either. They would be pheasants in a shoot.

Bayonet practice was particularly personal. Sacks resembling German dummies were hung from a platform while each rifleman charged it with a fixed bayonet, or sword. The drill occurred daily for several days and then they all got it. But what they didn't teach was the personal aspect. Standing before a six-foot German soldier with an eighteen-inch sword fixed to the end of their Lee-Enfield, then ramming it into the man's chest or belly and seeing the expression on the man's face and hearing the guttural sound they made when stuck. All of this assumes one was able to avoid the enemy's sword. Andrew swore he would kill Germans with marksmanship and not hand to hand.

--- 14 ---
Dardanelles Straits
March 18, 1915

Canopus received yet another direct hit from a Turkish shore battery, ripping equipment from decks and bulkheads and sending sailors in every direction. The blast tore off her main topmast and damaged the aft funnel, and the wardroom below the main deck. Gun crews scrambled to recover, unsure of where to direct their fire. Below decks in the torpedo bay, an NCO hung up a ships' phone and waived to Clem and a fellow torpedoman named Ainsworth.

"Fire control, forward!" he shouted. "Now!" Clem and Ainsworth grabbed their battle gear and entered a stairwell.

While Andrew, Philip, Sam, and Bertie continued their training in England, Clem and the crew of the *Canopus* had been transferred from the Falklands to the Mediterranean. Their mission was to participate in attacks on Ottoman coastal fortifications defending the Dardanelles. The plan was to gain control of the Dardanelles and Bosporus straits, capture Constantinople and open a Black Sea supply route to Russia. During this operation, *Canopus* and HMS *Swiftsure* were tasked with suppressing the guns in the fortress at Dardanus while the HMS *Cornwallis* engaged minor batteries at Intepe and Erenkoy. They were among 18 battleships with an array of cruisers and destroyers attacking the narrowest point of the Dardanelles where the straits are one mile wide. *Canopus* and *Swiftsure* had entered the straights in the early afternoon and closed within a thousand yards of the north shore. At 2 p.m., they opened fire. After a two-hour barrage, Ottoman soldiers inside the fort returned fire.

On deck, Clem made his way forward. There was so much black smoke it looked like dusk had fallen. The forward superstructure was ablaze; shells and ammunition were exploding. Running along the deck, he could barely keep his footing because the vessel was shuddering. Clem fell back against a deck hatch as another shell hit, this time amidships at the second funnel. He and Ainsworth grabbed a water hose that had been abandoned by another seaman only to be thwarted by bodies and injured men who lay bleeding and groaning on deck. Fire crews sprayed water on the spreading flames, the thick black smoke of burning oil making each breath painful. Clem's head slammed against the deck railing as another explosion blew part of the aft deck away. Dazed, he slid to the deck, holding tightly to the railing, scenes of Rawhead whirled in his head. Ainsworth and another sailor lifted him to his feet and rushed him below.

Further up the channel, minesweepers retreated from heavy and accurate Turk shelling. The first officer of the *Canopus* hung up a ship's phone in the bridge after speaking with the ship's teleoperator.

"Captain, the minesweepers are retreating. *Irresistible* and *Inflexible* have struck mines."

The captain shook his head. "We can't sail through a minefield! This is what we get when civilians man minesweepers!"

In the distance, near the narrows, the *Inflexible*'s hull struck another mine they had failed to detect.

--- 15 ---

"We've been called up, Ma'am," said the tallest of three Rawhead farmhands standing in the cheese parlour wringing wool caps in their hands. Mary and Joseph had been wondering why the men had not arrived for work that morning and were about to send for them. It certainly was not like them to be late.

"I see. Do you know of any men who might take your places? At least until you come back?" The men shook their heads. "Most of the men I know are gone," one hand replied. "You might try the schools."

"Well then, take good care of yourselves, gentlemen." Mary said. "There will be jobs for you when you come back."

"Thank you, ma'am, Mr. Bebbington," the men said, doffing their caps. They turned and walked through the parlour door. Mary took Joseph's arm and watched their help head down the drive.

"How will we manage, Joseph?"

"The best we can," he replied. "That's all we can do."

Hearing the dinner bell, the family assembled around the table. Five chairs were empty and would remain so until the five brothers returned.

--- 16 ---
Ballantyne Castle
Harthill

On a Wednesday evening, William Cutter dined with the Bryden family. He was working in the estate office when Gilbert Bryden extended the invitation. A waiter poured wine.

"…and you see, sir, some tenants are concerned about the loss of labour on account of the war effort." Cutter was saying. "They're asking to have their rents adjusted accordingly."

"Yes, Cutter, but the families have children, do they not?" Bryden challenged. "Not everyone has gone to war. Just those over seventeen, and temporarily, I might add. The war is likely to end soon."

"Do you honestly believe that, sir?" Cutter was astounded. "This talk of ending the war by Christmas is madness. They said that about last Christmas and it's 1915 now."

"Will you have to fight in the war, Mr. Cutter?" Chloe asked.

"No, my dear," Cutter assured her. "I was injured in the last one, the Second Boer. I'll try to serve in the Home Guard, if they will accept me."

"May we host another dance for the yeomanry, Father? Before they go?" Lindsay asked. "I think they are so handsome and gallant. They deserve another dance!" Gilbert Bryden told her he would consider the idea. "Did you serve with the yeomanry, Mr. Cutter?" she looked at him directly.

Cutter's eyes had drifted to Heidi Bryden seated across the table from him. She is so beautiful, he thought. He was lost in contemplation and didn't hear the question. His own dear wife Emily had been gone two years now from influenza. He remembered sitting with her in the hospital, holding her hand until she drew her last breath. Heidi caught him looking at her and smiled at him.

"Cutter, did you not hear my daughter's question?" Gilbert Bryden asked, bringing Cutter out of his thoughts.

"Oh, I'm sorry," Cutter answered. "What was your question, Miss Lindsay?"

"I asked if you were with the Cheshire Yeomanry in the Boer War."

"No, Miss. I was in the King's Shropshire Light Infantry."

"Were you an officer?" Bethany asked.

"Yes. I was a lieutenant. It was a long time ago." As memories of those days appeared in his head, his discomfort of the subject became visible.

Cutter looked at Heidi again as she demurely touched her napkin to her lips. She had smiled at him. *What could she be thinking? And how could her husband leave her? I could never abandon a woman like her. For any reason.* He was surprised that he felt so strongly about it. He looked down at his plate and tried to quell his disquiet.

--- 17 ---
Salisbury Plain, England

Despite suffering months of disease and hardship, the 9th Battalion continued to train. When they moved into the more comfortable billets at Basingstoke, "Kitchener Blue" uniforms were issued. By Christmas, they were khaki. Andrew's 13th Rifle Brigade received green uniforms. Old Metley rifles were replaced by Lee Enfield .303's. The men began to think of themselves as soldiers and embraced the esprits de corps expected of them. News of the Marne, Ypres, Neuve Chappell and Gallipoli battles and their shocking losses were met with dismay. The sinking of the *Lusitania* both rallied and sobered the men. Petty complaints and disputes within the ranks died away. Their mission was clear.

One morning Philip listened to a training class on gas attacks. Balanced on one knee with two dozen other soldiers, Philip watched an NCO instructor and his Bedlington Terrier "Andy" standing before them.

"Poison gas is being used for the first time in this war," he warned.

Just then a squadron of planes passed over. "Hang on, gotta let the planes get outta the way!"

Philip looked up at the marvel of aircraft and again wondered what it was like to fly. The buzz of the planes died off as they turned to the channel.

"Don't lose your gas mask or keep a pair of socks in it like the poor fellow in the London *Punch* story! You may escape a gas attack for months, then receive one. Almost always there are gas cylinders sitting in your trench or in the enemy's. A shell or bullet might hit and burst them, so take great care of your mask. It will save your life! If your mask leaks or by chance you lose it, and you bloody well better not, piss on a handkerchief and hold it tight on your face with your eyes closed. Run sideways away from the gas. Find a source of water and wash your eyes and exposed skin. That's a last resort."

Philip turned to Heathcote. "Piss on a handkerchief?"

"The acid in the urine 'elps block the gas," guessed Albert Birch who had taken a chemistry class in school.

Heathcote shrugged. "If it works."

"So long as it's not your piss!" Philip grinned.

The NCO went on. "One more thing, don't take your mask wallet off your shoulder or leave it on the ground or forget it when you're working behind the lines, maybe on a warm day with your jacket off. And don't forget to 'elp the animals during an attack." he said, gesturing to the dog sitting patiently beside him. The NCO then proceeded to fit a special-sized gas mask on Andy. Philip and the others laughed when they saw the little fellow behind the big eyes of the mask. The dog wagged his tail.

But the NCO's expression was serious. "We have masks for 'orses, mules, donkeys, oxen. But not pigeons."

Lt. Colonel Dauntessey, Col. Harkness's replacement, moved the battalion from Basingstoke to billets in Andover for the winter. In March they returned to Salisbury for more drilling. On April 16, Philip was promoted to Lance Corporal. That night, Philip wrote home and included the temporary red ribbon insignia in the envelope. When Mary received it, she saved it to use as a bookmark in the family Bible. She pinned the letter to the kitchen wall, along with the others he had written. Two months later, the 9th Battalion marched to billets in Folkestone. This would be their jumping off point to the war. Philip had never been to Europe and was anxious to see some of it.

--- 18 ---
Off Anzac Cove, Gallipoli Peninsula
April, 1915

On the bridge of the *Canopus*, Captain Grant observed Anzac beach through his binoculars. French, British, and Australian troops had been landing for hours and were facing relentless fire from Turk defenses.

"It's a bloody nightmare," Grant swore.

A ship's officer entered from the radio room. "Captain, *Albion* signals they have run aground on a sand bar. They are requesting a tow. Her rudder and propellers won't answer."

The Captain glowered at the beach and the horror unfolding before him. The shore was thick with soldiers fighting to reach higher ground. He watched as scores fell in the face of machine gun fire and artillery shells. Grant had never seen anything like it in his career. He felt like weeping.

"Sir?" the officer asked again.

Breaking away, the captain nodded. "Proceed west of her and rig for towing. Increase fire on the high ground!"

"Aye, aye, sir," answered the officer, quickly leaving the bridge.

From the deck of the *Canopus*, a group of sailors, including Clem, hauled in a messenger line from the *Albion* that had been retrieved by a launch. Within an hour, *Canopus* engines throttled up and the steel cable straightened.

"She's still firing!" Clem said, pointing at the *Albion*. "Even as she's aground!" There was a roar of cheers. With its engines churning revolutions for full speed, the *Albion* gradually slid free of the sand bar to cheers from the decks of both ships. Turk shore batteries continued firing mercilessly while several Turk guns aimed their fire at the tow cable joining them.

"We're not going to make it unless we increase fire on the forts!" the captain bellowed to his officers. *Canopus* towed *Albion* amidst heavy fire until they were three miles west of Gaba Tepe.

"Recommend we withdraw for repairs, sir," the first officer suggested to the captain.

"We're ordered to maintain shelling of the fortifications, Lieutenant."

"Captain, the main turrets report substantial damage and we're losing fresh water. If we can get to Malta or Mudros, we can drop the *Albion* there, tend to our wounded, refit the *Canopus*, and return within days with full crew and magazines. The *Lord Nelson* and *Glory* can maintain fire from our position."

"Very well," Captain Grant relented. "Signal *Inflexible* to that effect."

Canopus and *Albion* withdrew. After a brief retrofit in Malta, they took on supplies and *Canopus* returned to the Gallipoli Peninsula a week later. Reports arrived from shore as they approached. The campaign had turned into an appalling failure; casualties numbered in the tens of thousands.

--- 19 ---
Royal Victoria Station
London

Now a rifleman with the 13th Rifle Brigade, Andrew stood with others before the stone arch leading into Royal Victoria Station in London. It was one of several gateways to the war where families and soldiers parted. Thus far, Andrew's battalion had travelled through billets at Wendover, Halton Park, Chiltern Hills, High Wycombe, Hughenden Park, Daw's Hill, and Windmill Hill near Ludgershall. They heard rumors they would be home by Christmas 1915 but they were suspicious because that's what they'd been told in Salisbury the year before. He had accumulated stories to tell his family at the dinner table, if he did get home.

Andrew enjoyed a cigarette with his company while he watched soldiers telling loved ones goodbye. Families and sweethearts kissed their soldiers and cried. A train whistle shrilled imminent departure as goodbyes became extended farewells. Finally, NCOs stepped off the trains and ordered the few remaining soldiers on board. In a cloud of steam from the train, the men disentangled themselves from their sweethearts and climbed reluctantly onto the train. One young couple was so distraught with the idea of parting, NCOs pondered sending them home as a goodwill gesture to all watching. But the teary-eyed rifleman finally stepped away from his lover and got on the train. Andrew had said his goodbyes to his family at Rawhead months ago, but he wished he had a girl who would cry on his shoulder and write to him. His memories of Rawhead became a comfort to him.

"Riflemen!" an NCO barked. "13th Rifles! Departing gate three for Southhampton!"

The riflemen hefted their packs. Andrew picked up his Enfield .303 and looked it over. It was clean and shiny. He had fired it in practice several thousand times and rammed many a stuffed sack with its sword, but he had never used it to kill. He slung it over his shoulder and walked towards the train. At 10 a.m. the battalion departed for the Southhampton docks.

Later that afternoon, they boarded the iron paddle steamer *Mona's Queen*. Andrew heard faint singing and walked to the rail to observe the waving crowds. He joined in as they sang *Keep the Home Fires Burning* by Ivor Novello,

They were summoned from the hillside,
They were called in from the glen
And the Country found them ready
At the stirring call for men.
Let no tears add to their hardship
As the Soldiers pass along,
And although your heart is breaking
Make it sing this cheery song.

[Chorus]

Keep the Home Fires burning,

While your hearts are yearning.
Though your lads are far away
they dream of home.
There's a silver lining,
through the dark cloud shining.
Turn the dark cloud inside out
'till the boys come Home.

With the Isle of Wight to starboard, *Mona's Queen* churned down the Solent Strait towards the English Channel en route to Le Havre. Seagulls wailed and dipped in the sullen sky. Andrew and the others looked toward England and wondered if they would ever see her again.

Unbeknownst to Andrew, Philip and the 9th Battalion Cheshires were already in France. They had departed England on the HMT *Omrah* from Folkestone twelve days earlier. The 13th Rifle Brigade became part of the 19th Division of the British Expeditionary Force (BEF). Philip's battalion proceeded to St. Omer, and Andrew's to Nortbeqourt. The two towns were roughly ten miles apart.

--- 20 ---
Cheshire Yeomanry Camp
Langley Park, Cheshire

Since activation, Robert Bryden and the Cheshire Yeomanry had moved from Chester Castle to Kirby Cane Hall in Bungay, Norfolk, roughly eighteen miles away. From there, they rode on to Langley Park near Macclesfield where they were ordered to build huts for billets. After a flurry of recruiting, the regiment was now at full strength. Equipment and uniforms had been issued, horses branded and shod, and all ranks had signed a declaration that they would be deployed overseas. There was intense excitement over the pending deployment. Robert Bryden rode with his squadron down the streets of Langley Park in a Sunday parade with squadrons on either side of him and a fourth directly behind. Crowds waved, cheered, and tossed confetti. Wilkinson and others could not help but return woos to young ladies.

Unlike the New Army being raised, the yeomanry was already trained. It was assumed they would see action early on, but after several weeks of training in one location, they would move on to another. Football and rugby were played to maintain fitness and comradery. This routine went on for months.

Bryden stood on the sidelines of a playing field at Langley Park watching a rugby match between squadrons. A rugby ball rolled out of play to his feet, which he picked up and threw back without much interest. No word had come down as to when they might be deployed. Restless men had been granted weekend passes to visit home. Declining morale and boredom had descended over the camp.

One afternoon, the regiment doctor, Captain Tillerson, requested that Bryden meet him at the billet dispensary.

"These men have syphilis, sir," Tillerson informed him.

Bryden looked at the three men standing at attention in their underwear. "And how is that possible, gentlemen?"

The three men avoided his stare. "I want an answer," Bryden commanded.

"We was just on leave, sir," one of the privates stammered. "Recreation, sir."

"You were given passes to be with your families! What possessed you?" Bryden asked.

"How was we to know the girls had the pox, sir?" Private Taylor whined.

Bryden began pacing back and forth in front of the men. "Do you realize that contracting a venereal disease is equivalent to a self-inflicted wound?" Bryden spat. "They are shooting men for this in France." Jaws dropped.

"You…you're not going to shoot us, are you, sir?" Private Taylor asked in horror.

Bryden turned to the doctor. "What do we do with them? I haven't seen this since the Boer War."

"There's only one thing we can do, sir." Tillerson answered. "They have to be taken to Cherry Hinton Camp near Cambridge for quarantine. Probably for the rest of the war."

Bryden rolled his eyes at the ceiling and fumed. "Were any men in the other squadrons affected?"

"Two cases of cerebral meningitis from A Squadron, but no syphilis, sir."

Bryden looked to the three men with disgust. "It just had to be 'B' Squadron. My squadron." He shook his head. "Very well, doctor. I'll form a detail and have them escorted to Cherry Hinton."

"And with your permission, sir, may I recommend to the colonel that we cancel all leave until further notice? We don't want an epidemic." Bryden nodded his agreement.

Privates Taylor, Stephenson, and White of "B" Squadron were escorted south to Cherry Hinton Camp. To the disdain of nearby townspeople, the camp census had grown upwards of 200.

--- 21 ---

Mary and Joseph were enjoying a quiet cup of tea when there was a flurry of knocks on the door. Opening it, Mary saw the three eldest boys from George Plunkett's scout troop, Eddie McFie, Ernest Hewett and Lewis Briscoe. They wore army, rather than Boy Scout, uniforms and had white patches on their sleeves.

"Mrs. Bebbington, we had to tell you! We've joined the King's Liverpool Regiment," Eddie McFie informed her. "They're calling them Pals Battalions. Entire towns are forming them so friends can serve together."

"Where is Mr. Plunkett?" Mary asked.

"He joined already. He's in Salisbury, training soldiers."

"You're just boys!" Mary exclaimed.

"Don't worry about us, Ma," Ernest Hewitt assured her. "We're already trained in camping and survival and first aid and cooking and marksmanship. We have an advantage. Oh, here's your mail. Edgar gave it to us back there."

He handed Mary the mail. It contained a postcard photo of Sam and Bertie posing smugly in their ASC uniforms. They carried crops and sported bandoliers across their chests. "Sam and Bertie must be having quite a time!" Briscoe said excitedly, looking over her shoulder at the picture.

Joseph appeared next to Mary and took the mail.

Mary looked at the boys. "You should be in school not fighting a war."

"We'll be eighteen by the time they ship us out," Lewis Briscoe announced.

"But this is not scouting, boys," insisted Mary. "It's war. Killing and dying."

"It's an adventure, Ma," Ernest Hewitt said. "We'll write to you. Eddie has one of the new Kodak brownie boxes and we can send photographs!" Seeing her concern, he stepped forward and hugged her awkwardly. The other boys hugged her as well.

"Oh, you dear boys…" Mary fussed. "Why don't you just wait until it ends?"

"Why?" Ernest said. "We can help make it end."

After being given biscuits and cakes for their journey, the scouts marched off. "We'll see you at Christmas!" Ernest called happily.

The boys paused down the road to look at their former campsite. Ernest Hewitt waved a distant goodbye just before they disappeared behind The Clump.

Mary clutched Joseph's arm. "First my boys and now my scouts," she said. "They're all gone." She stared worriedly at the postcard of her sons, tears rolling gently down her cheeks, an emptiness in her heart.

--- 22 ---
Cheshire Yeomanry billets
Bungay, Suffolk
June 1915

The squadron leaders of the Cheshire Yeomanry met with Lt. Commander Philips-Brocklehurst.

"Sir, we've been training for almost a year now with no word of deployment!" Major Glazebrook of C Squadron said. "We're more than ready."

"The men are restless, sir." Major Bryden added. "Getting into mischief while on leave."

"I understand your concern, gentlemen." Philips-Brocklehurst said. "But the general staff does not readily deploy the yeomanry. Out talents must fit the conflict."

"But sir, at this pace the war will be over before we see any action," Major Verdin said.

"Let's hope to God it will be!" Philips-Brocklehurst replied fervently. "But there's talk of Salonika. And the Serbs have been begging for help in their defense against Bulgaria for some time. That may very well be our next destination."

The situation in Serbia was desperate. A pro-allied temporary government headed by Eleftherios Venizelos had been established in Salonika, against the will of the neutral-leaning Greek leader, Constantine I. For an entire year, Britain and France had been promising Serbia they would send military forces there. The situation in France had deeply depleted allied resources, which was the main reason for the delay in sending help to the Serbians. The squadron leaders tried not to leak the news that they would be going to Salonika but the rumor managed to get out. The story successfully eased tensions in the Yeomanry for the time being.

Approximately one third of volunteers were rejected for enlistment in the first year of the war. But in June 1915, the age range and minimum height requirements were relaxed to eighteen to forty-five years and five feet, two inches tall. Previously ineligible men were now able to enlist. After six weeks of training, they were sent directly to the front. Casualties were staggering.

--- 23 ---
Ballantyne Castle
Harthill

Heidi Bryden spent the morning riding through the estate. It was June in Cheshire, her favorite month of the year. Not quite hot but warm. She had resided on the estate for six years and still managed to find new trails. One such trail led her to the ruins of Beeston Castle, perched on a rocky sandstone crag 350 feet above the Cheshire Plain. It had been built in the 1220s by Ranulf de Blondeville, 6th Earl of Chester, on his return from the Crusades. It was partially demolished on Oliver Cromwell's orders in 1646 to prevent its further use as a stronghold. *What a pity Ballantyne was not located here*, Heidi thought. She rode on, but headed leisurely back to the estate. While in route, she happened upon a clear pool fed by a spring and went for a swim. William Cutter had followed her and watched from a distance as she emerged from the lake and dried off in the sun. She sat on a flat sandstone rock beside her clothes and began to comb her hair. Ashamed, Cutter looked away and rode on. When she left Ballantyne that morning, he followed her as a precaution, as he often did. He thought of asking to accompany her but did not feel right about it. If they were seen together, there would be talk. Though not proper and certainly not expected, Cutter was indeed in love with her, and he didn't have the courage to announce his feelings.

"God help me," Cutter whispered. "I think I must leave this place, or go mad."

--- 24 ---
Cheshire Yeomanry Billets
Lowestoft, Suffolk
July 1915

The Yeomanry moved again, this time to Lowestoft, the most easterly town in England and the first place in the UK to see the sunrise. With still no word on deployment, they were assigned home defense duties. Food supplies in nearby towns had been depleted. Despite strict orders, soldiers were caught foraging from nearby farms and villages. Some were charged with desertion, though those charges were later dropped. The battlefront had commanded the attention of the army quartermaster and the ASC supply lines since the beginning of the war. Supplying units camped all over south England had almost become an afterthought.

After being told supplies would not arrive for days, Robert Bryden recommended to LTC Philips-Brocklehurst that he dispatch a detail to visit the Quartermaster Corps in Salisbury. Bryden decided to join the detail himself along with A.G. Wilkinson because food shortage had become so urgent. He vowed he would bring back supplies that night if he had to pay for them himself. Upon arriving in Lufton, a small village on the fringes of the plain, the detail met an ASC horse company supply convoy who had stopped to water and feed their animals. Bryden rode up to an ASC lieutenant and they exchanged salutes.

"Lieutenant," said Bryden. "I need food and supplies for my battalion in Lowestoft. Can you direct me to…?"

"Not these supplies, sir!" he warned, shaking his head. "This train's headed to Folkestone. You best keep going to headquarters. Supplies are short all over!"

Bryden and his detail moved on and were met with similar responses from other convoys.

As they approached Winchester, Bryden's detail rode beside a long convoy of horse-drawn wagons. Wilkinson observed a young ASC soldier talking to a mule as if they were old friends. He laughed.

"That bloke back there is talking to a bloody mule!" Wilkinson mused.

"I'm tired of you, Jen" the young soldier said gently to the mule, wielding a crop in her face. "You want me to start using this on you?"

"Bertie?" Bryden yelled. He dismounted and ran over to him. "Bertie, what the hell are you doing here?"

"Major Bryden!" Bertie replied. "I'm…well, we're taking these supplies to the Folkestone Docks for sending on to France. That's what I do. How about you?"

"Listen, Bertie, I need food for my men. We're camped at Lowestoft and we're out of supplies. I've never seen such disorganization."

Bertie looked about. "We're trying to correct that, sir. Here sir, take these three wagons. It's food and should last you until we can get the mix-up worked out."

"I can't do that. How will you account for them?"

"I'll find a way," Bertie said smiling. "Learned a few things."

Bryden directed his yeomen to lead the wagons down a cross road away from the column. "I'll see that the horses and wagons are returned," Bryden assured Bertie.

"Good luck to you, sir." Bertie offered. He walked quickly in the direction of the transport. On a second thought, Bryden followed him. "What are your orders, Bertie?"

"None yet sir, but they say Salonika. It's just rumor. They won't tell us for sure."

"Us, too. Do you know where Salonika is?"

Bertie shook his head.

"Greece. A long way from here."

Oblivious, Bertie just stared at him. He had been working since dawn and was exhausted. He didn't care where he was headed, Greece, or the moon for that matter. He just wanted to deliver supplies to hungry soldiers then find a place for a few hours of sleep.

"Listen, Bertie," Bryden went on. "Stay away from the fighting. Leave that to me and the combat units. Just take care of your animals and you'll be fine. I'll see you when I get there."

"I heard they shot a nurse," Bertie said in a low voice.

Bryden nodded. "Edith Cavell. Yes, I know. My men know of it, too, and I can hardly hold them back. They said they'll swim to France if we don't get orders soon. But leave the fighting to us, you understand? With any luck we'll be there soon!"

(Edith Cavell was a British nurse from Norfolk who was famous for saving the lives of soldiers from both sides. She was arrested for helping some 200 Allied soldiers escape from German-occupied Belgium. Accused of treason and found guilty by German courts martial, she was executed by firing squad on October 15, 1915 in Brussels. On the eve of her execution, Cavell was quoted as saying, "Patriotism is not enough. I must have no hatred or bitterness towards anyone. I can't stop while there are lives to be saved.")

"Yessir," Bertie said. "Thank you, sir." He saluted and Bryden returned the gesture. Wilkinson smiled and touched his crop to his hat brim.

"And one more thing," Bryden offered as Bertie looked at his transport, now rounding a bend one hundred yards away. "Ships are being sunk. When aboard, stay near the upper decks. That way, if your ship gets hit, you'll have a chance to get off. And wear a bloody life jacket!"

Bryden extended a few pound notes. "No, thank you, sir. I'm all right," Bertie told him, embarrassed.

"Then at least take these..." Bryden said as he stuffed a pack of cigarettes into Bertie's breast pocket. He sneaked the pound notes in the pocket as well.

"I don't smoke, sir," Bertie replied. "But I've lots of friends who do."

"Goodbye, Bertie." Bryden said. "And thank you."

"Goodbye, sir." Bertie said, breaking into a trot to catch up with his unit.

On the return ride, Wilkinson drew a small flask from his saddle bag and sipped from it.

"What did you do that for?" Wilkinson inquired, offering the flask to Bryden.

"Do what?"

"Give him cigarettes and money," Wilkinson replied. "He's just a mule driver. It's his job."

"A.G., one day you just may become an officer."

--- 25 ---
Near Loos, France
September 1915

Philip and the 9th Battalion were told they would function as support for battalions fighting the German army near a French coal mining town called Loos. In the early hours of the morning, great numbers of British troops were running through communication trenches toward the front. The Allies were attempting to capture German positions from Loos to the La Bassee Canal. The 9th and 11th Battalions were ordered to attack positions at Rue Douvert just north of Givenchy. The names of the places meant little to Philip. He just understood that he was about to experience his first fight.

The single file trench march came to a halt. "What's the bloody holdup?" Heathcote asked.

Sergeant Corns arrived. "One more thing," Corns said. "When the order is given to attack you are not allowed to stop and care for wounded soldiers. You have all been issued emergency field-dressings. If you're hit you'll have to treat your own wounds. And try to get back to our lines. Pass it on." Corns continued down the trench. Philip and the others exchanged looks.

Six hundred yards away, on the far left of the column, the battle was to begin with a gas attack of the Germans by the Allied 2nd Division. There was no wind. Hundreds of canisters of chlorine gas were launched, landing immediately in front of the German positions. The Germans hurried to don their masks. As the 9th Battalion nervously waited to move through the trench again, there was a commotion far up the trenches. Philip saw a flag on the side of the trench flutter from a breath of wind. The gas, intended to kill the Germans, was now floating toward Allied lines. Screams from soldiers could he heard in the distance as they breathed in the lethal gas. Some had forgotten their training and not put on their masks. Philip's platoon reversed its march. Then it began to rain. Their opening attack had failed completely.

Minutes later, the 9th Division began shelling another German position, a slag heap known as "The Dump". Machine gun and musket fire began up and down the line. Philip could see a Lewis gun emplacement sixty yards from him, but it was not firing.

"Lance Corporal Bebbington!" barked Corns. "Take two men and see what's holding up that Lewis gun!" He pointed at it.

"Yessir!" Philip answered and nodded to Heathcote and Ellis.

The three climbed out of their trench and ran to the Lewis gun which stood in a small crater surrounded by sand bags. Philip saw the crew pouring canteens of water all over the gun.

"Do you need any help, sir?" Philip asked the young lieutenant in charge.

"It's fouled with mud!" he yelled. "Pour water around the breach!"

A hundred yards away, past No Man's Land, Heathcote saw a group of Germans climb out of their trenches and creep towards them. The Germans had been monitoring the British position with a periscope. An enemy troop leaned away from the glasses and a second peered through. They grinned and nodded at each other when they saw the trouble the British gun crew was having. It was a weakness, a hole in the line, while the 2nd Division was being killed by their own gas.

"We need to fall back, sir. The Germans..." Heathcote said as he gestured toward the Germans coming toward them.

"We got to get this gun working," the lieutenant cried, frantically pulling on the breach.

Philip, Heathcote and Ellis raised their rifles and began firing to provide cover. The enemy soldiers returned fire almost immediately, bullets striking the ground on all sides of the emplacement. The three men increased their rate of fire on the German advance.

"They'll be on us in a minute, sir!" Philip yelled.

The lieutenant had finally gotten the Lewis gun to cycle, so a crewman snapped in a fresh magazine and the gunner brought the Lewis gun to life. After several multi-second bursts, there was a metallic snapping sound and the firing stopped. In a fury, the lieutenant cursed and continued trying to clear the gun, the Germans were now forty yards away. The lieutenant looked at Philip with resignation. "Take your men and get out of here!" he ordered. "Cover fire from the trench."

"But, sir—" Philip started.

"Get out! That's an order!"

Philip, Heathcote and Ellis turned and scrambled back to the relative safety of the trench. Ellis was hit in the back and collapsed, so Philip grabbed his collar and dragged him into the trench. They began firing through the thick smoke and past the Lewis gun position at the advancing Germans. Covering machine gun fire from the enemy trench opened up. Out of his mind with frustration and fury, the lieutenant pushed one of the gun crewman away from the Lewis and continued trying to unjam it himself. He had trained for months on the operation of the Lewis gun and knew he could get it working. In the last act of his life, the lieutenant looked up at a large German just yards away and reached for his Webley revolver. Reloading his own rifle, Philip watched from the trench as the lieutenant and the two in his crew were shot and killed with German Mausers at close range. Two more Germans arrived at the Lewis gun and fired their rifles into the lieutenant's lifeless body.

After the assault, the Germans turned to withdraw. Philip and the others never stopped firing but the smoke, range, and darkness impaired accuracy. Finally, he took careful aim and fired one last shot through the thick smoke, hitting the big German fatally in the neck. The other two ran to their trench and dropped down the gradual slope, out of sight.

Philip had killed a man. Perhaps more, but one for sure. A .303 round in the middle of the neck was a kill shot. He eased himself down into the trench while Heathcoat continued firing. Philip checked Ellis. He was dead.

A black ammunition runner appeared from a communications trench with a bundle of Lewis cartridge bandoliers. He looked at Philip. "Delivering Lewis gun cartridges, sir!" the out-of-breath British private reported. "Got word you needed some." Philip noticed the ammunition courier's dark hands were shaking. Philip shook his head, pointing over his head at the dead Lewis gun crew.

"Their gun was jammed." The runner slowly peered over the trench at the Lewis gun location. There was no movement. Philip studied the courier as he lit a cigarette. "Where are you from?"

"Bermuda," he replied.

The courier gathered himself and moved on down the trench taking the bandoliers with him. No one said anything for an hour until orders arrived to move east. Later, after rotating from front duty, Philip tried to identify the brave young lieutenant and his crew. No one could tell him.

Weeks later, Philip learned he had been promoted to Corporal. He had no idea why.

Philip c. 1915
Photo courtesy of the author

--- 26 ---

Andrew and the 13th Rifle Brigade entered France at Le Havre and moved toward the Front by train and then by 40-man horse-drawn wagons. The rattle and thunder of distant heavy artillery could be heard dozens of miles away, lighting the night sky. The brigade's columns were met by long lines of casualties being evacuated from the Front. Andrew prayed he would not see Philip among them. Perhaps he had been given a blighty wound and a ticket back to Rawhead.

An observant man, Andrew learned from experience. He was not impressed with France. He thought he would see a pretty girl or two and sleep in comfortable billets, and expected to receive wine and cheers from the Frenchmen they had volunteered to liberate. But his experience was the opposite. Andrew thought the women were plain, far different from the Kitchener recruitment posters that hung in every tavern and railway station from Folkestone to Edinburgh. The billets were flea-infested barns made of mud and straw, offering little comfort from the elements. One private jokingly said the French billets were made by assembling long tree branches and throwing mud at them until enough stuck to hold them together.

Cases of bubonic plague and other diseases were reported. The French people were familiar with the sight of arriving soldiers. They knew all about the losses at Mons and Ypres and they desperately wanted the war to be over so they could begin rebuilding their lives. Andrew read the names of the towns on signs as he passed them and thought how different they were from town names in England: Hazebrouck, Mentque, Nortbecourt, St. Omer, Arques. They made out the word Champagne on one sign and Andrew supposed they might be offered a sip of the bubbly that night. An amused captain enlightened him: the town's name was Jardins en Campagne St. Sylvester Cappel, not Champagne. The town of Champagne was 300 miles to the east.

"Bloody French names," Andrew swore under his breath.

He and his battalion bathed in a canal just outside of the town. It had not yet been ravaged by the war. They did not own suitable swimsuits and were initially embarrassed to be seen naked and splashing about. But they found the locals indifferent to the sight of hundreds of unclothed men. Had they done this in England, they would have been court martialed en masse, Andrew knew.

Andrew and Philip shared the same experience of open-air bathing. Andrew hoped they would both live to wonder about it together. The locals were merely thankful the Englishmen had some sense of hygiene, as the German soldiers, in their experience, took no such care. The next morning, they relinquished their billet to a largely inebriated French battalion who gifted their English counterparts with bottles of wine. Andrew enjoyed it. We got our champagne after all, Andrew smiled to himself.

Within days, the brigade arrived at Le Bizet and began learning about life in the trenches. Trenches were dug in a zigzag manner to ostensibly minimize damage from attack. Support trenches paralleled the front-line trenches and were connected by communication trenches. Dugouts were added for command and medical posts. The soldiers constructed ladders to use for climbing out of the eight-foot-deep trenches, and for attacking. The dugouts were built to avoid shell splinters because shells throw their fragments forward on detonation. The trenches served as homes for the soldiers until they were ordered out to attack or retreat, or until they became so fouled and water logged they were more dangerous than the Germans.

Companies that saw little activity relieved each other in the trenches to cut down on boredom. Listening patrols sometimes ventured out under cover of night to gather intelligence. After two nights in Bailleul the battalion boarded a train for Godewaersvelde and Doullens and then marched to St. Amand and Pas.

An NCO asked for volunteers to re-dig trenches that had been bombed out. Andrew stood up. He was anxious to see something of the front. The damp and cramped trench billets afforded little sleep anyway. The digging detail formed and began the trek to the destroyed trenches, rounding the foot of a low hill to arrive at their destination. They could see remnants of trenches, but most had been bombed to uselessness. The area was strewn with damaged wire and timber supports which they knew would make digging difficult.

Then they got a taste of what lay ahead for them. The private in front of the party stopped in his tracks and held up his hand, signaling a halt. All around them, dozens of soldiers lay in pieces, though some were whole and looked to be sleeping. Men were decapitated, brains spilled from their cavities while others lay beside their own entrails. One soldier laying on his back had his arms and legs extended out like a starfish. His eyes were wide open, staring perplexed at the heavens as if asking what had just happened. Insignia identified the men as Sawney. Andrew surmised the attack had been sudden because rifles were slung, covers were on the actions and he could spot no spent casings. No one spoke as the digging party walked the scene. Two men fell to their knees and vomited.

"Should we take them back to town, sir?" the NCO asked the lieutenant.

"This isn't a grave detail, sergeant," he reminded the man.

"Well at least can we retrieve their tags and pay books."

"Our orders are to dig trenches," the lieutenant said. "We'll report the location when we return."

What happened next would forever change Andrew's romantic notions about going off to war. The German position that had attacked the Sawney contingent had been carefully observing the British digging party. Without warning they opened fire on the same spot they had shelled hours before. Artillery shells began exploding all around the party and machine guns and rifles filled in between shells. Seven men fell before the 13th Rifles understood they were under attack. Instinctively, Andrew and the others leaped into bombed out trenches. The sound of the exploding shells was deafening. Some men permanently lost their hearing in that moment. Then it stopped just as abruptly as it began. They heard shuffling and clanking sounds from the German position. The lieutenant, wounded in the arm, raised a periscope over the edge of his trench with the help of another soldier. Peering into the eyepiece, he saw Germans climbing out of their trenches and running toward them.

"Swords!" the lieutenant screamed. The patrol fixed their bayonets and loaded their rifles. "Standby Lewis gun!"

They waited until the Germans got within range. Andrew took careful aim at a German with a large, drooping mustache.

He chose him because he was at the head of his group. If he fell, the others might be frightened enough to turn back, or at least slowed to move around the body, Andrew reasoned. Through his gunsight, he aimed above the top lip and below the nose as he was taught.

"Fire!" the lieutenant shouted.

Andrew squeezed the trigger and the German fell backwards holding his rifle. A peace-loving dairy farmer had killed a man. He took a breath and resumed firing.

They thought they would spend the day digging, but instead had walked into a firefight. Finally, they stopped the German advance and the Lieutenant ordered withdrawal before the artillery could resume. The swords had not been necessary after all. They ran for a minute in the open then dove into a communication trench as soon as they reached it, then ran along the bottom of it until they reached the town of Campagne. Andrew made a mental note to never volunteer for anything again.

--- **27** ---

Edgar, the postman, filled his bowl with soup at the kitchen table at Rawhead. The family had finished lunch and returned to work, but Edgar was still at the table. Mary and Joseph were in the garden weeding, but paused to sift through the mail Edgar had handed them.

"Has he no home?" Joseph asked Mary observing Edgar through the window. "He eats more than Sam did, but never puts it on."

"He's on his bicycle all day, Joseph, and he keeps us informed of things," Mary replied, defended the man.

"Yes, but I thought the Royal Mail paid him," Joseph complained.

Inside, Edgar helped himself to more bread and butter.

"There's post cards from Sam and Bertie," Mary said. She read the back of one aloud and smiled. "'If thou wants a fight just come down to Ripon and I will give thee a whipping'."

Mary tacked the cards on the kitchen wall next to the pieces already received from Clem, Andrew, and Philip.

Mary and Joseph
Photo courtesy of the author

Later, Will Evans strolled into the kitchen for a tea break with Martha. As they sipped tea and talked in low tones together, Will looked over the steadily increasing collection of mail from his brothers-in-law on the wall. After their tea, Martha returned to the cheese room and descended the stairwell to the cheese cave. On his way back to the fields, Will stopped at the wall of letters. He studied photos of each brother, their uniforms and messages, and tried to guess where they were at that moment. He felt unsettled that a card from him was not on the wall with all the others.

--- 28 ---
Cheshire Yeomanry Billets
Lowestoft, Suffolk
October 1916

Robert Bryden was sound asleep in his quarters. It was a cold autumn night and the small coal fire was not putting out much heat. He rolled over and tugged at his two blankets. A hum from outside began to grow louder, but he thought it was yet another squadron flying overheard on a night training mission. A flash of light caught his eye followed by a distant rumble. Another flash and explosion jolted him fully awake. Leaping from his bed to the window he noticed several guards together pointing at the night sky, joined by other officers roused from their slumber.

"What's the trouble?" Bryden asked the closest sentry.

"Not sure, sir. A Zeppelin maybe?"

Fiery explosions erupted not more than 300 yards away, shaking the earth. Realizing what was happening, Bryden ordered, "Douse all watch fires and lamps! Pass the word!

A sentry began firing his rifle at the sky, followed by another.

"Cease fire!" Bryden yelled. "What the devil are you shooting at?"

The hum of the engines faded slowly and the bombing stopped. It was indeed a Zeppelin raid. The raids were becoming more common. The damage was minimal, the small bombs completely missing any actual military targets.

A week later another incident occurred. "A" Squadron was quartered at the Yarmouth Hotel, from which they had a clear 180-degree view of the North Sea coast. They saw several ships on the horizon and thought they were seeing the British Navy for the first time. A British destroyer was close to shore and sailing at flank speed. Shells struck the ship and columns of water erupted around it while some of the shells landed close to shore, signifying the first attack on British soil since the Norman Conquest of 1006, though shells had struck Britain during the Napoleonic wars a century before. The incidents abated and the ships sailed out of sight. Together, the two events seemed minor, but in fact were a warning of what lay ahead for the Allies.

--- **29** ---

Sam and Bertie continued to transport men and materials to embarkation points along the channel. After a year of serving in the ASC, they heard they were to accompany an allied expeditionary force, but the destination was not disclosed. A supply column left Salisbury and proceeded to Devonport where equipment, arms, troops and animals were loaded onto the HMT *Royal Michael*, an 8,900-ton passenger liner on loan from Cunard. After orientation and a lifeboat drill, the ship put to sea well after dark. Rotating details of sixty ASC and combat soldiers were assigned duty around the clock to ready antiaircraft guns, watch for submarines, and maintain lifeboats.

Sam, Bertie and many other sailors suffered from seasickness. They took turns vomiting over the side while Max Wainright and others looked on with amusement. "How's about a cheese sandwich, Red?" Wainright taunted. "Never been on a boat before, eh?"

Bertie and Sam threw disgusted looks at Wainright as they wiped their mouths on their sleeves. "And you have?" Bertie inquired.

"Of course, all the time!" Wainright assured them. Captivated soldiers and sailors listened intently. "Took the ferry to Boulogne, then a train to Paris a number of times. Oh, those were wonderful times. The ladies! Are ya sure I can't interest you blokes in some cheese?" Wainright leaned forward. "Maybe a little Gammelost, Camembert or Limburger on a cracker? Where we're headed you best try what they call feta cheese!"

Sam and Bertie had long since emptied their bellies but leaned over the rail anyway, dry heaving.

"Or maybe some of your Cheshire, or perhaps that lovely American cheese?"

Miserable and irritated, Sam lunged at Wainright. "You lousy bastard!" Two seamen and an ASC sergeant intervened and separated them.

"Save it for the 'uns!" the sergeant barked.

"Easy, mate, easy!" Wainright grinned. "Just tryin' to 'elp."

He flicked his cigarette over the side and walked away.

"What do you say we toss him overboard tonight?" Bertie suggested as Sam rejoined him at the railing.

One day later, the *Royal Michael* was struck by a torpedo and sank off the Pelion coast of Greece.

--- **30** ---

"What is it, Mum?" Mollie asked.

Mary felt weak and lowered herself on a chair. She had been baking bread all morning and had eaten almost nothing. Perhaps that was all it was.

"I don't know," Mary said faintly. "I felt shaky for a moment. I've never felt like that before."

Mollie made her mother a cup of tea and went to find Joseph. Mary took a sip of the tea and rubbed her eyes. Minutes later, Joseph arrived.

"Mary?" he asked as he knelt before her, a concerned look on his face. "What's the matter?"

"I don't know. I am not tired. I feel as though something has happened to one of the boys. Something terrible."

"Sam said in his letter that he and Bertie were shipping out," Joseph said. "Andrew and Philip are in France. And Clem is at sea."

"I am afraid, Joseph." Mary admitted, placing her hands on his arm. "I fear for them."

--- 31 ---
Pelion coast
92 miles south of Salonika, Greece

Max felt solid ground and was grateful as he could not swim much further, nor could the horses and mules following. Bertie dismounted and waded to shore. The surf was illuminated with plankton and provided just enough light to negotiate the rocks. Several mules and horses appeared around him, and still others from behind. Bertie finally stepped onto dry sand. He placed two fingers to his mouth and whistled to attract the remaining animals coming in from the surf. Exhausted and numb, his legs gave way and he collapsed. To his right, a sea turtle laid her eggs. Oblivious of the strange animal watching her, the turtle finished her annual ritual by raking sand on top of the eggs, before returning to the sea. Bertie closed his eyes and drifted into sleep. It was beyond the season to lay her eggs but the unusually warm October sea temperature tricked her. She sensed another location would be appropriate next year, for this cove was getting too crowded.

Bertie woke on sugar white sand at the foot of a Grecian cliff. The hilly countryside beyond was lush and green. His mouth was dry and swollen and his face was already singed from the morning sun. Opening his eyes, he observed a blue land crab standing on the back of his hand and brushed it off. From what he could see, he and the crab were the only life on the beach in both directions. He scanned the horizon for ships, but there were none, just rocky outcroppings and reefs surrounded by turquoise-blue water.

Where are the animals? he wondered. He stood and took a few painful steps. Feeling his swollen feet, he sat to remove his boots. A cup of water and sand drained from each. *They couldn't have drowned,* he thought. *How would I have made it here?* There were no tell-tile hoof prints anywhere. A faint whinny answered his question. He climbed to the top of a large, jagged rock and looked down.

"Dear God…" he said under his breath.

Before him was a sight for all time. Bertie counted nine horses and four mules casually drinking from a pool of water fed by an inland creek. Several other horses were apart from the others, feeding on sea oats and wild onions that had grown out of a large dune. Bertie climbed down the rock, walked to the group and they welcomed their friend as he mingled among them. He found Errol, hugged his neck and slid his hand back to the "921" brand on his rump.

"Errol, you beautiful thing!"

Like one of the band, Bertie knelt before the refreshment and drank deeply. *Slightly brackish, the water was not the nectar from the Droppingstone Well,* he thought, *but it wasn't sea water,* either. He thought a moment about Sam and where he might be, or if he was at all.

Errol and Max stepped over to him, as if to ask what was next. Bertie rubbed their snouts affectionately. Max raised his head above the others, and looked to the surf.

"I'm sorry I couldn't save all of you," he said, wiping away a tear. "I'm sorry."

From a shipboard briefing, Bertie knew that Greece was neutral in the conflict and not welcoming of the Allied forces. The Salonikan mission was to oppose the Bulgarian advances as part of the Macedonian Front, with the ASC providing logistical support. He could sit and wait for a possible rescue but that seemed unlikely. The Salonikan Force had to move up through the Ionian Sea and offload. He decided to wait a day or two before moving so he and the horses could rest up and rehydrate. He might even try what the horses were eating. Bertie estimated that over half the cargo of animals on the ship had drowned and half again the horses and mules he managed to lead away from the ship. After such an ordeal, he swore he would not let them fall into enemy hands. If he couldn't reach Allied forces, perhaps the local residents might help him. Perhaps. War was not for horses, he thought. They belong on a farm pulling a plough in the early morning hours then enjoying a pleasant country ride with their master on Sundays. Or competing in a ploughing match and rewarded with an apple or carrot, whether they won or not. If only I could bring them home, Bertie thought. Then I could have my own holding.

The next morning, Bertie saw something on the far eastern end of the cove. It was a body wearing a life jacket with "HMT Royal Michael" stamped on it. He did not recognize the poor soul, but his clothes were that of a sailor. He pulled him up the beach and into a grassy clearing and after digging a grave, he removed one dog tag and marked the grave with large stones. He looked to the dog tag and chain in his hand and placed it in his pocket. Perhaps the army will come for him after the war.

The next day, Bertie fitted Errol with a rein formed from a piece of hemp rope he found on the beach. He mounted and set off slowly through the ravine. Except for Max, the rest of the animals instinctively followed Errol. From low tide, the defiant horse stood in a swath of sea foam watching the others. The mineral rich sea water felt wondrous to Max. The onions and sea oats on the beach were infinitely better tasting than the weevil-infested grain he'd been fed since being purchased by the army, and still better than the infrequent food received from an alcoholic Salisbury farmer two years prior. Bertie looked back and saw Max standing, alone and free as the gentle surf bathed his underbelly. The last horse in the column, a young mare, sensed an absence and stopped. The horse marked with "618" on her rump looked back at Max and nickered, wondering why he was not following.

Bertie beckoned Max.

"Come on, Max! We're leaving!"

But Max stood unmoving. He heard the plea from his mounted friend but insisted on staying put. He knew better. Whatever purpose he was trained for in Salisbury and then enduring a lengthy cruise in a swaying, wooden barn followed by a test of his swimming abilities, earned him his freedom. No, he would not go. This is his place, his time, his life.

"Well then, you're free now, Max" Bertie said under his breath. "You're free."

Bertie yanked on Errol's rein and left the beach. Not wanting to part from Max, 618 trotted out to join him.

"Oh, bloody hell," Bertie said. "Okay then, go stay with him!"

Riding without a saddle was an experience Bertie remembered as a boy at Rawhead, but one he had not repeated. He had to re-learn how to ride this way. Balance was critical, his father once told him a decade earlier. Sitting in direct contact with the horse a rider had to become aware of muscle and bone when riding this way.

After a day's ride on stony beaches and goat trails, Bertie and his equine entourage were ten miles north of their landing point with still no sight of a village or humans. Unbeknownst to him, he was only five miles from a coastal fishing village. He was certain that heading northeast and then due north along the coast would eventually take him to Salonika. Direction could be estimated from the position of the North Star Polaris. Something he learned from the scouts at Rawhead, though he was too old for scouting. The landscape was not unlike the Peckforton Hills, Bertie thought, but the crystalline turquoise water was beyond his imagination. Just follow the contour of the ridge and keep the ocean in sight he constantly told himself. At one point, he took to the water again to get around a steep ridge. Further north, he had to backtrack a few miles and go inland for a while.

Sam arrived in Salonika along with British and French troops. After the sinking of the *Royal Michael*, Sam's lifeboat was picked up by a trawler and later transferred to a French transport. The Salonika Force comprised only one corps, commanded by a Lieutenant General Bryan Mahon. Though Sam made inquiries, there was no word of Bertie, nor was there any interest in searching for him or others who were missing. The Aegean around Salonika was teaming with German submarines. Bertie had either made it to shore or had drowned. If he made it ashore and was able, Bertie would try to rejoin the Salonikan force, but that would be a trip.

What was he to tell his mother if Bertie was dead? He was Bertie's older brother and he was supposed to take care of him. And Bertie was just supposed to take care of the animals. Not fight or drown or get shot. This was not supposed to happen.

"What's the hold up?" an NCO yelled at Sam. "Let's move!"

Sam started the engine of his supply lorry and drove it off a ship onto the docks.

--- **32** ---

Once he reached the outer edge of a recently ploughed field, Bertie decided to stop for the night. He knew now that he was on the right path. A small grove of apple trees offered all a welcome refreshment. He herded the horses into an old hay shed and found a comfortable, dry place to sleep apart from them while the animals muzzled around and unearthed hay to eat. He mounded straw into a bed, and resting on it, pulled more straw over him. Sleep came easily.

A light knocking woke him. Sunlight filtered through holes in the shed walls. He crawled out of his straw bed on his knees and saw Errol kicking at the shed wall. "Errol, what are you doing?" He grumbled. Bertie reached the door and shoved it open.

A young girl of about sixteen stood in the doorway. Surprised, she backed away, brandishing a pitch fork at him.

"I'm sorry," Bertie said, gesturing around the inside of the shed. "My horses and I were tired and needed somewhere to sleep."

Not frightened anymore, the girl said something in Greek.
"I'm on my way to Salonika," Bertie said a bit loudly.
"Salonika? Thessaloniki?"
"Thessaloniki," the girl repeated, perking up.
"Thessaloniki?"
"Yes," Bertie nodded affirmatively. He pointed in several
directions. "Which way?"
The girl looked around as if to get her bearings. She
beckoned Bertie to follow her. He whistled for the animals to
follow them out of the shed and up a grassy promontory. He
looked down on a narrow valley extending to the north with a dirt
road alongside a stream. She pointed up the valley.
"Zagora, Thessaloniki," the girl said. Bertie looked
puzzled. She held out the first and second fingers of her hand and
made them "walk" down her upper arm to her wrist. There the
walking fingers stopped. "Zagora," she said. Then she continued
walking her fingers across her palm and pointed at the ground.
"Thessaloniki," she stated.
Bertie nodded and smiled that he understood. She was
saying that from where they stood, he must go to the town of
Zagora and from there he could reach Thessaloniki. Grateful,
Bertie smiled and nodded again. The girl gave him a charming
smile, then reaching into her apron pocket, she withdrew
something covered in a cloth and offered it to Bertie. It was
cheese, Bertie thought. Greek cheese.
"Katsikísio tyrí," the girl said proudly.
"Cheese," Bertie acknowledged as he accepted it
gratefully. "I make cheese at home." Bertie lifted the cheese and
sampled it. To his delight, it tasted great. A bit saltier than
Cheshire but the texture was similar. It wasn't Rawhead
Cheshire, he thought. But still wonderful. "Feta."
"Feta," she said with a smile.

She was lovely, Bertie thought as he ate. Maybe he would come back some day to visit her.

Bertie searched his pockets for a gift. He could find nothing, except the cigarettes Robert Bryden had given him weeks ago near Salisbury. They had disintegrated in the sea. He extracted the pound notes. Unfolding them, he stared in disbelief.

"Well I'll be…" Bertie uttered.

He extended the notes to the girl and she accepted them with another smile.

"It's not Greek money but I'm sure someone will take them," he assured her, knowing she did not understand his words. He took hold of Errol's reins and turned in the direction she indicated. The girl watched until he reached a wavy grove of poplars a quarter mile down the valley. Bertie waved at her one last time and she waved back. He and the horses disappeared into the trees.

Losing sight of the soldier, the girl looked at the crumpled pound notes he had given her and slid them into her apron pocket where the eggs had rested. She recognized that the bills were money though not Greek drachmas. Her father would know what to do with them, she thought.

After several hours, Bertie and his entourage of horses and mules paused at the base of a rise in the foothills east of Mount Pelio. It was a warm day and he was enjoying the birds playing in the underbrush, the babbling of the stream, and the sun on his head. Curiously, the horses began to snort and shake their heads. Bertie noticed an unusual odor as they made their way onward. The smell grew more powerful the closer they came to the rise and he recognized it. He had lived on a farm after all. The wind shifted and the smell became so overpowering he had to pull up his shirt to breathe through the cloth. When they reached the top of the rise, he saw it.

They were in the middle of a battlefield. It made no sense that there had been fighting in this area. He shook his head, baffled. He was south of Salonika and the Balkans. From the condition of the dead horses, Bertie estimated the conflict occurred just days before. Errol stooped to sniff the bloated carcass of a horse covered with flies. Killed by gunfire, Bertie guessed from the wounds. In disgust, Bertie yanked on Errol's rein to steer him away.

He was struck by the eerie stillness. He looked around the blackened yard that was littered with bodies of men and animals. Around the edges of the field, he saw poppies bobbing in the tall grasses. It occurred to him that he had been in the war for over a year and was finally seeing the end of an ASC supply chain. He had been far from the conflict but had heard of the truckloads of casualties being carried away from the Front. He thought of his brothers in France. Clem was on a ship somewhere. And Sam. Where was he? Had he and the others been rescued from the *Royal Michael*?

Bertie studied the uniforms on the bodies. The skirmish was not between British and Bulgarian soldiers, but concerned Greek police or militia and men with no uniforms. Who were they and what had they done wrong? Bertie stopped near a fallen horse and removed the saddle. He took a revolver from a headless Greek soldier's hand and checked it for ammunition. All had been fired, no doubt in the last moments of the man's life. Bertie's stomach clenched and he vomited.

He scavenged for revolver shells and dropped some in his pocket, then looked farther down the road. If he lost his way, he could look for the ocean and find his way by that. Maybe he would meet a British or Serbian unit.

Leaving the field of dead behind, Bertie passed a disabled wagon with a map flapping against a wheel underneath it. He stopped and picked it up. After looking it over, he was certain he was on his way to Salonika. He had no food but he wasn't hungry. The poppy field had left him nauseous.

A bearded Greek farmer stared at the British pound notes in his hand and looked at his daughter. "Where did you get these?" he asked her in Greek.

The girl pointed to a distant field. "There. A man with horses was sleeping in the shed and asked where Thessaloniki was. He was nice. I think he was a soldier."

The farmer stuffed the notes in his pocket and started toward his horse.

--- 33 ---
Lake Doiran, Balkans
50 miles north of Salonika

Sam was distressed. He had been driving supplies to Lake Doiran and environs for a week and still had received no word of Bertie. He was listed as "missing". Sam had written his family shortly after he arrived to tell them about Bertie's circumstances. He wasn't sure it would get past the Army censors or mail ships sinking.

As much as France and Belgium welcomed the British Army in Europe, Salonika on the Macedonian Front did not. British ASC transport personnel were harassed every place they stopped to feed and water animals or refuel trucks there. The demand for men in the European theaters was so great that no additional ASC workers could be spared for transport duty in Salonika. As a result, the ASC was drawing mule handlers from the local population, straining relations with the Greek government. Matters worsened when malaria, dysentery, and diphtheria spread indiscriminately through the camps. Soldiers perished at the rate of six per day.

"They're calling it a sideshow," Max Wainright reported at the evening's mess on the shore of Lake Doiran. "The real show is in Europe while we're here in the Balkans tending bloody mules!"

"All I can think of is my brother," Sam said, puffing furiously on a cigarette and staring at his plate. "I told our mother I'd look after him."

"How can you do your job and worry about your brother and mother at the same time?" Wainright asked. "You know how many soldiers are in the same lot you're in? He's got a good chance, Red. He was a couple miles from shore and had good horses! He's probably eating fish and drinking ouzo with a pretty girl in a Greek fishing village! And we're eatin' this," he held up his plate. "Tastes like puke in a tin. But the vodka's all right." Wainright tossed the tin into the fire. "What I wouldn't give for a wedge of ripe Camembert right now," he muttered. "And a glass of French Chardonnay."

"Will you shut up? Bloody hell! My name isn't Red! It's Sam! And my brother's name is Bertie!" Sam stormed off.

"He'll turn up!" Wainright shouted back, unfazed by the sudden outburst. "I've a sense about these things!"

--- 34 ---

The day after he met the Greek girl, Bertie entered yet another valley. He halted the column of horses and mules trailing behind him. Sensing something, he lifted his arm. "Hold up," Bertie called to the animals. "Woahhh."

He looked around and behind him. To his left, he saw dust rising above the tree line. He turned to the right and observed a similar cloud swelling over a growth of high brush. Alarmed, he kicked Errol into a run. Then, two groups of riders appeared from out of the dust on both sides descending the valley slopes toward him. Bertie attempted to whip Errol into a gallop but the other animals held them up. He withdrew the revolver he had found on the dead man, looked at it briefly, then tossed it into the brush. He could not outrun them. With any luck, they were Serbian or Greek. If they were Bulgarians the skirmish was over.

The group of riders converged on Bertie, surrounding him and the animals with their guns drawn. Except for the young girl, Bertie had never seen a Greek, Serbian or Bulgarian, but had learned to recognize insignia. The uniforms looked like the ones he had seen on some of the dead men three days prior. An older man moved closer to Bertie and spoke to him in Greek. "I am a British soldier," Bertie said clearly. He started to reach inside his shirt but stopped when they cocked their revolvers. Bertie raised his hands and pointed to his chest. The Greek leader leaned over and ripped open Bertie's shirt. He lifted one of his dog tags and read it quickly.

"Stratiotaki," the leader announced. "Vretanós stratiótis!" Whatever the man said, it could not have been good. The two dozen riders looked sternly at each other and back at Bertie. "Anazítisi ston stratióti!" the leader ordered. Two Greek riders dismounted, pulled Bertie off Errol and searched him, then went through Errol's saddle. They found the folded map, a compass and several rounds of revolver ammunition.

"I am British!" Bertie said slowly and loudly. "My ship was torpedoed. I am trying to get to my unit in Saloni…Thessaloniki." A rider handed the revolver he had retrieved from the brush to the leader.

They understood the word Thessaloniki. The leader pointed north with his revolver. Bertie hurriedly remounted Errol and spurred him to move, looking back only to be sure the other animals were following.

--- 35 ---
Cheshire Yeomanry billets
Lowestoft, Suffolk
February, 1916

The Cheshire Yeomanry had been in Lowestoft for nearly eight months. The thorny supply crisis had eased, but more syphilis cases and other diseases were being reported. Cerebral meningitis had become an epidemic. Many men preferred to remain in camp rather than venture into town. There was some mention of deployment, but nothing definite. They continued to train, more to ease the boredom than to hone their fighting skills.

Robert Bryden inspected his company standing at attention with their polished rifles and clean uniforms. He found little to complain about. Overhead, he made out the faint sound of an engine which grew louder as it approached. An aircraft appeared at 1,000 feet up. Bryden and the troops were trained to identify aircraft, but only from drawings, and passing airplanes were not an uncommon sight. This one dipped lower and circled twice. For a second, Bryden saw an Iron Cross on the wings. Then something fell from the craft. The object corkscrewed downward and struck the side of B Squadron billets, exploding on impact. A swoosh of air and heat pushed them back. Another bomb dropped and hit a small inn.

"Take cover!" Bryden yelled. "Lewis gun crew!"

The yeomanry, still standing at attention, scattered grabbed their rifles and fired at the aircraft. It circled once more and turned away. They continued shooting and readied a Lewis gun but the plane disappeared. The bomb destroyed the officer's quarters but no one was injured. A similar incident occurred two weeks later but miles to the north where A Squadron was billeted.

Within two days word arrived that the Cheshire Yeomanry would be transported overseas as infantry. Their horses would be used elsewhere, probably Salisbury. This stunned them. They had been a proud and honorable cavalry unit since 1797. But they were heartened to hear they were going to participate in the war at last. Passes for one-week furloughs were issued with a small detail remaining for defense duties.

Bryden traveled to Ballantyne eagerly. Entering the foyer of Ballantyne, he heard harp rhythms from upstairs and found his way to Heidi. In the ensuing few days, they spent their time making love, walking the grounds, exchanging news and funny stories, and riding in the cold, wintry drizzle. In a rare break from the weather, they rode in full gallop beside each other and extended their arms to touch the other's finger tips. They were joyous moments, perhaps the last they would have together, they each thought.

On his last day, he saw his father. They met in the castle foyer, a waiting Rolls Royce purring in the driveway. "You can't insure my life this time, Father," Robert said. "No one would underwrite it."

Gilbert forced a tight smile. "I think I might find a firm…for a premium. But don't be ambitious, Robert," his father advised. "'By ambition fell the angels'," he quoted Shakespeare.

"Then you've changed, Father," Robert said. "Ambition was always the center of your being. I, on the other hand, have never been ambitious. Dutiful perhaps, but not ambitious." Tacitly choosing not to argue anymore, they shook hands and Robert started toward the waiting car. Heidi ran past Gilbert Bryden and out the door to her husband.

"Robert!" she called. They embraced and kissed.

"You are my guardian angel, Heidi," Bryden said. "I'll be fine. I love you."

After Robert's departure, Gilbert Bryden hurried to Roland C. Voight & Sons in Liverpool and renewed the policy on his son's life. He had been correct; the premium was hefty.

Once all ranks returned to Lowestoft, the regiment proceeded to Lowestoft Station. Their overseas destination was classified but they figured they were headed to the Mediterranean because they were departing from Devonport, as opposed to points nearer Belgium or France. On March 3, 1916, the Cheshire Yeomanry boarded the HMT *Haverford*, a 12,000-ton American transatlantic ocean liner loaned to Britain as a troop ship.

Most of the yeomanry stood at the rail when the ship cast off. Just then, they saw a soldier push his way through the dock crowd with a duffle bag over his shoulder. He ran toward the ship yelling, "Wait! Waaaaaait!"

On the deck of the *Haverford*, Bryden and the others strained to see who the soldier could be. As he reached the bottom of the retreating gangway, they recognized him. It was Private Taylor, the soldier diagnosed with syphilis and sent to Cherry Hinton months earlier, for quarantine and Salvarsan. Taylor tripped on a mooring line and fell flat on his face on the dock. The watching yeomen onboard laughed and whistled while a sailor lowered the gangway again and escorted the soldier onboard. Bryden met him as he approached the deck. Taylor saluted his commanding officer.

"Sir!" he said. "Private Taylor reporting for duty." He held out his papers.

"What are you doing here, Taylor?" Bryden asked. "You were quarantined."

"I'm cured, sir!" Taylor reported happily. "Doctors discharged me with a clean bill of health!" Bryden examined the papers quickly. He was tempted to send Taylor back to Cherry Hinton but he noticed the expressions of the men crowded around them. Something in their manner suggested he should choose otherwise. Taylor had earned his passage. "Come aboard, Private."

"Thank you, sir," Taylor said gratefully and stepped off the top of the gangway onto the deck. "Learned my lesson, so I did, sir." He turned to the bewildered Officer of the Deck and saluted. "Oh, sorry, sir. Request permission to come aboard?"

"Granted," the OOD said.

"Where are Privates White and Stephenson?" Bryden asked.

"Still down with it, sir." Taylor replied, wincing slightly.

Bryden glared at the young soldier. "If I hear about you visiting another brothel, I'll shoot you myself!"

"Yessir! Thank you, sir!"

--- 36---
HMT *Haverford*
3 miles east of the Isle of Wight, England

After they passed the Isle of Wight, two navy destroyers slid alongside the *Haverford*. The two ships were assigned to escort them across the English Channel, providing cover. But to everyone's dismay, the escort destroyers stayed with them only as far as Cape Ushant on the southwestern end of the English Channel. There, they dropped back as quietly as they had arrived and slipped away into the darkness.

The *Haverford* was crowded and offered little room for walking or exercise. The soldiers slung their hammocks from all parts of the ship. They were ordered to wear their life jackets during all daylight hours.

On March 8, 1916, Robert Bryden was summoned to the deck. "What's going on?" Bryden asked reaching the stern rail.

The OOD pointed to the aft starboard quarter. Bryden squinted. There was something roughly 1,000 yards away that resembled a swarm of flying fish or a breaching whale. Bryden gestured for a pair of binoculars from the officer beside him. Looking through them, he made out the conning tower of a submarine barely breaking the surface. "We're cheese, sir!" a Private said, nervously.

"No," Bryden corrected. "We're Cheshire cheese. There's a difference, Private."

The Private gave Bryden a baffled look. He did not understand his commanding officer's attempt at humor. But Bryden recognized he must exhibit confidence before his men, even if he felt fear himself.

Bryden lowered the binoculars and looked up at the ship's bridge. Anxious ship's officers were looking through binoculars as well. Not being a sailor, Bryden had to defer to their judgment about ship maneuvers. He knew that if the submarine was German and determined to sink them, nothing would help. Perhaps they were cheese.

After a disconcerting half hour, the submarine fell back and disappeared below the surface. A cargo ship passed the *Haverford* as it rounded the coast at Gibraltar. Two hours later, a radio message revealed the cargo ship had been torpedoed and was sinking fast. It must have been that submarine, Bryden concluded. The Captain of the *Haverford* decided to avoid the danger of a rescue attempt. They had been lucky so far. Prevailing opinion on board had it that the enemy submarine captain had a conscience and had opted to sink a cargo vessel instead of a ship containing 1,200 men.

They spotted a blinking light on shore. The ship's signalman communicated in Morse code that she was the *Haverford* headed for Alexandria with 1,200 passengers aboard. Many on the ship understood Morse so they were able to make the connection. At dawn, Lt. Colonel Wilson spoke to the men assembled on the main deck.

"Gentlemen, you probably know by now that our destination is Alexandria, Egypt, and not Salonika," Wilson said. "Our mission is to reinforce the 53rd Welsh Division and assist in the capture of the Senussi-occupied Baharia Oasis, which is about 200 miles south of Alexandria. The Senussis are a local tribe and part of the German-Turkish alliance. The bloody hot climate will make our job more difficult and a bit unpleasant. But I know you'll all persevere. Our ongoing mission is to protect the Suez Canal. Please assemble your gear and prepare for disembarkation."

On March 13, a torpedo boat appeared on the port side and escorted *Haverford* into Alexandria harbor. Robert Bryden and A.G. Wilkinson stood on the dock and watched as open cattle trucks arrived.

"And we were complaining about the conditions in England!" Wilkinson exclaimed. "It's much worse here! We're to travel in 30-man cattle trucks. Bloody hell!"

"We all wanted to enter the war," Bryden reminded him. "Now we're in it. Horses would not do here. We'll probably be riding camels."

Wilkinson was amazed. *Camels? What a prospect.*

After a rough truck ride, they arrived at a village near the Nile River called Bini Salama, joining four other yeomanry regiments already there. Bryden and the other officers noticed there were no tents or supplies anywhere. They were sweating in uniforms that were more suitable for the colder temperatures of Salonika.

It took nearly a month for pith helmets, lighter uniforms and other appropriate equipment to be issued. They camped there for several weeks, plagued by sandstorms, sand flies, and intestinal ailments caused by consuming local water and food. Lt. Colonel Wilson remarked to the officers that they seemed as far from the war as they ever had been in England and now were in an even worse situation. They were unclear as to who they were supposed to fight and with what. The squadron majors sat with Lt. Colonel Wilson.

"I realize you are disappointed, gentlemen," Wilson told them. "I've sent Major Glazebrook to the Suez to take the matter up with the Duke of Westminster and to see if he can't arrange for us to be included in the next transport to France."

"That could take months, sir." Bryden said. "What are we to do until then?"

"We will begin building blockhouses every twelve miles between Minia and the Baharia Oasis. That's 120 miles due west of the Nile. This will give us the best chance against the Senussi. We can store supplies in the blockhouses and protect communication lines, the commander explained.

"There's nothing out there but sand, sir," Bryden commented. "Reports say the Turks are in the Sinai."

"The Senussi support the Turks. It's going to be hard work with not enough water during the hottest months of the year."

"Yessir," Bryden agreed.

"Once a month we'll rotate your men out for a week at the beach in Alexandria."

Bryden and the other majors exchanged appreciative looks and saluted. They passed the news to their squadrons and issued instructions to prepare for the desert construction work ahead.

News going home was confusing. During the *Haverford*'s voyage, other ships had been torpedoed, triggering rumors in Cheshire that the *Haverford* had been lost. When Heidi Bryden heard this, she frantically made inquiries. Anxious families and friends swamped Chester City Hall and regiment headquarters, but it would be weeks before the War Office could inform the people of Cheshire that the *Haverford* had landed safely in Alexandria.

In his tent at the Blockhouse B2 construction site, Bryden wrote short, cryptic letters to Heidi knowing they were likely to be censored. One or two of his missives might make it to Cheshire if they were not carried aboard an unlucky ship, he surmised. He would like to have kept a journal even though they were forbidden out of fear they might fall into enemy hands. Some men managed to keep them anyway.

April 2, 1916

My dearest Heidi,
I have safely reached my destination and am retired for the night. This place is not quite Cheshire but it does have its amenities. Scenic vistas, warmth. I think that is it. We travel by night as it is so hot and we are dismounted. Strange we trained on horses and now move by lorries and camels. At one stretch we sailed down the Nile in a kind of sailboat called a Felucca. Quite an experience. I will write again soon.

All my heart,
Robert

--- 37 ---

In January 1916, the disastrous Dardanelles campaign was abandoned and forces were evacuated. Casualties numbered upwards of 150,000. After loading casualties aboard the *Canopus*, Clem visited the ship's sick bay and strummed songs on his ukulele for the wounded soldiers. He had become proficient at playing the instrument since he acquired it in 1909. The music soothed the spirits of the injured, hurting soldiers.

After Gallipoli, *Canopus* rendezvoused with a hospital ship to transfer her casualties. She was assigned to the British Eastern Mediterranean Squadron to transport troops but saw no further action. In April, she returned to England, stopping at Chatham to offload men for antisubmarine duty, finally arriving at Plymouth a few days later. A lengthy retrofit began while she served as a barracks ship. Clem watched ships coming and going as he stood at the stern rail of the *Canopus*. Clem concluded in a letter home:

Rest easy, Mother. I believe the war is over for me.

--- 38 ---
Blockhouse 3
50 miles east of Baharia Oasis, Egypt

Blockhouse construction went on. Eight men and two officers were ordered to take turns in 10-day stints as security patrols of the area. The first patrol returned safely but the second and third did not return at all.

"The last patrol was due back two days ago," Wilson said to Bryden. "Take a platoon and search for them."

"Yessir."

"Remember this is the land of Senussi tribesmen," Wilson advised. "They use irregular tactics and travel by night."

Bryden and his men set out in two Ford lorries at dawn the next day. After two days they found nothing but tire tracks leading nowhere. On the third day, a private spotted an object on the horizon. They arrived within an hour and found one of the missing patrols. All had been shot, their lorries burned, and guns, ammunition and supplies stolen. They had been ambushed. Bryden recognized one man and took a knee beside his body. It was Private Taylor. "You should have stayed at Cherry Hinton," Bryden whispered.

He decided to return to base and report what they had found, despite the urging of his men to find the perpetrators. Perhaps they could entice the enemy to tail them, coax them into the open and then attack. Two days out of Minia, the patrol camped for the night in the shelter of a giant dune. Bryden posted sentries in camp and atop the dune.

Sergeant Ryan woke Bryden in his tent at 12:02 a.m.

"What is it?" Bryden asked.

"Something, sir." Ryan whispered.

Crouching behind a lorry, Bryden took Ryan's binoculars. "Just there, sir," Ryan whispered, pointing a finger. "To the right on the lower crest of that dune."

Bryden searched the terrain some two hundred yards away but saw nothing. "Can't see anything in the dark," Bryden muttered.

Then he saw it in his peripheral vision. In the dim light of a waning moon, he made out several figures running along the top of the dunes. Sergeant Ryan lit a cigarette, carefully hiding the flame in cupped hands.

"Put that out!" Bryden hissed, swatting at the cigarette. Then a shot rang out, striking Ryan in the shoulder, knocking him to the ground. Soldiers of the patrol began returning fire.

"Are you all right?" Bryden asked, louder.

"Just creased me, sir!" Ryan replied, rising on one knee, clutching his shoulder. Then a second shot hit him in the center of his forehead, removing the back of his head, killing him instantly.

The Lewis gun opened up, panning back and forth aimlessly at the dunes.

"Cease fire! Cease fire!" Bryden yelled at his men, searching the horizon. The shadowy figures on the dunes were gone. Bryden needed a strategy. He knew they were being baited and they learned from reconnaissance later that the Senussi had indeed been in the area.

Sergeant Ryan and another soldier who had died in the skirmish were buried that day. Bryden said the Lord's Prayer over their graves and the patrol returned to camp. A few days later, a detail went out to retrieve the bodies for burial in the Coptic Cemetery in Minia but they could not find the graves. Bryden's men had constructed wood crosses and he had marked the exact location on a map and they were unable to locate the corpses. The Sahara had claimed them. Bryden concluded a lengthy letter to Heidi with these words:

If there is an enemy to fight here it's the climate, the terrain and...ghosts.

--- 39 ---

Near Montauban-de-Picardie, France
July 1, 1916

The village of Montauban lay two miles north of a river named after the Celtic word for tranquility. The goal of the Somme offensive was three-fold: to relieve enemy pressure on Verdun, stop further movement of German troops toward Russia, and wear down German troop strength. In the months following the battle at Loos, elabourate preparations were made. Trenches were dug, miles of railways and trench tramways were built, and tons of supplies were installed. The Germans prepared their own trench system which included redoubts and fortresses on every topographical feature including knolls, villages and wooded areas.

July 1 marked the first day of the Somme Offensive. Eddie McFie, Ernest Hewett, Lewis Briscoe and the rest of the Liverpool Pals anxiously waited in a six-foot trench. The cool temperature at dawn belied the heat that descended as the morning progressed. The Pals were entrenched on the extreme right flank of the French and other British forces. Light artillery and musket fire rattled in the distance. An NCO arrived from a communications trench.

"Any word, sir?" Briscoe asked.

The NCO shook his head. "We need a scout."

Eddie McFie smiled. "That's me, sir!"

The NCO produced a map and compass, rotating it for orientation.

"We need to know what's beyond the ridge here," he said, pointing at the map. "Also, approximate troop numbers and machine gun emplacements. If you're not back by...," the NCO looked at his watch, "0730, the show begins."

"See you soon," McFie said with a confident wink, accepting the NCO's field glasses. McFie crawled out of the trench and made his way toward the river.

--- 40 ---

"*A mask! Give me a mask! For the love of God, please!*"
screamed a lieutenant as he ran along the top edge of a trench.
None of the dozens huddled in the trench recognized him but he
had come from the direction of a neighboring artillery battalion.
A cloud of yellowish green gas flowed towards them. Another
canister burst almost in front of the lieutenant and he changed
direction. There were no masks to spare. Finally, a soldier
grabbed his ankles and pulled him into the trench. He threw a
towel to Andrew.
  "Piss on it! It will help filter the gas! Hurry!" Andrew
quickly relieved himself into the towel.
  "I need more!" Andrew pleaded.
  "Here, I'll help!" said the soldier next to him and within
seconds the towel was drenched with urine.
  "Put if over his head! Cover his hands!"
  The soldiers quickly draped the wet towel over his head
and held it tight over his face.

The gas enveloped them. They watched as the deadly, green vapor slowly spilled into their trench filling every space. They winced in pain when the gas made contact with exposed skin. The hapless lieutenant coughed and convulsed as gas entered his lungs. Another soldier held the lieutenant as he shook. "Try not to breathe so much, sir!" Andrew told him. Over his shoulder he yelled, "I need another wet towel!" A soldier stuffed another handkerchief inside his pants and urinated on it. He handed the sodden cloth to Andrew who held it against the lieutenant's face. Agonizing minutes passed. Then a little breeze slowly shifted the gas. No more canisters landed near them and within minutes the creeping death dispersed.

Andrew pulled the wet, smelly rags off the lieutenant's face. Another soldier poured water from a canteen over his head and into his eyes.

"Thank you," the lieutenant coughed. "For the first time I'm glad you bastards drank all the tea…"

--- 41 ---

Philip and the 9th Cheshire Battalion were in a trench no more than a mile from Andrew's. They had not seen each other for nearly two years. Mail from home was intermittent, if any came at all, and there were no other ways to learn for certain where relatives in uniform might be at any given moment. They overheard comments now and then about troop movements, and soldiers could estimate where relatives and friends might be. They were thankful to not be in the same unit as a cousin or sibling. The idea of witnessing a loved one's death in battle was too disturbing to contemplate. One day, while passing another soldier in a communications trench, Andrew thought he saw Philip. The soldier was walking in the opposite direction and the trench was narrow and packed. Andrew turned and called his name but he had to keep moving. He could not tell whether he heard him or not.

An artillery barrage preceding a gas attack had fragmented Philip's company, then gas canisters landed on all sides of the trench he was in. Everyone donned their gas masks and Philip peered carefully over the trench wall with a periscope. He could see German helmets moving in the enemy's trench. The enemy soldiers cycled their rifle chambers and one of them cocked a Maxim machine gun. Philip lowered himself back into the trench and handed the periscope to Ellor who backed away from the instrument to check his rifle.

"What do we do?" Ellor demanded. "There's only the five of us."

Philip climbed back up and peered over the top without the scope. A bullet ricocheted off his helmet. They heard a German bugle signal the attack and dozens of Germans began pouring out of their trenches. Philip glanced through his field glasses then shoved them aside. He pushed Ellor. "They're coming! Down the comm trench! Move!"

Four of them hurried away in the opposite direction of the attackers. Philip started to follow but hesitated. Quickly scanning the equipment at his feet, he lifted an empty metal map cylinder, thought a second, then reached into his coat. He pulled out a wad of blank letter paper and slid it into the case, making sure the edges of the paper were clearly visible. He upended a satchel and spilled five grenades into the mud. Then he tied one end of a wire to a nearly withdrawn ring pin and slid the other end into the metal cylinder containing the paper.

The four others were fifty yards east, running for their lives through ankle deep mud. Philip was gaining on them from behind while bullets began striking the inside top of the trench. The youngest soldier stopped and fell against the mud wall, out of breath. "Keep going!" yelled Philip, now thirty yards away.

"I can't run anymore!" Birch gasped.

"It's rugby!" Philip yelled. "You've got the ball. Run!"

"Where's Bebbington?" Philip appeared down the trench and caught up with the stalled group of four.

"Go! Go-go-go-go-go!" screamed Philip as he neared them.

The Germans ran across No Man's Land and began firing into the British trench. Seeing it was empty, they slowed their fire. A group of Germans reached the position the five British soldiers had recently vacated. A large blond German saw the map case and jumped into the trench to pick it up. At first glance, he did not notice the wire and grenades. He pulled out the paper and frowned when he saw the pages were blank. Then the grenade exploded, blowing the German against the trench, his arms flying in three directions. Three of the four grenades taped to the rigged grenade had detonated, killing two more Germans who had jumped into the trench behind the big blond. The fourth exploded a second later, killing none but steering approaching Germans away. Shells began pounding the trench behind Philip and his men. They continued running down the communication trench away from the bombing. They escaped.

After a two-week rotation at the Front, Philip moved back to the 9th Battalion's billets in a deserted, burned out village. The few soldiers who were uninjured laid in their bunks quietly smoking. Birch sat picking his bare feet.

"Bloody hell," Birch said as he picked at black splotches on his feet.

"Best you start keeping your feet dry," Ellor joked. "That trench foot will kill you out there!"

Laughter. Ellor nodded at the corporal bars on Philip's sleeve. "Corporal Bebbington now, is it?"

"That's right. You better stay in line now," Philip quipped.

"Hey, Birchy, Bebbington's been promoted again!" Ellor called.

"Is that how we get promoted?" Birch asked. "Send an NCO to the Front for two weeks then put in for his job, 'cause he's finished?"

"Pretty much," Philip said, lighting a cigarette. "Everybody gets a turn. Next week, you blokes'll have my job."

News of the Somme Offensive began to trickle in. On the first day alone, an estimated 57,000 British soldiers were killed or wounded. July 1, 1916, became known as the bloodiest day in the history of the British Army. After fighting for four months, they gained only three square miles of territory.

The Allies achieved their objectives the first day, only to lose heavily over the next few weeks in nearby Guillemont. The Liverpool Pals advanced with their French comrades and seized Montauban, one of the few successful Allied victories of the day. As the number of men in the Liverpool and other Pals battalions dwindled, replacements slowly arrived. Companies of the 9th Cheshire Battalion were very heavily engaged and saw intense trench fighting amid torrential machine gun fire. They dug and re-dug trenches under enemy fire, and carried materials forward through communication trenches. Badly injured and shell shocked, Captain George Plunkett was sent home after spending several weeks in a field hospital.

--- **42** ---

In good weather and bad, Mary Bebbington drove the twelve miles from Rawhead to Chester Market almost daily. It was raining and her long skirt was drenched. She hauled Cheshire cheese, milk, eggs and vegetables, whatever she could manage to pull together. She parked the cart in the open-air market and began greeting familiar customers.

"'Ow's eggs going today, missis?" a woman called.

"Pennies apiece, ma'am." Mary answered. The woman noticed Mary's wet gown. "You'll catch the influenza, missis' if ye don't take care."

"I haven't in forty years, Mrs. Bodnick. I am blessed that way."

"Rain has narrow shoulders," the woman smiled. "It will get in anywhere!"

They laughed at the old joke. Mary continued selling her fresh produce and chatting with her regulars through the morning. She barely recognized a tall man who was hobbling with the help of a cane across the market.

"Mr. Plunkett!" she called out. "Mr. Plunkett!" Plunkett stopped and looked around. Seeing Mary, he crossed to her and sat down on a produce crate.

"How good to see you! Have you news of my Boy Scouts?" Mary asked him. "The older boys? Eddie, Lewis, and Ernest? They came to see me before they left."

He was not the healthy, enthusiastic scoutmaster she remembered from years earlier when he rode his bicycle onto Rawhead and introduced himself to her. He seemed much thinner now and lost somehow. He looked at the ground, his mouth moving.

"Mr. Plunkett?" Mary prodded.

He hesitated. "They were killed at Montauban France months ago," Plunkett finally managed. "Eddie McFie is listed as missing."

Mary's hand grabbed the side of the cart as grief seized her. She eased down to sit beside Plunkett, grappling with the news. Thunder rumbled above them. Around her, farmers hawked their goods and haggled with customers. She ceased to hear them. Why had Edgar not told her? He was always so full of information.

"Oh, no. No, no, no," Mary murmured in a low voice.

She stood and touched George's shoulder softly, then walked to her horse and trap. Aboard, she absently spread her wet skirt over her flanks and flapped the reins. The rig lurched forward. George Plunkett watched numbly as the cart disappeared in the rain down Princess Street.

Before reaching the farm gate, Mary stopped the horse and slid from her seat. She ambled through the east field toward the area near The Clump where the Boy Scouts had set up their camp years ago. The rain had stopped but the dormant field was awash in mud and draped in mist. Reaching the campsite, her gaze went to the old fire ring, encircled by stones and log seats.

The arrangement had shifted slightly over time. Grass had grown up where the pup tents had stood. She sat on one of the logs and stared into the fire ring remembering the merry flames that had once danced there. Images of warm summer afternoons flitted through her mind. She had marveled at the skills those boys had practiced there, and recalled the laughter, the stories, the delicious sausages they had roasted on sticks. They were such good cooks. The thought of never again seeing their dear, happy faces brought tears spilling down her cheeks. They only wanted to do good things, she remembered. Mary lowered herself down onto the mud and wept.

Mary, Joseph, and Martha on the horse and trap
Photo courtesy of the author

--- **43** ---

Heidi Bryden watered the flowers in the greenhouse at Ballantyne. The groundskeepers would have done this but it was one of her favorite places and she liked to perform some of the duties herself. William Cutter appeared outside. She did not notice him and he watched her for a moment through the glass panels. She was as beautiful as ever, he thought. She was filling a large pot with dirt and begonias. When she attempted to lift it, Cutter rushed in. "Let me help you with that" he offered gallantly.

"Oh, thank you, William."

"Where did you want to put it?"

"On the back patio," she answered, brushing soil from her gloved hands. "I'd like it to get some rain."

He followed her to the spot and set the pot down. Their eyes met. She smiled at him and his heart skipped a beat. "You look lovely, Heidi," Cutter told her.

"Why, thank you, William." She considered him a moment in silence. Not as handsome as Robert, but nice-looking over all, she mused. "Was there something you needed to see me about?" she inquired politely.

"No. I was on my way to meet Ernest Black and I saw you and—" Embarrassed, Cutter's voice trailed off. He smiled at her, gave a little wave and walked away. Heidi watched him for a moment, then wandered back to the greenhouse, her thoughts curious about William Cutter.

--- 44 ---
Port of Salonika, Greece
August 1916

A British Army major strode briskly down a hallway and knocked on a door marked LTG George Milne. General Milne of the 12th Army Corps had replaced General Mahon after the latter had been reassigned to Egypt.

"Come!" A muffled voice called from inside. The major entered.

Milne sat behind a desk conversing with two ASC officers.

"The Greeks are prohibiting the sale of petrol and they've placed a guard on the Standard Oil yard," one of the officers told Milne. "And they're balking at the amount we offered for bulk grain."

"Tell them we will seize the petrol facility and granary if we have to!" the general replied irately. The two ASC men nodded curtly and left, closing the door behind them.

"Sir, there's a Greek army unit outside," the major said. "The commander asked to speak with you."

"In regard to what? They're neutral. I didn't think they had an army. Handle it, major."

"He insists on speaking with someone in charge, sir." The major coughed. "He has a British soldier with him and wants to exchange him for horses."

The general's mouth dropped. "What?" He stood up, closing a file on the desk and reaching for his service cover. "Take me to him."

Milne followed the major out of the harbor master building into the hot, midday sun. Greek labourers were busy offloading transport ships docked at the wharf, a dozen men on horses milled around in front of the building. Bertie was slumped in a saddle, hatless and reddened from sunburn.

"What's the meaning of this?" Milne asked, blinking in the bright light.

The Greek leader began speaking. A British officer, fluent in Greek, translated.

"He says they found this man south of here on the Pelion coast road. He had a Bulgarian map and compass on him," the British translator said.

Milne looked at Bertie. "Who are you?" he asked.

Bertie saluted, wearily. "Private Bert Bebbington of the Fourth New Armies Horse Transport Company, sir." His lips and tongue were swollen from dehydration. He was slurring his words. "My ship, the *Royal Michael*, was torpedoed and sunk, and I made it to shore."

"But that happened...what, six months ago?"

Bertie nodded. "October. I was held in a jail in Zagora." Milne looked at the Greek leader and back at Bertie.

"On what charge?" The general demanded.

"They thought I had something to do with the killing of some Greek soldiers near where I came ashore."

The Greek leader spoke again through the translator. "He says he wants to keep the horses and mules this man had in his possession when they found him. He wants to exchange them for this fellow."

"What horses and mules?" Milne asked Bertie in confusion. "I thought you said you swam ashore?" Before Bertie could clarify, the general told him to get off the horse and follow him. He wanted to discuss this inside, out of the heat. The Greek leader, Bertie, the translator and the adjutant major trailed behind him into the building.

"I appreciate your returning this soldier to us, Captain," Milne said briskly to the Greek through his translator. "But the animals this man had with him belong to the British Army and will be returned."

"He says no British soldiers were supposed to be south of Thessaloniki and that we are in violation."

"In violation of what?" Milne asked, outraged. "Protecting his country from the Bulgarians? Tell him we are grateful for his assistance but the animals are essential to our mission here. This man's ship was torpedoed. What was he supposed to do, swim to Salonika?"

Hearing the translation, the leader slapped his thigh with his cap angrily and shook his head. Milne looked at Bertie who was swaying with fatigue. "Major, please escort this man to hospital. I'll meet with him later."

The Greek patrol leader left Milne's headquarters in a huff fifteen minutes later. Milne and his adjutant went to talk with Bertie in hospital. When they found him, he was sitting on a padded table, sipping water from a glass. A nurse was cleaning a wound on his head.

"So, you were on the *Royal Michael*?" Milne asked him, a bit suspiciously. "What possessed you to risk your neck for those animals?"

"I am a muleteer and horse driver, sir. They were in my charge," he told Milne. "I happened by the scene of a recent dust up between the Greeks and some farmers and everyone was dead. I saw the map and the compass and took 'em, thinking they might be useful."

"They were in your charge...the animals..." Milne repeated. "Right." He looked at his paperwork. "Who is your superior officer?"

"LTC May, sir."

"Mmm. He's in hospital. Sick. Private, your ship was miles off shore when it went down. Did you realize how far you were from shore when you went in?"

"Yessir," Bertie admitted with a sigh. "I thought there was a good chance I could get them ashore."

"Few places on earth are as dangerous as the waters around Salonika. Yesterday, a supply ship from Egypt was torpedoed." Milne said. "Three hundred muleteers and drivers were lost. How am I supposed to supply the Salonikan Force without muleteers and drivers if all this is going on?"

"Sir," Bertie asked the major. "Were you able to retrieve the animals?"

"They will be returned, mark my words. I sent some men with the Greeks to bring them back."

"Thank you, sir." Bertie said, standing to leave, his wound properly dressed. He reached into his pocket and withdrew the dead sailor's dog tag and handed it to Milne. "This man washed up a day after me."

A sharp explosion shook the building, sending everyone diving for cover. It was a bombing raid. Two airplanes circled the waterfront, dropping incendiary bombs. Outside, men began running for cover as the attack ensued. Symbols on the planes indicated they were Bulgarian. The planes left as quickly as they arrived. For the rest of the day, the army battled the fire which resulted in the destruction of a warehouse containing 5,000 tons of hay and grain.

--- 45 ---
Near the Nile River
September 1916

In September 1916, LTC Wilson became ill and was admitted to hospital in Alexandria. LTC Phillips-Brocklehurst replaced him.

"We are moving back to the Baharia Oasis," Phillips-Brocklehurst briefed his officers as he grabbed his satchel and pistol. "The Senussi are evacuating the Baharia Oasis for Siwa." He headed out of headquarters in Minia.

Robert Bryden received orders to cease work on Blockhouse B5 and the light railway and move to cut off the Senussi. The yeomen travelled in armored cars, Ford cars, transport wagons and camels. Two aircraft from Alexandria were dispatched to locate the Senussi and provide aerial bomb support. But again, they were too late. The Senussi's equipment and even their tracks had been covered by sand.

"It's as if God himself was on their side!" Bryden exclaimed as he slammed his wagon door closed. "They played us!"

He stared across the vast desert landscape searching for a sign of the Senussi departure. A wisp of smoke possibly. A distant gunshot. The reflection off a piece of metal. But there was nothing, just sand and searing heat. Lowering his binoculars, he looked at his feet and kicked a piece of dried camel dung off the slope of the dune. Not even fresh muck as a clue!

For days, the yeomen caravan searched the only possible route the elusive enemy could have taken. Bryden sent small patrols ten miles in both directions along the route but the Senussi had vanished. The tribesmen had prevented the yeomen from fighting the Turks, waiting until the very last blockhouse, B6, was completed. Then they evacuated the oasis. With the Senussi gone, the yeoman force moved on to Baharia and secured it, though no one was sure why.

Robert Bryden was disillusioned with the entire affair. In the ten months since their arrival in Egypt, dozens of yeomen died of disease or had been picked off one by one by an enemy they had never seen. Even if he wanted to remain and share in the defeat of the Senussi, he had been ordered to leave. Bryden was no longer anxious to fight. They were battling the climate, terrain and disease, not a flesh and blood army. The enemy was out in the desert but it was constantly on the move. It used hit and run tactics, mostly by night. The Senussi had successfully kept the yeomen from engaging the Turks in the Sinai for months, which had been their plan all along. The building of block houses proved a colossal waste of time and the project was abandoned.

Philips-Brocklehurst was reassigned to command the 9th Battalion Cheshires. He had spent thirty-two years in the yeomanry and was fifty-six years old. Now he was being sent to the trenches in France for the winter. The general feeling was that if any soldier deserved to go home it was him. Following a subdued farewell celebration, he departed and Robert Bryden became second in command of the yeoman regiment. Ordered to

Alexandria to prepare for action in Palestine, Majors Bryden and Glazebrook took the railway north. They gazed at the Nile River from their seat as the train chugged along. "Well, at least the railway got completed," Bryden glowered.

--- 46 ---
Near the Somme River
October 1916

On October 6, LTC Philips-Brocklehurst arrived in the Somme to take command of the 9th Battalion Cheshire Regiment. After being briefed on the unit's status, he was at a loss to understand it. He had come from the desert in Egypt where he had fought tribal bands who used guerilla tactics. Now he faced the devastation of a very real Front. After assessing what was left of the battalion, one of his first duties was to backfill NCO ranks and to process personnel requests from the War Office. Philip was next in line to be called to his field desk.

"Corporal Bebbington, you've been recommended for promotion to the rank of Lance Sergeant," Philips-Brocklehurst told the young man standing at attention before him. "I want you to know I heartily approve."

"Thank you, sir," Philip said. "I don't know what I did to deserve it."

"You've been serving as a Corporal since what, August?"

"Yessir."

"The other NCOs of the 9th are wounded or dead. Most of them, anyway." Philip knew that the 9th Battalion had been reduced but not that all the NCOs had fallen. "Have you a recommendation for corporal for your platoon?"

"Heathcote, sir."

"There will be a meeting at 0630 tomorrow at the field tent. Please be there."

"Yessir." Philip saluted and turned to leave, then paused. "I heard you came from the Cheshire Yeomanry in Egypt, sir."

"That's right."

"May I ask of Major Bryden?"

"He was fine when I left Alexandria. Been playing a bit of a cat and mouse game with a Sudanese tribe along the Nile. How do you know him?"

"He's the landlord of the farm where I'm from."

"I see. He's a fine man."

"Yessir."

--- 47 ---
Near the Ancre River, France
November 1916

Andrew and dozens of other riflemen fired repeatedly across a snow-covered "No Man's Land" as Germans began to attack their position from Beaucourt Trench. In the preceding days, the 13th Battalion of the Rifle Brigade had moved from bivouacs in Hedauville to their appointed place of assembly near the Ancre River, a tributary to the Somme. Heavy snow hindered travel but they were familiar with the cold and damp weather by now. Andrew continued to fire from his trench, remembering his Mad Minute training. He stopped only to reload a clip from his bandolier. His short stature and the depth of the trench forced him to stand on an upended ammunition box to peek over the berm while those around him rested their boots firmly on the trench floor. They were being overrun and he was afraid. Trembling. *Perhaps this will be it for us*, he thought, reaching for another cartridge clip.

Following the initial skirmish an NCO arrived and saw Andrew lying at the bottom of the trench, clutching his hand. Another rifleman lay dead next to him. Andrew removed a handkerchief from his pocket and the NCO helped wrap it around his injured hand then moved on. He shifted his rifle to shoot with his left hand. Seeing that Andrew's section had stopped firing, the Germans increased firing in that area. Andrew fixed his left index finger on the trigger of his rifle and steadied the forward grip with his wrapped hand. He resumed firing, cycling, and firing again. Pain from his right hand became unbearable, the end of his rifle dipped to the ground. Across the field, dozens of Germans fixed their bayonets and advanced through the smoke. Andrew reached for his bayonet and fixed it on the end of his rifle. He was breathing hard and sweating.

He knew the attack had changed and he was going to have to stick a German. He was going to wait before resorting to his bayonet. The Germans were now upon them so Andrew climbed out of the trench and fired a shot, hitting a German in the chest. As the German fell, another appeared and lunged. Andrew deflected his rifle away with his own. After seconds of furious grappling, Andrew crouched on his knees and shoved his rifle upward using both hands. He thought his sword hit the German's belt but in fact he had gored him savagely.

The fighting went on into the night, back and forth, until it finally ceased when the command to withdraw was given. German and British soldiers who were still alive withdrew to their respective trenches. The pink sky of dawn emerged, and Andrew, exhausted, wounded, dirty and numb from cold, moved through communication trenches to a dressing station for medical treatment.

By November 15, ninety-three men of the 13th Battalion were dead including runners and aid station staff. The Battalion Chaplain, who had fought in the Second Boer War, was killed while helping casualties to an aid station. Eleven officers were wounded.

Battalion headquarters was unsure how to continue. The Battle of Ancre was the last big British assault at the first Battle of the Somme. Though deemed a success, the win came at a terribly high price. Andrew had fought his second major battle of the war in the worst of winter conditions.

Dismissing his own injuries, LTC Pretor-Pinney watched the dozens of injured soldiers being rushed into a large dressing station in Albert. One soldier had been so badly damaged he had to be carried from the battlefield in a basket because he had lost all four limbs. Such instances coined the term "basket cases". An exhausted, blood spattered medic arrived at Pretor-Pinney's side. The lieutenant colonel was laying on a stretcher and propped up with a bundled blanket. The medic listened to his chest with a stethoscope. "Doctor, I need you here!" the medic called across the tent.

Pretor-Pinney looked at the faces of his soldiers around the tent. He recognized many from training in Salisbury. Ten feet away, Andrew sat in a chair with the number one etched on his forehead with a grease pencil. He was holding his bandaged right hand up with his left, awaiting treatment. He had received morphine for the pain but felt weak and thirsty from blood loss. The air was heavy with the smell of chloroform and Dakin antiseptic.

Trained in the method of battlefield triage, doctors and nurses worked busily to save soldiers with the number two on their foreheads. This meant if they received immediate treatment, they might be saved. A one signified the man's wounds were not life threatening and he could wait. A three meant the man would not likely survive even if treated. Pretor-Pinney, who bore a two, looked at Andrew. Their eyes met and Andrew returned an encouraging smile. To date, Andrew recalled having spoken directly to him only once before. It had been in Salisbury, during an inspection.

"What a mess they've made of my battalion," Pretor-Pinney said weakly. Tears pooled in his eyes.

"Doctor!" the medic yelled, looking wildly back and forth between his patient and the physician. "Doctor, please!" Finally, a blood-stained surgeon rushed over and examined Pretor-Pinney's injuries. He listened to his chest. After a few seconds, he looked dully at the medic and shook his head.

"He's a three," the doctor said and hurried on to another patient. LTC Pretor-Pinney died minutes later; he was fifty-two years old.

A day later, Andrew lay in a field hospital bed when a captain from his unit arrived.

"How did this happen, private?" the captain asked Andrew, pointing to his bandaged hand. The NCO who had come to Andrew's aid after being shot in the trenches stood by with a doctor.

"I was shot in the hand," Andrew replied.

"While you stood in a trench?"

"Yes, sir."

"Sure you didn't shoot yourself?"

Andrew looked to the NCO and doctor with a puzzled look. "Yes, sir."

"How did it happen?"

"I…was firing at the enemy from within the trench."

"The trench you were in is eight feet deep and you were hit in the hand?"

"I stood atop a box when firing, sir."

"I see."

The three men walked away. Outside the hospital, the doctor rubbed his chin.

"I've been seeing more and more of these injuries, sir. In the hand, in the foot."

"Three months' pay it was self-inflicted to get a blighty home," the NCO said.

"You can't blame a soldier for being afraid," the doctor offered.

"We don't know for sure," the captain said. "Where are the others with wounds to extremities?"

--- 48 ---

LTC Philips-Brocklehurst's field office had been moved again and hastily erected after he had taken command of the 9th Battalion. A battle-weary major on crutches was inside a tent amidst a pile of rubble that had once been a small French hamlet. He hovered over his new adjutant watching him type an order. Philip entered and saluted.

"Lance Sergeant, you have been with the battalion since September of '14." He looked at Philip after reading from a piece of paper. "The army needs experienced NCOs for training purposes back in England. Interested?"

Philip nodded affirmatively. "Yessir." He had seen enough of the trenches.

"I'll have orders for you within the hour. You can catch a lorry to Le Havre."

The major went on to open another file and read. Sensing the young sergeant was still there, he looked up at him. "Did you have a question, Lance Sergeant?"

"Why me, sir?" Philip asked bluntly.

The adjutant stopped typing and looked at Philip.

"Because the 9th Battalion has been decimated. We've lost over 700 men. Haven't seen losses like this since the Marne in 'fourteen. That makes you a rarity. We're short of experienced men like you. Good luck, Lance Sergeant."

"Thank you, sir," Philip replied and saluted. He never saw his unit again.

--- 49 ---
Minia, Egypt
February 1917

"Redundant?" Robert Bryden asked, standing before three seated officers at a table. "I don't understand, sir." Robert Bryden had been in Egypt a year almost to the day when he was summoned from Baharia to regiment headquarters in Minia.

"You and Glazebrook are going home," LTC Wilson said. "The Cheshire and Shropshire squadrons are being absorbed by the 10th Kings."

"And why, sir? May I ask?"

"Sayyid Ahmed and his Senussi were defeated at Siwa by a force of armored cars from Sollum five days ago. The threat no longer exists. The Imperial Camel Corps, the Sixth Company and the Light Armored Car Patrols under the Duke of Westminster will deal with any further trouble from that quarter," the colonel explained.

"Palestine...?"

"We've more than enough officers for action in Palestine."

Bryden remained perplexed. "This doesn't make any sense at all, sir."

"Unfortunately, it's a rather political matter. The Shropshire Yeomanry will supply the four senior positions. They have seniority over the Cheshire's. You may take a position at headquarters in Chester if you wish."

"I must protest, sir." Bryden said. "I have been an officer in the Cheshire Yeomanry for twenty years. What on earth have I done wrong?"

"Nothing that I know of. I should think you would be keen to see English soil and your family again, Major."

"But--"

"That's all, Major. You can catch the next transport for England."

"Sir." Bryden saluted and started for the door.

"Oh, and take that drunken fool Wilkinson with you," LTC Wilson added, his face puckering with distaste. "Or turn him over to the Turks. Your choice. He's done more for them than us, as far as I can see."

"Has something happened, sir?" Bryden asked.

"He was arrested last night for drunkenness...again. C Company doesn't want him anymore."

In March 1917, Robert Bryden returned to England after weathering a bitter political upheaval within the Yeomanry. With the formation of the 10th Battalion King's Light Infantry Brigade, the Cheshire Yeomanry and the Shropshire Yeomanry were merged. They were then absorbed by the 10th King's. As such, redundant officers were ordered home against their wishes and those of their troops. The goal was to use discipline and common experiences to avoid disagreement and maintain morale.

Following the traditional farewell celebrations, the officers departed Egypt for home with a few exceptions. Glazebrook journeyed south to Kenya to inquire about joining the British East African force stationed there. After some apprehension from Wilkinson, LTC Wilson offered him a position with the British force in Salonika and he accepted.

The fact that Bryden had not been required in the amalgamated unit, was humiliating and one not easily overlooked. It meant he would never command another unit again. Disconsolate, Bryden packed for his voyage home. There was some consolation to the whole affair. Before the war, he had introduced LTC Verdin to his sister Lindsay at a yeomanry dance at Ballantyne. Prior to the dance, she had lamented to him that she thought herself undesirable at nearly eighteen. They married within two months and they were a good match, Bryden thought. He realized that introducing them made him a successful matchmaker, like his father tried to be. It would be good to see them after all.

In the coming weeks, the 10th Kings departed for Palestine to confront the Turks. Six months later they would sail for Marseilles on the HMT *Omrah* to fight in the last stages of the Somme conflict.

--- 50 ---
Portsmouth, England
March 1917

Robert Bryden's transport ship escaped the threat of German submarines once again. Bryden thought this simply miraculous. Although a member of the Anglican Church, he did not consider himself a religious man, but was convinced something or someone was protecting him. Perhaps Heidi and her daily prayers combined with his carried a little more weight. He had seen men in his command perish, both in the Second Boer War and in the Sahara, and found the loss of his men in Egypt particularly troubling because of the trifling nature of the conflict. It distressed him that he was denied the chance to fight the Turks in Palestine.

Twelve days after leaving Alexandria, Robert Bryden's ship landed in Portsmouth. He watched happy families welcome soldiers returning from the war. Longing for the peace and comfort of home Bryden caught a train to Chester and hired a hackney to drive him to Ballantyne Castle. He asked the driver to drop him at the entry road so he could surprise Heidi who was, despite the wintry day, probably in the garden. Walking in that direction he inhaled the crisp, pine-scented air and noticed the grounds had been improved. There were new trees and shrubbery, more low walls and terraces made of field stone. John, a groundskeeper spotted him and waved.

"You're home, sir. How good it is to see you again!"

"You too, John," Bryden replied, grinning. "Where might I find Mrs. Bryden?"

John pointed to a section of the garden and Bryden walked toward the greenhouse catching a pleasant, familiar fragrance. Quietly peering through the glass doors, he spied Heidi on her knees absorbed in digging and planting. He knocked on the frame.

"Would you care for a cup of tea, madam?" Robert asked in a deep, formal tone.

"Oh no, tha—" she responded, not recognizing the unfamiliar voice. She turned to see her husband in his yeomanry uniform smiling at her, his face bronzed by a year in the Egyptian sun, his hair lighter. "Robert!" she squealed. "You're home, you're home!" He reached for his wife and kissed her. "You didn't say you were coming home, Robert!"

"I wanted to surprise you. And I knew just where you would be!" Robert kissed her more deeply. "Where are the children?"

"School. Did you not get my letter?"

Robert frowned, shaking his head. "Letters, mail. How I long for the day when I can speak into a…device and talk to you from anywhere. Imagine that."

"Geoffrey is at Harrow and Matthew is at Oxford," she said, still trying to recover from her surprise. "How long before you must return?"

"The war is over for me, sweet Heidi," he told her, taking her gloved hands in his. "Maybe adjutant duties at the Old Bank

Building in Chester now and then. Come, there's a million things I want to tell you."

--- 51 ---

Morning light peeked through the windows of Robert and Heidi's bedroom. Robert was on his back dozing, and Heidi was snuggled next to him. She caressed his chest. "Awake? Heidi whispered.

"Yes," Robert smiled with his eyes closed. "For a while. I'll have to get used to the comfort of this bed again. I've been sleeping on an Egyptian torture contraption." They laughed and kissed.

"And those hanging beds they have on ships," she said, rising. "What are they called?"

"Hammocks. They're not so bad, once you get used to them."

"I'll draw a bath," she said, walking into the bathroom. "But I must warn you, the plumbing needs work."

Robert sat up and looked out the window. It felt extraordinary being home. No bugle calls, no truck engines roaring to life, no orders waiting for him to write or fulfill. He was relieved he had no more letters to write to the relatives of fallen soldiers. He could feel none of the gastrointestinal distress he had experienced in Egypt. The weather was also a welcome change. From the heat and sand of the desert to the verdant, overcast chill of his island home. He breathed deeply with satisfaction and lifted his watch from the bedside table. He figured it would be late morning in Cairo now and wondered what his men in the 10th Kings were doing. They would be deep in Palestine by now.

"Have you heard anything further of Sam and Bertie Bebbington?" Heidi called from the bathroom.

"No. Still in Salonika, I should think."

Heidi appeared in the bathroom doorway. "Their ship was sunk."

"What?"

"Their ship was torpedoed in the Mediterranean. Near Greece."

"When?" Robert swung his legs to the floor and put on his robe.

Heidi thought a second. "It must be a year now. Perhaps more. I thought you would know." He shook his head and turned to her.

"How would I know? He's in the Service Corps," he said. Minutes later, dressed in his uniform, Robert Bryden sped down the driveway in his Rolls Royce. Heidi watched from the front door with concern, the war separating them again.

--- 52 ---

Robert Bryden saluted a guard as he entered Chester Castle.

"All we know is that the ship he was on, the *Royal Michael*, was torpedoed off the Pelion Peninsula in Greece. That was in…October 1915," an officer said, studying a paper on his desk. "Survivors were picked up and delivered to the Salonikan Forces with General Mahon. From what I understand, they are now entrenched in the Balkans with French troops."

"Is there a list of survivors?"

"I would have to look into it," the officer replied. "If he had been listed as missing or killed, his family would have been notified. Ships are being sunk all over, Major."

Bryden slowly walked out of the Cheshire Yeomanry headquarters reading a crumpled newspaper. Maybe City Hall would know. As he drove past Chester Castle, he saw a long queue of both young and old, mostly short men extending down Princess Street. The youngsters look like they're sixteen, Bryden thought.

He knew the government had lowered the minimum height for army service again. If any man stood 5' or taller the army would take him. *The Conscription Act* increased the maximum age to forty-one and specified the only men not likely to be called up were those who were widowed with children, serving in the Royal Navy, ministers of religion or working in one of the reserved occupations. A second act in May 1916 extended liability for military service to married men. An amendment extended the upper age limit to fifty-one.

As Bryden drove, the voice of George V replayed in his head after reading an appeal to the Empire from the newspaper:

> *At this grave moment in the struggle between my people and a highly-organized enemy, who has transgressed the laws of nations and changed the ordinance that binds civilized Europe together, I appeal to you. I rejoice in my Empire's effort, and I feel pride in the voluntary response from my subjects all over the world who have sacrificed home, fortune, and life itself, in order that another may not inherit the free Empire which their ancestors and mine have built.*

At Rawhead, Martha finished reading the King's appeal to the family:

> *I ask you to make good these sacrifices. The end is not in sight. More men and yet more are wanted to keep my armies in the field, and through them to secure victory and enduring peace. I ask you, men of all classes, to come forward voluntarily, and take your share in the fight. May God bless all of you.*

Will Evans contemplated the photos on the wall.

--- 53 ---

By April 1917 the British Salonikan force, under General George Milne, held 90 miles of front, including the key strategic position at Doiran. The Allied force, consisting of French, Italian, Russian and Serbian troops, launched an attack. In support of the offensive, the Salonikan force attempted to capture Bulgarian positions around Doiran. Bertie moved to the Struma River Valley, driving over the mountains north of Lakes Beshik and Langaza, performing supply and construction duties for the British and French troops camped there. Intermittent fighting continued and with the advent of warm weather, malaria and dysentery returned to ravage the troops.

Feeling dizzy and feverish, Bertie reported to a field hospital. "I think I need some aspirin," Bertie mumbled to a nurse. A moment later he stumbled and collapsed. The next morning, he woke in a hospital bed.

"Good morning, soldier," a doctor said as he touched a stethoscope to his chest.

"Where am I?" Bertie blurted.

"You're in hospital."

"What's wrong with me?"

"You have malaria." Bertie looked puzzled. The doctor explained, "It's a tropical disease caused by a parasite and transmitted by mosquitos." Bertie stared at him. The doctor listed the symptoms, "Fever, chills, headache, nausea, vomiting, muscle cramps, fatigue. Sound familiar?"

--- 54 ---
Rawhead Farm
July 1917

Before reporting to Training Reserve Brigade in Rollestone, Philip was given ten days of leave and returned to Rawhead. Although it was a weekday and food shortages persisted, Dave managed to acquire a small beef roast in exchange for ten rabbits to welcome Philip home. Everyone was present around the dinner table except for Bertie, Sam, and Clem. Martha had invited a friend, Minnie Davis, who was a nursing student at Witnington Hospital in Manchester. Philip and Minnie met and exchanged polite conversation.

"What does that patch mean, Philip?" Martha asked, pointing to his uniform.

"My rank," Philip answered, peering at his insignia. "I'm a lance sergeant."

Will Evans had noticed Philip's uniform when he arrived at Rawhead.

"You didn't tell us you were promoted," Mary said. "How did that happen?"

"I'm not sure," Philip replied. "I was told all the non-commissioned officers were killed." The table went silent.

"How?" Jim asked.

"Jim!" Mary scolded. "We don't want to know."

"So where will you go now?" Mollie asked.

"To a training unit near Rollestone," Philip answered. "I'll be working with soldiers who have been injured so they can be sent back to the war."

"Dear Lord," Mary said. "Haven't they done enough?"

After supper, Philip wandered outside and strolled up a path through the east field. It was a cool, quiet evening. Birds chirped in the hedgerows, a brown hare emerged into the open and daylight slowly faded. Will Evans came up beside him.

"Hello, Philip," Will said.

"Will."

"Must be great to be back."

Philip nodded. "How are you and Martha? Happy?"

"Yes. Your father torments me every now and then, but I manage."

They laughed.

"I wanted to tell you that I joined up today," Evans told him. "As a litter-bearer and ambulance driver. With all the driving I do here, I figured I can do that."

Philip eyed him. "They need all the litter-bearers and ambulance drivers they can get."

--- 55 ---
Training Reserve Brigade
Rollestone, Wiltshire

Philip reported to Training Reserve Brigade Rollestone. A camp near the Salisbury-Bustard Road had existed there since 1904. When the war broke out, the camp expanded, with hut installations in addition to tents, and became part of the Larkhill Garrison. The ASC supply depot, where Bertie and Sam had been assigned in 1915, was not far away. Across the road, the Royal Flying Corps (RFC) had established the No. 1 Balloon School.

Descending from a lorry onto what he thought was firm ground, Philip sank to his knees in mud. *Bloody Hell*, he grimaced to himself. Army camps teemed with menace; disease, cold, heat, humidity, bad food, pests, and muck. Once he got out of the service, he vowed he would not set foot in an army camp for the rest of his life. Drawing his boots out of the sucking mud, he wondered why conditions had not improved in the three years he had been in the Army.

The training brigade was designed to help wounded soldiers heal and return to their battalions at the Front. Training involved a combination of strengthening exercises and sports. New soldiers, originally rejected for service, arrived from all parts of the UK at neighboring camps, as well as men who at first try were considered too old, too young, too short, too thin, overweight, and frail or married were now accepted. By 1917, the hale and hearty ones were all gone.

"Step forward and extend your bayonets!" Philip shouted from a platform that had two straw sacks hanging from it. Two trainees stepped forward and rammed the bags with their bayonets. "Don't think about it, just do it!" Philip bellowed. "It's you or the Huns!" More recruits followed until all had attacked the sacks. Later, Philip stood above trenches as a dozen soldiers with only their heads exposed, hurled scoops of earth into the air. "Come on, lean into it."

Mills bomb and rifle practice, map and compass and other training exercises were redelivered, but with actual front-line experience added. After several weeks of this, the men played football and rugby for hours of conditioning. Philip coached, umpired and played as well.

A sergeant major, who was a Sawney miner before the war, walked to a clearing and stepped up on an open lorry bed waving his arms. "Come on over!" he called. "I got somethin' to say! Gather 'round, mates."

Philip joined two dozen other NCOs gathering around the man. The sergeant major cleared his throat and spoke.

"If any of ye want to go to 'eaven quick, now's yer chance!" Philip could hardly understand the man, maybe because of his natural Tyneside accent or his obvious injury. A hideous scar extended from his left ear to the base of his neck.

"B'ttalion 'eadquarters is askin' for 'olunteers to become officers and fly aircraft in the bloody Flying Corps to take the place of kilt ones! If any of ye is 'ligious an' 'eels like meetin' 'iz maker, step 'orward out of ranks n'mark your name. But 'member, if ye make a mistake or get shot up it's a long way down! An' ye burn when ye get there!"

There was a long silence as the NCOs in his audience gave each other puzzled looks. None of them rushed forward out of enthusiasm to accept his offer and they had good reason. Many of them saw aircraft in action over France and had seen plenty of them crash. Some were shot down, some experienced mechanical failure in mid-air, and others simply ran out of fuel, stalling and hurtling out of the sky. A few of the NCOs in attendance had seen crash sites too. They remembered the smell of human bodies burned to a crisp. The aroma of roasting meat wafted over the crowd from the mess tent nearby. Philip looked down, feeling queasy.

The sergeant major was studying the group. They were looking away, anywhere but at him. "At's what I thought," he said finally. He made the speech every few weeks as part of his duties and got the same reaction everytime. "Smart thinkin.' Grub's ready. Diiiismissed!" The sergeant major saluted smartly and stepped off the box.

An RFC captain had been listening from the back of the crowd. He frowned and approached the sergeant major. "Sergeant Major, flying is not that unsafe," the captain offered. "How can we recruit new pilots if you tell them they will die if they learn to fly? What kind of salesmanship is that?"

"Just bein' honest, sir. Most cadets die inside of three weeks, and that's in school. In France, they're lucky if they get past two!" The group of NCOs began breaking up, discussing in low tones the message the sergeant major had delivered.

NCOs tended to be well-informed and Philip believed what the sergeant major said. Crashes in flight school averaged three per day. He stepped forward and signed his name anyway. He thought it might be useful to have such a skill if he made it out of the war alive. Flying mail or passengers. Think of that. Philip walked into the HQ tent and came to attention before the RFC captain and camp CO.

"So, you want to fly?" the captain asked him.

"Yessir."

"Are you afraid of heights?"

"Heights, sir?"

"Yes, you know from climbing trees or looking over cliffs or such," the captain clarified.

Philip thought about it. "No sir. I think the tallest I've ever been was the York Minster when my parents let me climb the steeple stairs on my twelfth birthday."

"Not dizzy?"

"No, sir. It was exciting. At the time. I liked seeing the gargoyles up close."

The captain stood and lifted a model of a D.H.1 aircraft from his desk so Philip would look at it. "You'll have to become an officer," the captain said. "Four and a half weeks training at university, put in for a transfer to the RFC, then six weeks flight training. You'll need at least 15 hours of flight time before going solo."

The British Army was not trying to deplete its ranks of experienced soldiers; quite the contrary. But the RFC's efforts to recruit pilots had failed miserably. In response, the War Office issued orders to field units and training depots to formally request volunteers for flight training. It was an easy choice for Philip and others like him. Death in the air was infinitely preferable to death in the stinking muddy ditches of France. Getting shot was one thing, but being blown up or gutted by a bayonet was far from appealing. But if you had to choose how you died, the worst way may have been suffocating from poison gas. They had seen rats gnawing at corpses waiting weeks for recovery and burial. If they crashed, at least their body would be incinerated. That way the trench foot would escape him, he mused. Philip was on his way to becoming an officer and a pilot in the Royal Flying Corps.

--- 56 ---
22 mi south of Lake Doiran
Greece

Sam felt dizzy. He considered whether he was hungry or if something had been wrong with the food he had eaten. He didn't know, but his head was spinning and he could no longer drive. He turned his lorry out of a two-mile-long convoy crawling from Salonika to Lake Doiran. Stopped on the roadside, a face appeared in the cab rear window. "Why are we stopping?" asked a soldier.

"I'm sick," Sam told him. "Can't drive." Two men helped Sam out of the cab and into the back. He was taken to hospital once they arrived at Lake Doiran. Illness preyed on the Salonikan Force, raising hospital admittances into the thousands. The problem was so acute that more leave days were granted. An alternate route to England was established to circumvent the ever-present submarine danger near Salonika. Troops rode trains to Bralo, Greece, then in lorries to the Port of Itea, then they took a ship to Taranto, and finally to England via Italy or France. This took weeks.

Bertie was assigned to help build a road over the mountains from Bralo to Itea. By the time Sam arrived in Southampton, he had pneumonia. Doctors told him he was home for good.

--- 57 ---
Central City District
Salonika, Greece
August 1917

On Saturday, the 18th of August, Bertie, and hundreds of other ASC corpsmen were summoned back to Salonika. A kitchen fire had escalated into a massive conflagration. And strong winds whipped the fire across houses and businesses, destroying the central city district. Two ASC fire engines had almost no effect. The summer drought had substantially reduced water reserves controlled by the Allied Forces. As a result, it made condition worse. In the army's view, the camps and hospitals that served the Allied Front had priority over its use.

"Extra Mature!" yelled a familiar voice. It was his old cheese shop friend, Max Wainright from London. "Where the bloody hell have you been?"

"On holiday," Bertie replied, wiping sweat from his brow. "Hospital with malaria."

"I thought you were dead, Mature!"

"Not yet," Bertie replied. "Where's Sam?"

"Got a blighty home. Diphtheria. Took the long way back. Mostly overland."

They had little time to talk and moved on. The British contingent was working around the clock fighting the fire. They were using military lorries to transport fire victims and their belongings to temporary settlements outside the city. By the time it was over, the fire destroyed one third of Salonika. Men of the Salonikan Force helped build shelters for the estimated 80,000 citizens who were left homeless. Days later, Bertie learned of Max Wainright's death. The cheese shop keeper died a hero by entering a burning home to rescue a child.

I'll go see his family in London, Bertie assured himself. If I ever get out of here.

--- 58 ---
Near Ypres, Belgium
September 1917
(The third battle of Ypres at Passchendale)

"Can you give me a lift to the British side?" said a tall Royal Army Medical Corps driver. "Lost my ambulance back there."

"Get in," shouted his US Army equivalent. "Clarence Harper, 103rd US Army Ambulance Service (USAAS), volunteer," he told William Evans as he climbed in. Harper had been driving the ambulance for six days straight, ferrying wounded soldiers between regimental aid posts and advanced dressing stations. His fatigue was evident.

"I'm Will Evans, Royal Army Medical Corps." Evans studied Clarence a moment. "How about I spell you, mate? You look knackered."

"Not now," Clarence shook his head. "Engine's acting up, you know?" A shell burst ahead of them, sending a shower of gravel over the roof and bonnet. They drove another thirty minutes under heavy fire when a US Army soldier frantically waved at them from the side. Harper slowed and opened his window.

"There's wounded down there." The soldier told him, gesturing. "But the road's impassable."

"We can make it," Clarence assured him. "Please honey, don't fail me," he mumbled, patting the dash. He turned the ambulance down the road the soldier had indicated. Shell bursts intensified around them almost as if the ambulance itself was the target. Evans looked at Clarence.

"They know this is an ambulance, yet they fire on us!" he said with disgust.

"The Germans have been ordered to bomb Allied hospitals," Clarence answered. "Why spare ambulances?" Another shell struck the side of the road they were on. After another mile, they stopped at a blown-out section of road.

"We can't cross that," Will Evans declared.

Harper cranked the wheel to the right. "Off the road we go!"

They arrived in a blackened field of craters. Soldiers immediately appeared from trenches hefting injured soldiers. Clarence and Evans got out and opened the rear doors. After seven men were loaded, Clarence started to shut the doors, but more wounded were brought forward.

"We can't take any more!" Clarence told them wearily. "I'll come back."

"What about up front?" one of the soldiers asked. Without waiting for an answer, he helped another injured soldier into the cab to sit squeezed between Clarence and Will. Another was strapped to the hood.

The ambulance swung around and started back. Evans pulled a map from the floor and studied it. "Where can we take them?"

Clarence rubbed his face. "I know an aid station up that way. Best we can do."

As the ambulance laboured up the road, Will looked at the injured soldier slumped next to him. He was bleeding from a chest wound and appeared near death.

"It's gonna be okay," Will murmured gently. "You're on your way home, mate."

The soldier opened his eyes when he heard Will's voice and stared at him.

Just then a gas alarm sounded and everyone in the ambulance that was capable reached for their gas masks. Will pointed through the window to a soldier in the field stumbling through debris. He was trying to get away from a cloud of gas. Clarence stopped the ambulance and got out.

"What are you doing?" Will screamed through his mask. "Are you crazy?"

Clarence ran to the wounded soldier and hurriedly placed his own mask on his face.

"Clarence, put your mask back on!" yelled Evans from the lorry cab. He leaned over and pulled the driver side door shut to help block the fumes. Harper hauled the soldier over his back and ran toward the ambulance. The soldier was heavy and Clarence slowed. He was thirty yards away from the lorry when the fumes enveloped them. Clarence started coughing, trying to hold his breath, and closed his eyes. His face and hands started burning.

"Clarence, put your bloody mask on!" screamed Evans.

When they reached the ambulance, Evans got out and helped the wounded soldier and Clarence into the back. He pulled a blanket over Clarence's face. "Can you hold this on his face?" Will yelled to the soldier nearest him. Evans sat in the driver seat. The vehicle refused to start. He tried again and again. The deadly gas surrounded them. The carburetor was smothered, he realized.

"Oh, dear God!" Evans cried. "Come on!" After several more tries, the vehicle roared to life and bumped ahead up the muddy road.

--- 59 ---
Officer Cadet Battalion 3
Bristol University
September 1917

Officer Cadet Battalion No. 3 Bristol was one of three schools operating in the university cities of Bristol, Oxford, and Cambridge. The mission of the newly established schools was to train candidates before they received officer commissions instead of after, effectively raising the standard by weeding out the less qualified candidates. Officer Cadet Battalion No. 3 maintained a complement of 400-600 cadets when Philip reported there in September 1917. He was one of 73,000 who obtained infantry commissions after being trained in an OCB. The cadets received drill, physical training and a wide-ranging course in tactical work over a four-month period. Subjects included field engineering, trench design, mining, anti-gas instruction, Lewis gun, revolver practice, topography and military law. Over-riding, clear emphasis fell on the officer's first duty; the wellbeing of men under his personal supervision. Philip had to complete OCB before he could transfer to the RFC. Fortunately for Philip, he was in good physical shape and familiar with at least some of the course material.

--- 60 ---

The tall dense shape of The Clump stood before Andrew like a sentinel. A milk lorry turned onto the hedge-lined Coppermine Lane behind The Clump and stopped. Andrew got out with his army bag and waved a thanks to the driver. He had been away from Rawhead for two-and a-half years. A familiar weather-worn sign provided direction:

⇐ *Droppingstone Farm 0.5 mi*
Burwardsley Hill Farm 1.2 mi ⇨
⇐ *Rawhead Farm 0.2 mi*

The lorry turned towards the Burwardsley Hill Farm. Andrew raised his right hand and studied it. The index finger, thumb and one-third of his palm were missing. What was once his right hand now resembled a bird's claw. He began to exercise the remaining three fingers by drawing them to the palm and releasing repeatedly. He worried about what kind of a job he could perform with a maimed hand such as his. There had to be something. Though the war left him handicapped, Andrew felt fortunate. He was one of a thousand men of the 13th Rifle Brigade who had passed through the Gate of Goodbyes train station, though by 1917, fully half of them were dead. By the end of the war, 768 were dead.

A man on a bicycle appeared. It was good old Edgar.

"Andrew!" Edgar exclaimed, extending his hand and nearly falling from his bicycle. "You're back!" Edgar noted Andrew's injured right hand and switched to his left. They shook hands. "I hope you're back for good! Can I take your bag up to the farm?" Andrew nodded.

"Tell me, Edgar, how much money does a postman earn?"

--- 61 ---
Royal Victoria Hospital
Southampton, Hampshire

After a long overland journey to avoid submarine infested waters, Sam arrived in Paris and spent three weeks in a hospital that had once been a church, then shipped to the Royal Victoria Hospital at Netley. Half the patients in the hospital census were suffering from tropical diseases and the other half from wounds inflicted in the war. The census averaged 4,000 per day at any one time. Low priority casualties, those not requiring constant care, were housed in large Red Cross tents in neighboring fields.

Recovering from pneumonia, Sam had little more to do than watch the activity taking place in and around the enormous stone structure. Opened in 1856, the Royal Victoria Hospital was Britain's largest military hospital. Before the Crimean War in 1855, no large British Army hospitals had existed for treating casualties. The site at Netley was chosen because of its proximity to the port of Southampton where hospital ships could dock. The main building was one quarter mile long, had 140 wards and over 1,000 beds. Because the regular force was overseas, most of the Royal Victoria's staff were reservists or Red Cross Voluntary

Aid Detachment (VAD) nurses. Sam was one of approximately 50,000 patients who passed through the doors of the institution during the war years. The hospital was credited with losing less than five percent of those who were admitted during that period.

Sam walked the grounds in his robe. It was a rare, sunny day, soft, white clouds decorated the azure sky. Anti-aircraft batteries occupied several locations around the hospital and he wandered near one to observe them. The enemy had invoked a vicious, new policy of bombing hospitals. Sam moved on to Cemetery Wood where a burial was taking place. A man with crutches appeared next to him. "I heard they were hiding the cemetery back here…out of view of the hospital," he said to Sam. "I guess they forgot about our tents being back here. What's your name?"

"Sam Bebbington, Army Service Corps. And you?"

"Clarence Harper, US 103rd Army Ambulance Service." He sat on a bench and doubled over, coughing. "Were you shot?" he asked Sam when he could speak. Sam had heard that type of persistent coughing before and knew Clarence was a chlorine gas victim.

"No," Sam replied. "I was shot at, though. Came down with diphtheria and then pneumonia. How about you?"

"Gassed."

"A Yank, eh? Sam was curious. Where from?"

"Greenville, South Carolina."

"What did you do before…in Greenville?" Sam asked, making conversation.

"Farm," Clarence Harper coughed again. "And make furniture, and other things. I was a newspaper reporter, too. I volunteered for the Ambulance Service. Wasn't fit for the Army. Seemed to be the thing to do at the time for typesetters and reporters. That writer Hemingway is doing the same thing. What did you do in…England, is it?"

"Farm," he smiled. They laughed at their commonality. "Well, my family runs a dairy farm in Cheshire. We make the best Cheshire cheese in England! My brother-in-law is an ambulance driver too but not because he wasn't fit. He objected to the war for a long time. So, they made him drive wounded."

Clarence shook his head. "There's no worse duty. I'd have preferred a rifle." They watched silently as a plain pine coffin was lowered into the ground and another one arrived on a cart. "I must go back in for some oxygen," Clarence admitted ruefully. "It's been a pleasure, Sam."

Sam had seen enough, too. Maybe mail was waiting for him back at his bed.

--- 62 ---

Mary Bebbington watched Edgar dismount his bicycle and dig into his shoulder bag. Tending her flower beds, she ignored him. It was a little game she played with herself. If Edgar sought her out it was good news. If he avoided her and searched for Joseph or one of the boys, it was bad news. Almost daily, Edgar and other mailmen called on the fathers of Cheshire to hand over bad news. How he knew the contents of their mail baffled her.

"Mrs. Bebbington!" called Edgar. Mary closed her eyes and heaved a sigh of relief. She turned to greet Edgar who was negotiating the latch on the entrance gate. "I've a letter for you!" He told her excitedly. "It's from Buckingham Palace!"

Mary accepted the envelope and studied the front. It bore the official mark of The Crown. "The Queen?" Mary gasped. "What could she want with me?"

"It won't be bad news," Edgar suggested. "They don't do that, unless of course one of 'em did something extraordinary like save a whole unit, but we'd hear of it in the *Gazette* if that were the case, right?"

Mary glared at him. "My sons are capable of that!"

Edgar looked at the ground. "Well, of course they are," he murmured contritely.

Mary waved to Sam in the cornfield. Sam shut off the mechanical hay thrasher and trotted in.

"Sam, would you ring the bell?" Sam looked at the letter in her hand. "Is it Bertie?" he asked her, a worried look on his face.

"I don't know....do as I ask, please, Sam!"

"Yes, Mum." Sam hurried off.

Mary entered the house and closed the door. Holding the letter gingerly in front of her, she slowly made her way to the family room. She studied it. The writing. The printing. The quality of the paper. The Royal mark. The address of the palace. She was looking for some indication of the letters' content before she opened it.

What has happened to one of my boys? She fretted. Has Philip crashed? Did Clem drown? Have they found Bertie?

Outside, Sam, Dave, Jack, Tom, Andrew, and Mollie trooped into the farmhouse, dusty and smelly from their work. A summons that took them away from their chores was rare as there was simply too much work to be done. They seldom saw each other between meals and, unless there was an emergency such as a fire or a serious injury, a summons like this did not happen.

They found seats in the small room. Joseph sat beside Mary, Sam by the door, Dave, Jack, and Mollie by the window. Mary held the unopened letter in her lap.

"What is it, Mum?" Sam asked after a weighted pause.

"What does the Crown have to say to working people like us?" Joseph asked irritably. He took the letter from her and ripped it open. Mary's worried eyes went to his, anxiously. Joseph read aloud.

Buckingham Palace
London
October 3, 1917

Dear Mr. and Mrs. Bebbington,

> *We are informed that your family has contributed five of your sons to the defense of England. We thank you for your patriotism. Godspeed, and may they come home safely.*

George R. Mary R.

Suddenly furious, Mary snatched the letter from Joseph. She rushed to the fire and threw the letter into the flames.

"Mary! What the devil?" exclaimed Joseph in surprise. He reached to retrieve the letter, but it had disappeared into ashes.

"They took my sons and sent them to die!" she squawked. "What do we need with their thanks? They already took my scouts. No bloody letter will ever bring them back!"

--- 63 ---
Officer Cadet Battalion 3
Bristol University
January 1918

Philip and his class were abruptly awakened from a Bristol University dormitory just after 4:00 a.m. and marched to a neighboring field in full pack. Twilight had barely touched Bristol and physical training instructors had officer candidates sweating it out on the PT field. Standing out amongst the howling voices of the instructors were cheeky, always motivating British accents urging candidates to push themselves, but also to ensure the future officers conducted training safely. While crawling through mud and leaves with a compass in his right hand and rifle in his left, questions were screamed at Philip and the others with earsplitting volume.

"How do you expect to lead men in battle if you haven't been there yourself?"

"Did you think OCB was just a classroom course with weekend trips to town?"

"You see those men up there?" an NCO yelled, pointing to a company of recruits on their bellies twenty yards ahead.

"They are your men! They are your first duty! You earn their loyalty!"

--- 64 ---
Struma Valley, Balkans
April 1918

Bertie arrived near the Balkan Front after another long, dusty journey carrying supplies. He unstrapped his mules and, after removing their burdens, led them to a watering trough. He gave each an affectionate pat as they drank. Then he picked up the sound of a horse in distress. In the distance, he saw an infantry captain straining to subdue a brown gelding. The animal was rearing and stomping the ground while the captain yanked hard on its lead. When the officer picked up a stick and began flogging it, Bertie ran to the horse's aid.

"Easy, easy, fella!" Bertie yelled as he grabbed the reins away from the captain.

"Stand down, Private! I'll not have this beast defy me!" the captain roared. He struck the horse's rump repeatedly.

"Sir, there's no need for that!" Bertie exclaimed. He recognized the captain as A.G. Wilkinson from their meeting in Salisbury. He then saw the 921 tattooed on the horse's rump. Bertie noticed signs the poor beast had endured many beatings since Bertie had last seen him nuzzling a mare at the beach off the Pelion coast road. "Errol!" Bertie cried. Wilkinson swung at the horse again and Bertie, stepping between them, tore the stick from the captain, knocking him down. The two rolled in the dirt, grunting and punching each other. Errol skipped nervously out of the way. ASC soldiers from the supply tents hurried over to separate the two men. Once they were subdued and facing each other, the captain swung and struck Bertie hard in the face. An infantry major and more soldiers joined the party.

"Here, what's the meaning of this?" The major glared at Wilkinson.

"This man struck me!" Wilkinson replied.

Recovering, Bertie wiped blood from his nose and mouth. "The captain was abusing this horse, sir!"

"I don't care what he was doing!" the major said. "Striking an officer is a Courts Martial offense!" He gestured to two NCOs. "Place this man under arrest."

"Yessir," the NCOs said, and led Bertie away.

The major turned to the captain. "Didn't you receive instruction in the care and training of horses? Report to the command tent at once."

"Sir." The captain saluted and stalked off.

The major walked over to Errol and looked him over. Marks of excessive whipping and other signs of abuse were clearly visible.

The next morning, Bertie stood at attention before several officers at HQ in Salonika.

"Private Bert Bebbington, 4th New Armies Horse Transport Company, Army Service Corps, having been accused of striking an officer and after hearing all evidence and testimony we find you guilty as charged. Have you anything to say before sentencing?"

Bertie spoke in the most respectful manner he could. "Sirs, it is my duty to take care of the animals in my charge. I take that duty seriously and I was trying to do it to the best of my abilities yesterday. I've known that horse since my ship was torpedoed and I saved him and others from drowning. The captain was whipping him for no reason, sir. Errol didn't deserve that kind of beating."

The three-officer panel exchanged uncomfortable glances. They were bemused that Bertie referred to the horse by name but they knew dedication when they saw it. After brief deliberation, they decided to drop the charges against Bertie on the condition he transfer to the Labour Corps. He accepted.

By the spring of 1918, influenza, sand fly fever, pneumonia and malaria had fully ravaged the British Salonikan Force. An estimated 160,000 hospital admissions had occurred since 1915. Once stabilized, they were rotated back to England via the lengthy overland route. Bertie's first project with the Labour Corps was strengthening the Itea Road which constituted the first leg of the route. Sam was one in a group of 2,000 who were initially sent to England on the Itea Road. Since arriving in Salonika, both he and Bertie made repeated inquiries about each other, and were even in proximity at times, but neither was able to learn what had happened to the other.

--- 65 ---
RFC Upavon Aerodrome, Wiltshire

When Philip entered flight school in early 1918, there were over 100 training squadrons, 30 specialist schools and nearly 7,000 aircraft in the UK. Pilots were instructed in all aspects of air combat in a multi-month course that included 50 hours of solo flying, up considerably from the 15 hours given at the height of the war.

Philip handed his army discharge papers to the gate guard at the Upavon Aerodrome. "An 'ow's the weather in Bristol, sir?" the guard inquired as he quietly read:

War Office
Park Buildings, St. James's Park, S.W.I.
21 March 1918

Sir,
I am directed to inform you that No. 14679
P. Bebbington, 9th Battalion, Cheshire Regiment
has been appointed to a temporary commission as

Second Lieutenant in the Royal Flying Corps, and
to request that you will carry out his discharge for
the purpose stated with effect from 22nd February
1918.

I am, Sir, Your obedient Servant,
S. Pinkerton, 2nd Lt.

"Cold and miserable," Philip answered.

"Me step-sister's family's from there," he told Philip, handing him his orders and identification. He pointed to a sprawling two-story building in the center of the aerodrome. "They started serving supper an hour ago, if you's a mind."

Philip took his papers and thanked the corporal. He was indeed hungry, so he headed directly for the Officer's Mess.

Mechanics on the aerodrome were servicing F.E.2bs and D.H.1 trainer aircraft. Overhead, a squadron of F.E.2bs approached and he stopped to watch them. Nightfall was still a few minutes away and visibility was clear, though an orange band to the west hinted at rain later that evening. Out of the west, four F.E.2bs began a slow descent toward the airfield. They served as bombers and fighters along with single-seat D.H.2 pusher biplanes and Nieuport 11s. He knew the F.E.2b was the main reason German air superiority over France had ended. Fascinated, Philip climbed over a rail fence to get a closer look at one. Glancing up at the sky, Philip collided with a ranking officer.

"Oh, I am terribly sorry, sir!" Philip exclaimed. He quickly noted the officer was a colonel. "I was trying to see them land!"

"Well, you landed me instead," the officer replied smiling, retrieving his hat and a large bouquet of flowers from the ground. "Beautiful, aren't they?"

"Yessir!" Philip agreed. The planes were completing their landing. One bounced three times before it settled. "Beautiful, indeed."

"I meant the flowers, lieutenant! The squadron needs practice, however." The colonel hurried to a waiting car. Late for a dinner date maybe, Philip mused, looking after the colonel. He would remember his clumsy introduction to the Central Flying School.

The CFS was formed on the training grounds in June 1912 just outside of Upavon Village. The school was established to supply the military wings of the newly formed RFC, with pilots. Back in 1913, the first night landing in England took place at Upavon. The same year, Winston Churchill, First Lord of the Admiralty, flew in a Farman biplane while visiting the airbase. Early in the war, pilots serving at Upavon developed the CFS Bomb Sight which was used extensively on the Western Front.

After a quick meal, Philip found his quarters and turned in. He was too excited to sleep and spent a restless night.

"This aircraft is an F.E.2c, a 'pusher' biplane," a flight instructor explained to a group of pilot trainees seated on the ground. "Notice that the engine is mounted behind the pilot. The reason for this is to avoid having to fire a Lewis gun through the propeller blade, effectively shooting the bloody plane down. It also provides a clear view for the observer-gunner. With a wingspan of fifty feet and a maximum weight of 3,300 pounds, this is a very big aircraft. The upper center section alone is nearly sixteen feet wide. The horizontal stabilizer is the size of a wing itself. The drag it creates only allows a cruise speed of seventy-five miles per hour. A hefty price," he finished. Philip and the other students listened intently as the lecture went on.

"She is fitted with a Beardmore 120 horse power, liquid-cooled, inline engine." The instructor walked to the front of the aircraft. "This section, resembling a bathtub, is called the nacelle."

A student sitting beside Philip extended his hand.

"Hello, I'm Stuart Henley."

"Philip Bebbington."

"Where are you from?"

"The Somme."

Henley thought a moment. Anyone who came from that part of the war and lived to tell about it must have a few stories.

"No, I mean, in England?"

"Cheshire."

"That's a big county."

"Chester. Grew up on a farm called Rawhead. How about you?"

"Scotland. Edinburgh."

The instructor continued. "When you stand up to shoot, all of you from the knees up is exposed. There is no belt to hold you. Only your grip on the gun and the sides of the nacelle stand between you and eternity!"

Philip swallowed and exchanged a look with Henley. The instructor continued. "Toward the front of the nacelle is a hollow steel rod with a swivel mount where the gun is anchored. There's a second gun mounted between the observer and the pilot. This one fires over the F.E.2c's upper wing to protect the plane from rear attack. You stand right up out of the nacelle with your feet on the coaming to adjust and fire this gun. You don't have to worry about anything except getting blown out by the blast of air or tossed out if the pilot makes a wrong move. There are no parachutes or belts."

After the class, Henley and Philip climbed a ladder to look at the interior of the plane. Henley seated himself in the cockpit while Philip remained on the ladder, waiting his turn.

"It's not going to go well for the observer if this noses over!" Philip speculated. "Hope our pilot is worth his salt."

After the field introduction, Philip sat at a desk in a classroom and looked at the cover of his notebook:

> *The "Ideal" Royal Flying Corps Loose Leaf*
> *Note Book, Course 48A, Class 10*
> *P. Bebbington, Cadet*
> *April 1918*

He opened it and began taking notes. Instructors Lieutenant Mace and Captain Williams, conducted a class on aircraft instrumentation, often pointing to an already crammed blackboard:

> *Instruments:*
> *Air speed indicator*
> *Altimeter*
> *Compass*
> *Inclinometer*
> *Oil gauge*
> *Petrol gauge*
> *Pressure gauge in petrol tank*
> *Pulsometer*
> *Pump for maintaining pressure in petrol tank*
> *Revolution indicator*
> *Thermometer*
> *Watch; for time duration of flight*

The students filed into another classroom and sat at desks. After a one-hour lecture on navigation, Philip stood and looked out the window at a trainer plane.

"School," Philip muttered to Henley with disgust. "I spent the last four and a half months in school learning to be an officer of all things. When do we start flying?"

"In five minutes, lieutenant," Lt. Mace answered as he walked past.

Having watched the others find their seats, Philip figured out how to maneuver into his Avro 504 trainer seat successfully.

"Switches on," Lt. Mace called to a grounds man who was standing in front of the propeller blades. The man reached up, grabbed one propeller blade and gave a hard-downward swing. Philip studied the controls in front of him and heard the engine catch and roar to life. Wheel chocks were pulled away and the instructor seated behind eased the plane forward. The Avro trainer rumbled down the runway, picking up speed, bounced once, then rose smoothly from the grass airstrip. Trees appeared in Philip's line of sight and he wondered nervously if they would clear them. Another Avro appeared to his right and veered off. The nose of Philip's plane lifted, the ground fell away and the trees slipped below them. He would never forget the first time he went aloft. A dairy farmer's son flying, he marveled. They flew over Southampton and within minutes were soaring over the English Channel. Flying 500 feet above the surf, he saw the cliffs of Dover directly below them. Philip was thrilled. After an hour in the air practicing turns, slips and stalls, they returned to Upavon and landed effortlessly.

He climbed down and stomped his feet as one of them had gone numb some time earlier. Engine fumes overwhelmed him. He rubbed his face hard and leaned over, vomiting on his boots.

"What's wrong?" asked a mechanic on a ladder nearby.

"It's the smell," Philip managed.

"Castor oil from the engine," the mechanic informed him, knowingly. "We can't use crude 'cuz it hardens from the cold at high altitude. 'Ere, 'ave some uh 'dis." The man pulled a small flask from his hip pocket and uncorked it with his three remaining front teeth. Philip sniffed the mouth of the bottle and pondered the label.

"Blackberry brandy?" Philip guessed.

"It's the only stuff that works! Proven in France. A shot before take-off and three once you're back. 'At's the medicine."

"Thank you," Philip said taking a swig. *It was not a bad remedy*, he thought as he felt his stomach settle.

The mechanic walked away and Philip followed him, sipping the brandy as he went. The mechanic started to repair exposed wires and cables. Philip wanted to learn more about the engines so he watched the man work. "Looks like a smashed piano," Philip chuckled. "How do you manage all the wires?"

"Easy," said the mechanic with a straight face. "We sit a bird inside and see if he gets out. If he does, we know a wire's missing!" Another mechanic watched Philip's face to see if he bought the tale.

"Bloody mechanics," Philip muttered and handed back the bottle. The mechanics looked at each other and laughed heartily. The clowns probably tell the same joke to every new pilot, Philip supposed. They ought to make them fly these death traps, he thought.

The next morning a most peculiar arrangement of tail wheeled aircraft greeted Philip and his flight school classmates. Ten two-seat trainer planes had been rolled onto the field. The men were expecting a day of airborne instruction, but that was not how it turned out.

"Okay, you Huns," the instructor quipped. "You'll recognize the aircraft behind me as trainers. The one important distinction is five feet of wing has been clipped from both sides."

The students studied the clipped wing aircraft, wondering how planes with short wings would be used. Probably assembled from damaged aircraft, Philip surmised.

"The aircraft cannot fly with the reduced wing area. This change is intentional. The purpose of these aircraft is to teach you how to taxi and bring your aircraft to full throttle. You will not become airborne at full throttle in these airplanes. Once you master these tasks, you will begin airborne flight instruction with a mentor. Find your assigned aircraft."

RFC instructors had borrowed this method from French flight schools. The clipped planes were affectionately dubbed "penguins". After hours of practice, the students should be able to taxi from side to side to see ahead, then keep their aircraft straight for takeoff. An instructor and student conducted a preflight inspection and climbed into the cockpit of a flightless penguin. The other students jockeyed for the best view. "Switches on!" yelled LT Mace. A mechanic swung the propeller clockwise and the engine sputtered to life. Then he pulled the wheel chocks away.

"Proceed to taxi!" the instructor yelled to the student. The penguin eased into motion and rolled away from the group. About one hundred yards down the runway, the penguin started turning in circles. Some in the class laughed. Captain Williams snapped, "We'll see who's laughing when it's your turn!" The group quieted. Thirty minutes later, the students were each assigned to a penguin. Philip stood next to his instructor.

"Climb aboard," the instructor invited.

Normally, the pilot's position was raised so he could see over the observer-gunner, but in the penguin he sat next to Philip.

A mechanic climbed onto the wing root and balanced himself while he filled each of the six brass primer cups from a squirt can of fuel. He then clambered to the ground and eyed Philip. "All switches off," Philip called. The mechanic slowly rotated the two-bladed prop. The man signaled "read." Philip checked all the cockpit controls one last time: fuel selector main tank to carb, air selector to hand pump, air pressure to two and one-half psi. He looked at the sight glass gauge on the side of the tank and saw it was full. Then he moved the spark advance to retard.

"Clear!" Philip yelled and selected two on the magneto switch which allowed the engine to run on both of its power generators. He then turned the booster magneto switch to on.

While Philip was thoughtfully engaged, the engineer stood before the engine, angling himself to avoid the rotating propeller. The engine would rumble to life with a spin of the booster mag if all went well. Otherwise the engineer would have to manually swing the propeller to start the engine. It roared to life and the mechanic stepped clear.

Philip was anxious to get into the air. He knew the instruments from hours of practice in soap crates and now he was in an aircraft with clipped wings. He saw an officer drop a flag well in front of the line and the penguins eased forward.

The taxi effort became a circus. The ten penguins started off in a straight path but soon began veering to the left or right nearly hitting each other. One hundred fifty yards down the field the penguins became scattered. Some had eased off their throttles and were sitting motionless while others zigzagged precipitously in irregular paths at full throttle. One crashed into another, shearing off the plane's tail. The two students climbed out of their destroyed aircraft yelling angrily at each other. Then they started throwing punches and their instructors intervened.

"Take your foot off the bloody rudder pedal!" screamed Philip's instructor. His penguin was traveling in a tight circle to the left because his foot was pressing hard on the left pedal. Philip lifted the offending foot and the penguin straightened out. But soon he was heading into the path of another plane.

"Press the right pedal or you'll hit him!" the instructor screeched.

In the aerodrome tower, a flight operations officer was watching the spectacle through field glasses. Several more penguins collided. The fight between the two students resumed once their instructors stepped away from them. The operations officer began laughing and pointing and soon more officers joined in.

Clipped wing instruction never failed to inspire hilarity among viewers. LTC Patrick Underwood saw the others enjoying the spectacle and wandered over to the window. He took in the calamity, shook his head and managed a tight smile. "The bright future of the RAF," he pronounced as two more aircraft smacked into each other.

Over the next weeks, Philip learned an observer's duties, navigation, radio communication, bombing, gunnery, and aerial maneuvering. As pilot and commander of the aircraft he was obliged to know all of the actions required to make the aircraft and effective fighting machine. It was at this time when the Royal Naval Air Service merged with the RFC to form the Royal Air Force (RAF).

--- 66 ---

Edgar continued to deliver mail on his bicycle until 1918. One afternoon he arrived at Rawhead on a motorcycle equipped with a sidecar. Tom begged a ride and Edgar took him along for the rest of the day's deliveries. He appreciated that he could complete his route faster.

After running an errand in Broxton, Tom passed an automobile garage with a motorcycle parked in front of it. He had seen it there previously and decided to stop. Dismounting his horse, Tom looked the motorcycle over with keen interest. "It's a 1907 Indian Single Cylinder," said a voice. A mechanic appeared, wiping his hands on a rag. "Needs work, though." Tom had not taken his eyes off the machine.

"Go ahead and sit on it if you like," the mechanic offered. Tom swung his leg over the old motorcycle and eagerly gripped the handles.

"Would you sell it?" He asked staring at the man. The mechanic rolled his eyes.

"I suppose. Ten pounds?"

"Could I work for it on weekends?" Tom inquired. The mechanic nodded.

"If it's okay with your mum."

Jack on sickle mower in front of The Clump, c. 1918
Photo courtesy of the author

--- 67 ---
RAF Upavon, Wiltshire
September 1918

The group's motto, omnibus princeps, first in all things, was appropriate for Britain's oldest squadron. Since it formed in 1914, Number 33 Squadron had participated in almost every major British military operation. One of the RFC's original three squadrons, Number 33 was remolded at Filton in January 1916 from what remained after Number 12 Squadron departed for France.

Major P.B. Joubert de la Ferte, took command of the squadron at Filton and saw it through its workup period. The squadron moved east to Kirton-in-Lindsey in late 1918 and took on Home Defense duties or in other words to intercept enemy airship raids on the North Midlands. The venerable squadron continued the task through the remainder of the war, employing F.E.2cs, D.H.1s and Avro 504 aircraft.

"I'm assigning you to coastal patrol flights." Joubert de la Ferte told Philip. "You'll fly two missions per day from Kirton-in-Lindsey Aerodrome."

"Not France?"

"We have pilots there already. Too many now because they're not being shot down as fast. Your plane will be armed, but your days in France are over."

Leaving HQ, Philip saw Stuart Henley.

"What'd they give us?" Henley asked, pausing to light a cigarette.

"Kirton-in-Lindsey," Philip told him, frowning. "Lincolnshire. We're to fight werewolves in the Moors."

"What?"

"Middlesbrough to Dover twice a day," Philip translated.

"Aircraft?"

"F2s and 504s."

"Biffs and Avros? They're antiques!"

"And the F.E.2.c. The newer aircraft are reserved for the offensive, I guess."

"Yes, but what about Zeppelin raids on England?" Henley asked. "I know it hasn't happened since July when that Canadian seaplane downed one in a Camel. What was his name?"

"Culley,"

"Yes, Culley, that's him!" Henley shook his head in wonder. "Extraordinary young chap off the *Redoubt*."

"Well, let's look at it this way. We just might survive the war."

--- **68** ---

"Listen to this!" Jack was reading from a newspaper at the family table. "It's from the London *Gazette*: 'November 1, 1918. British Army confirms five brothers of the name Souls from the village of Cotswolds Dales in Great Rissington have been killed. Albert Souls, 20, Frederick Souls, 30, and Walter Souls, 24, in 1916, and Arthur Souls, 30 and Alfred Souls, 30, in 1918. Albert and Walter Souls were of the Second Worcester Regiment and later transferred to the Machine Gun Corps. Arthur, Alfred, and Frederick were members of the 16th Battalion Cheshire Regiment. Upon hearing of the death of his twin, Alfred, in the spring offensive, Arthur Souls reportedly lost the will to live. During an engagement at the Bretonneaux Plateau he performed an undisclosed fatal act of valor for which he is to be awarded the Military Medal.'"

He laid the *Gazette* on the table. The silence in the room was deafening. Joseph, Mollie, Dave, Jack, and Tom looked at Mary. "Their poor mother," she whispered. "God help the mothers." She withdrew slowly into the cheese parlor with Joseph following.

Joseph moved beside Mary as she lifted a wheel of cheese from a bin and slid it onto the table. "They are coming back, Mary," he murmured gently. "The war may be ending." She turned and hugged him, weary of the years of worry and uncertainty. Joseph leaned forward and stamped the cheese wheel with its label:

Cheshire Cheese, Aged 3 months
Rawhead Farm, Ballantyne Estate

--- 69 ---

It was a sullen, overcast day in Cheshire. Mary chose to work indoors making cheese, mixing bread, preparing their meal. As their elder brothers had done, Dave, Jack, and Tom had quit Bickerton School to work on the farm. Through the kitchen window, Mary watched Tom wheel his motorcycle out of the barn into the courtyard. She went to the kitchen door. "Where are you off to, Tom?" she called.

"Just going for a ride, Mum," Tom told her. "Maybe to Cholmondeley Castle and back." After checking the petrol level, he sat astride and used all his weight to press down on the kick starter. The machine rumbled to life with his first effort.

"If the war doesn't take our men, a girl certainly will," Mary laughed to Mollie. Watching Tom, Mary imagined he would become a machinist or mechanic at the iron works in Chester. That might lead to something. Or maybe he could finish school and go to university. She did not believe her youngest son was destined to be a farm labourer or a miner. Nor a soldier, she prayed, the memory of that patronizing letter from the Queen still stinging her heart. She had not encouraged him to join the Boy Scouts for fear it might persuade him to enlist in the army. It was November 1918 and the war that was supposed to be over by Christmas 1914, but would soon be starting its fifth year. Please God let it end before it takes Dave, Jim, and Jack, she prayed silently. It had to end before Tom would be old enough. Dave was seventeen now and already had his physical at Chester Castle. He was just waiting to be called up. The army wasn't picky any more.

Tom waved to her as he drove past the window and was gone.

One hundred miles to the east, Philip walked to headquarters alongside his observer when Stuart Henley waved at him from a F.E.2c. Philip had just returned from a coastal patrol flight. He stopped to see what Henley wanted.

"Want to come along in the observer's seat?" Henley asked. He was going through his preflight checks.

"Where?" Philip asked.

"Liverpool to Penzance and back. We'll fly over that farm you talk about!"

Philip checked his watch. "Back by three? I'm seeing a young lady tonight," Philip smiled.

"Climb aboard!"

Philip climbed into the nacelle and checked the Lewis gun, not that he would need it. Minutes later they were aloft, and within an hour, Philip recognized the Peckforton Hills and the Rawhead Escarpment. He turned around and gestured to Henley, who eased the F.E.2c down in response and descended several hundred feet. Philip pointed down and to the left and Henley smiled and gave a thumb's up. Just east of the escarpment, he saw a patch of cleared land and guessed it must be Rawhead Farm.

Mary walked out of the kitchen with a big basket of wet laundry. She heard the drone of Philip's plane, put the basket down and looked up at the sky. She did not know Philip was in the plane but she thought of him as she watched the little aircraft circling. Finally, the F.E.2C flew on toward Liverpool.

Tom pulled over and stopped near a petrol station. He unscrewed the fuel cap on the tank and looked in. He could make it back to Rawhead if he only went as far as Noman's Heath then turned around, so he headed off and passed Cholmondeley Castle, the seat of the Cholmondeley family since the 12 Century. The original structure was replaced only at the start of the 19th century with a massive, crenellated castle. It took Tom fifteen minutes just to travel the length of the grounds. After reaching Noman's Heath, he turned onto a gravel road he knew led to Bickerton. From there, he could take a short-cut across the fields to Rawhead. He would have to open and close a few gates along the way.

A mile down, a milk lorry approached an unmarked intersection. The driver reached for a cigarette and matches on the dash and bent his head to light up. Glancing up and down the crossroads, he proceeded across, even though he could not see past the thick hedgerows on the right. Too late, Tom squeezed the brake tightly as the lorry came from the left. His bike swerved to the left and Tom went flying head over heels. He saw the ground and sky tumbling around him, then landed with a sickening thud on a grassy slope.

From Liverpool, the F.E.2C descended to 200 feet and followed the coast. They flew over Holyhead, Pwhelli,

Aberystwyth, Fishguard, and Swansea on the Welsh coast. Philip loved seeing the view from the air. To their dismay, they observed no Zeppelins or foreign vessels. Off Bideford, just a few miles northeast of Penzance and the mythical ruins of King Arthur's Castle at Tintagel, Philip gestured for Henley to descend. They passed over a small naval vessel, circling once. The sailors waved from the decks and the British flag it flew confirmed a false alarm. At Penzance, the F.E.2C turned northeast and began the homeward leg.

Thirty minutes later there was a large bang. Philip turned to face Henley who was also looking behind at the engine, which was trailing smoke. Looking down at the instrument panel, he was alarmed to see the oil pressure was dropping fast. Henley turned back to face Philip and drew a finger across his neck, signaling they were in trouble. From training, they knew their best chance of survival was to make the aerodrome where crash crews were always on alert, but they were still miles away. Henley eased the F.E.2C down to 500 feet and began lowering the flaps. Philip checked his restraints and started surveying the terrain ahead for a suitable landing spot. A minute later there was a loud crack from the starboard wing and a sputter from the engine. Then another bang and the engine quit completely. The F.E.2C began gliding downward fast.

If Henley dove any lower, he would hit trees. He dared not maneuver, losing precious airspeed and lift in the process. Despite his efforts, the heavy F.E.2C plunged. They were going to be the first ones at the scene of the crash. Philip tightened his seat belt again. Henley worked the controls, which were becoming sluggish for lack of airspeed. He remembered from flight school how furious a struggle it was to survive a crash. The F.E.2C, as with all World War I aircraft, had no hydraulic lines to transfer mere pounds of human hand or foot pressure to hundreds of pounds of leverage on the flaps, ailerons, and rudder.

Philip wished he was at the controls for this flight but had to rely on the younger pilot's skill. *My life is again in another man's hands*, he thought. Why did he agree to go? He had a choice this time. He felt his heart pounding from adrenaline.

The plane hit a grassy field hard. Bouncing once, the tail lifted forward and they cartwheeled. The last thought Philip had before turning upside down, and blackness, was whether there would be a fire.

--- 70 ---

Mary walked back from the south field after delivering bread, cheese, and apples to their workers. The dogs, Bo and Wendy, trotted beside her. She opened their pen but stopped after seeing the silhouettes of two men in uniform standing at the courtyard gate. She shielded her eyes from the sun and tried to make out who they were. It was too early for Edgar, but he had a motorcycle now so it's possible he was ahead of schedule. Or was it William Cutter come to collect the rent? Could it be a telegram from the army? She could read the name in the *Gazette* or on lists posted at Chester Castle, but that would be quite impersonal of the army. God in heaven, who could she have lost? Bertie was in the eastern Mediterranean and had not been heard from for some time. Philip was with the RAF in Kirton-in-Lindsey. Clem had been on the *Resolution* in Portsmouth since mid-1916 working on a retrofit. Sam had returned months ago from the Balkans, and Andrew was back from the Somme with only half his right hand and perhaps half his usual self. Perhaps one had perished from typhus, diphtheria, pneumonia, malaria or some other disease she had never heard of. She knew illness was killing soldiers at twice the rate as the battlefield. Her hands held her chest and her mouth moved in fervent prayer as she neared the uniformed figures. She saw it was Constable Billings and Edgar. He looked at her stone-faced.

"What is it, Edgar?" she asked faintly. Her eyes searched his hands for a telegram. But there was no telegram.

"Thomas has been killed," he blurted. Joseph came out of the barn wiping axle grease on a cloth.

"His motorcycle crashed near Cholmondeley Castle on the Whitchurch-Tarporley Road."

Having delivered the terrible news, poor old Edgar could say no more. He stared numbly at the ground. Sam arrived and looked questioningly at his mother. Mary could not feel her legs. She slowly sank to the earth and sat still with her legs folded under her. She did not understand what Edgar was saying.

"Take your mother to the house," Joseph told Sam, his face ashen. "Find Mollie and Martha."

"Tom is at the Bickerton Clinic, Joseph," Constable Billings said. "I can drive you there."

"Sam, after you take your mother inside, ride to Brown Knowl and fetch Father Bentley," Joseph told their son. "Ask him to meet us at the clinic."

Edgar was crying. Joseph looked at him. "I found him on the side of the road," Edgar managed. "His motorcycle was in the field all messed up. Not a soul around. Bloody people must have hit him and kept going." Edgar stumbled to a trough and splashed water over his head.

"We'll find out what happened, Joseph," Billings declared quietly.

"Why am I God's chosen bearer of all dreadful news?" Edgar asked of his reflection in the water.

--- 71 ---

Mary held up a photograph of Philip standing and half-hidden by a bandage wrapped around his head. He was grinning as if proud of the injury. Another photo was of Thomas standing with his motorcycle in the courtyard. She flipped Philip's picture and read the note on the back:

Your humble son after the crash.
Concussion, black eyes, split lips, a cut forehead.

Philip.

The little Brown Knowl Chapel in Bickerton was packed with mourners, some standing in the aisles and in back. The community had become all too familiar with the service for the dead. They had endured the loss of many young men killed in the war. Tom Bebbington's death was terrible, but not a shock. The war was over and four of the five Bebbington brothers who had gone off to fight in it had been spared, perhaps Bertie as well. It was a cruel irony that their youngest died in his hometown and not in France or elsewhere. Minister Thomas Bentley nodded at Mary, who walked to the pulpit. Eyes still red, her face only a mask of courage, she read aloud in a strong, clear voice:

> *"Where is my wand'ring boy tonight?*
> *The boy of my tend'rest care,*
> *The boy that was my joy and light,*
> *The child of my love and prayer?*
> *Oh where is my boy tonight!*
> *Once he was pure as morning's dew,*
> *As he knelt at his mother's knee;*
> *No face was so bright, no heart more true,*
> *And none was as sweet as he.*
> *Oh where is my boy tonight?*
> *Oh, could I see you now, my boy,*
> *As fair as in olden time,*
> *When prattle and smile made a home a joy,*
> *And life was a merry chime!*
> *Oh where is my boy tonight?*
> *Go for my wandering boy tonight;*
> *Go, search for him where you will,*
> *But bring him to me with all his blight,*
> *And tell him I love him still."*

It was a poem written by the American Baptist minister and hymn composer Robert Lowry in 1877. Mary reseated herself beside Joseph. She wanted to say something personal about Tom but could not bring herself to do it. What was there to say? He had lived such a short life. After the benediction, George,

Sam, Clem, Jack, Dave, and Edgar carried Tom's coffin out of the chapel. At Mary's request, the coffin was constructed of pine from The Clump and was buried in the chapel cemetery.

Robert and Heidi Bryden made their way through the crowd of mourners after the burial. "We are so very sorry, Mary." Bryden said, taking her hand. "If there is anything we can do."

"Could you please find Bertie?" she pleaded. "At least, tell me if he is all right."

--- 72 ---

The hammering of the steam tractor in the east field grew louder. Mary opened her eyes but didn't move. She had been in bed for days, overcome with the shock and grief over Tom's death. Mollie brought her tea and slices of buttered bread with jam. Mary managed a few sips of tea but could not swallow any food. She told herself that work might distract her but she could not summon the strength even to rise from her bed. When her father died years ago, her mother told her the pain of losing a loved one became more bearable with time. Time was the only answer. But that advice didn't apply now, when the hurt was new and raw. Her work could wait until she could cope with the fact that her baby was dead and lying in the cold ground. Hot tears slid down her ample cheeks. She closed her eyes and pressed the blanket to her face.

Moments later, she heard knocking at the kitchen door. She groaned, hoping that whoever it was would give up and find Joseph or Mollie. But the rapping became more insistent. She crawled out of bed and wrapped herself in a warm shawl.

Opening the door, she stared with swollen eyes at the young woman at the door.

"Good morning," the woman smiled tentatively. "I hope I'm not disturbing you! I'm the District Nurse. Minnie Davis." She reached out to shake Mary's hand.

"Oh," Mary said in consternation. She shook Minnie's hand weakly. "I wasn't expecting visitors today. We've had a death in the family."

"I am so sorry," Minnie said, taking a step back. "I came to look in on Lieutenant Bebbington. I can come back tomorrow?"

"Oh, Philip, my son. He's just there." Mary pointed through the window to the east field. Minnie squinted in that direction. She could just make out the form of a man standing in silhouette. "He's been out there all morning," Mary told her.

"I'll just pop out to see him, shall I?" The nurse nodded at Mary and walked to the stairs. "Thank you, ma'am," she called over her shoulder. "My condolences, as well." Mary watched her briefly and then wandered back to bed.

On the hill, Philip was deep in thought. Rawhead was quiet and peaceful, very different from the ravaged farmlands he had seen in France. He had received word of Tom's accident by telegram while he was in hospital recuperating. His injuries prevented him from attending the funeral. Henley had survived the crash. A farmer and his son pulled them from the wreckage and, to Philip's everlasting relief, there had been no fire. Now he imagined how Rawhead might look, had the war reached Cheshire. Like Ypres, he thought, his mouth twisting. Prior to 1916, Ypres was a well-preserved, classic, medieval city. Now it was a blackened heap of rubble. He remembered the cold, wet, filthy trenches he'd lived in for weeks and the men he had shared them with who were no longer alive. When he departed Folkestone on the *Ivernia* with the 9th Cheshire Battalion, there were 33 officers and 988 other ranks. Now, 713 of those men were gone. The 10th Battalion fared even worse. Ninety percent of them had been killed, mostly from heavy artillery bombardments at Bazentin. By 1919, losses to the Regiment had reached 8,420. All the men he had known were gone. Heathcote, Corns, Clayton, Ellor, Birch and dozens more.

Looking down, his eye caught something half-buried in the crumbled earth. It looked like a piece of his old cricket bat, the one he had broken back in 1911. He picked it up and took a slow practice swing with one-hand, remembering that long-ago game. For an instant, he managed a smile.

"Hello," called a faint voice. Philip placed his weak hand in his uniform tunic. He glanced back and saw a young woman trudging toward him.

He straightened. "Hello, Miss..." Philip struggled to remember her name. She had large brown eyes and short dark hair that curled softly from under her cap. He thought her attractive.

"Davis," she supplied. "Minnie Davis." Philip walked toward her.

"From the Bickerton Clinic. Yes, I remember. Please forgive me." He gently replaced the piece of bat on the ground. "What brings you to Rawhead, Miss Davis?" he asked.

"I came to check on you and make sure your injuries are healing properly. How's your arm?" She looked around for something he could sit on and led him to a stone wall at the edge of the field. She took his hand with her left, pushed his sleeve up and felt his forearm with her right. She inspected it for swelling, any abnormal sensations of heat. "Do you have any pain?"

"Some." She sat on the wall beside him.

"I can give you something for that. Will you continue flying after the war?"

"No. Too many pilots now."

"Then you'll stay and work the farm then? I imagine your mother would like that." Philip gazed across the fields, his expression blank. He didn't reply.

"Did you miss the farm while you were away?" she persisted. He was withdrawn, like many soldiers she had met in the course of her duties. She knew he might benefit from talking about his war experiences. It was a mild day and she felt comfortable sitting on the wall with him in such a peaceful place. She decided she would like to know more about the young lieutenant.

"I missed Rawhead and my family," he answered truthfully. "I don't miss farming."

They walked and talked for an hour, Minnie asking questions and Philip answering in a thoughtful, though halting manner. They made their way back across the field to the gate where her bicycle rested. As Minnie peddled away, Philip came into the kitchen and poured a cup of tea. Mary emerged from her bedroom, still wrapped in her shawl.

"That was Minnie Davis, the district nurse," Philip informed his mother. "Came by to see about my arm."

"That's not the only reason she came by." Mary winked at him, feeling a bit better. Philip frowned at his mother.

"I don't take your meaning," he said.

Mary turned to a large bowl of bread dough she had started. "She came to see you, of course." Philip watched her knead the dough, embarrassed. "I only met her a month ago, Mum. And she's a nurse! She's doing her job!" He sipped his tea. The thought of Minnie Davis being interested in him romantically struck him as absurd. "I'm a trained pilot and observer. Why do you see things that I don't?"

"The district nurse doesn't ride her bicycle around to check on bandages and broken arms. She has enough patients at the clinic and sanitarium. And expecting mothers. She came to see you, my dear, handsome RAF officer," she bantered, her eyes twinkling with mirth.

Philip went to the gate and looked after Minnie. She had stopped and was picking up sticks from the field. Firewood for hot water, Philip surmised. She continued on around The Clump and out of sight. He remembered she was going to see a pregnant woman after leaving Rawhead. It occurred to him her visit had lightened his burden somehow.

--- 73 ---
Firth of Forth Estuary, Scotland
November 21, 1918

Deep inside the *Resolution*, Clem stood at the ready in the torpedo bay. The war was over. The armistice had been signed ten days before. Clem and his group were not expecting orders to attack but they remained at their stations, wary and alert.

"Clem!" called Percy Wilde as he poked his head in the bay. "Come up on deck. You must see this! It's quite a sight!"

Clem followed Wilde up several stair wells to an open hatch at main deck level. He took in the astonishing sight before them. Over a hundred ships were traveling in formation towards the estuary of Scotland's River Forth. Accompanied by American and French ships, the British Grand Fleet included 33 battleships and 90,000 men. Squeezed between two columns of 40 British ships were the balance of the German High Sea Fleet. They were destined for internment. Ahead of the *Resolution* was the HMS *Revenge*, and immediately behind it, the HMS *Royal Sovereign*. These were three of the nine ships comprising the First Battle Group. Clem and Percy Wilde were ordered to don protective gear and gas masks and man a deck gun crew. The other British ships had readied similar teams for action in the event of a double-cross by the enemy.

From his F.E.2c, Philip and his observer had a better view of the internment convoy. Henley was his wingman, flying another F.E.2c 100 yards to his right and slightly below. Philip and Henley's eyes met and they both gestured downward. Two thousand feet below them were over 100 enemy naval ships chugging north under escort. Philip's chest swelled with pride. He would never forget the sight as long as he lived.

After reaching Newcastle, Philip eased the yoke to the left and pressed the port rudder pedal to return his aircraft to the aerodrome. Air crews from the northern sector would take over from there. Within an hour, he touched down at Kirton-in-Lindsey. Shutting the engine shut down, he removed his goggles and flight cap and finger-combed his hair. A mechanic held out the customary bottle of blackberry brandy but Philip declined. Henley taxied his F.E.2c next to Philip's and cut its engine.

"The ghastly war is over, gentlemen," LTC Hendrick announced from his desk as a group of pilots entered HQ together. "Thirty-Three Squadron is disbanding. Orders."

Philip was astonished. "Why?"

"It's time we all went home, don't you think, Lieutenant?" he asked jubilantly. "We're all on the unemployed list as of right now." Hendrick handed Philip and Henley their discharge papers.

After a celebration at the officer's club, Philip left Kirton-in-Lindsey aerodrome in a lorry. He hoped that somehow the RAF would require his services longer and summon him back, to continue coastal patrol flights or train new pilots. But he knew England was awash with pilots now. He was going back to farm work and cheese making. Pilots were a commodity, like so much cheese and milk. He found the prospect wholly unappealing. He was a pilot now, not a farmer.

Clem on the HMS *Resolution*, c. 1917
Photo courtesy of the author

Heading west over the countryside, Philip was deep in thought. The towns he passed through appeared the same as when he saw them in 1914. In contrast, the cities and towns he had seen in France and Belgium in 1916 no longer existed. By 1918, they were in ruins and the surrounding land had seen abhorrent death by the tens of thousands. An estimated 800,000 mules and horses had been killed, all noble creatures who played a humble and yet important part in hauling supplies to soldiers, and the saving of the wounded. Of the farm and domestic animals that were lost, one could only guess. He thought of Sam and Bertie and what they had seen in the Balkans. By the time Philip's 9th Battalion had reached Messines and Aisne, the cities were heaps of rubble surrounded by flooded craters. He would never see the true Europe that he had learned of in books at the Bickerton School.

But he was not sure he wanted to. How could they rebuild after such memories and destruction?

Philip's lorry stopped in Malpas and he jumped out carrying a single duffle bag. A hackney drove up and a red-headed driver leaned out.

"Where you headed?" he asked.

"Rawhead Farm near Bickerton."

"Where is that exactly?"

"Ballantyne Estate," Philip told him.

"I think I know that place. Wanna ride?"

"No, that's okay. I've been sitting in a truck for hours. I'd like to walk for a bit."

He sauntered down Old Hall Street. An old, embattled chapel sat on top of the hill overlooking two main streets lined with tidy houses. Philip stopped at the Red Lion, a brick tavern with origins in the early 17th century. He knew the famous old inn had entertained royalty in the distant past. King James I had visited there in the year 1600. The tavern proudly displayed the chair the king had occupied when he had supped there 320 years before. Once a busy market town, Malpas was now a quiet village with a crossroads dissecting it.

Thirsty, he imagined a pint might go down easy. But when he glanced in the window of the tavern, he saw a soldier with his head propped on a table. Multiple empty pint glasses stood in front of him. On second thought, Philip decided to skip the beer and continue home.

After another two hours, Philip stood at the entrance to the Broxton Clinic, not five miles from Rawhead. Perhaps Minnie was inside.

"She's at the sanitarium today," a nurse told him. "Chester."

Philip decided a detour was in order and he hitched a ride with a lorry driver. The Cheshire Lunatic Asylum opened in 1829 under the auspices of the *1808 County Asylum Act*. Its mission was to accommodate people who suffered from severe mental challenges, although "lunatics" is how the patients were described. Part of the facility had been closed long before the war, but due to the influx of injured veterans, it was re-opened to provide care for them. The original section of the three-story building was constructed of brick and detailed with stone. Additional facilities included stables, repair shops, and a mortuary, all bordering the main courtyard alongside the sanitarium. The kitchen, brewhouse, storehouse and laundry were housed in the basement. Staff offices and quarters were in the main area, and behind the building were the exercise yards and a well.

In 1918, the impact of the war drew the mostly all male medical staff to the armed forces. The staffing crisis was aggravated by the fact that the asylum had to house patients from Winwick and still others from the Chester Workhouse, as these institutions had been taken over as war hospitals. The only answer was to employ more women and break the outdated practice of male attendants nursing male patients. Although the war had ended, the asylum along with the rest of the country was dealing with with a devastating influenza epidemic and the wards were filled. It was not until 1920 that all the male staff returned.

Minnie opened a card from her father, Samuel Davis. It read:

Greetings from the 33rd Divisional Signal Corps.
Yesterday – War and Misery
Today – Hopefulness
Tomorrow – Peace, Perfect Peace

Just a little card to greet you,
Whether you are far or near.

And wish you a merry Christmas
And a bright and happy New Year.

From,
Your Old Dad

She wiped a tear and made a mental note to look up where Pakistan was in the world. From a previous letter, she knew he was there. The asylum library would have an atlas. Her father had now served in two wars and had been to so many places as a career soldier she could no longer keep track. He had been in the Signal Corps for some time now as a telegrapher and she was relieved. From discussions with Philip, such duty was mostly not at the front.

Philip walked down a second-floor hallway which was shabby and in need of repair. The air had a sickeningly sweet smell tainted with disinfectant with hints of old urine and feces. Philip supposed the staff and patients could get used to it as he had from walking among aid stations and the dead in France. In wheelchairs and chairs were veterans from the war bearing injuries of every kind. There were paraplegics, a quadriplegic, and some with missing fingers and hands. One patient in a wheelchair, facing away from Philip, suddenly reached and grabbed his arm as he walked past, startling him. Looking up at Philip was a horribly disfigured soldier. He placed the stumps of two fingers to his mouth. Philip forced himself to smile and produced a cigarette from his breast pocket. He placed it in what was left of the soldier's mouth and lit it. Philip gently patted the man on his back and gave the lighter and remaining pack to him. The soldier nodded a thanks and wheeled on.

After some searching and needing of fresh air, Philip came upon a nurse pushing a patient down the hall.

"Pardon me, I am looking for a nurse," Philip asked. "Minnie Davis."

The nurse turned and pointed. "Three doors down, sir."

"Thank you."

Minnie then walked out of a patient's room with blood stained sheets and towels.

"Philip!" she exclaimed. "What on earth are you doing here?"

They embraced. "Is there somewhere we can talk?"

Minnie led Philip outside to a bench in a flower and vegetable garden in the rear of the asylum. Gardeners and patients were busy tending a plot, a worker pushed a cart holding freshly picked flowers out of a greenhouse.

"When I have my own place, I should like to plant flowers of every variety," Minnie said. "And roses. My mother and father had a fine garden in Liverpool before they moved to London. I miss the life we had before the war."

"You will have another one," Philip replied. He looked around. "How is it here? Working here?"

Minnie gave Philip a somber look and shook her head.

"Hard," Minnie said. "I was a midwife before the war and much preferred that. Here I…I have never seen anything like this place."

Philip held her close and kissed her temple. "I don't know what I will do now," Philip went on. "I can work at the farm until I find something else."

Minnie,
Photo courtesy of the author

PART III
1919 - 1937

--- 74 ---
HMS *Resolution*
Portsmouth Harbor
March 1919

Clem paused at yet another sailors' auction taking place on the deck of the *Resolution*. Clem reached into his duffle bag and pulled out the ukulele he had purchased at a similar auction on the *Canopus* ten years ago. He strummed the opening bars of *The Jolly Sailor's Description of a Man O War* one last time then laid the instrument on the wool blanket spread out in front of him. He continued on to the Torpedo Office. Sailors looked at him and wondered how he could part with it.

Entering the office, Clem waited his turn in the queue and finally stood before his commanding officer who was studying paperwork on a table.

"Seaman Torpedoman Clement Bebbington reporting as ordered, sir." Clem said, coming to attention.

"At ease, Seaman," the officer ordered.

LT Middleton filled in some blanks on Clem's enlistment papers. He also signed a personal letter and offered it to Clem for approval. "Please read it over," Middleton said. Clem read the discharge letter silently:

Torpedo Office
HMS Resolution

Able Seaman C. Bebbington, Seaman Torpedoman, Royal Fleet Reserve, has served this ship for the last two years, during which time he has been employed on work in connection with the high-tension electrical installation. He has performed his duties in a highly satisfactory manner and I have found him to be most thorough and valuable. I have no hesitation in strongly recommending him for suitable employment at his discharge.

G.B. Middleton, Lt, Royal Navy.

Clem rolled up the papers and slid them inside his coat pocket. "Thank you, sir," he said and saluted.

"Good luck, Seaman," Middleton said, returning the salute with a smile. Clem shouldered his sea bag and headed for the gangway. He stopped to collect his pay, and swept the pound notes and coins off the table into his hat.

"Your share of the prize money is one pound six schillings," the paymaster said.

"Seaman Clement Bebbington requesting permission to leave ship, sir." Clem asked the OOD. The officer made a note in his log and saluted.

"Permission granted." The OOD said. Clem then saluted the ensign and descended the gangway to the dock. Minutes later, he passed through the gate for the last time. He paused for a moment to look back at the entrance marquis and several young recruits wearing civilian clothes and carrying suitcases. They reminded him of himself as he must have looked ten years ago. He felt elated to be free, but also felt an ache in his chest. He made many friends and seen so much over the past decade. A groan from a tug in the harbor sounded as if bidding him farewell.

"Last tram to Southampton!" a gate guard yelled at the group of departing former seamen.

Clem swung his sea bag over his shoulder and hurried to board the bus to begin his journey home. He had learned that Andrew, Sam, and most recently Philip were back at Rawhead.

--- 75 ---

Late in the afternoon, two lorries trundled up the snow-covered driveway to Rawhead. When they stopped at the gate, Robert Bryden emerged from the passenger side of the first one and met Mary and Joseph in the courtyard. Sam and Dave came out of the barn. Mary was startled to see the driver was Oliver Goldford, the man living in the cave under the Raw Head escarpment.

"I believe I've found Bertie," Bryden announced.

Mary covered her mouth, her eyes wide with surprise.

"He's alive and he's arriving at Liverpool on a ship tonight. I came to take you there. They're short of ambulances, so I'm bringing my lorries."

"Ambulances?" Joseph asked.

"Sam, Dave, would one of you come with me?" Mary asked. "Please make up a bed for Bertie," she said to Mollie.

Mary and Dave climbed into the back and the lorries departed. Mary slid along a bench inside the lorry to the rear window of the cab. It was open.

"Where did you find him?" she asked Robert.

"Palestine," Bryden shouted over the engine noise. "He was shipped there with the Labour Corps months ago. That's why I couldn't find him sooner."

Mary caught the driver's eye in the rearview mirror. "Mr. Goldford, how good to see you."

"He's our newest employee!" Bryden announced, looking over at Goldford. "A rare find. We're most fortunate."

A cold, briny wind whistled over the docks of Liverpool as hundreds of civilians and military personnel pressed forward looking for their missing soldiers. A heavy snowfall the night before made the situation worse. Pandemonium ensued. Long lines of sick and injured soldiers on litters were carried down ship gangways to waiting ambulances and lorries. The vehicles arrived and departed in a disorganized manner. The lorry driven by Oliver Goldford and carrying Robert, Mary and Dave pulled up and Dave jumped out of the back and helped Mary out.

Robert Bryden joined them in front of the lorry. "He'll be on the *Chyebassa* or the *Lake Erie*."

"Stay here, Mum! We'll find him!" Dave disappeared into the crowd and Bryden strode off towards the harbormaster's office. Mary could see the *Lake Erie* docked right in front of her but she stood alone amid the chaos anxiously watching a queue of stretchers extended from the ship down the gangplank. Police blew whistles and gestured frantically to establish order and clear lanes for arriving ambulances. Mary moved forward to view the blanket covered men on the litters more closely. She grabbed a military policeman by the arm.

"Please, where did this ship come from?" she asked. He waved her away, shaking his head. Mary stopped another policeman and tugged on his coat. "Please, sir!" Mary called. "Where did this ship come from?"

"Tripoli!" he informed her, raising his arms to push back the crowd. "Please step back, all of you! Clear a path for the ambulances!" Mary turned toward the *Chyebassa*, stopping to allow a stretcher to pass. She began rushing from stretcher to stretcher and ambulance to ambulance.

"Bertie!" Mary called. "Bertie!" She suspected that even if he were near, he would not have been able to hear her. The noise of the traffic and crowds was overwhelming. Then she saw Dave coming out of an ambulance.

"I can't find him anywhere, Mum," Dave moaned. "Maybe they've already taken him to hospital." Two hundred feet away, a stretcher emerged from the *Chyebassa*. Weak and fevered, the patient stared at the sea of faces, searching for a familiar one. He caught sight of his mother and younger brother and lifted his right arm from under the blanket. Dave spotted the distant stretcher and the soldier's raised arm. On a hunch, he rushed forward, shoving and pushing through the crowd. Reaching the litter Dave could not be sure it was Bertie because the man looked so different. Dave reached into the man's shirt and read his octagonal identification tag. It said, Bebbington B., Army Service Corps, 501571. He gently took his brothers' hand in both of his, overwhelmed by the toll time and trial had taken on his smiling face.

"Bertie?" Dave asked, bewildered. This isn't him. There's been some sort of mistake and this fellow's wearing Bertie's tag. "There's been a mix up," he murmured to the man.

"You're all grown up now, Dave," Bertie whispered, his eyes searching his brother's face. Dave waved in Mary's direction. "He's here, he's here!" He shouted. He could not believe what he was seeing. "My God, Bertie," Dave murmured. "Where have you been?"

"On holiday," Bertie managed, grinning crookedly. Sam remembered the last thing Bertie said before their ship was torpedoed. Mary made her way to them, and looking at Bertie's skeletal face, she burst into noisy tears. It was unbearable to see how wasted he was.

"Oh, my poor boy," she crooned, tears coursing over her chin. She stroked his hair and face and felt for his arms and legs, feet and hands. He was in one piece but severely undernourished. She shook her head and wondered what he could possibly have been through. She thought he was only supposed to take care of animals. He was twenty-six years old and looked fifty years older.

"He's had a terrible fever," volunteered one of the ship's nurses, coming up beside them. "Malaria. And diphtheria." Mary began to sob into her hands. Dave put his arm around her. They followed along as Bertie's stretcher was loaded into a waiting ambulance.

"He'll be at Liverpool Infirmary," the attendant told them as he closed the doors. An army officer approached Bryden. "Sir, may we use your lorries? We have a great many patients to transport."

"Of course," Bryden said. He joined Mary and Dave. "I'm staying here tonight." He and Goldford turned and walked toward the *Cheybassa*, while Dave and Mary boarded another lorry to Liverpool Infirmary.

On the way to the hospital, Mary sank into a reverie. She was remembering the Septembr 1914 morning when the boys left for the army. They were dressed in their best clothes and carried their small bags. They were so excited, so eager to start their big adventure. Andrew even took his rifle with him the first time, but left it home only after he found out the Army would issue him one. Clem had left for the navy five years before his brothers but had been able to return on leave several times.

She recalled feeling terrible fear, not knowing if she would ever see her sons again. She was more confident that Sam and Andrew would manage than she was about Bertie. She worried about him the most. Of the five who had participated in the war, he had been the second oldest, at twenty-one, to go. He had been such an innocent, a child at heart. Mary knew he should not have gone, but also that she could not have prevented him. He wanted to go. "See you at Christmas, Mum," Bertie told her cheerfully when he hugged her goodbye. They had shaken Joseph's hand and hugged their sisters, Martha and Mollie. Then they had climbed into the wagon, happily waving, and departed. Mary remembered it as if it had been yesterday, then came out of her reverie and caught Dave watching her.

"Bertie's going to be all right, Mum," he assured her stoutly. Mary looked at her lap and nodded. Many years later, Dave told his children that was the only time he had ever seen his mother cry.

--- 76 ---

Supper following Clem and Bertie's homecoming was a
solemn occasion at Rawhead. They were the last of the brothers
to come home. The entire family was there—Joseph, George,
Annie Foster, Andrew, Sam, Mary Artbury, Philip, Minnie
Davis, Clem, Dave, Jack, and Martha and William Evans. Bertie,
recently released from hospital and still very weak, hobbled in on
a crutch with Mollie's aid and sat down. All sat with their hands
in their laps, quietly waiting for Mary and wondering what she
would say. They were hoping for some laughter and reflection as
they had not had any for years. In his ten years of Royal Navy
service Clem had returned to Rawhead only twice. Andrew had
been in the Somme for nearly two years with no leave before his
hand injury returned him. Philip was in France for over two years
and spent his remaining service in southern England, first with a
training brigade and lastly with the RAF. Sam had been sent
home after bouts of diphtheria and pneumonia. Bertie's odyssey
kept him from home for almost five years.

Mary finally appeared from the hallway with the family bible. All stood as she entered. Large and heavy, the bible showed signs of considerable wear. She placed it on the table and opened it to the first page showing the names of Joseph and Mary, followed by the children as recorded after their births. It was the first time they could recall when she ever appeared at supper with the book. A grace prayer was a custom, but there was never a Bible verse read aloud. Mary looked at the names of her children and the dates she gave them birth. She touched the name of Tom next to the date of his death. She lifted a red ribbon to reveal a verse near the book's middle. Philip recognized the ribbon as his temporary NCO insignia. He had sent it home in a letter, saying proudly "I've been decorated!"

"I recall it was Sam's turn to say grace the last time we were together." She said, "But I thought...a different kind of blessing is right."

She observed the empty chair next to Philip where Tom used to sit. She read from Psalm 91:

"Those who live in the shelter of the Most High,
will find rest in the shadow of the Almighty.
This I declare about the Lord:
He alone is my refuge, my place of safety;
He is my God, and I trust Him."

The boys nodded, having heard and spoken the prayer often to themselves during difficult moments of their service. Whether there was a god or not, it gave them comfort.

"I was told by a friend in chapel that it's called *The Soldier's Psalm.*"

She laid the Bible in her lap. "I prayed for all of you and God answered. But...I'm afraid I didn't ask for Thomas."

Several looked to Tom's empty chair. Joseph took her hand.

Bertie observed the spread of food and could only think of water. Nothing looked appetizing. Wanting to break the silence, Philip looked at a wedge of Cheshire cheese before him and reached for it. After slicing a piece and spreading it on some fresh bread, he placed it in his mouth. Clem noticed and nodded. It was the best food he had tasted in years and would be part of his daily staple from that day on, Philip decided. As well as many other cheeses, he also enjoyed the fresh tomatoes as he hadn't seen any since his enlistment. He would grow them in his future gardens and take pleasure eating them from the vine. The family followed in suit, accepting helpings of roast beef, Yorkshire pudding, potatoes, carrots, and mushy peas.

"I'd like to start making cheese again, Pa," Bertie offered. "If that's alright."

"When you're well enough, Bertie" Joseph answered.

"There's a good cheesemaker you should meet over at the Bradeley Green Farm." Mary said. "Her name is Ivy Threadgold."

Philip smiled. "They're at it again, Bertie. Finding us wives!"

The family had found laughter again. Match making would have its way. Andrew Bebbington married Elsie Booth, a farmer's daughter and Bertie Bebbington married Ivy Threadgold, a cheese maker's daughter, in the summer of 1919 at the Westley Methodist Church in Chester.

--- 77 ---
**Scapa Flow, Orkney Islands, Scotland
June 21, 1919**

A month later, Clem's former ship *Resolution* and other ships comprising the First Battle Squadron were emergency recalled to Scapa Flow, Orkney Islands where the German fleet had been interred. At 10:30 a.m. on June 21, 1919 German Rear Admiral Ludwig von Reuter sent a pre-arranged signal out to the German fleet:

Paragraph eleven. Confirm.

Below decks, German sailors opened sea cocks allowing sea water to flow into the ships. Allied crews looked on helplessly as the German ships sank into Scapa Flow harbor. So began the largest scuttling of ships in world history. Boarding parties were dispatched. The *Baden* was run aground, as well as the cruisers *Nürnberg*, *Emden* and *Frankfurt*, but all other major ships sank where they were anchored. Although efforts were made to prove that the scuttling had been authorized by the Supreme Army Command in Berlin, nothing could be established. Nine German sailors were shot dead by Allied boarding parties and machine gun batteries. Some say they were the last casualties of the war. But in the years to come, untold numbers of veterans slowly succumbed to injuries sustained in the war.

--- 78 ---

Like his father and his father before him, Robert Bryden made rounds to the farms to look over conditions and the books. Today, it was Droppingstone and Rawhead. William Cutter and Bryden headed up the entrance road in an estate car.

"Any special questions on the Droppingstone Farm, sir?" Cutter asked of Bryden.

"Not especially. It's always been well run."

Cutter handed a ledger to Bryden and he began studying it.

"There is one thing, William." Bryden said. "The tenant is near retirement, correct?"

"Yes sir," Cutter replied. "Next year. We'll begin looking fo—"

"Offer it to Bert Bebbington."

"I…don't know him well." Cutter said. "Shouldn't we at least talk with him?"

"Bertie's a good man. I can vouch for him."

After arriving and having a pleasant review of Rawhead's books, Bryden looked about.

"I don't see Bertie," Bryden said. "Is he well?"

"He is well, sir." Joseph said. "He should be in the east field ploughing this morning."

In the east field, Bertie adjusted straps on two large draft horses. Thus far, half the field had been completed. As Bryden approached, he observed Bertie speaking to the horses and smiled.

"Major Bryden!" Bertie called out. "It's good to see you, sir."

"How have you been, Bertie?" Bryden said.

"Well enough to work."

"It must be good to be home again,"

"Oh, it is, sir. And you?"

"Fine. It's been quite a ride, the last six years, eh?"

"Yes sir, I'm afraid I didn't do too much."

"Well, I was a soldier and they asked me to fight," Bryden said. "And to take care of my men. But I lost…twelve in my charge and got sent home. I'm afraid I didn't do too much either. They asked you to take care of the horses and from what I hear, you more than did that."

"Thank you, sir."

Bryden started to leave. "Bertie, how would you like to take over Droppingstone?"

Bertie's face went blank. "Take over?"

"Yes. The current tenant is retiring soon and…I need a good tenant to work it."

"I would like that very much, sir."

--- 79 ---

The year 1920 brought not only all five Bebbington sons back to Rawhead but was also was the occasion of Gilbert and Ella Bryden's Golden Wedding Anniversary. It was also the instance of Geoffrey Bryden's birth, the second child born to Robert and Heidi Bryden, after Matthew. Estate tenantry and gentry from across Cheshire attended and toasted the Brydens under a large tent on the Ballantyne lawn. As the Brydens held their newborn, they looked upon Reverend Moreland of All Saint's Church as he addressed the crowd.

"It is with great pleasure to announce the Golden Wedding Anniversary of Gilbert and Ella Bryden, and also the birth of Gilbert Bryden's grandson Geoffrey, future heir to this magnificent estate," Moreland stated. "This birth has caused widespread pleasure, especially among the tenants. There is no position on earth more important or desirable than that of a large landed proprietor, if he be an upright, consistent, kind and generous landlord, and beloved by his tenantry. It is these noble qualities which your tenantry admires about you."

Gilbert and his wife nodded thanks, followed by prolonged cheering from the crowd.

"We know that your grandson will follow on in your footsteps."

Joseph, wearing the best clothes he could manage with his shirt buttoned to the top, leaned to Mary. "I would belove him more if he lessened our rent!"

Mary smiled and playfully elbowed him. After the ceremony, guests enjoyed the refreshments and lined up to greet the new addition to the Bryden family.

A fortnight after the celebration, seventy-eight-year-old Gilbert Bryden died in his sleep and his son Robert, now forty-three, became Squire Bryden of Ballantyne Castle. A mile-long cortege extended from the castle to All Saint's Church. In Ballantyne Estate tradition, the bearers of Bryden's coffin were seven estate tenants, among them Joseph Bebbington and Oliver Goldford. At the gravesite, over 200 tenantry, yeoman and families from across Cheshire sang the hymn *Peace, Perfect Peace*, and said goodbye to their beloved landlord. As they sang, Robert Bryden contemplated the burden now upon him. Heidi looked to him beside her as he was not singing. She offered her hymn book and pointed to the current verse. He smiled and sang with her. After the mourners departed, cemetery workers placed Gilbert Bryden's coffin into the family mausoleum.

On a Tuesday morning at 2:04 a.m. there was a loud knock on Robert and Heidi Bryden's bedroom door. After some stumbling about in the dark, Bryden opened the door to face their butler Lloyd Green.

"Sir, the school is burning!"

Bryden turned to a bay window and looked across the estate towards Harthill. A flicker of light in the distance illuminated his face.

Minutes later, Robert Bryden arrived at the school to find it engulfed in flames. Estate workers and nearby residents frantically tossed buckets of water at the flames. Bryden joined the effort to extinguish the blaze, even attempting to enter the building, but was held back by others. A fire brigade wagon arrived minutes later but it was of little use. Harthill School was destroyed.

Hours later, Bryden and Cutter walked through the ashes. Bryden took a broom handle and poked and prodded the smoking embers. The headmaster followed.

"How could it happen?" the headmaster pleaded. "The hearth fire was put out and no candles had been lit."

Bryden searched the ashes at his feet and kicked at it. He stooped down and picked up a half-burned text book and opened it. "Elementary Mathematics", the title read. He glanced down at its publication date—1902. He tossed it away, frustrated. Bryden made his way to an unburned area and pulled a piece of wallboard away from an electrical panel. He examined the wiring and shook his head in disgust. It was all old knob and tube wiring. He looked to the headmaster.

"We will rebuild it," Bryden said, dusting off his hands. "And it will be magnificent."

Instruction was temporarily moved to the Ballantyne Castle library where Ella and Heidi assisted the headmaster with the children. After an inquest, the cause of the fire was attributed to faulty electrical wiring with mention of a damaged chimney as a possible contributing cause. It was an awakening to Robert Bryden. He was so alarmed he had his estate employees rebuild it with all modern features including the latest text books from London. It included a play yard, kitchen and library. It even had indoor plumbing. When completed, the schoolmaster was so pleased he began a ritual of having the children greet Robert Bryden whenever he returned from his travels. The children would break from their lessons and line up in front of the school to wave as he passed. If enough notice was given, a banner was prepared that read "Welcome Home, Major Bryden" and held across the school entrance. The friendly waves and smiles from the children always elevated his spirits. On one occasion, it brought him to joyous tears. The greetings would forever serve as a reminder of his duty to support charitable causes.

One of an English landowner's other duties was to inspect the estate from horseback from time to time. In that Ballantyne was now his, or at least under his responsibility for the time being, Robert Bryden rode through the estate in November 1920. It had been some years since he had done so and the school fire literally struck a fire under him. After many hours of riding, he still had not seen all of it. Yet, he had seen enough. He concluded the castle itself was a shamble although he used the term "disrepair" in discussions with William Cutter. Many of the rooms had moth-eaten rugs and curtains. The tapestries needed restoration while others were completely rotten. The plumbing was "unfit even for an Egyptian latrine" and had badly designed leach fields that leaked into the scenic estate pools, Bryden explained at dinner. Although most rooms had one or more fireplaces, various spaces and stone floors failed to benefit from their heat. The chimneys themselves were damaged and posed a fire hazard. Guests of his father, on many occasions, concluded in private that it was among the dampest of castles they had visited. One guest even referred to it as a "poor monk's monastery". Such comments eventually got back to the squire so Bryden decided that he would modernize the castle and estate and would seek his wife's help in doing so. Many of the other estates had already been down this path and he was way behind.

After months of planning, the Brydens chose an architect famous for his creation of a Parisian village, but mostly because he was a distant relative of Heidi's family. The project replaced the original pipes and radiators and installed white and green marble flooring in the outer hall. It took almost two years to re-roof, re-wire, re-plumb, re-decorate, and basically re-everything else. The Brydens even had a rudimentary fire control sprinkler system installed, complete with the new fire-activated heads. Such a system was added to Harthill School as well. Bryden also had the garden replanted and terraces added with more than 350 varieties of trees and many different rhododendrons, azaleas, and camellias. The grounds men were overwhelmed, but happy to see the long-awaited enhancements. Upon completion of the modernization, local assessors valued the estate at twenty million pounds Sterling. Heidi Bryden went on to celebrate with many galas and elegant parties in the years to come and would spend hours in the garden and greenhouse nurturing the flowers. After finally realizing it was her favorite place on the estate, Robert Bryden had a small, private pool built within the floral garden confines as an anniversary gift. It was constructed of Italian marble and tile and supplied by water from a small boiler. The elegant pool would serve as a romantic refuge for years to come. The Ballantyne Estate was again a grand residence, worthy of the vision Robert Bryden's grandfather had decades earlier.

In September, Mary and the family enjoyed a Sunday afternoon in the north field of Rawhead. As always, the tradition was to play cricket or football and to drink homemade ginger beer. The table was set with a "ploughman's lunch", although it would not be called that for many years. Always cold, the lunch consisted of crusty bread and cheese, pickled onions and chutney, cold meats, ham, pate, and a slice of pork pie. Slices of a Bedfordshire Clanger, a sort of elongated suet crust dumpling filled with meat and potatoes, rounded out the menu.

Guests were always welcome, including sons and daughters of nearby farms. One such girl, Margaret Large, arrived with her sister, at the invitation of Philip, who had stopped at their farm with Minnie while on her nursing rounds. He thought Dave might fancy her.

Dave and Margaret shook hands and exchanged pleasant smiles. Philip led Margaret around to meet the others as Dave studied her. Margaret sat in a chair and watched the game as it resumed. Dave summoned strength to do something profoundly athletic to impress her. After swinging overly hard at a pitched ball, he comically lost his balance and fell. Jack and Jim and others laughed. He looked to Margaret to see if she had seen his unruly swing; but fortunately, she had been distracted.

Jack wound up his arm for a pitch.

"Make it a daisy-cutter, Jack!" Sam called from the field.

"Who wants to walk up Burwardsley Hill?" Philip asked.

Margaret stood. "I'd like to go."

Dave dropped his cricket bat. "I'll go too."

"Oh, come on, Dave!" complained Jack from the field. "We've got a game on!"

Dave started walking towards Philip and Margaret who were already headed down the entrance road.

"Tired of cricket," Dave shouted back.

Jack removed his cap and scratched his head. "Well, now, what's up with him?"

After a pleasant hike, several weeks of courting, and finding excuses to visit the Large's Woodhouse Farm during weekdays, Dave proposed to Margaret Large at the top of

Burwardsley Hill. They were married at St. John's Church and honeymooned in Colwyn Bay, Wales.

--- **80** ---

On an early July morning in 1923, everyone was busily tending their chores when Jim stormed into the Rawhead kitchen in a huff. He leaned on the table heavily with both hands and out of breath, staring down at a large pile of flour.

"Jim, what's wrong?" Mary asked while kneading dough. She was certain he had been arguing with his father again.

Jim said nothing and ran upstairs. Moments later, Joseph stormed in.

"Where is he?" he asked.

"Oh, leave him alone, Joseph" Mary said. "Everyone has been working hard all day!"

"Everyone but Jim!" Joseph implored. "He was supposed to fix the west cattle gate last week and half the curst herd got out and are all over Cheshire! Drat the boy! He's more plague than profit! The dogs are doing his work!"

Jim clambered down the stairs with a suitcase, nearly falling from a stumble and started for the door. Mary and Joseph turned to him.

"You've work to do!" Joseph demanded.

"I've done enough for a lifetime!" Jim yelled. "I'm not a slave!"

He opened the door and stormed off through the courtyard. Mary rushed after him.

"Jim, please!" Mary said to his back. "I'll talk to him."

Joseph appeared in the doorway behind Mary.

"If I continue to work for him, I'll never be finished!" yelled Jim as he walked briskly down the road.

"Jim!" Mary screamed, but it was no use. Jim was gone.

Seeing a stone, Jim angrily kicked it down the road but it bounced back in his path. He kicked it again with the intention of it veering off into the field but strangely enough it landed back in his path. Jim took it as an omen.

Later that evening, after spending hours searching Broxton and Bickley for Jim, Philip and Minnie found success at the Mayflower Tavern. Philip remembered the pub after having a pint there with friends. All taverns have a story, and the one told of Mayflower was that the door was always propped open as it had been since 1799 when an aging widower decided he didn't want to farm anymore and set off for a new world. Philip peered inside. The pub was filled with farm labourers and tradesmen, smoking and sipping pints, sampling pub food, and playing darts. Some veterans wore their uniforms, obviously as a ploy to get free drinks. Philip and Minnie entered the musty, smoke filled tavern and observed Jim and Mabel Jean across the tavern sitting in a dimly lit booth. Several empty pint glasses sat before them. Philip and Minnie eased themselves through the Friday evening patrons, many of whom were regulars and thoroughly imbibed. Philip pardoned himself as he walked between a grubby farm mechanic and his dart game.

"Jim." Philip said, sliding into the booth across from him. "What the devil is going on? We've been looking all over for you."

"We're going to America," he said, looking at Mabel Jean.

"What's in America?"

"I don't know. Has to be better than shoveling manure for Pa."

"But...you're not even married!"

Mabel Jean took Jim's hand.

"We can be married on the ship," Mabel Jean said. Then she turned to Philip. "Why don't you and Minnie come with us?"

Philip was in shock. America. Marriage. Minnie. To leave Rawhead forever...and the family.

"Come with us, Philip!" Jim went on. "It'll be fun. And we can help each other get started. There's even work for pilots! For heaven sake, Jeremy Pluck married a girl he met at the Nantwich Cheese Fair and he's younger than us."

"You do intend to marry Minnie, don't you?" Mabel Jean asked.

Embarrassed, Philip and Minnie looked at each other and smiled. "What is it with everyone? Clem, Bertie, Sam, Andrew, Dave all getting married one after another as if there's no tomorrow!"

"That's just it, Phil, there may not be." Jim advised. "You ought to know."

Jim had never made much sense but what he just said was quite profound.

"Jack and Mollie are the only ones left with any wisdom. Who will work the farm?" Philip said. "Robert Bryden just hired Bertie and Ivy to work Droppingstone, so he's gone."

"Jack and Dave," Jim said. "And Martha and Will."

"Come on, Phil," urged Mabel Jean.

"We haven't really thought about it," Phillip answered after a moment of reflection. He looked to Minnie.

"We have," Jim said looking at Mabel Jean.

"Tell me, just when did you two arrive at this latest bit of foolishness? Before or after the ale?"

"Before," Mabel Jean said, taking another sip."

"So you get in another scrape with Pa and then go to a grogshop to get over the bay and decide to get married?" Philip asked.

"I'm not over the bay," Jim said looking at Mabel Jean. "Just a bit...seasoned."

"You're off, Jim!" proclaimed Philip rolling his eyes. "Both of you are completely off!"

A grey-bearded tavern keeper appeared. "Another round of bitter, sir?"

"Yes," Jim said. "And two clangers?"

"Right-o. And a bitter for you two fine folks?" The tavern keeper asked Philip and Minnie.

"What on earth is a clanger?" Mabel Jean asked. "I know what a banger is."

"It's a meat and potato-filled pastry with a wee bit of sage," the bar keeper answered.

"Yes, but why is it called a clanger?" Mabel Jean asked further.

"Cuz' it's shaped like a bell clanger!" Jim answered, chuckling.

"You got me, sir," the tavern keeper answered. "Me wife makes 'em."

Philip sat back in the booth and looked to the tavern keeper. "I think we'll have whiskies."

Two weeks later, Philip drove Jim and Mabel Jean to the Liverpool Docks. They said their goodbyes and boarded the RMS *Laconia*, bound for New York City. Philip and Minnie married several months later and decided to honeymoon in London. On their way to Chester Station to catch a train to the south of England for their honeymoon, Philip asked the hackney driver to stop.

"Why are we stopping?" Minnie asked.

"I want to see something in the cathedral," Philip said.

Inside, Minnie and Philip stood holding hands in the South Transept of Chester Cathedral. Before them were the names of 8,420 soldiers: the Regimental Roll of Honor. A similar memorial to the Cheshire Yeomanry stood under the organ loft.

A woman and her children stood at the wall as well. She touched a name.

"Who is that, Mummy?" her little girl asked.

"That's your daddy," the woman replied, wiping a tear.

Philip searched the names and found those he knew and touched them as well. Ellor, Birch, Heathcote. As he touched each name, their faces appeared in his head. He silently read the verse above the wall taken from "John Bunyan's *Pilgrim' Progress*": *And all the trumpets sounded for them on the other Side.*

After the honeymoon, they boarded the *Laconia* to join Jim and Mabel in America.

A Cunard ocean liner, RMS *Laconia* was built as a successor to the 1911 *Laconia* which had been torpedoed on February 25, 1917. The new ship was launched on April 9, 1921, and had her maiden voyage on May 25, 1922 from Southampton to New York City. Like her predecessor, *Laconia* would suffer the same fate at the outbreak of World War II with 1,600 lives lost. Years later, after hearing of the sinking on the radio, Philip remarked that it was as if all their ties to their former life in England had been severed.

The headlines about Charles Lindberg and Amelia Earhart peeked Philip's interest in aviation so he inquired about becoming a commercial pilot, but met little interest. There were far more pilots than aircraft to fly. One day, while wrapping meat in a newspaper for a grocery customer, Philip noticed an ad from an insurance company for a "Safety Engineer". I could do that, Philip thought. It proved to be an eye-opening experience into what workers had to deal with in industry.

--- 81 ---

Within months of Jim and Philip's arrival in the United States, Clarence Harper was admitted to the US VA Hospital in Lake City, Florida. He had lived much longer than the minutes to weeks it took to die for most soldiers exposed to poison gas. Many wished they had died on the battlefield than endure years of suffering. Since war's end, Clarence had been treated for recurring respiratory bouts from his exposure in Belgium. Upon returning, he resided with his family in Greenville, South Carolina and later Fairburn, Georgia where he met and married a graceful southern girl, Jewel Wilson. A newspaperman before the war, he was now a full-time patient and moved with Jewel to a small cottage in Lake City, not a mile from the hospital. It was there that they had a child, Dorothy Nell. After a pleasant morning visit at his bedside, Jewel and young Dorothy kissed him on his cheek and left for the grocery.

Later that day, a young nurse entered the crowded ward to deliver the day's mail. She stopped at Clarence's bed and adjusted the oxygen mask on his face.

"Good afternoon, Mr. Harper," the nurse said cheerfully, sifting through a stack of letters. "You've a letter from England! From a Mr.... William Evans of the Rawhead Farm in Cheshire. I think I should like to visit England one day. I hear it's beautiful there."

Clarence was asleep. The nurse placed the letter under his hand and left to check other patients. Minutes later, one last breath left Clarence Harper's eroded lungs and the letter slipped to the floor. He was buried in Fountain Inn near Greenville. Jewel and Dorothy returned to Fairburn.

--- 82 ---

Robert and Heidi Bryden had just finished dinner and enjoyed a quiet cup of tea. Ella Bryden and two of her visiting daughters and their husbands had excused themselves from the table to leave them alone. They marveled at the new dining room with its shimmering marble floors and paneled walls and spoke of small pleasantries as dishes were removed.

"The Fête is coming," Heidi said. "We must begin to plan for it."

Bryden nodded. "Yes, that will be something. Many are looking forward to it. There're no more wars to go to. Especially for redundant officers."

"Oh, not that again."

"It's an eternal nightmare, Heidi. I try to forget…but it keeps coming back." He shook his head and took a sip of tea. "Redundant."

"Robert, that is only partly correct. Your father wanted you home."

"What?"

"The casualties in Egypt were growing, mostly from disease."

"What are you saying? How do you know so much of this?"

Heidi stood and walked around the table to him. She sat and took his hands into hers.

"Robert, you were his only son. He was not going to lose you. He knew that after Palestine, your regiment was going to the Somme. So, he arranged to have you sent home."

"Arranged?" Bryden said, shocked. He slowly stood and began pacing around the room. "Dear God."

Suddenly it all made sense to him. He was too good an officer for the regiment to just send him home as surplus in a war where thousands were dying every day. If he was surplus in Egypt they would most certainly have sent him somewhere else in the war. It was not spiritual intervention or fate after all. It was his father...and Heidi.

"And I wanted you home, too." Heidi said. "There's too much good you can do here! For your tenants and employees. And the families of soldiers who have been killed and injured. And Cheshire. If you died, who would continue that legacy?"

Bryden hunched over the dining table. Finally, he looked to Heidi.

"You were his only son, Robert!" Heidi implored. "And my one love. You have two sons, tenants, charities, people who need you here. Please forgive me, my love. Please understand."

Bryden was furious but maintained his composure.

"Heidi, do you know how many men from my battalion died in Palestine and in the Somme while I stayed here?"

"You were not well! You did not have the mindset anymore for war. You would have been killed, and needlessly!"

Robert could manage no further words and slowly retreated to his study.

"Robert!" Heidi called after him in tears. "Please!"

JON BEBBINGTON

--- **83** ---

May 1924 brought the long-awaited Ballantyne Great Fête. It was usually held every five years or so but had been delayed on account of the war. The Fête included events and amusements such as horse jumping, plough matches, a pig chase, a cheese contest, a dog show, a treasure hunt, a rowing race on the lake, and a stock show, followed by dancing and fireworks. There was even a palmist, whose services many ladies, including Mary, found amusing. The Fête was held on the terraced lawns at Ballantyne Castle in the most splendid weather seen in Cheshire. Hundreds of guests walked about, taking in the sights and listening to a band while generous amounts of food and beer was served under tents. On tables were cooked goslings, ducklings, chickens, and mutton joints surrounded with innumerable embellishments which the tenantry took delight in providing. Charles Dickens himself would have approved of such a spread.

In planning the events, Robert and Heidi Bryden arranged for the annual Chester Hunt to coincide with the Fête as the opening event. Reserved largely for ladies and gentry, the Cheshire Hounds was an exclusive club founded in 1763 where riders wore scarlet coats with gold buttons and white jodhpurs and hunted twenty-five square miles around Tarporley, Nantwich, Chester, Kelsall, Whitchurch, and Malpas.

Bertie swore under his breath as he watched the riders assemble in their finery. "I'm as good as these grandees," he muttered. He had keenly watched the event since he was a boy. A day with magnificent hunter horses following a pack of experienced foxhounds presented splendid scenes. It took riders through woods, marshes, rocks, streams, thickets and over hedgerows. Maintaining the sport was costly, nearly £6,000 per year including the salaries of the huntsmen and two whips. A pack consisted of sixty hounds made up of thirty males and thirty females. On hunt days, the pack was divided, males one day and females the other. Today it was males. The objective was for the hounds to catch and kill the fox with the encouragement of the scarlet clad riders. Fortunately for the foxes, most got away. If a fox was chased up a tree, it was set free. But the hunt was also a kind of race through the countryside as a test of rider horsemanship and was keenly observed by spectators from various locations. First to return to the starting line from the end of the hunt was the goal of the race. Wagers among riders and spectators were not uncommon.

Mounted, Robert Bryden looked about the excited crowd and found Heidi standing with Geoffrey. Their eyes met and he extended a gentle smile and nod. The gesture warmed her. The past year had been difficult for their marriage, but they worked through their differences. He observed Bertie in the crowd and steered his horse over to him.

"It's a great day for a ride, sir," Bertie said, stroking Bryden's magnificent horse.

"Have you ever ridden in the Chester Hunt?" Bryden asked.

"No, sir. But I rode the tenantry hunt down in Shropshire last year."

"Are you familiar with the course and rules?"

"Of course, sir. I've been an avid watcher for many years."

Bryden smiled at Bertie, seeing his eagerness. He rotated his crop and extended the handle to Bertie. Ivy looked on from the crowd.

"Then ride it."

Bertie's face went blank. "What do you mean?"

"Ride for me today Bertie," Bryden said as he dismounted. "I'm not quite up to it."

It was not just a kind gesture to his friend, Bryden thought. He honestly did not want to ride that morning. At his age and all he had been through, declining such sports was wise. Heidi didn't want him to ride either, and frequently urged him not to. He chose to take her advice this time.

Bertie accepted the crop and stroked Bryden's horse. "What's his name?"

"Julius." Bryden said. "As in Julius Caesar."

"The hunt is in five minutes," Bertie said. "I haven't any riding clothes."

"You'll find suitable accoutrements in the tack room," Bryden said pointing over his shoulder. "And, Bertie—"

Bertie was on his way to the tack room before Bryden could finish his sentence.

"Bertie!" Ivy protested, holding their new baby, Jeffrey. Geoffrey Bryden, now seven years old, ran from his governess to his father.

"Father, may I go?" asked Geoffrey.

Bryden smiled and ruffled his son's hair. "One day soon you will, Geoffrey," Bryden said. "But the hunt can be dangerous and you must practice your riding skills a few more years before I'll allow you to join these scoundrels." He intentionally described the riders as scoundrels to needle two scarlet coats nearby. They all exchanged good natured grins.

Ivy helped Bertie find suitable riding clothes. While he was changing, she looked for a place where she could change her wet baby. She opened a door that led out into a garden. Before she could close it, she saw William Cutter and Heidi Bryden standing under a floral arch kissing. Cutter's hand was entwined in her hair and her arms were wound around his chest. Sensing someone was there, Heidi's eyes found Ivy's. Ivy quickly closed the door and backed away, shaken. She looked for Bertie, but he was gone.

After a fifteen-minute delay in the start of the hunt, Bertie was finally mounted on Julius. He nervously looked among the other riders. What have I gotten myself into now? Bertie asked himself. All hunt riders were dressed in a black riding helmet, white pants, a scarlet coat with gold buttons, high black riding boots, and held a riding crop.

"I don't know, Robert." Lord Crewe said. "He's not a member and I haven't seen him at any competitions."

"He'll be fine, Crewe. Bert's the best horseman I've ever seen."

"If it's okay with the others and the judges, I have no objection."

Slowly, nods of approval were extended to the new rider, Bert Bebbington. The change aroused much curiosity amongst them. Bertie looked about. He was in the company of extreme wealth. Among the others were Lord Crewe, Lord Doddington, the Earl of Chester, the Marquis de Cholmondeley, the Baron of Halton, and Lord Delemere. Wives and daughters within the families also rode and were equally talented, if not better, in their equestrian training.

Looking around, Bertie observed A.G. Wilkinson in the distance. Their eyes met and Wilkinson ceremoniously saluted Bertie with his crop. Bertie did not return one, suspecting full well what was behind the gesture. He reached down and rubbed Julius' neck while Wilkinson pulled a small bottle from his saddle pocket and took a swig.

A revolver shot launched the Hunt and twelve male hounds dashed into the countryside. Moments later, the twenty riders took off galloping and the two hapless foxes were released from a hutch. Terrified, they ran in opposite directions. The riders chased one toward a fence and a ditch that ran in the direction of Cholmondeley Castle. The fox jumped and darted in expected fashion. The master of the hunt hooted his horn. Several of the riders were unseated, one landing in a stream and one in the ditch. A lady was thrown while trying to jump a very high fence. The Duke of Westminster was leading, followed by Bertie and the rest. There were some 200 spectators including the Duchess of Westminster, the family of the Marquis of Cholmondeley, Lord and Lady Arthur Grosvenor, and others who watched through binoculars from various vantages along the route.

As the last scarlet coat disappeared into the Peckforton Hills, crowds at Ballantyne moved towards another traditional event; the ploughing match and the shoot. If the Hunt and the pheasant and grouse shooting was a sport reserved for gentry, the ploughing match was most certainly reserved for the tenantry.

Andrew was as keen on the shoot as Sam, Dave, and Jack were on the ploughing contest. His hand injury was a shooting handicap, but it was no matter. He could still shoot on his left. As Andrew unpacked his shotgun from a worn case, a rapid series of explosions went off near him, instinctively sending him diving for the ground. He grabbed his shotgun and pulled it close. He looked around for the source; it turned out to be children lighting fire crackers ten yards away. The children and guests laughed and smiled but Andrew was petrified. He had not heard such resonances since the war and struggled to process them. Visions from the war flooded his head; being shell-shocked for days after heavy artillery bombardments, Mills bombs detonating mere feet away, gutting a German with his rifle sword, and cries from soldiers as they lay wounded or dying alone in the night. Will these visions ever go away? Is death my only freedom from them? Must I hide from nightmares by staying awake? Perhaps it's the price I must pay for surviving, he thought. Guests turned and looked upon Andrew and pointed, wondering what was up with him. Seeing her husband on the ground with his hands covering his ears, Elsie ran to his aid. She knelt down and lifted him.

"It's okay, Andrew. Just children playing. You're safe." Elsie had seen this happen before, sometimes triggered by loud noises and sometimes from nothing at all. On several occasions she observed Andrew just staring into space as if in a drunken trance. Some nights he could not sleep, and began sorting mail downstairs after midnight. His symptoms were those of 'shell shock'. Though common in returning soldiers, the condition was not well treated at the time. He began to sob but choked his emotions back. Embarrassed, Andrew slowly regained his composure and stood with the help of Elsie. He looked about at the guests watching him, laughing. After dusting himself off and picking up his shot gun and case, Andrew and Elsie slowly walked on to the shoot.

Robert Bryden stepped onto a small stage with an announcing cone and issued the impending start of the ploughing contest. The crowds hurried to a large field where thirty-one estate farmers stood ready with their horse and ploughs at the starting line. It was a single furrow, single horse-drawn race judged for straightness, firmness, evenness, depth, shape and uniformity. A good ploughed furrow had to be straight with a smooth trough and with clean, even sides. Sam, Dave, and Jack looked to each other along the starting line and smiled. Now this is their idea of fun, they all thought. There was a revolver shot in the air and the race was off. Judges walked carefully along the sides and centerline of the field observing the furrows of each contestant.

Two miles away, near Cholmondeley Castle, Bertie was in full gallop with Julius. The fox dashed across a stream, confusing the hounds, and disappeared into a thicket. The other riders negotiated the many hazards, making jumps and crossing streams. Bertie and Julius jumped a hedge easily and continued on while the rider behind, Lord Crewe, got a refusal from his horse and stopped before the hedgerow. Still another scarlet was met with a refusal behind him. Three other riders rushed past and barely made it over the hedge, some skimming the hedge top with their hoofs. Out of the trees, Wilkinson came up alongside Bertie and Julius. Wilkinson gave Bertie an evil smile but Bertie ignored him. Bertie knew he had to get away from him. He was going to do something and being first back at the Fête was not enough.

After an hour of hard riding, the fox disappeared up a tree and the hounds jumped and howled around it. Riders pulled up, horses breathing hard. Everyone was exhausted. Riding to hounds was a physically demanding exercise for both horses and riders. The hired whips arrived and leashed the hounds to take them back to Ballantyne.

"Another great hunt!" Lord Crewe proclaimed. "Now, back to the start!"

Nine riders began the leg back to the stables. There were several routes back and some split off to find their own way. Bertie chose a longer trail, not caring if he won the race. Mainly, he wanted to elude Wilkinson. The path led through a dense wood. He checked behind him and saw he was alone.

He and Julius emerged from the wood and cantered toward a tall hedgerow. Trusting his rider, Julius sailed over it, landing in the road on the other side. Suddenly, Wilkinson appeared on their right side. He had taken a path that merged laterally with Bertie's trail.

Wilkinson closed the distance between them and whipped at Bertie with his crop. Surprised, Bertie retaliated with his whip but was too late. Wilkinson pulled ahead onto a narrow trail through a forested area and Bertie followed twenty yards behind, winding his way through the maze of trees. He had ridden these trails many times over the years and knew a shortcut on this one. He slowed and turned Julius onto a narrow path that was hidden by brush. They walked quickly into a boggy area, ducking to avoid low branches. When they came out, he looked back and saw he was ahead of the other man. He picked up his pace and narrowly avoiding another branch, jumped Julius over a decayed log. In his haste to again overtake Bertie, Wilkinson followed and hit the same branch, sailing face-first into the bog. Bertie halted to make certain Wilkinson was all right. After a moment, he limped out of the trees and Bertie resumed his ride to the finish line.

He joined seven riders galloping over an open field toward the cheering crowds. Bertie and Julius crossed the finish line first and heard the crowd erupt in triumphant cheers. Other riders arrived, one bleeding from the head. Bertie leaned over Julius' sweaty neck and stroked him gratefully. Lord Crewe came up beside Bertie as he dismounted.

"Jolly great show, son!" he exclaimed. "Where'd you learn to ride?"

Lord Delemere's daughter Josephine waved her crop at Bertie and smiled her congratulations. A lovely girl, Bertie observed. Her long blond hair was fastened into a bun at her nape for the race. She unpinned it and shook her hair upon her shoulders. People crowded around him talking excitedly, extending congratulations. Ivy finally found Bertie and rushed over to him. They embraced, then she noticed the raised red welt on his forehead. "What happened?" she asked.

Bertie shrugged and took her hand. "Just a low branch. It's nothing."

Wilkinson was last to arrive, covered in mud, a red welt also on his forehead. He looked about angrily and saw Robert Bryden watching him from a distance. Disgusted, knowing he'd been soundly defeated by a tenant farmer, he whipped his horse and rode off the grounds.

Sam, Jack and Dave hovered at a beer stand, covered to their thighs in dirt. They talked enthusiastically about the ploughing match. Mary sat with the palmist and listened to him tell her fortune, Joseph watching with amusement.

--- 84 ---

"It's none of our business, Ivy!" Bertie pleaded as he unbridled their horse and trap in the courtyard of Droppingstone. The events of the Ballantyne Great Fête and Chester Hunt had lasted all day and both were exhausted. In fact, it was still going on and would continue into the late evening with dancing and fireworks later.

"He's your friend!" Ivy said as she removed items purchased at the Fête from their buggy.

"He's my landlord," Bertie corrected, adjusting the bandage on his forehead. "And William Cutter is the land agent. We could lose the farm!"

"Robert Bryden is our landlord, not William Cutter!"

"I won't be disloyal to any of them, Ivy. I tell you it's none of our business! The matter can only harm us. Maybe they are just friends— "

"Friends don't behave like that, Bertie!"

He faced her. "Like what?"

"Kissing."

"If it amounts to anything," Bertie said. "Major Bryden will discover it soon enough and make amends. It's his problem, not ours. Promise me you'll say nothing, Ivy. We should never have gone today! Andrew was not well. Dropped out of the shoot."

Bertie suddenly leaned to one side and started to collapse.

"Bertie!" Ivy screamed.

Ivy caught him and eased him to his knees. His mind was spinning with the onset of fever.

"You didn't take your quinine, did you?"

Bertie leaned against the wall and tried to stand.

"Actually, I think it's from the ale..." Bertie joked. "I can't drink like I did in the army."

Ivy released him and hurried inside. She returned with a box of quinine pills and placed one in his mouth.

"Swallow, Bertie" she said gently and gave him a sip of water from a cup. She helped him stand. "Let's go lay down." She helped him up the stairs and into bed.

"I'm all right," Bertie said, wiping sweat from his brow. He shivered, hoping the quinine would take effect soon.

"Please, Bertie just rest. Why did you have to enter the hunt, anyway?"

She pulled a wool blanket to his neck and applied a damp cloth to his forehead.

--- **85** ---

As with all wars, changes were made at their conclusion, and the yeomanry was no exception. Before the war, the regiment assembled for training in May. Now it was held in late July because it allowed a longer period in summer in which to train before Camp, and Camp was where the Yeomanry would perform military exercises for weeks. Before the war, there were fifty-four yeomanry units but now only fourteen remained as cavalry. All fourteen units were re-equipped and advised that the day was coming in which horses would be replaced with mechanization, though horsemanship and parades would continue for ceremonial purposes. Shortly before the conclusion of training, the regiment won the Inter-Yeomanry Challenge Cup for shooting, an award it had never won.

Camp was held at Prestatyn near the River Dee. Many new subalterns joined the Yeomanry, some being the sons of former squadron commanders. In celebration, Robert Bryden held a gala for the yeomanry officers. At the midpoint of the evening, Bryden presented the ceremonial "Silver Horse" trophy to the company which had achieved the highest standard of horse management during training. It was the most coveted of all squadron trophies.

Outside, Wilkinson and a young lady guest had strolled away from the ceremonies. He led her into the stable and began kissing her passionately.

"Please, A.G...." the lady said. "Noooo."

"No, what?" Wilkinson asked. "We're alone."

He slid her dress away from her neck, revealing her breasts. As she tried to restore it, Wilkinson pulled it down again. There was a ripping sound. She struggled and pushed at him. He pushed her onto the straw-covered floor.

On a foot path near the stable, Lt. Colonel Verdin and his wife Lindsay Bryden strolled. Hearing a scream, the officer ran to the stable and began to struggle with Wilkinson. The girl ran up the path to Lindsay, who covered her with her coat.

Later, after the dance hall was closed off from the castle foyer, a bloodied and drunk Wilkinson was brought before Bryden by several other officers. He was led into the estate office and the door was closed. Bryden studied him and the scratches on his face.

"What happened?" Bryden asked of several yeoman officers holding Wilkinson.

"I caught him assaulting a female guest in the stable," he said.

"Is this true?" Bryden asked of Wilkinson who seemed to be in a daze.

"We were just...enjoying the evening," Wilkinson offered.

"Please, ask the doctor to see to the lady," Bryden said. "Quietly." A yeoman officer departed the office. "And summon the constable." Another officer nodded and walked out.

"Stay with him here until the constable arrives," Bryden ordered, then left.

Bryden opened the door to the dance hall and walked over to Lt. Colonel Wilson who was dancing with his wife. After listening a moment to Bryden, his expression became pallid and they both walked out of the hall.

In the succeeding days, A.G. Wilkinson was faced with criminal charges. But instead of causing further embarrassment to the regiment, and with Bryden being Sheriff, he was offered the option of resignation, and he took it. Bryden also barred his former friend from the estate.

--- 86 ---

The Ballantyne Estate in October 1926 was a sight to behold. The weather and grounds were as near perfect as it could be. With fall approaching, there was precious little time left to enjoy it before the long winter. Robert Bryden knew he had to be in Chester for a meeting with a magistrate that afternoon as part of his duties as the Sheriff. Afterward, he would meet Heidi and the children at a fine dining house called "The Grouse" for supper, but he had no appointments between noon and then. It was a rare blunder by his staff to leave gaps in his daily schedule, but perhaps intentional. For once, he had an appointment with himself.

After putting on his riding clothes, he noticed Heidi through a bedroom window walking through the garden. In their nearly twenty years together, he had never seen such a sight. Or perhaps he never took notice. Her cherry brown hair and jade green eyes could be seen, even from there. She's more beautiful now than ever before, he thought. He felt so useless, so unworthy. A sense of hopelessness came over him, as it had many times in the past. What have I done in my life that made her proud? Or anyone? He felt the need to go to her.

In the foyer of Ballantyne, William Cutter waited for his employer to join him for the estate ride, hearing of it just minutes earlier. Cutter observed Bryden as he descended the staircase and met him at the foot.

"William, I'll meet you at the stables straight away!" Bryden said as he headed out to the garden.

"Yes, sir," Cutter answered to Bryden's back. "Did you have a mount in mind?"

Bryden looked at Cutter over his shoulder before losing sight of him. "Julius, I should think. We need a good workout!"

Cutter thought he heard him say 'Julius', but was not sure.

Heidi did not see her husband enter, but she knew he was there. She always felt his energy and love when he was near her.

"I was...just there," he said pointing up to their bedroom window. "And I saw you. I don't think I've ever seen you so beautiful."

Heidi laughed. "Robert, you know I always enjoy the garden at this time!"

Bryden grew serious. "Yes, but I never saw you. Always been wasting time somewhere else."

"Your passion for riding has deprived you of many opportunities to be with me," she teased while placing some clipped roses she had just harvested into a basket. "What more must I do to make my husband notice me?"

"Come riding with me."

She laughed. "I would have to change."

"I'll wait," he said, pointing to the stables. "You'll save me from Julius! You said a long time ago you would protect me. And you have. For twenty wonderful years."

"Oh, don't ride the hunter, Robert!" she said. "He's not gentled yet."

"He's broken. I rode him last year before and after the hunt. You've ridden him many times!"

"Horses behave differently with different riders, Robert, I keep telling you! I have a way with him, that's all."

"Then come with me," Bryden insisted. "I'll ride one of the twins and you can show me how to handle Julius!"

"I would much prefer a walk," Heidi said. "I must be in Chester at three and you have your meeting with Lord...whomever."

He slid his arms around her and kissed her. She eased him away to study his face. She felt an uneasiness about him; a kind of vacant loneliness. She had seen him that way on a number of occasions.

"What's wrong, Robert?"

"We must spend more time together, Heidi," he said. "In all our years, I have been away much too long. What a waste. And now it's almost 1927."

"Not so long," Heidi said. "We'll have many more, Robert. And we'll have a silver anniversary too, like your parents."

He suddenly felt reassured. It was her voice and confidence in him that made him strong he thought, not his father or the estate and its millions of pounds. And certainly not the Yeomanry, of which he was so proud to be part of, at least before 1915. She was like a drug, like quinine, that eased his bouts of misery. He straightened and kissed her hand. Not letting go, he held her hand to his cheek. As rich as he was, he felt that he was just a brief caretaker of a stack of bricks and nothing more. On many instances, he pondered how close he had come to death and escaped it, only wishing later the circumstances had taken him. Perhaps then he could have made his mark in the world, like in a *Gazette* war dispatch. His father would have liked that. Eleven men and two women had died under his command since joining the yeomanry in 1895. All people who would never again smell the fragrance of life or feel the warmth of the sun again.

"I'll meet you and the children at The Grouse at five?"

"Yes, my love." Heidi said. They kissed and he left.

She noticed Cutter standing in front of the stables looking at her.

"The car is waiting in front, ma'am."

"Thank you, Lloyd." She said, and walked into the castle.

In the car, minutes later, Heidi turned to look through the rear window at Ballantyne.

Julius Caesar was a bay gelding purchased from the Tollemache Estate four years ago. He was indeed spirited but not, as Robert Bryden thought that day, beyond the skill of a Cheshire Yeoman. Cutter and Heidi had ridden him many times, Bertie in the Chester Hunt, and he several times, but twice with difficulty. Bryden had been thrown only once on the estate, the time when Bertie came to his aide. He also had his horse shot from under him in South Africa and was thrown several times in Egypt, one from an engine backfire and the others from gun percussions. But there was the time near the Suez when he was thrown for no reason at all. Bryden knew that being thrown was always a risk and dealt with best by knowing how to land: Let go of the reins, clear the stirrups, bend the knees, curl into a ball, and roll with the impact.

William Cutter was waiting at the stables with Julius and a Kabardian mare named Bess. Cutter watched Bryden walk confidently along a gravel path that weaved through trim shrubbery. He held Julius' bridle firmly as Bryden mounted him. Sensing who the rider was, Julius stirred.

"Are you sure you won't let me take him, sir?" Cutter insisted. "He's fresh, you know. Just up from the field."

Bryden looked at his agent, puzzled. "What is troubling everyone today? First Heidi, now you?"

Cutter massaged Julius chest to calm him. "Just looking to your safety, sir."

"Well, no thank you, William," Bryden answered. "I'm taxed and need a good release! I'm to meet my family in Chester this evening for dinner."

This news bothered Cutter though he was careful not to show it. Bryden struggled a bit to control Julius and followed Cutter's lead by leaning forward and rubbing his neck. As experienced as Bryden was, he was careful to note the skill exhibited by his peers without admitting any weakness, a trait he learned from his father. Cutter easily mounted Bess and led them out to a pebbled estate trail that opened to the fields. The head forester, Ernest Black, greeted them. He began to explain a complaint he had about hired help.

Suddenly, Julius bolted, unseating Bryden to the ground. Bryden rolled and halted his motion by extending his upper arm.

Cutter was instantly off Bess to his employer's side. "Are you all right, sir?" he asked. Black helped him to his feet.

"That bloody animal is a nuisance!" Bryden joked as he stood and dusted himself off. "Bert Bebbington rode him at the Fête, and he was fine. In fact, he was first back to the finish line! I'll take him for a jaunt up the hill. That should teach him!"

"Sir, I must insist," Cutter said. "Please ride a less phantomy horse."

"Without getting my way?" Bryden remounted Julius and kicked him into a gallop. Black and Cutter watched as Bryden ran Julius up the hill. They reached the summit two hundred yards away without stopping and disappeared down the other side.

Ernest Black continued his complaint. "…and the blacksmiths, sir, well they say they could make a better wage on the Cholmondeley Estate–"

"Then tell them they should go!" Cutter said, carefully listening to Black but with his eyes never leaving the summit of the hill. "I'll be back later to discuss it!"

He quickly remounted Bess and followed after his employer.

On the other side of the hill, Robert Bryden was in full sprint on Julius, nearing the estate pool. He had never felt Julius' full power until that moment and focused on maintaining the speed but with considerably more control. He noted a young boy walking the field a hundred yards to his left.

Ahead was a split-rail fence which converged from both sides to a gate over a narrow creek at the base of the hill. Bryden could see that the gate was closed. He had jumped the five-foot fence several times before with other horses but not with Julius. Deciding to jump, Bryden whipped Julius's rump with his crop. He knew it was against his wisdom to try this jump with a temperamental horse, but he had been in worse situations in South Africa and then again in Egypt and the Suez. And, he had his wife's love and prayers. What could possibly harm him now?

William Cutter reached the summit of the hill but could not see them. His eyes slid across the horizon and below it, trying to find some change in contrast that might reveal Bryden and Julius. He saw that the east gate had been left open 150 yards below him and made a mental note to talk to Ernest Black about estate carelessness. He looked north, seeing workers near the pool about a quarter mile away. Cutter looked again down at the open gate and edged Bess forward a few feet to better his view. To his left, he observed the young boy Bryden had seen minutes before who was now running speedily towards the gate.

Then he saw them.

Julius was lying on the ground just past the gate amongst splintered rails.

"Dear God!" Cutter uttered. He kicked Bess into motion and descended the hill.

Robert Bryden had never been shot or seriously injured before and he suddenly wished he had as it would have prepared him for what pain really was, and he was in horrible pain. He felt Julius hit the top rail and trip on his hind legs, sending Bryden at full force into the ground. Julius fell after him sending his one thousand pounds of body on top of him, crushing much of Bryden's lower half. He saw Cutter approach and dismount but then closed his eyes as it took too much effort to keep them open. He needed to remain still as he had been trained and to rely on his friend's aid and judgment. An image of Heidi in the garden appeared in his head. His last thought was how upset she would be after missing their dinner appointment in Chester. The young boy arrived at the gate, horrified. Cutter recognized him as Ernest Black's son Clive.

"Go to the castle and tell your father that Major Bryden has been injured!" Cutter told Clive. "He needs a doctor." The boy hesitated. "Go!"

Clive Black turned and ran as fast as he could towards the castle.

Minutes later and several hundred yards away, children stood in front of Harthill School watching the goings on at Ballantyne. Cars and lorries began arriving and estate workers ran about. Something had happened. An estate worker, galloping on horseback, was halted by the schoolmaster.

"What has happened?" the schoolmaster asked.

"Major Bryden has been badly injured!" he answered and rode on. The schoolmaster gathered the children and ushered them inside.

Robert Bryden died at Ballantyne Castle at 6:10 p.m. on that Monday evening. Beside him were his wife Heidi, and his sons Matthew and young Geoffrey. He never regained consciousness since the accident several hours earlier.

Outside the castle entrance, a crowd of estate workers, their families, and tenantry had formed, hoping for news of the squire's recovery and to offer help. Children from Harthill School had been dismissed for the day. Cars, lorries, carts, and riders came and went. Mary and Joseph arrived by carriage from Rawhead as the news dispersed through the crowd. Mary saw Thomas Harding of the Bank Farm standing next to his wife who was sitting on a stone bench.

"How is Major Bryden?" Mary asked.

"He's dead," Harding said in a daze. "We just learned of it."

Mary covered her mouth with her scarf and tears welled in her eyes. She could not manage to speak.

Joseph walked over to Harding. "How did it happen, Thomas?"

Harding pointed to the green dales behind the castle. "He was riding just there on the hill when his horse lost control," he said vacantly. "Ernest Black's son Clive said his horse smashed through the gate and collapsed onto him."

Joseph looked among the crowd to see if he could hear tenants discussing anything more.

"There's to be an inquest next Thursday!" a voice said. Joseph looked to the voice; it was John Booth from the Hill Farm. "Superintendent Amherst is coming over from Broxton."

Joseph took Mary's arm. "Come, Mary," he said. "We can do nothing here. Let's go home." He looked into her face. "There's work to be done."

Robert Bryden had been taken into the library where a bed had been brought down. After watching her husband draw his last breath and pass from this life, Heidi Bryden retreated to their bedroom upstairs. Geoffrey was led away by the governess. The castle staff knew she wished to be alone but stood outside her door. In the bedroom, ticking from a massive grandfather clock reminded her of the preciousness of time and how much had been lost that day and over the years.

An hour later, there was a gentle tap on the door. Heidi ignored it while she sat in a chair facing the bay window. The tap continued.

The door slowly opened. It was William Cutter, still wearing his riding clothes, soiled and with blood stains. Heidi observed him briefly but turned back to the bay window. She was trying to see in the garden what her husband had that morning. Cutter entered but left the door ajar. There was a long silence as he stood watching her.

"I'm sorry, Heidi," Cutter said from across the room. He slowly walked to an ottoman and sat, still some distance from her. He rubbed his face, trying to summon an explanation of what had transpired earlier that day. "I begged him not to take the hunter. He insisted."

The clock ticked away.

Heidi remained still on the far side of the room, trying to remember her husband's rare words of love that morning and then replaying them in her mind. Not knowing what to do, Cutter slowly stood and approached her. Sensing his nearness, Heidi rushed to him and began beating his chest furiously with her fists.

"What have you done?" she screamed. "What have you done? I don't want you here anymore! I want you off Ballantyne now!"

"Heidi, I—"

"Get out!" she screamed. "I asked you to look over him! You were paid to take care of him!"

Hearing the screams from the hallway, Matthew Bryden rushed in. Seeing them struggling, he stepped between them.

"Leave," Matthew said to Cutter. "Please, William."

Cutter slowly backed away, out of the room. Two maids entered after him and closed the door. Cutter mindlessly descended the staircase to a crowd of estate staff in the foyer. Amid questioning eyes, Cutter eased his way through them and out the castle entrance.

On the morning of Robert Bryden's funeral, Bertie opened a trunk in the attic of Droppingstone Farm, revealing his RASC uniform and campaign medals. None of the medals were for notable deeds or bravery but in recognition of service during the war. The 1914-15 Star Medal, the British War Medal, and the Allied Victory Medal. He put the uniform on and rode separate from Ivy over to Ballantyne. Arriving at the stables, he was met by the estate blacksmith, John Clyde who was shoeing one last horse before the funeral service. Bertie knocked on a stable post.

"Hello, Mr. Clyde," Bertie said. "I was wondering if I could borrow Julius for an hour."

Bertie stood before him wearing his dress ASC uniform with shined boots, polished buttons, and cap.

After a moment, Clyde nodded. "Sure, Bertie."

Six years after Gilbert Bryden's death, another mile-long cortège extended from Ballantyne Castle across the meadows to All Saints Church. Dignitaries from England and Scotland came for the service. Forty-two children from Harthill School looked on, wearing the best clothes their parents could muster. After the service, six estate workers carried Bryden's casket to Harthill Cemetery. In front of the Bryden mausoleum, over 500 tenantry, Cheshire Yeomen, and families from across England sang one last hymn, "*Nearer to God*". Robert Bryden's casket was slowly carried inside and placed into an empty crypt. On the back wall was an ornately carved marble cross. Outside, on the walls, were panels where memorials were inscribed. Bryden's grandfather had the structure built so that the family had views of the church yard, school, and Ballantyne Castle.

Reverend Moreland read from Thessalonians: "Who shall be punished with everlasting destruction from the presence of the Lord, and from the glory of his power; When he shall come to be glorified in his saints." Then from John he continued, "Jesus said unto her, I am the resurrection, and the life; he that believeth in me, though he were dead, yet shall he live: And whosoever liveth and believeth in me shall never die. Believest though this?"

William Cutter observed Heidi Bryden through the crowd but looked away, not wanting her to see him. Mourners opened their hymnals and began to sing. Mary and Joseph Bebbington held each other as they reverently sang a familiar hymn from memory. Oliver Goldford brushed tears from his eyes. A.G. Wilkinson, wearing civilian clothes, stood alone and apart from the others. The service went on.

"Major Robert Bryden was a model landlord who lived happily among his tenantry and had the highest regard for their welfare," Moreland said. "As an officer with the Cheshire Yeomanry for twenty-six years, he led soldiers in South Africa and Egypt. He was High Sheriff of Cheshire, a county magistrate, and a past president of the Cheshire Agrarian Society. In these positions he set a high example of public service. The people of Cheshire mourn and join in sympathy with the Bryden family.

"Let us commend Robert Bryden to the mercy of God, our maker and redeemer," Moreland continued. "We therefore commit his body to the ground; earth to earth, ashes to ashes, dust to dust; in the sure and certain hope of the Resurrection to eternal life."

As the ceremony concluded and mourners started to leave, Matthew Bryden, Geoffrey, Cutter, Heidi, and the others slowly turned to see a rider at the cemetery fence wearing a British Army uniform, holding the bridal of a caparisoned horse with colored ribbons. It was Bertie and a very well-behaved Julius Caesar. Bertie's uniform bore insignia of the now Royal Army Service Corps, as conferred by warrant in November 1918, of which he was very proud. Empty riding boots were placed back to front in the stirrups, symbolizing that Major Bryden is looking over his troops one last time. Bertie saluted the grave of his friend, followed by companies of Cheshire Yeomen and other veterans in attendance. Out of uniform and not permitted to salute anymore, A.G. Wilkinson had departed. Bertie finished his salute, slowly turned and calmly led Julius away on foot.

An inquest was held on Tuesday afternoon in the Ballantyne Castle library. Messrs. Taylor, Lester and Co., solicitors of Chester were present to represent the family. Superintendent Amherst of the county police, Matthew Bryden, Ella Bryden, Heidi Bryden, Dr. Crawley, county coroner, Dr. Henry Lakin of Chester, and the head forester, Ernest Black and his son Clive were also present. All sat in chairs set in an arc before C.J. Stockbridge and a small table near the door. A stenographer recorded the proceedings. The inquest was underway when Cutter knocked twice and entered.

"William Cutter, sir," Cutter said to Stockbridge. "Land agent for the Ballantyne Estate. My utmost apologies, I was... detained."

"Please be seated, Mr. Cutter," Stockbridge said, pointing his pen to the only vacant chair.

Cutter closed the door. He wished he had not lied of his whereabouts that morning. He was not detained, but had stood for hours on the Raw Head escarpment looking towards Harthill and beyond. From there, he could see long distances, whether it was clear or not. As the stenographer finished noting the agent's arrival, Cutter walked to the only empty chair, opposite the room from Heidi Bryden. He looked to her. Their eyes met briefly but she looked away.

"Please go on, Dr. Lakin," Stockbridge said to the coroner.

"I arrived at 3:30 p.m. on Monday to find Major Bryden suffering from injuries to several parts of his body. Upon examination, I found that his pelvis, hip, and leg were fractured on the left side and in connection with these fractures was a deep incision about four inches deep. This wound caused a hemorrhage, though there were fractured ribs on the same side, some of which had punctured his lungs."

Heidi Bryden sighed and leaned to her side, comforted by Matthew. Some noticed, and Dr. Lakin allowed her a moment before continuing.

"There was a small wound on his left temple and his left eye was swollen and bruised. My examination also revealed various internal hemorrhages." Lakin shifted in his seat. "Given these injuries, there was nothing I could do except dress his wounds and ease his pain with a shot of morphine. Dr. Tarver arrived moments later and confirmed my assessment. I pronounced Major Bryden dead at 6:10 p.m. on Monday October

4. The immediate cause of death was shock from injuries sustained in the accident nearly four hours earlier."

Heidi Bryden clenched Matthew's coat, deeply wanting to go to her room.

Dr. Crawley, the coroner, was now being questioned. "Dr. Crawley, what was the cause of the deep incision you described?"

"I do not know," Dr. Crawley responded.

Charles Birch, esquire, leaned forward and pointed to Crawley with his pipe.

"Um, Dr. Crawley, wasn't the injury caused by Major Bryden's collision with the gate?"

"I believe it may have been from Major Bryden's impact with the gate, yes, sir."

"Please, just describe what you are certain of, Dr. Crawley." Stockbridge insisted.

"Yes, of course. I do not know exactly what caused the wound."

After two hours of testimony from other witnesses, the inquest adjourned for half an hour. Some gathered for tea in the dining room. Just after 4:00 p.m. the inquest resumed.

"Mr. Cutter, you accompanied Major Bryden on a ride over the estate," Stockbridge inquired. "What time was that?"

"We departed the stables at about 2:00 o'clock in the afternoon."

"And what happened then?"

"We entered an estate trail and stopped to speak with the head forester, Mr. Ernest Black."

"And what was said?"

Cutter adjusted his seating. "I had been meaning to speak with Mr. Black about clearing a large area near the Ballantyne Hill Farm. For the planting of barley. I thought this was a good time to discuss the matter as it required Major Bryden's approval. Our conversation shifted to an employee's complaint regarding pay. Major Bryden then attempted to turn his horse away and was thrown. He landed safely and laughed it off."

Heidi straightened to observe Cutter's testimony.

"Are you saying he was thrown before the accident?" inquired Stockbridge.

"Yes, sir," Cutter answered. "But he was fine. Uninjured."

Stockbridge flipped back through his ledger. "Why did you not—"

"Sir," interrupted Cutter, "as I stated earlier, I warned Major Bryden several times to take another horse, mine or one of the others, as I knew the hunter was fresh and a bit spirited. Major Bryden refused. He was intent on riding Julius."

"And Julius is the name of the animal?"

Cutter eased back, trying to calm himself. "Julius is the name of the horse, yes, sir."

"And what kind of horse is Julius?"

"He is a seven-year-old bay gelding of good breeding, sir." Cutter explained.

"Why?"

"Why what, sir?"

"Why would Major Bryden ride such a dangerous horse?"

"The horse was not dangerous, sir. Just spirited, strong, and fresh. Many horses are that way."

"Then what is your opinion as to why he would ride such a...'spirited' horse, Mr. Cutter?"

After a long pause, Cutter said, "He said he felt he needed...a good ride." Heidi closed her eyes and looked to her lap. She brushed away tears.

In the dining room, maids readied refreshments for any adjournment of the inquest. Outside, estate workers and town folk stood, waiting for any word.

"They have been in there for hours," a maid said to another. The library door opened and attendees of the inquest began exiting. Matthew Bryden stopped and nodded to the maids, signaling the verdict.

"What does that mean?" one maid asked, observing Bryden's nod.

"It has been ruled an accident."

Days later, an obituary was published in The *Observer*. At the Rawhead Farm table, Jack Bebbington read aloud to the family:

> *"The Tragic Death of Major Robert Bryden, Killed in a riding accident. He died on Monday evening from injuries received midafternoon on his estate. The Brydens of Ballantyne Castle are one of the most respected of Cheshire's squires. Major Bryden was the kindest of landlords and had the highest regard for his tenant's welfare. An officer with the Cheshire Yeomanry, he bravely led his soldiers in South Africa and Egypt. An ex-High Sheriff of Cheshire, a county magistrate, and a past president of the Cheshire Agrarian Society, he was a model public servant. Cheshire grieves his untimely and catastrophic death."*

Jack looked up from the paper. "It goes on to discuss the inquest and various accounts," he said, turning the page. "Ruled an accident."

"Why on earth would he ride such a horse?" asked Dave, as he spread butter on some bread. "He had his pick!"

"One can ride horses all their life and never know them," explained Bertie, looking out the window, reflecting on his experience with animals. "Animals can be unpredictable, no matter how skilled the rider!" Bertie looked at Jack. "What of his horse? Julius?"

Jack nodded. "I don't know."

Later, Mary and Jack stopped at All Saints Churchyard in Harthill and walked to the flower covered Bryden Mausoleum. They read a new inscription:

ROBERT BRYDEN
OF BALLANTYNE CASTLE
MAJOR, SQUADRON B, CHESHIRE YEOMANRY
NOV 21st, 1876 – OCT 4th, 1926
BELOVED SQUIRE AND LANDLORD

"Just fifty years old," Jack uttered as his mother placed some wildflowers before it. "His son Matthew will inherit the estate. I wonder what he plans for Rawhead and the other farms."

William Cutter stood before his former desk in the Ballantyne estate office packing his personal things.

"Mr. Cutter?"

He turned to see Bertie at the door.

"Bertie," he answered.

"Mr. Cutter, I've an offer for you," Bertie said.

"Let me buy Julius. I could use him at Droppingstone."

"I...am no longer the estate manager, Bertie," Cutter said. "But I understand he is to be put down. Killed a man."

367

"But it was an accident, sir," pleaded Bertie. "It wasn't his fault. He would be harmless on a farm."

Cutter looked away.

"Bertie, it's out of my hands. I wish I could help."

Cutter solemnly left the office with a box under his arm and walked past Bertie into the foyer.

"Mr. Cutter, I never believed what they said about you. I know Major Bryden was not just your employer. He always spoke highly of you."

Cutter slowly turned and looked to him squarely. "Thank you, Bertie."

Weeks later, A.G. Wilkinson's body was found near a footpath in the Delemere Forest, partially eaten by wolves. It was determined he had taken his life by gunshot.

--- **87** ---

"We'll be needing a new land agent," Matthew Bryden said as he finished reading the January 3, 1927 *Observer* at dinner. The headline read:

Economic Crisis Ahead, Says Babson

Heidi looked at him with surprise.
"What do you mean? William Cutter is the land agent." She said.
"He left for South Africa yesterday on the *Fastnet*."
This was news to Heidi. "But why?"
Bryden wiped his mouth with a linen napkin and helped himself to more sausage.
"To take a position with the South African government," he said. "I suspect he's off Portugal by now."
"Was he not happy here?"
"I suspect the tragedy weighed on him."
"But he was not at fault."

"The estate doesn't blame him," Bryden said. "But he'll want to sort it out."

Heidi stood from the table. Please excuse me, Matthew." She had inquired enough.

"Mother," Bryden called to her from the table. "I've been meaning to speak with you about something." He got up from the table and met her.

"There's a dowry house available for your new residence."

"New residence?" she inquired. "I am no longer to stay here?"

"It's…customary for widowers to live in one of the dower houses with their children. I'm sure you and Geoffrey will find the house quite comfortable. You will have a maid, gardener and cook at your disposal, of course. I will be starting my own family here, you understand."

"Yes," Heidi replied. "Yes, of course."

Heidi felt terribly alone. It wasn't so much leaving Ballantyne as it was a reminder of Robert. She had no one now.

At Droppingstone Farm, Bertie and Ivy enjoyed tea with their children. Bertie had worked endlessly with her for years to master the art of cheese making, but the prospect was elusive. Finally, after letting a batch age for eight months, Bertie placed a small wheel of Cheshire on the table. He carefully removed the wrapping and cut a wedge and then a sliver and placed it in his mouth. It was not moldy or distasteful. It was not too salty, but full-flavored, mild, crumbly, dense, tangy, and a bit nutty. He looked to his wife. She tasted a piece and after an eternity, nodded favorably.

"Mrs. Nunnerly would approve," Ivy said. It was a momentous occasion. Bertie had joined his wife in becoming a master cheesemaker. He took Ivy in his arms.

Ballantyne blacksmith John Clyde walked into the Droppingstone Farm's cobbled courtyard with a horse. Hearing the steps, Bertie turned and walked with Ivy to the doorway. It was Julius.

Bertie slowly walked over to Julius.

"A gift from Major Bryden," said Clyde.

Julius's eyes looked around the unfamiliar courtyard and then to Bertie. Bertie slowly stepped towards the now infamous horse. Julius backed a step, not sure of the somewhat familiar human before him.

"Easy, lad." Bertie slowly stepped closer, eventually reaching him. Julius sniffed Bertie's hand and was instantly relieved.

Bertie began stroking his mane. Julius nudged him playfully with his nose. Bertie crouched, lifted his leg, and surveyed the scars from the accident.

"You remind me of a friend of mine," Bertie said. "Actually two friends. Max. You won't throw me, will you?"

Julius nudged Bertie again.

Bertie climbed onto Julius' back and laid over Julius' neck. He stroked his sides and neck, remembering Max, Errol, and the other animals he led ashore the Pelion Peninsula in Greece. *What had become of them?*

"No more hunting for you. No Service Corps, either. Just easy rides on the farm."

Ivy watched the pair ride into Droppingstone's east field and disappear over the rise towards the well.

--- 88 ---

News of the stock market crash on October 3, 1929 reached Cheshire. In Britain, the effects were known as the "Great Slump" and saw a period of economic downturn extending through the 1930s. It was Britain's largest and most profound economic depression of the 20th century. Although the Great Depression originated in the United States and quickly spread to the world, the effects on British farms were less severe. Unemployment rose but rents generally remained the same. In America, Jim and many others lost their jobs when their employer threw himself out of a New York City high rise. But Jim soon got work as a bread truck driver and later as a road inspector.

While cooking dinner, Mabel Jean felt sharp pain in her chest. Doctors and their medications were of little help other than to ease her pain. Philip, Minnie, Jim and Mabes spent as much time as they could together, realizing that Mabel was shy of this earth. They went to shows in New York City, camped on Long

Island and at the Finger Lakes upstate, and exchanged memories of Rawhead over dinner. Mabel continued to fade.

--- 89 ---

Matthew Bryden was not like his father Robert, grandfather Gilbert or his great grandfather Robert. Upon Heidi Bryden's departure for the dowry house in Clangston, he married a Ms. Charise Mariani, an Italian Corsican who went by the name of "Ilaria". Soon after, he was elected Joint Master of Cheshire Hounds. Within a year he took a methodical look at farm rents, many of which were low compared to milk and cheese prices which had risen considerably since the war. So, in 1930 he astounded neighboring estates by introducing farm rents linked to the price of milk. He also surveyed the farms comprising the Ballantyne estate and decided to modernize and amalgamate several, much to tenantry protests. Other estates followed in suit. Some families were displaced and expressed their woes to Mary at Chester Market.

"Me landlord swears he will send me a papper," one tenant farmer said.

"Oh, dear," Mary said, wondering if the same would happen at Rawhead.

The tormented farmer walked off.

But Matthew Bryden assisted most in finding another arrangement. When the *Observer* began to incur financial difficulty from lagging sales, he approached the Board with offers of assistance which they unanimously accepted. Within weeks he became Chairman.

--- 90 ---

The summer of 1930 was particularly hot in Cheshire. It was only June and with three months of work yet to be done in the stifling heat, thought Joseph. He was seventy-two years old and still working the fields. Joseph wished he had brought a jug of water before making the half mile walk to repair the north cattle gate as Jack had taken the horses for ploughing the Clump field. Reaching the gate, Joseph suddenly felt a pressure within his head, then a sharp pain. He covered his forehead with his hand and dropped his hammer.

In the field, Jack was driving a plough and having some difficulty with the horses. Unbeknown to him, they had been underfed the night before and were awry. He halted them.

"What's wrong with you guys?" Jack yelled. "Is Bertie the only one you'll listen to?"

Sensing something, he looked towards the farmhouse and then to the east field, seeing a distant figure leaning against a sandstone wall. He raised his hand to his brow and squinted against the bright sun. A moment later, he watched his father collapse.

"Pa!" screamed Jack as he dismounted the plough and ran a quarter mile to his father.

Joseph broke his fall by leaning on the wall and momentarily tried to stand. Jack arrived and lifted his father's head. "Pa, what is it?"

Joseph looked at him and smiled. "Call your mother, Jack."

On the morning of her husband's burial, Mary Bebbington sat in her favorite chair. In her lap was the large family bible. She opened the front cover and wrote, "d. June 17, 1930" next to Joseph's name. She touched his handwritten name at the top of the cover, as if to summon strength from it. Although it was a day of passing, she was not grief struck. I will see him again, she told herself. She pulled a folded marriage certificate from the back cover.

Reflecting, Joseph was everything she had hoped he would be: A good husband and father, though Jim might have something to say on that. They bore twelve children, five of whom, by some miracle had survived the war. All but Mollie had married. She looked through the parlour window. From there she could view the Cheshire plain and sometimes even as far as Liverpool. She summoned a memory of the day they met. In those days she was considerably thinner. Her hair was long and brown, not the bunted, gray bore it was now, she thought. He was tall and gangly, though strong with chiseled features with straight black hair. Only Bertie shared a resemblance and the rest of the children, hers.

The year was 1884. It was the latter half of the Victorian era which coincided with the Belle Époque era of continental

Europe and the Gilded Age of the United States, periods characterized as peaceful and prosperous. Chester Arthur was President of the United States, the cornerstone for the Statue of Liberty was unveiled on Bedloe's Island in New York Harbor, and Eleanor Roosevelt was born. A Dr. John Harvey Kellogg patented "flaked cereal". In London, the infamous Coldbath Fields Prison for debtors was ordered closed. On their marriage record, Mary's occupation was recorded as "spinster", and for Joseph, "labourer". She was twenty-one and he twenty-eight. Her father was a farm labourer and Joseph's father was a shoemaker journeyman in Broxton.

"It's time, Ma," Bertie said gently from the gate, his voice returning her to the present. She stood up and walked to him with her round, characteristic smile known to lift the heaviest of hearts. She saw the grief in Bertie's face and placed her hand gently to his cheek.

"Your father will always be with us, Bertie, and we with him." Bertie started to cry and turned away. "He was so proud of you."

Bertie walked a few steps to a window and wiped away tears. In the courtyard, two carriages were waiting. The burial plot she chose was near the top of the Brown Knowl graveyard next to Tom, overlooking the farm not more than a mile away. Here, she felt, Joseph could continue to watch over the family as he had since their marriage forty-five years ago. And Tom was at his side.

She had his marker carved to include her when that time came. The stone read:

IN LOVING MEMORY OF JOSEPH, THE BELOVED
HUSBAND OF MARY BEBBINGTON
DIED JUNE 17, 1930 AGED 72 YEARS.
ALSO OF THE ABOVE, TOM ERNEST, SON,
NOVEMBER 6, 1918.

After the service in Brown Knowl Chapel, Joseph's Clump-pine coffin was carried off by Sam, Bertie, Clem, Jack, Andrew, and George. The gathering included Sam's wife Mary, Andrew and Elsie, Dave and Margaret, Martha and William Evans, Bertie and Ivy, Clem and Myra, George and Anne, Mollie, and neighboring farmers and their families. Only Philip and Jim were absent, although they attended church that day in Montclair and sent a telegram. Having not spoken to his father since he left England years earlier, Jim almost did not go.

"I'm sorry, Mary," a familiar voice said near a tall, weather-worn tombstone dating to 1820.

It was Heidi Bryden and William Cutter, Matthew Bryden, and his wife Ilaria.

"Joseph will be remembered," Matthew Bryden said. "A model tenant and tireless farmer."

"Thank you."

When the family returned to Rawhead, they found that a cooked ham with fruit and sweetbreads had been delivered and neatly arranged at their dinner table. As the family pondered the food, Mary stepped outside to the departing estate worker who had delivered it.

"Please thank Mr. Bryden for this," Mary said.

The worker looked at her. "But it's not from the estate, ma'am. It's from Mr. Cutter."

The Clangston dowry house was quite a change for Heidi Bryden. She had grown accustomed to being a country squire's wife with servants tending her every need, though such luxury was too much she thought. In the small garden behind the house,

Heidi and Cutter strolled a path. Heidi stopped to sniff the fragrance of a yellow rose. A gardener walked by with a basket of what appeared to be herbs.

"Good afternoon, ma'am," he said.

"Good afternoon, Giles," Heidi said. "And what are those?"

"They are called Proud Carpenters," the gardener answered. "Good for healing."

Heidi took a stem from the basket and continued on.

"William, what caused the wound in Robert's side?" Heidi asked, looking into space.

Cutter looked to her and said nothing for a long moment.

"I don't know, Heidi. We've been all through that. The gate?"

He took her hands. "Heidi, I didn't kill him. As much as I love you, please believe me."

Heidi looked into his eyes and studied him. Cutter dropped her hands and stepped away. Heidi could see that he was distressed.

"All those years I prayed you were mine and not his," Cutter went on. "I'm sorry for having those thoughts, as they are not Christian. I just…saw you alone for those long periods when he was away. I even heard you crying at times when he was in Egypt. But he was my employer. And he was also my friend. Do you understand?"

Heidi slowly walked to him and rested her head on his chest.

"Take me away from here, William" Heidi said. "Far away."

Days later, news of William Cutter and Heidi Bryden's wedding was the talk of Cheshire. They were married by a justice of the peace in Chester and subsequently departed for South Africa with young Geoffrey.

Cutter had begun to correspond with Heidi Bryden within months of Robert Bryden's untimely death. He had written four letters in two months with no word from her. He swore he would not write another. Three weeks later, a pile of mail was laid on his desk at Cape Town City Hall. He stared at the mail a moment and then noticed a letter bearing the familiar post mark of Chester, England.

--- 91 ---

In all Mary's years, nothing prepared her for what would round The Clump on an April morning in 1931. While milking a cows, Mary and Jack felt the floor and walls of the barn begin to shake. Then there was a rumbling sound from outside. Jack stood up and quickly walked out to see what it was. When Jack had not returned after several minutes, Mary went to see for herself. Outside, Jack stood at the court yard entrance gate unmoving. Beyond him was a long queue of lorries extending from The Clump to the farmhouse. In the lead lorry, Matthew Bryden stood on the passenger side running board with a white scarf flapping leeward from his neck. He looked back, waving and howling to the drivers as if in some great mounted Yeomanry charge. Arriving, he stepped off the lorry dressed in new work clothes and boots. Rather a sight, Mary thought.

"Good morning, Mary!" Bryden said looking around the farm. "I've come to get some bricks."

"Bricks, sir?" Mary inquired.

"Yes…the Chester Zoo project is running short of bricks and I think the farm might be able to spare some!"

"But we have no bricks here, sir," Mary said.

"You've many," Bryden said pointing to several three-foot walls extending from the house in several directions, one all the way to The Clump.

"But, sir, they are part of Rawhead. Couldn't the zoo quarry them? There's lots of quarries in Broxton."

"I wouldn't think of it! Cost too much. Not when I can have a say!" Bryden stomped off into the north field waving for the drivers to follow him. The lorry drivers pulled their vehicles off the dirt road and roared past the garden. Mary watched aghast as some fifteen estate workers, some of whom she recognized and knew in church, began dismantling a three hundred-foot long wall that extended from the farmhouse to The Clump. The workers hurriedly stacked the bricks onto the lorries. Parts of the wall in several sections collapsed from the scampy process in which they worked.

"But sir, you can't!" Mary shouted, running after him. "Those walls are—"

"Mine," interrupted Bryden. He stood firmly facing her. "I'm sorry, Mary, but it's for the good of the county!"

Baffled and hurt, Mary withdrew to the safety of her garden and watched as Ballantyne estate workers changed what had been built since 1865. As one of the directors, Matthew Bryden had been an enthusiastic partner of the Zoo's founder, George Mottershead when he approached him weeks earlier in 1930 with plans to build a zoo for Chester. Having been wounded in the war, Mottershead spent several years in a wheelchair pondering alternatives. As a child, he remembered visiting a now closed zoo in Manchester and was so upset seeing large animals in small cages, and he said to his father, "A proper zoo would not have any bars." Despite this, his collection of animals grew and he began to search for a suitable location for the venture. He finally chose a location in the Chester suburb of Upton for the price of 3,500 pounds sterling. An earlier venture with an affluent physician in developing a small zoo in Shavington had fallen through.

"What is going on?" Jack asked from her side.

"The future, I'm afraid." Mary answered. "The only certain change." Hours later, many of the walls built at Rawhead since 1865 were gone. Jack held his mother to his side.

"We'll fix it," Jack said. "I know some quarry owners."

"Not until the zoo is done," Mary said. "Mr. Bryden would just come and take them."

In the years following, Mary would visit the Chester Zoo often and recognized the bricks forming many of its walls and structures. She was proud to tell zoo patrons that her farm, Rawhead, was a big part of it. She took comfort in knowing the farm had helped provide a home for its animals.

--- 92 ---

As with life everywhere, there were comings and goings. At Rawhead, Jack was the last of Mary and Joseph's boys to marry. He was now twenty-seven and a grocer's daughter named Martha Jones had intrigued him for months. He had noticed her in Brown Knowl Chapel and at her father's store on many occasions. After a several-week courtship, they married, with Dave as the best man. In the coming years they would bear five children.

The tenants of Rawhead Farm had dwindled to just Mary, Jack, Dave, William, and Martha, plus hired labourers. The work got done, but cheese making in the county was slowly being overtaken by milk production. More money could be made that way. It was the future. Instead of growing hay for cattle, farms grew more corn and also changed how milk was produced. Instead of having the cows produce the main bulk of milk in the summer to make the cheese, milk was now produced year-round. Farmhouse Cheshire was still made on many farms and sold at the shows but large-scale production had shifted to factories because the small farms, including Rawhead and Droppingstone, could no longer get the help they needed as wages were higher elsewhere. Although the quality of the cheese was still maintained by strict standards set by the Milk Marketing Board, Mary and Ivy often remarked that it was never the same. The distinctive tangy richness seemed to fade from all the changes. The MMB had come into existence. As such, local dairy farmers found it was easier and more profitable to sell their milk to the MMB rather than continue to make cheese. Branding, such as adding distinctive logos, some with the Cheshire cat face and other art faded. Sam and Bertie's war time friend, Max Wainright, had accurately predicted what was to come and go.

In America, Mabel Jean succumbed to her illness and was buried in Prospect Hill Cemetery in Caldwell. As mourners began to leave her grave, Jim and his daughters Dottie and Jean remained and knelt beside it. Jim kissed the coffin and rested his head on its flower-covered lid.

"I will miss you, Mabes," Jim said. "You are my love, my life, my girl guide, my girl scout."

He slowly stood and looked to Philip and Minnie waiting for him at the car with their sons Philip and Harvey. From under his arm, Jim placed his old brown Boy Scout campaign hat on the casket.

"I'll be back tomorrow, Mabes," Jim added.

Later that year, Jim Bebbington remarried. But he would continue to visit Mabes' grave and left flowers. On birthdays, he left a Boy Scout hat. Thrift stores always seemed to have them.

--- 93 ---
HMS *Queen Mary*
Liverpool Docks
November 1936

In her seventy-one years, Mary Richardson Bebbington had never left England. In fact, she never really left Rawhead except for short trips to Chester and nearby parishes as the boys always did any necessary traveling. But in 1936, an invitation from Jim and Philip to visit them in America was the relief she needed from thoughts of Joseph and Tom...and now Mabel Jean. With Dave, Jack, and William and Martha taking care of Rawhead, she thought it might be the holiday she never had. Mollie had joined Jim and Philip a year earlier to help with their children. It was the one time in her life that she disobeyed her "responsibilities of running a dairy farm were just too great" rule. Aboard the *Queen Mary* at 5 p.m., she waved good-bye to Bertie and Jack in the crowd on the Cunard Lines dock below.

It was a cold, drizzling day in Liverpool. Such weather and being on a ship departing for a southern latitude created an atmosphere of excitement on deck. As the ship nosed away from the dock, passengers gradually made their way to their cabins to dress for supper. Mary remained on deck until the sight of her sons faded. It was a strange feeling, seeing England from the sea. Perhaps it was how her sailor Clem and four soldiers felt when they left England for the war.

Mary looked down at her two large suitcases…but they weren't there! "Oh, Lord! Where are my bags?"

She looked around in a panic, fore and aft, up and down. Then a handsome young ship's officer appeared.

"May I help you, madam?" he inquired.

"My bags! My bags! They were right here!"

"They were taken below to your cabin, madam. Your name?"

"Goodness! Mary Bebbington." The officer produced a clipboard and quickly searched for her name. "Ah, yes. Here we are. Mary Bebbington – Deck Six. Everything is fine, madam. Allow me to escort you to your room."

The officer led Mary to an elevator and they descended to her deck. He opened the door to her cabin and proceeded to show her around. He then pulled a lifejacket off a shelf.

"And lastly, here is your life jacket," the officer said. "There will be a drill this evening so when you hear the announcement, please put it on and make your way to Lifeboat Station No. 4." He laid it on a small table.

"Are there enough lifeboats?" Mary asked, remembering the *Titanic*.

"Yes, more than enough madam," the officer said. "We don't make that mistake anymore. May I have the honor of your dining at my table this evening?"

Relieved, she answered, "Why…yes, I'd be delighted. How lovely."

The officer left and closed the door. Mary curiously looked about the cabin and then looked to the lifejacket on the table and examined it. She thought of the *Lusitania*, and Bertie and the soldiers, sailors, and animals who had been cast into the sea during the war. But no sad thoughts, she told herself.

After six days at sea, Mary arrived in New York and was greeted by Jim and Philip at 11:05 a.m. Jim's employer told him to take his best car to go fetch his mother. Philip greeted her at the gangway and they hugged.

"Oh, Philip," Mary said. "It's been thirteen years!"

They drove sixteen miles to Philip's home, had dinner and retired early.

Mary began to keep a journal:

11 November 1936

This is Armistice Day and a holiday here, so my son Philip took us all to the service at the war memorial in the park. Harold Davies, is Captain of the American Legion and asked me to speak at the memorial. I did not know what to say. So he asked if I could speak in a few weeks at the legion hall and I said I would. We came home from dinner and my son Philip took me for a lovely drive to the aerodrome where I saw the airplanes coming and going, just like in England. We passed a lot of farms and my son told me the fields we saw were most likely the only fields the farmer had and they were so small, just to exercise his cows in. The farms are so different. I did not see any hedges, and there is no shortage of water. The houses are all nicely painted–not many old places. We saw the penitentiary, where naughty people are sent.

Mary's days were full, going on long drives, visiting different markets, spending time with Mollie, who had emigrated several years earlier. Mary wrote letters home, read letters, had tea every day, and went to church every Sunday. She asked the location of the veteran's hospital and spent many days spending time with injured veterans. Curiously, she even asked to see a new mortuary to see all the advancements that had been done in the burial business. Mary was a naturally inquisitive woman and was simply fascinated with America. It was vastly different from her life as a dairyman's wife in Cheshire.

One afternoon, Philip came home and was visibly shaken. Minnie and Mary were having tea.

"What's the matter, Philip?" Minnie asked.

Philip shook his head. "I inspected a slaughter house today on Staten Island. Saw how they make sausage and hot dogs. Horrible. Just horrible."

Philip entered the back yard and surveyed their small vegetable garden, mostly dominated by tomatoes. And that is what they ate that night for supper. As a boy at Rawhead, he thoroughly enjoyed bangers and sausage for breakfast but had never actually visited a butcher shop to see how they were made, despite an invitation from Clem many years ago. From that day onward, Philip never ate another pork product and for many months still, any other meats. It reminded him too much of the Somme.

Philip asked what Mary was going to talk about at the American Legion Hall meeting that evening. She had been thinking about it for weeks and even that very moment as she gazed out the window at the snow-covered landscape. She dozed off for a nap and thought of her speech.

Flakes of snow began to dust the hats of Friday evening crowds on Bloomfield Avenue after weeks of uneventful, yet bitterly cold weather. The American Legion Post No. 34 hall was crowded with veterans who had eagerly awaited the evening's events for weeks. Members, their wives, and guests were dressed in evening clothes and uniforms. The men wore corsages and medals and the women evening dresses. Philip Bebbington had been a member of the post for the past twelve years and had mentioned his mother's visit to Harold Davies at a recent meeting.

Harold Davies stood. "Ladies and Gentlemen, we have some distinguished visitors here tonight, and one is from Great Britain. Please welcome Mrs. Mary Bebbington of Chester, England." The guests applauded as Davies helped Mary to the podium.

"It's a pleasure to be here tonight. I've never done anything like this before! It is so nice to be with my people and their friends! I've had such a lovely time here. Oh my, where do I start? Well, thank you for inviting me to speak with you tonight. You are so fortunate to live in America. Everything is so fresh and clean and there are so many parks. Montclair is a gorgeous city with spacious lawns and homes, like castles. It's just a big dream. I must tell you I had quite a start yesterday. My son Philip came home and told me he had lunch in prison. I then asked my son, 'Well, why did they send you to prison?' My son replied, 'Because my job sometimes takes me to such places to inspect lifts and elevators!'" She covered her heart. "Good Lord!"

Laughter. Mary looked about the room. "I know that many of you were in the war. I am so happy you're here! I have ten sons and two daughters in England. Our landlords order us to have large families to work their farms, you see!" More laughter.

"Five of my sons were in the war. Two of my sons are here tonight." She gestured to them. "I know…many mothers and wives have not been as fortunate as I. And I pray all of you who have seen war can help those who have suffered so much. And continue to suffer. War…is so terrible. I know this because I have seen it in the eyes of my sons and other soldiers when they came home. I have seen it in the faces of boys who camped on my farm as Boy Scouts. They cannot bring themselves to tell me what happened to them, or where they've been. I can't begin to imagine. Queen Victoria, the Kaiser, Constantine, and the Czar were all related. How could they do this to each other's own people? What is worth more than the lives of millions of people?"

It was a hard question. Philip looked around the room. The gaiety of the night had ceased. Faces of many legionnaires before her appeared lost in memories from 20 years ago. Harold Davies sensed the uneasiness.

"Well…" Mary said, looking at Harold Davies. "…I don't know what more to say."

Davies stood. "Thank you, Mrs. Bebbington. I think we might have some questions from the audience?"

Instantly, many hands are raised. Mary smiled, not knowing whom to choose.

She pointed to a man in the front row. "Where else will you visit before you return to England?" he asked.

"Well, there is one place I want to go and that is up to the veteran's hospital at Lyons where the wounded American soldiers are. I just want to see them and tell them how wonderful they are."

An attractive young woman in the middle of the audience raised her hand. Mary nodded to her.

"May I ask what you think of the King Edward affair?" There was welcome laughter.

A scandal in the royal family was occurring at the time. King Edward was in love with Mrs. Wallis Simpson. She was not only an American, but also a married woman already once divorced. Yet, in order to marry her, King Edward had to relinquish the British throne...and he did, leading to his abdication in 1935.

"As a young woman, I had one love," Mary said as visions appeared of the day she met Joseph, the day he asked her to marry him in the parlor of her father's farm, the joyous times they had with the children before the war and after, and at breakfast on their last day together six years ago. "And although King Edward has had many romances, I believe he really does love Mrs. Simpson and he should marry her."

"Would you like to say anything about youth movements in Great Britain?" asked another.

"I have a 100-acre dairy farm called Rawhead and Boy Scouts come every summer and have their camp on my farm," she said, reflecting on her days spent with them, recalling their youthful faces. "They invite me to their meetings and I tell them stories around their campfires. They are wonderful boys and they do many little things around my farm. They call me 'Ma'. I loved to have them there. Most of them became soldiers in the war...and some never came home. I am glad to hear that the veterans in Montclair have a scout troop. The Girl Scouts even have a section on my farm."

"What is your opinion of the United States Social Security Act?"

"It is a wonderful thing. We've had something like it in England since 1912, known as the English Health Insurance Act of the Realm."

Mary barely noticed the slight hand raised from the table below her. The hand belonged to a disfigured American legionnaire. Mary looked down at him and smiled. The man struggled to stand on his own with the help of a cane, proudly brushing away the assistance of his wife and another legionnaire sitting next to him. "Mrs. Bebbington, what is your idea of world peace?"

After looking at him for a moment, Mary answered, "I wish the people who talk about going to war, whatever it costs, could see the soldiers suffering from chlorine and mustard gas poisoning; their faces covered with scars, blind, always fighting for breath, with their voices a mere whisper, saying that their throats are closing and they are choking. I... have hope that at some time there would be a big meeting of all the nations. Groups such as the American Legion, the British Legion, and the French Legion, all boys who fought in the war, can stop such a horrible thing as war."

The man stepped closer and rebutted, "But do you think that the British Government will be involved in another war in Europe? England seems to be preparing for such an event."

"I pray that won't be so. The people of England want peace." She hesitated a moment, thinking. "When the sun is shining, we must have an umbrella, so if it should rain we will be protected. That is why armament is so pronounced. England...has been caught so many times unprepared." The ghostly legionnaire stared at her, unwavering, wanting to believe her.

A young woman raised her hand. "What is your recipe for a happy marriage?"

"Good cooking and a sense of humor." Mary quickly replied. There was welcome laughter. *That was an easy one*, Mary thought.

"What happened to the cheese?" asked a man with a notepad, likely a reporter. It was an interesting question. Someone must have mentioned that it was made at Rawhead.

Mary thought a moment and smiled. "Oh...the cheese...that marvelous tasting Farmhouse Cheshire cheese. It is said that it was so prized that the Romans built a wall around Chester just to protect where it was made," she said proudly. "We still make it at Rawhead and at the nearby Droppingstone Farm, which my son Bertie manages. It's also made on many other farms, though it's mostly made in factories now. I have not seen it in shops in Montclair. It seems you will just have to come to Cheshire to find it."

Minutes later, as Mary was helped off the stage, guests crowded around her to ask more questions.

"Tell me more about King Edward and Mrs. Simpson," the attractive young woman asked. Mary could not believe the attention a tenant farmer's wife from rural England was receiving from strangers in a country she was visiting for the first time.

A man entered the hall and announced that President Roosevelt had defeated Kansas Governor Alfred M. Landon by a landslide. There was overwhelming applause at the news.

Two men fiddled with a projector near her as a slide show about the war in Spain was next on the schedule. The attendees began to gather near the bar and a band started playing the music of Benny Goodman.

On the other side of the hall, in an empty sea of wooden chairs, a woman of about Mary's age, though considerably thinner sat alone. In her hands were photographs of several men in American World War I uniforms. She had been crying. Through the crowd, Mary saw her. The voices of the legionnaires and their wives around her faded. She lost her easy smile as she studied the woman. Then she slowly walked towards her.

Lost in despair, the seated woman did not notice Mary standing beside her. Mary sat down and extended her hand to her. She touched one of the photographs.

"May I see them?" Mary asked gently. The woman looked up at her with tearful eyes and slowly nodded. Mary accepted the photos and looked through them, feeling emotion from each. "These are your sons?"

The woman nodded. "And my husband."

"How many have you lost?"

She looked at Mary. "All of them," whispered the woman. "I suppose I am not as blessed as you…"

--- 94 ---

Philip, Minnie, Jim and his new wife Erma, Mollie and Mary left the First Presbyterian Church in Caldwell following the 10:00 a.m. service, and paused on the steps. It was April 1937 and after six months in America, it was time for Mary to go home.

"What a delightful service, Philip. "Not too different from Brown Knowl. Except they call it church and I call it chapel."

"Why don't you stay, Ma?" Philip asked. "Pa's gone. And Tom. Mabel Jean."

Mary smiled. "England is my home. And the responsibilities of running a dairy farm…"

Seeing Philip grin, she stopped and hugged him.

"Jack and Dave can take care of Rawhead," Philip said as he held her. "I'm sure the Brydens would approve. And Bertie's just across the road at Droppingstone. Or maybe Martha and William could…"

Mary took Philip's hands into hers and said nothing more on the matter. Philip knew that it was impossible to talk his mother out of a decision. Though her visit was a joyous one, he knew he would not likely see her again. Philip brushed a tear away. He remembered her rule of not crying in public. Only once in her life did she break that rule. It was the day she, Dave, and Sam saw an ashen, near skeletal Bertie on the docks of Liverpool eighteen years earlier. Mary Bebbington was always able to place death in perspective. To perish was simply a stage in life. A passing. And from her eternal faith in God, she knew she would see that person again. But she had no tolerance for suffering, and needlessness. God has much to answer for in that regard, she thought.

Philip looked up at the sun, enjoying the warmth on his face, remembering its scarcity in Cheshire.

"Well, we have one more day together," Philip said. "And it looks like it's going to be a fine one. What would you like to do, Mum?"

Mary watched a one-legged man cross Bloomfield Avenue on crutches. As he arrived at the other side, he turned and looked to her.

"I think I would like to visit the veteran's hospital at Lyons to see the boys there," Mary said. "And then let us have supper with Jim and Irma. Roast beef and Yorkshire pudding. Like we always did on Sundays…at Rawhead…"

AFTERWORD

Three and a half years after Mary Bebbington returned to Rawhead, Germany signed the Tripartite Pact with Italy and Japan and a year later Germany sanctioned Austria and invaded Poland. England was drawn into another world war.

Sam, Clem, Dave, and Jack remained for a time at Rawhead, but gradually left farm life to pursue other things. George retired as Postmaster of Norbury but volunteered as organist for a local chapel. As a postal worker, Andrew resided above the Burwardsley post office with Elsie. Bertie served in the Home Guard during World War II and he and Ivy remained tenants at the Droppingstone Farm, continuing the tradition of making award-winning Farmhouse Cheshire cheese. Dave and Margaret ran the Little Hill Farm, also on the Ballantyne Estate. Sam and Jack purchased their own farms. Clem briefly had his own farm and later became a driver for a large dairy. Oliver Goldford married the former Ballantyne governess and they resided in a Harthill cottage. Geoffrey Bryden was killed at Monte Casino in February 1944 while serving with the Welsh

Guards. William and Heidi Cutter never returned to England. Awarded the Victoria Cross posthumously for his actions at Montauban, Eddie McFie's remains were never found. Mollie joined Philip and Jim in Montclair but she died of appendicitis several years later.

Mary Bebbington died of cancer in 1947 at the age of eighty-two and was buried at Brown Knowl next to Joseph and Tom. A memorial to Mollie is inscribed at the foot of Mary's grave. Shortly after, Rawhead was rented to another family. In America, Philip continued to work as a safety engineer for industry and became a city councilman.

The setting of this story has changed little since 1908. A red sandstone brick farmhouse and many of the original outbuildings and walls still exist, though modern farm implements have been added over the years. Now 500 acres, Rawhead continues to operate as a dairy and as a pheasant shoot for the current tenant. Today, authentic Farmhouse Cheshire cheese is difficult to find. Only a few dairies in Britain produce it and the remainder is purchased by the locals with little left to export.

Rawhead can be experienced by hiking the Sandstone Trail, a meandering ridge of 300 million-year-old Triassic sandstone that rises dramatically from the Cheshire plain along the backbone of central Cheshire, from the Shropshire border to the Mersey River.

Rawhead c. 1995 (photo courtesy of the author)

ABOUT THE AUTHOR

Jon Bebbington was born in Morristown, New Jersey and raised in Rancho Palos Verdes, California. He received a Bachelor of Science degree from UCLA and two master's degrees from the University of Colorado. Early in his career he worked for a nonprofit legal organization and later as an engineer. He has traveled the globe pursuing his many interests including sailing, rock climbing, scuba diving and family history in the US and England.

The author lives in South Carolina with his three rescued dogs Andy, Darla, and Emma. He is currently at work on his next novel.

RAWHEAD